To:
Casey Pharris
And family

John 3:16

With LOVE,

Sherry Dee

TRIALS OF A CHRISTIAN COUPLE

Sherry Dee

WESTBOW
PRESS®
A DIVISION OF THOMAS NELSON
& ZONDERVAN

WestBow Press books may be ordered through booksellers or by contacting:

WestBow Press
A Division of Thomas Nelson & Zondervan
1663 Liberty Drive
Bloomington, IN 47403
www.westbowpress.com
1 (866) 928-1240

ISBN: 978-1-9736-2998-6 (sc)
ISBN: 978-1-9736-3000-5 (hc)
ISBN: 978-1-9736-2999-3 (e)

Library of Congress Control Number: 2018906536

Print information available on the last page.

WestBow Press rev. date: 06/13/2018

DEDICATION

I dedicate this book to my second eldest, Sherida, a single parent, home school teacher, as well as fulfilling her career from home.

She gave up many hours to assist putting this story into book form. Her dedication and devotion I deeply appreciate and cherish.

My prayer is you always allow God to lead and guide you in his ways, Sweetheart.

CHAPTER ONE

As the groom escorted his bride down the church steps, rice was thrown on the handsome couple by their friends and family.

"Are you ready to run to the car?" Kelley questioned, looking down into Darla's eyes.

"Do you expect me to run in heels, Husband?" She inquired, looking up into her handsome groom's eyes, with sparkles in her eyes.

"No, I guess not, hang on." Kelley ordered. Sweeping his bride off her feet into his arms, he ran toward his now fully decorated car.

Assisting his bride inside his car, Kelley quickly drove away. Driving through their small desert town, the handsome groom and beautiful bride were soon followed by many in their cars, blowing their car horns. As Kelley neared the interstate, their friends turned back toward town.

"Kelley, who will cut the wedding cake?"

Kelley put his arm around his young bride's shoulders pulling her closer to his side.

"Whoever would like. I say allow our friends and family to enjoy the reception, while you and I enjoy our honeymoon. Do you agree?" He questioned, looking into her eyes.

"All the way, until death do we part." Darla answered happily, leaning her head against her groom's strong shoulder. Kelley pulled his bride even closer to his side, then kissed her on top of her head.

Looking up into Kelley's eyes, her face aglow, giving him a loving smile, she lightly kissed his lips. Returning her head to his shoulder, she silently thought of the specialness and excitement with being a bride. The passing car lights, with the bright stars above against the darkened night, seemed to add to the romance she felt surrounding them. She felt like an angel, with her groom as her gift from her Heavenly Father.

As they neared the mountains, leaving their desert land, the cool mountain air with the smell of sweet pine filling the car, made their drive more romantic.

"You make a very beautiful bride, Mrs. Peterson." Kelley complimented with pride in his voice.

"Thank you." Darla replied with a pleased smile and sparkles in her eyes as she looked into Kelley's eyes.

"You make a very handsome groom and in my book the most handsome groom ever." She added.

Kelley lightly kissed his wife's lips, briefly taking his eyes from his driving, her words bringing a pleased smile to his face.

"Are you happy, Dar?"

"Happy? I am the happiest I could possibly be. I feel like Cinderella with you as my prince. Now that my name is Mrs. Kelley Peterson, I will be happy each day for the rest of my life." She answered with a beautiful smile.

"I will do my best to always keep you as happy as you are now." Kelley assured, sincerely.

"I do not doubt you in the least and I intend to do the same for you."

"Baby doll, I have just been granted the desire of my heart. I will always be full of happiness." Kelley shared with a pleased grin, bringing a soft laugh from his wife, she sharing his excitement.

Turning off the interstate onto a narrow mountain road, Darla looked up at Kelley's face.

"Where are you taking me, Husband?" Darla asked excitement in her voice.

"I am taking you to a special place." He answered, glancing down, noting the excitement on her face.

"Be patient, we are almost there." He added.

"I am trying to be patient." She confessed with a laugh, her excitement too great to conceal and her open honesty bringing a grin to Kelley's face.

"Here we are, Mrs. Kelley Peterson." Kelley informed as he parked his car near a tiny cabin.

Darla sat in awe, as she slowly, silently took in all God's beauty of nature, surrounding their honeymoon cabin.

"Darla." Kelley spoke as he now stood outside the car, offering his hand to her to assist her from the car.

"This is beautiful, Kelley! This has to be a glimpse of what heaven is like."

"Beauty is what I think when I am with you." Kelley informed her, taking both of his bride's hands into his, patiently allowing her time of observing their surroundings.

"When I am with you, I think of heaven and happiness." Darla shared with an excited beautiful smile, hugging her husband's neck tightly.

With his arms around his wife's waist, he pulled her close to him, hugging her in return.

"Thank you for waiting for me and not taking another for your wife." Darla said happily with sparkles in her moist eyes.

"You are most welcome." Kelley replied with a sensitive, understanding smile.

"How long has it been since I kissed you?" He asked, looking into his wife's eyes with romance in his.

"It has been too long." She answered with an excited laugh over her forwardness, her cheeks flushing.

Looking into his bride's eyes, with the look of a man deeply in love, Darla silently looked into his eyes, waiting for his lips to meet hers at his timing. Gently, bringing his wife closer, he kissed her long yet gently several times as she allowed him to.

"What do you say we make our wedding official and carry you over the threshold, Mrs. Peterson?" Kelley asked politely, his arms still around his thin bride's waist.

"I say you better."

"Yes, Ma'am." Picking his bride up into his arms, Darla kissed his lips as he carried her.

"I can't see where I am walking, silly." He informed, with a pleased grin over her play, Darla releasing a tickled laugh.

With Kelley sleeping soundly, Darla quietly left his side. Slipping out from under the covers, she tiptoed to her suitcase, removing her robe. With her robe tied snuggly around her thin chilled body, she quietly unpacked her and Kelley's suitcases. Picking up her lovely wedding gown from a chair with great care, she hanged it in the closet. Before closing the closet door, she admiringly looked at her gown once more. Her heart swelled with both pride and happiness.

Vacating the bedroom, she slowly walked through the front room, then the kitchen admiring the rugged, but attractive cabin Kelley had chosen for their short, yet special honeymoon away from the entire world, a very special place, where they in private, could express their love freely toward one another, deepening and strengthening their love, and creating an even stronger bond between them.

Holding her hand up, looking at her wedding ring admiringly, she smiled a beautiful, happy smile. Her heart was full of joy, excitement and love for her dear husband.

Quietly opening the front door, she went outside into the darkness having only the many stars above, lighting her path. Her heart swelled even more as she once again, slowly observed her beautiful surroundings nature had supplied. Admiring the cabin from a distance, she noted how inviting and romantic the cabin looked tucked among the many pine trees. The cool mountain breeze, gently swaying the trees branches, as though moving in time to music.

Wrapping her robe even tighter around her thin chilled body from the refreshing mountain air, she neared her husband's car. Admiring the beautiful decorations their friends and family had put on the car. She proudly ran her fingers over the decorations, each participant expressing their happiness for the bride and groom.

"I wondered where my bride ran off to." Spoke Kelley approaching her.

"I did not run off." She corrected with a gentle smile. Putting her arms around her husband's waist, she looked up into his eyes.

"I will never run from you, only to you." She added.

"I will expect this." Kelley agreed as he leaned against the car, pulling his wife close to him.

"Dar, is something troubling you?" Kelley asked with tenderness in his voice and gentleness on his face, as he looked into his bride's eyes, searching her eyes with his.

"No, everything is perfect, much more perfect then I ever imagined. I am so keyed up over our wedding, our marriage, this beautiful honeymoon cabin and your love for me that I can't sleep. I am so happy. I feel as though I am about to burst with happiness." She shared excitedly.

"I feel like a small child at Christmas time, one who just opened all the presents of her dreams." She added with a beautiful laugh.

"I am glad for your happiness, I feel the same way. I intend to make sure your happiness never fades."

"You taking me as your wife and adopting Heaven as your daughter believe me, is more than I ever expected would happen. I thought I was doomed when I learned I was pregnant last summer. I wore your college class ring faithfully, but I seriously doubted that even you could forgive me of my foolishness as a sinner." She shared with a happy smile as tears streamed down her cheeks.

"You choosing to allow us both to be a part of your life and your ministry for the Lord, are all the happiness I need. This is certainly much more than I am worthy of." Darla added.

"Thank you for the kind words." Gently removing his bride's long hair from her face where the wind had blown it, he kissed her lips.

"We must clear the air in this matter Babe, once and for all. Are you not a born again Christian?" He asked, looking into his wife's eyes.

"Of course."

"When you re-dedicated your life to the Lord a year ago, He erased all your sins. Whatever happened prior to your re-dedication, the Lord has forgiven you. I will hear no talk of who is worthy or not worthy in our marriage. We both, equal servants of the Lord, are worthy of all the Lord chooses for us. We both are sinners saved by grace. My Bible reads 'For all have sinned and come short of the glory of God.' Am I not speaking the truth?" Kelley asked.

"Yes, Preacher you are speaking the truth." Darla answered blushing.

"You being a preacher's kid should know your Bible. You now being a preacher's wife, better practice what you preach." He reminded with a comforting smile.

"I believe you know me well enough to know I know my Bible." She defended, poking her husband gently in his stomach.

"I know you know your Bible. I know you are always the first to practice forgive and forget with others. It is past time you learn to forgive yourself." Kelley scolded lightly, bringing a laugh from his bride as she blushed.

"You do not play fair, you always seem to know me better then I know myself."

"So, my wife is guilty as charged?"

"I am guilty." She answered with a soft laugh, still blushing.

"Shame on you, how can you not practice what you preach, not heed to the scripture and not learn from the message I shared two weeks ago, defending our marriage?"

"I will do my duty, Kel, I promise. I will forgive myself."

"In all sincerity Babe, you must or you will be giving way to a hindrance in your life. A hindrance pulls one down, not allowing one to be free to allow the Holy Spirit to lead and guide you in His ways."

"I agree."

Returning inside the warm cozy cabin, Darla was able to fall asleep in the comfort of her husband's loving, protecting arms.

"Good morning Wife." Kelley greeted with a kiss, awaking Darla.

"Breakfast is almost ready." He informed, as he politely laid her robe on the bed for her.

"I will be right in." She said.

Slipping out from under her covers and into her robe, Darla entered the bathroom. With her face washed and her hair combed, she sleepily entered the kitchen to join her husband.

"I thought cooking was the wife's job?" Darla questioned, joining her husband at the stove where he busily prepared their breakfast. She slipped her arms around his waist.

"Believe me, when we return to the real world, I will gladly resign my role as chef. Until we do, I will be in charge of the kitchen." Kelley assured.

"This is kind of you." Darla said.

"I am a kind person."

"Are you kind enough to give your bride a kiss?" She asked.

"Yes, I am most kind in the kissing department." Kelley answered with a boyish grin. Putting his cooking utensils down, he put his arms around his wife lovingly, kissing her.

"I love you, Dar." He informed, looking into her eyes with tenderness on his face.

"I love you too." Darla replied happily, and then politely pulled away from her husband, allowing him to complete his meal preparations.

"You look cute in your apron." Darla said with a smile, putting her hand over her mouth to conceal her laughter.

"Cute?" Kelley questioned, looking as though he disapproved of her comment.

"I thought cute changed to the word handsome after the age of two." He said.

"Excuse me Sir, you look handsome, I wish I had thought to bring a camera." She voiced with a soft laugh, she observing while he hurried around the kitchen to complete their breakfast.

"Your wish is my command. There is a camera on the mantle."

Darla enjoyed herself as she took several shots of Kelley with his camera.

"Smile, Baby doll."

"Kelley, I am not dressed yet." She protested blushing, putting her hands over her face.

"Come on, Baby doll, one more picture so I can show every groom-to-be how their bride will look the morning after." He coached, enjoying his play.

"You thought it was funny me wearing an apron, I think you look beautiful." Though blushing, giving in, Darla allowed Kelley his wish.

Putting the camera aside, Kelley joined his bride at the table. Taking her hands in his, he reverently asked the Lord to bless their meal.

"I would like us to go fishing after breakfast for our dinner this evening, so I hope you brought some old clothes."

"No, I didn't." Darla answered again her face flushed as she thought of the newly bought outfits she had carefully chosen for her honeymoon.

"If you will remember dear, you refused to tell me where we were going on our honeymoon." She added.

"I wanted to surprise you." Kelley defended, innocent of harm intent.

"Surely you didn't go shopping for our honeymoon, did you?" He asked with flushed cheeks.

"Yes, I did." Darla answered.

"Oh, I believe I goofed."

"Yes, Kel, you goofed." Darla replied with a soft laugh, as she thought of her new outfits.

"You're welcome to a pair of my jeans and a flannel shirt." Kelley's solution bringing a laugh from his bride.

"I assure you, your pants are at least four inches too big around the waist and six inches too long. It is probably a must that we go fishing, am I right?"

"Of course, we have a beautiful lake just waiting for us." Kelley answered with a grin, as though eager to begin their outing, he began clearing the table.

"I love you, Babe." He added stopping briefly, giving her a kiss as though his words were enough for him to have his way with his plans, bringing a soft laugh from his bride.

"You had better get dressed, the fish bite best early in the morning." Kelley informed.

Kelley washed the breakfast dishes as Darla dressed for her first morning of married life.

"Kel…" Darla called from the bedroom. As Kelley beckoned to her call, she stood behind the nearly closed bedroom door.

"Promise me no picture taking when I leave this room."

"Sorry Babe, I learned a long time ago not to make promises."

"Kelley!" She called, with a nervous laugh.

"I will be outside, hurry up." He replied, ignoring her plea. He left their cabin with his fishing poles in hand.

Taking one last look in the mirror at her fishing attire, wearing Kelley's baggie jeans with the legs rolled up, a sloppy flannel shirt, which looked like a tent on her, she let out a long sigh then left the bedroom.

"Smile, Sweetheart." Kelley spoke as Darla stepped outside the cabin. Kelley laughing, as he filmed his bride, finding her outfit amusing.

"I thought I married a preacher not a photographer." Darla scolded with a weak smile, lightly punching her groom in his arm.

"I am going fishing and you are baiting my hook." She informed, pretending to be annoyed with his play, as she picked up a fishing pole.

"I think of myself as more than a preacher, Babe." Putting his arm lovingly around his wife's neck, Kelley pulled his bride closer to his side, walking toward the lake.

"I am a carpenter, a husband and a father also." He reminded with a happy-go-lucky smile, ignoring his wife's scolding.

"You forgot to mention you are a tease."

"That also." He agreed with a chuckle.

"I thought I left my brother at home." Darla complained, as Kelley politely assisted her inside the rowboat.

"Do I hear sarcasm at this early hour, still on our honeymoon even from a Christian, a preacher's wife?" Kelley questioned with a boyish grin, bringing a tickled laugh from his wife.

"Row the boat, smarty." Though she truly enjoyed Kelley's relaxed, playful mood.

"Yes, Ma'am."

Darla's thoughts quickly left Kelley's teasing to the beauty of the lake. The water was a pretty blue. It was so peaceful, with only the sounds of the nearby ducks swimming and the water hitting against the row boat.

"Kelley, put the oars down quietly." Darla said in a whisper, pointing to two beautiful deer drinking water at the edge of the lake.

"Are they not beautiful?" She asked excitedly.

"Yes they are." Kelley answered, quickly picking up his movie camera. The couple silently sat admiring the beauty of God's creations until the deer left their sight.

"This is truly a beautiful place." Darla shared happily, as Kelley baited his hook, tossing his line into the water.

"I suggest we go to your mother's, get Heaven and return, making our home here."

"I would love too, but there is the small matter of employment."

"We could live off our love; we seem to be blessed with a

surplus." Darla said, her words bringing a pleased smile to Kelley's face.

"The reality is, if you don't help me catch some fish, we will not have dinner tonight." Kelley turned his eyes from his wife to his fishing line.

"I don't care for worms. If I wouldn't be asking too much, would you please bait my hook?"

"I recall taking you to the fair when we were in high school and you wanted to spend most of our time with the livestock. You told me then that you love animals. You are presently a nurse, so surely you have seen gorier sights then earthworms." Kelley answered as though too involved with his fishing to assist her.

"Worms are not animals or people, Kelley." Darla voiced, not understanding him neglecting to assist her.

"Pick up a worm and put it on your hook if you want dinner tonight." Kelley ordered, as though he was becoming impatient with her as he continued to watch his fishing pole.

Looking at her husband, she silently questioned why he was insisting she do such a thing, especially since she detested worms, though Kelley seemed to pay no attention to her request.

Once again staring at the worms, she slowly picked one up. She held the worm out, away from herself as though she thought it might bite her. Slowly, carefully, she stuck her hook through the worm, shivering. Sighing a breath of relief, she took her eyes from her hook and worm and glanced at her husband, hoping he was pleased with his ridiculous insisting. Kelley sat with a pleased grin, filming her from start to end with his movie camera.

"Okay, Kelley Peterson, the joke is over." She informed, as though irritated as she tossed her line into the water.

"What are you up to?" She questioned as he continued to film her.

"Your brother assured me I would never get you to bait your hook when I shared our plans for this weekend with him. I assured him he was wrong, now I have my proof." Kelley explained with a chuckle.

"Bill, I should have known." Darla said with a sigh.

"Perhaps you should have brought Bill here instead of me, I am sure the two of you would have a blast fishing together."

"Dar, it was all in fun." Kelley assured her quickly putting the camera aside.

"At my expense, so if you are not careful, you may find the sofa in the cabin makes for an uncomfortable bed the remainder of our honeymoon." She threatened in her soft slow way, quickly bringing silence to Kelley. She pretended to remain annoyed as Kelley returned to his fishing pole, with his face now flushed.

Even though Darla had appeared annoyed with her husband's feistiness and teasing, she truly didn't mind. This was a side of Kelley she hadn't seen often since her youth. She was pleased that he felt completely relaxed and carefree in her presence.

"I will bait your hook for you, Dar." Kelley informed, breaking their silence.

"I will do anything for you, Baby doll to stay off the sofa." He added with a chuckle, bringing a tickled laugh from her.

"Bill forgot to inform you, I know how to get even."

"I know you and your capabilities. Bill didn't need to warn me." Kelley assured.

Completing their fishing, the young couple returned to the bank carrying a fine catch of fish. While Kelley tended to the fish, Darla entered the cabin to shower.

Slipping into a pair of slacks and a warm delicate sweater for the cool October mountain air, she found Kelley sitting on the sofa reading his Bible.

"You look nice." Kelley complimented lovingly, putting his arm around his wife's shoulders, as she sat down next to him and giving her a light kiss.

"Thank you."

"Dar, you don't have to go fishing again unless you would like to." Kelley said, compassionately.

"I would rather not." Darla confessed with a soft laugh, blushing over her fishing experience.

"Give me a minute to shower then I will take you on a romantic walk through nature." Kelley said, looking into his beautiful bride's eyes.

"This, I would like." Darla agreed looking into his eyes, pleased with his suggestion.

Kelley kissed her then left for his shower.

Getting up from the sofa, Darla entered the kitchen. Opening the refrigerator, she removed a soft drink. Leaning against the counter, she noticed two cameras. Going closer, she noticed the instamatic, which Kelley had allowed her to use when he was preparing breakfast. Secondly, the movie camera, which Kelley had used filming her. She almost laughed out loud at the realization before her. Kelley intended to hide the pictures of him in a photo album, yet he intended to flash her episodes on a screen.

Going outside, sipping her soft drink, she secretly plotted to film Kelley before their honeymoon ended.

"May I film you now, Mrs. Peterson?" Kelley asked, finding his wife smelling the different fragrances of the many flowers.

"Yes, husband, you may." She answered.

His filming completed, Kelley put his arms around his wife's waist. Looking down into her eyes, he kissed her several times.

"Have I told you this morning that I love you?" He asked, still looking into her eyes.

"Yes." Darla answered with sparkles in her eyes and her face radiant with happiness.

"I am right in assuming you really enjoy nature walks?" Kelley asked.

"You're correct, I love nature walks." Darla answered anxiously.

"Good, I realize I am in serious trouble if I collect strike two." Kelley replied with a grin, bringing a soft laugh from his bride.

"I do know you well, Mrs. Peterson." He added.

"With your deep understanding of me, we should get along just fine." Darla stated.

"Of course we will."

Taking Darla's hand in his, Kelley lead her down a path stopping often to film animals, beautiful wild flowers, scenery and one another. They laughed, they kissed, and they shared special sights. They were as happy and carefree as two small children visiting a zoo for their first time with no rules, simply enjoying one another, making one another happy, and allowing their love to grow deeper and deeper and more unique.

Excitement grew in Darla as she silently took in God's beautiful creations. Her eyes sparkled with both happiness and fascination. The narrow path soon brought the newlyweds to a large clearing with a small log cabin church facing the grassy clearing.

"I just happen to have a key to the church." Kelley informed with a mysterious grin, bringing a smile to Darla's face.

"Did your Irish father also give you a bag of magical dust for your wedding gift?" Darla asked with a soft laugh, sending Kelley into laughter.

"No, silly." He answered regaining his composure, putting his arm around his bride's shoulders, as they walked toward the church.

"I have something special I would like to say to you, I intend to film and record us and hopefully, I remember my speech." He explained, as he unlocked the church.

Opening the old shabby door, Kelley politely escorted his beautiful bride inside. With his movie camera set, he politely and with a look of sincerity led Darla to the altar.

"I am sorry the altar is dusty, Dar, you are wearing a new outfit." Kelley said his face flushed.

"It will wash." She assured him kindly, relieving her husband of his awkward realization, giving him a loving smile.

Kelley knelt down with his wife at his side, taking her hand in his, he looked into her eyes, his face growing serious.

"I told my dad, when first meeting you, I would marry you when I became a man. I don't believe he took me seriously, I was only seven." Kelley shared with a grin, blushing, bringing a tender smile from Darla.

"As teenagers we fell in love. Being in love, innocent, carefree from any real complications in life, we both set our goals professionally, for marriage, for servants unto the Lord as a team. We were a good team together. The Lord put us together and He blessed both you and me and His work. We both felt we could conquer the world, until Satan interfered, creating strife, pain and confusion. You became side tracked for a time and Satan used this to his advantage by trying to destroy you, our love for one another and the ministry the Lord had in his plan for our future. He surely must have thought he won when you became pregnant. Satan is a liar, and he is out to rob and destroy. But he lost Babe, and he will continue to lose, he must. The Lord chose you and me for one another. He chose us both, as a united team to be ministers for Him. Satan lost the battle completely when God joined us in marriage."

"I will always insist the Lord and His ways are our ways in our home. The Lord comes first, then you and me, thirdly our children, then others. With this lifestyle, God first, we will always have our needs met. Our love will only grow stronger and deeper. The Lord will bless us and our home."

"Sweetheart, I am both proud and honored to be your husband and Heaven's father. I will always love, comfort and protect you and our family."

"Thank you, Kelley." Darla spoke deeply touched, with tears streaming down her cheeks.

Kelley removed his handkerchief from his pocket and gently wiped the tears from his young bride's face, then put his handkerchief in her hand.

"Let us pray that the Lord will use us and for strength and guidance to do His perfect will." Kelley instructed closing his eyes and bowing his head, as did his wife.

Darla walked around her honeymoon cabin with her hand in Kelley's. This would be their last walk at their cabin, it was time to return to the real world, to their home, their jobs and their ministry for the Lord. Darla was filled with even more warmth, love and respect toward her husband. He had been the perfect gentleman in every way. He had made her life complete now, by taking her as his bride. Oh, how she intended to repay him by being the best wife possible.

"We best leave, Babe, it's getting late." Kelley suggested putting his arm lovingly around her shoulders as they started toward the car.

"We will have to come back here again, Kelley, perhaps for our anniversary. This could always be our special place." Darla suggested happily.

"I will bring you back, Babe." Kelley agreed opening his car door for her.

"For now, let us go pick up your daughter and go home." He added.

"Yes, please." She agreed, excited to see and hold her baby.

Both Darla and Kelley were quiet as Kelley drove the two-hour drive from the mountains to their desert community. Darla sat close to her husband with her head resting on his shoulder and he with his arm around her shoulders as he drove.

"Is Mom becoming anxious?" Kelley asked with an understanding smile, as Darla sat up, with Kelley exiting from the interstate.

"Yes, very much so; I cannot wait to see Heaven's big blue eyes, her happy face, and her tiny fingers. I will probably hug her endlessly." Darla answered with an excited laugh.

"I am sure Heaven will be just as excited to see you as you are to see her, you are a wonderful mother."

"Thank you. You my love are now a daddy." Darla reminded, pleased.

"That I am." Kelley agreed also pleased.

Pulling his car into his parents' drive, Darla impatiently waited in the car for Kelley to return with her precious daughter. Excitedly, Darla opened the car door as Kelley approached with Heaven.

"Here is Mommy, Sweetheart." Kelley spoke, placing Heaven on Darla's lap.

"Oh, Heaven, Mommy has missed you." Darla hugged her

eight-month old daughter repeatedly while Kelley momentarily observed, then put Heaven's belongings in the back of his car.

"Mama." Heaven said happily.

"Mom said you may get the rest of Heaven's things tomorrow evening when you pick Heaven up after work." Kelley informed, as he started his car.

"Okay." Darla agreed pleasantly, her eyes seemed to dance with sparkles and her face seemed frozen with a smile.

"I do believe, Mrs. Peterson, you are the happiest lady in the world." Kelley voiced with both pride and happiness on his face, as he began the twenty-mile drive to their home.

"I truly am. I have the most handsome husband and most beautiful daughter in the entire world. I intend to love and spoil you both." Darla said with an excited laugh.

"I am sure you will do just as you say." Kelley replied with a pleased smile.

"Believe me, Heaven and I will gladly allow you to spoil us." He added with a chuckle, bringing a smile to his young bride's face.

Arriving at their country home in Ragweed, even more excitement consumed Darla. She and Kelley's first home, she couldn't wait to begin being the perfect wife, the perfect family.

Turning the car engine off, Kelley looked at his young bride happily holding her daughter on her lap. "If you will stay put, I will unlock the door. Then my lovely bride, I will carry you over the threshold of our new home."

"You do realize I have Heaven in my arms, correct?"

"I assure you, I presently and will always, be able to handle both my pretty girls."

"Hmm, I like this; I will wait for my groom's return."

Vacating the car, Kelley unlocked and opened the back door. Returning to his car, he assisted his wife from the car by sweeping her off her feet, while still holding Heaven. She kissed her husband's lips as she had on their wedding night. Standing, holding his wife, he returned her kiss. Removing his lips from hers, he began to walk when Darla kissed him again, bringing a boyish grin to Kelley's face, he gladly returning her kiss, enjoying her play.

"Do you realize you are becoming heavy?" He asked, looking into his bride's eyes as though spellbound in love.

"No." Darla answered with an excited laugh kissing her husband again, ignoring his comment.

"I love being in love." She added, with her lips still against his as she spoke, bringing a pleased grin to his face.

"You may take me inside, Husband." She said with a gentle smile, giving his lips one last quick kiss.

"What time is Heaven's bedtime?" Kelley asked with a boyish grin, as he carried his bride inside their home.

"Considering the lateness of the hour, shortly." Darla answered excitedly, her husband still holding her in his arms.

"Hmm..." Kelley commented and then winked at his wife, bringing a laugh from her.

"Let us make your daughter happy and then one another happy." He suggested and then kissed his wife's lips lightly before putting her down.

Heaven raised her arms excitedly toward Kelley, bringing pleased smiles to the young couple's faces. Kelley took Heaven from her mother's arms into his.

"It is time you learn to say Daddy." Kelley informed gently loving his adopted daughter, comforting her in his strong arms.

As Heaven tired, Darla tucked her baby in bed for the night while Kelley unloaded his car of their belongings.

"We made this big old house look nice, Dar." Kelley remarked, pleased as they prepared for bed.

"I didn't think the day would come when we would actually be married, being allowed to live here as a family." He added.

"I know." Darla agreed with a tender smile.

"We finally are a family with our very own home. We will make this a happy home Kelley, and we will make one another happy."

"You bet we will." Kelley agreed.

Darla awoke early to find her excitement in her marriage as

when she had fallen asleep the night before, her first morning of married life in her home. She showered and dressed quickly for the bright sunny October Monday. With the coffee brewing, she sat down at the kitchen table, having her morning devotions before beginning her busy schedule for the day. She sincerely intended to be the best wife ever.

At six o'clock, Darla returned to the master bedroom where her husband of three days lay sleeping.

"Good morning, Husband." She greeted as she woke him with a kiss.

"Good morning, Babe, you look beautiful."

"Thank you, are you sure you are completely awake?" She questioned with a soft laugh, bringing a smile to her husband's face.

"Yes, silly, I still say you are beautiful." He answered, and then kissed her lips gently.

"Get dressed while I start your breakfast."

"I was warned wives are bossy, but I had no idea they began giving orders as soon as the honeymoon ended." Kelley voiced with a playful grin as he got out of bed, bringing a tickled laugh from his wife.

"Kelley, I was not bossing, I was suggesting." She defended blushing, as she ceased her laughter.

"Right." He replied as though doubting her, bringing laughter from her again.

"I am going to make your breakfast. Just for the record, you have time for a shower." She informed, as though bossing him, bringing a laugh from him.

Darla busily prepared breakfast for her wonderful husband. She wanted to please him in every way and she intended to make every morning a happy morning before sending him off to work.

"You smell nice." Darla said as Kelley joined her near the stove, putting his arm around her waist.

"Thank you."

"Have your coffee while I finish your breakfast." Darla suggested kindly, as she sat a cup of coffee on the table for him.

Kelley picked up the cup of coffee, sipping it. Going to the counter, he leaned against the counter silently, as Darla completed his breakfast.

"Your breakfast is served, Husband." Darla informed pleasantly.

"Thank you, Babe, but where is your breakfast?" He questioned, still leaning against the counter with his coffee cup in hand.

"I am not big on eating breakfast; perhaps I will have some toast later."

"Where is your medicine?"

"It's in the cabinet above the sink." Darla answered puzzled, as he began opening cabinets.

Kelley removed his wife's medicine from the cabinet, placing the prescription on the table. He then removed a plate and glass from another cabinet. Opening the silverware drawer, he removed eating utensils and a napkin until he had a place set for his wife.

"Kelley, why are you doing this?" Darla questioned, surprised at him removing half his food from his plate, putting it on her plate.

"Have a seat Babe, before our breakfast gets cold." He instructed kindly, pulling her chair out for her.

Darla silently took her seat with Kelley assisting her. He sat down then held his hand out for his wife's hand. With her hand in his, he asked the blessing over their food.

"Would you like for me to explain?" Kelley asked with a gentle smile, noting his wife's still puzzled expression.

"Please do."

"I have two sets of rules I have been given, one by my parents and one by your parents. Then I have Kelley's ideas about how to run my home. I am sure you have a few rules you are willing to give me also." Kelley explained with a chuckle, bringing a tickled laugh from his wife.

"Your parents said you are to eat three meals daily, take your prescribed iron medicine every morning and get sufficient rest, so you do not become run down. Now eat your breakfast and take your medicine, Mrs. Peterson." Kelley instructed with a gentle smile.

"Yes, dear." She replied, with a loving smile.

"My dad never sat down at mealtime until after my mother. He informed me I better be a gentleman to my wife or I will be answering to him." Kelley informed.

"I think it would be nice to begin each morning together over breakfast. Your body requires a proper diet and my body simply enjoys food."

"Okay by me, partner." Darla agreed in her soft gentle way, as she politely removed their dishes from the breakfast table and Kelley picked up his Bible for his morning devotions.

With Kelley silently reading, Darla left the kitchen for Heaven's room to attend to her fussing daughter. She enjoyed watching her full of excitement, hitting her bath water with her tiny hands as Darla bathed her and then returned to the nursery to dress Heaven for the day.

"Dar, I need to leave for work." Kelley informed as he joined his bride at Heaven's crib, putting his arm briefly around her waist and noting Heaven's excitement with his arrival, stretching her tiny arms toward him.

"Good morning, Princess." He greeted picking Heaven up, taking her into his arms as though he was the proudest of fathers.

"You learn to say daddy today." He ordered and then gave his bride a tender smile. With Heaven in his arm, he gently put his free arm around his bride, his face growing serious. Kelley reverently closed his eyes asking the Heavenly Father to both lead his family through their separate busy day and protect them.

Giving Heaven a kiss goodbye and returning her to her crib, he then looked into his young bride's eyes, putting his arms around her and stepping closer to her. "I love you, Mrs. Peterson."

"I love you too, very much." She looked into her husband's eyes, happily.

"Should I attempt to tempt you?" She asked with a mischievous smile.

"Tempt me." Kelley encouraged with a boyish grin.

"We both could call in sick on our jobs extending our

honeymoon an extra day." Darla suggested her face flushed with a soft laugh, knowing she had surprised her groom by suggesting they lie.

"I now understand fully how easily Eve tempted Adam." Kelley said with a chuckle.

"I must remind you again, Baby doll, we can't live on love alone." He added.

"This is a matter of opinion." Darla replied surprising her groom, more with her light play, bringing a tickled laugh from him.

"May I have a kiss before I am late for work?" He asked.

"Please, I thought you would never ask." She said with a tickled laugh.

"Give me a kiss, silly." Kelley ordered with an approving smile.

Darla felt the happiest she could possibly feel, as she left her home with her daughter to begin her busy work day. Arriving at her in-law's home, she removed Heaven from her car seat and her heavy, well-supplied diaper bag. Ringing the doorbell, she patiently waited for her mother-in-law.

"Good morning, Darla." Greeted Kelley's mother pleasantly, relieving her of Heaven's heavy diaper bag.

"Good morning." Greeted Darla, happily, putting Heaven in her walker.

"Mama." Heaven said holding her arms up, wanting her mother.

"Mommy has to go to work, Sweetheart." Darla said, her smile quickly disappearing as Heaven began to fuss then cry, desperately wanting her mother.

"I have to go, Heaven." Darla said quickly taking her baby into her arms, hugging and soothing her.

"Heaven will be okay, Honey." Mrs. Peterson assured, taking the baby from her mother into her arms. Heaven cried louder and her hardest, with being taken from her mother. Darla's eyes quickly became moist, feeling terrible for her baby's wishes.

"Honey, go to work, Heaven will be fine shortly."

Darla did as she was told. Leaving her in-law's home, she released tears as she went to her car. Her heart ached to return inside and comfort her daughter. Her morning of nursing duties at the doctor's office seemed to drag on. She loved her work, yet this morning her heart ached for her daughter's happiness. Her lunch break came none too soon for her. Picking up the office telephone, she dialed her in-law's telephone number.

"This is the Peterson's, Hello." Kelley's father greeted with his Irish accent, bringing a smile to Darla's troubled face.

"Hello, Dad Peterson."

"Aye, and a hello to you, Miss Darla, will you be joining Mama and me for lunch?"

"No, Sir, not today, may I speak with your wife, please?"

"Aye, one moment please."

"Hello, Darla." Mrs. Peterson greeted.

"I apologize for disturbing you at lunchtime." Darla assured quickly.

"I have been concerned about Heaven, is she okay?" Darla asked.

"She is fine now, don't worry, dear. I rocked her and sang to her until she felt content. Perhaps she missed you more than we thought while you and Kelley were away over the weekend."

"Perhaps she did." Darla agreed remaining troubled with her daughter's actions.

"I will hurry to end my work day to get Heaven." She stated.

"This isn't necessary, but you do as you feel you must, Honey." Mrs. Peterson said, understanding.

Darla left the office locking the door behind her. She walked to the corner pharmacy, sitting down on a bar stool waiting patiently for her turn to be waited on, with her thoughts on her unhappy baby.

"Darla Roberts!" Darla quickly turned around.

"Sonja!" Darla exclaimed getting up from the stool, hugging her dearest friend tightly.

"You look great!" Darla added.

"You look as beautiful as ever, I am sorry I missed your wedding. I couldn't get away from L.A. until Saturday. Of course, by then you and Kel were long gone. Your parents told me it was the most beautiful wedding ever."

"It was." Darla agreed, her eyes sparkling once again and her face aglow with happiness.

"How long will you be home?" Darla asked.

"Until Tuesday night, I have to be back for classes Wednesday morning. I am staying at your parents' house. I believe your mom intended to invite you and Kel for dinner this evening. I suggested in a very discreet manner that Kelley would probably like to have his bride to himself tonight."

"You, discreet?" Darla asked with a soft laugh.

"Yes, between Mom and Dad Roberts and the University, I have learned a few things." Sonja answered with a laugh.

"I am sure you have." Darla complimented kindly with a gentle smile.

"Are you ladies going to order or are you intending to take up counter space?" Martin asked with a grin.

"Martin, you have been asking this same question since we were in elementary school." Sonja teased.

"I will have a Coke please." Darla informed politely.

"Sonja? This is my treat." Darla said.

"In that case, a steak, salad…" Sonja teased laughing.

"We don't serve steaks as you well know." Martin reminded patiently placing Darla's Coke in front of her.

"A Coke will be fine." Sonja said.

"I have a hard question for you, Sonja." Martin informed, as he placed Sonja's Coke before her.

"Go ahead, I am capable of answering hard questions." Sonja replied in her forward blunt way as though challenging Martin, bringing laughter from both Martin and Darla.

"When are you going to meet someone crazy enough to tame you down and marry you like your friend here?" Martin asked.

"Probably never, I am having too much fun being single. Besides, I don't accept orders easily." Sonja replied.

"No, but you do speak the truth." Martin said with a chuckle.

"Most certainly, the truth will set you free, I enjoy being free." Sonja replied, winking at Darla.

"Enjoy your Cokes, I hear a sermon coming." Martin voiced and then left the girls to themselves, bringing laughter from them.

"Mom Roberts says you don't work tomorrow, so I would like to spend the day with you if you haven't any other plans." Sonja suggested.

"I would like this." Darla agreed, happily.

"What are you doing with yourself today?" Darla asked.

"I am looking for victims." Sonja answered.

"I don't understand."

"I have been looking up old friends to attempt to lead them to salvation." Sonja explained with a laugh, bringing a smile from her girlfriend.

"Most of our friends have either moved away or they are away for fall semester in college." Darla informed.

"I am sorry I'm working today, otherwise you could entertain me." She added with a soft laugh.

"I'm the visitor, Darla; you are supposed to do the entertaining." Sonja reminded.

"I know the way rules go, you are the one who has the gift of turning things around or upside down and still coming out on top, you heard me correctly." Darla assured, bringing a smile to her friend's face.

"I do kind of upset most people's apple carts by my forwardness. Your dad says I am one of a kind."

"What does Mother say?" Darla asked with a tickled laugh.

"She told your dad the mold was definitely broken after I was made. I believe both of your parents have given up trying to make a young lady out of me, I am Sonja."

"Perhaps they have given up attempting to change your personality, but they have great faith in you as a Christian. They love you as if you were their daughter and I love you as a sister." Darla assured, giving her friend a tight hug.

"This I have never doubted since seventh grade, when your parents took me in." Sonja shared happily.

"Good, walk with me to Dr. Paul's office, my lunch break is quickly drawing to an end." Darla suggested, pleased for her company.

Darla felt uplifted by her short visit with Sonja. Her afternoon work hours seemed to fly by. Leaving her work for the day with the departure of the last patient, her thoughts quickly went to her baby. Arriving at her in-law's home, she rang the doorbell then patiently waited.

"Come in Miss Darla." Her father-in-law offered.

"Mama says our Heaven has not had a good day." He informed, quickly bringing unhappiness and concern to Darla.

"Sister Peterson," Darla spoke as she entered the kitchen with her father-in-law.

"I am sorry Heaven has been unpleasant for you." She apologized with flushed cheeks, concern on her face.

"I am Mom to you now, dear, not Sister Peterson." Kelley's mother stated, in her kind way.

"Yes, Ma'am." Darla agreed with a pleased smile.

"As far as Heaven, I am sure being with her mother will solve her unhappiness." Mom Peterson comforted with a tender smile.

"I hope so." Darla removed her unhappy daughter from the highchair, taking her into her arms. Heaven laid her head against her mother, as though weary from her day of upsets.

"She has not taken a nap, so I am sure she is exhausted."

"I am sure you are exhausted also, then." Darla said, feeling for her mother-in-law, as well as her daughter.

"This day was long, but I am sure by Wednesday we will have our Heaven back to her old self. She will be fine, dear."

Dad Peterson kindly took Heaven's things to Darla's car for her.

"Dear, will you please tell Kelley to inform his telephone callers he no longer lives here? They call at all hours and his father is becoming annoyed. I put his messages in the small zipper compartment of Heaven's diaper bag." Mom Peterson informed hurriedly, before her husband returned.

"I will tell Kelley." Darla assured.

Reaching her car, Darla attempted to put Heaven in her car seat. Heaven began to cry, stiffening her legs, making it impossible for her mother to put her legs in the car seat.

"Heaven, what is wrong with you?" Darla asked, hugging her baby close to her, calming and comforting her.

"Shhh, don't cry Sweetheart, Mommy is here." She soothed, hugging and kissing her for several long minutes, until she calmed her crying. Darla attempted to put her daughter in her car seat once again and again Heaven screamed her loudest.

"Heaven, please, I can't drive a stick shift with you in my arms." Darla scolded, as she carefully forced her eight-month old daughter in the car seat.

Closing the passenger door and going to the driver's side of her compact mustang, Heaven was now screaming and kicking her feet. Darla quickly removed a bottle from her diaper bag, offering it to Heaven, but Heaven just threw her bottle, surprising Darla with her actions.

"Honestly, Heaven." She scolded, aggravated and concerned with her actions. Removing some Kleenex, she nervously wiped the milk from her dash where the bottle had hit. Retrieving the bottle from the floor of the car, Darla started her car with Heaven still screaming and throwing a tantrum.

"Kelley, you will get dinner sometime tonight." She spoke aloud, as she backed her car out of her in-law's drive.

Driving through the small town of Dunes with Heaven continuing in her crying state, Darla nervously looked at her watch as she waited at a red light.

"Oh, Kelley, I'm sorry." She silently thought, knowing he had been off work for nearly an hour.

"Heaven, please stop crying." She pleaded glancing at her baby, as the light turned green.

Reaching the highway that lead from the town of Dunes to

the town of Ragweed, Darla finished shifting gears. She wiped her daughter's wet face from her continuous crying with a Kleenex. Heaven lifted her arms toward her mother wanting to be held.

"Heaven, Mommy can't hold you now, Sweetheart." Darla soothed patting her, taking hold of her tiny hand as she drove, she began to sing, *Jesus loves you...* Near reaching her home after fifteen miles of comforting, Heaven finally fell asleep.

With five miles remaining, Darla silently prayed asking the Lord to calm her from her upsets and concerns toward her daughter before arriving at home to greet her husband.

Turning into her drive, Darla noted Kelley cooking the steaks she had set out for dinner on the grill. Kelley approached her car as she parked.

"Hi, Baby doll." He greeted pleasantly opening the car door for his wife.

"Hi." Darla greeted with a happy smile, as she got out of her car.

"I was concerned my wife forgot her way home." He informed, putting his arms around her waist.

"It has been a very long day." Darla replied with a nervous laugh, beginning to relax with her husband's strong arms around her.

"Would you like to talk about it?" He asked.

"No, I would much rather forget it." She answered, allowing her husband to pull her closer to him.

"Besides, I am with you now my world looks bright again." She added.

"Then it is okay to kiss you now?" He inquired as though impatiently waiting, bringing an excited laugh from his bride.

"Yes, I could use a kiss."

With Heaven tended to sleeping soundly in her crib, Darla gently kissed her head.

"Dar, dinner is ready." Kelley said, standing in the doorway of the nursery.

"May I have a minute to change?" She asked, quietly leaving her daughter's room.

"If you don't mind cold steaks."

"I will wait." She agreed, with a tender smile.

"Thank you." Kelley appreciated.

Taking his wife's hand into his, he asked the blessing over their meal.

"You know I have the park ministry tomorrow evening." Kelley stated.

"Yes."

"You told me when we were engaged, you would return to the ministry with me after we married. Will you be joining me tomorrow or are you not ready?"

"I'm not ready." Darla answered slowly looking into her husband's eyes, hoping her answer would not disappoint him.

"I need a little time to organize my married life, for example, you preparing dinner tonight." She explained her cheeks flushed.

"It was no problem to throw steaks on a grill and make a salad, I assure you." Kelley said.

"Nonetheless, I intend to prepare your dinner for you, so I am laying claims on the cooking department." Darla insisted.

"Are you complaining about my cooking?" Kelley asked quickly, teasingly.

"No, dinner is very good and you make a terrific chef." Darla answered pleasantly.

Kelley went outside to tend to the grill as Darla washed the dinner dishes. Returning inside, he kindly began drying the dishes when the telephone rang.

"Peterson's" Kelley answered.

"Darla is right here." He informed, handing his wife the telephone.

"It's your mother." He said.

"Hi, Mother." Darla greeted pleasantly.

"Are you busy, dear?"

"I'm just finishing dinner dishes." Darla answered, as she continued to wash and Kelley dry.

"At this hour?" Her other asked.

"Yes, we had a late dinner; my day has been rather hectic."

"What did you prepare for dinner?"

"Actually, I didn't prepare anything, Kelley cooked steaks on the grill."

"You were so late from work that Kelley had to cook?" Darla's mother questioned with disapproval in her voice.

Darla's face flushed with her mother's tone.

"Mother, Kelley didn't have to prepare dinner, he chose to." She answered, glancing at her husband who now stood leaning against the counter with a grin, shaking his head at his mother-in-law's scolding. Kelley's actions bringing a smile to Darla's face, quickly setting her at ease.

"I wouldn't allow you being late after work to become a habit, dear. Kelley shouldn't have to tend to dinner preparations after working hard all day." Her mother advised.

"I agree, Mother."

"If you have not made plans, Sonja would like to drive out in the morning to visit."

"I have no plans, I will be expecting her." Darla approved politely.

"Okay dear, I will tell Sonja. Love you, bye."

"Love you."

"Will you please tell my mother I am married and that I can do without her lectures?" Darla asked with a smile, as she hung the telephone up.

"If you sincerely want me to, yes I will." Kelley said.

"I'm not being serious. Don't add fuel to the fire, please." Darla said, bringing a chuckle from Kelley.

While Kelley studied his Bible preparing his speech for the park ministry to the people living on the streets, Darla took a long hot bath to help aid in relaxing her from her tense day.

Awakening early Tuesday morning, she was pleased breakfast went smoothly, fulfilling Kelley's wishes in regards to the breakfast hour.

With Kelley on his way to work, Darla tended to her daughter. She too was pleased with Heaven back to her happy-go-lucky nature. Heaven happily followed her mother from room to room in her walker, as Darla busily tidied her home.

"Hello." Darla spoke, as she answered the ringing telephone.

"Good morning, how is married life agreeing with you?" Her mother asked.

"I couldn't be happier, Mother." Darla answered with an excited laugh.

"Good, I expect to hear this twenty years from now also." She said with a soft laugh, bringing a smile to her daughter's face.

"How was your honeymoon?"

"It was beautiful and with the exception of missing Heaven, it was perfect."

"I'm very happy for you and Kelley, dear. Dad says Kelley is on cloud nine, apparently you both are."

"I have been concerned about the wedding reception. I sincerely hope no one was offended by Kelley and me not attending." Darla stated.

"No one was offended. Everyone understood with you and Kelley only having the weekend off from your jobs for your honeymoon. Kelley took care of everything nicely." Mom Roberts assured pleased.

"Kelley?" Darla questioned.

"You didn't know?" Her mother asked.

"No, Kelley didn't explain."

"Kelley left instructions for Bill and Cindy to cut the wedding cake. He said with Bill being the best man and Cindy the maid of honor, they were the best-qualified choice. Kelley said the reception was to be a party for all in attendance, for our love, support and prayers for both him and you."

"This is beautiful, Mother." Darla replied, deeply touched by her husband's thoughtfulness.

"Everyone thought so. I might add, Kelley also said he intended to have his own party with his bride." Her mother shared with a soft laugh.

"Kelley did as he intended, he made our honeymoon like a

party each and every moment. I told Kelley I felt as though I was Cinderella with Kelley as my Prince, fulfilling my every dream." Darla shared, proudly.

"Just remember all of this wonderfulness, dear and how special Kelley is, throughout your marriage, especially when the chips are down." Her mother cautioned wisely.

"I will Mother and if I temporarily forget, I'm sure you will remind me." Darla's comment brought a laugh from her mother.

"Sonja is on her way out, dear. Enjoy your day."

"Thank you and you have a nice day also." Darla said.

Darla did enjoy her day with Sonja. They had become friends as young girls and Sonja had even lived with Darla and her family for a brief time, receiving salvation while in their home. Their bond had never weakened even though they lived miles apart. They would always be family, always reuniting.

Showered and dressed in a nice pant outfit and sandals, Darla anxiously waited for Kelley to return from work.

"Hi, Babe." Kelley greeted as he entered the kitchen through the back door.

"We have a dinner guest." He informed, holding the door open for their guest.

"Hi, Sis." Darla's brother, Bill greeted.

"Hi, this is a nice surprise." Darla stated.

"Thank you. I told Kelley I don't want to intrude since you two have not been married a week." Bill apologized.

"Kelley has to leave shortly after dinner. Besides, you are more than welcome, regardless. Darla assured him.

"How was your day, Baby doll?" Kelley asked putting his arms around his bride, causing her to blush with her brother's presence.

"I had a nice day. You do have time for a quick shower before dinner." Darla informed, secretly hoping Kelley would remove his arms from around her.

"Are you telling me I am dirty, Wife?" He asked, bringing a laugh from Bill and Darla.

"Yes, I am."

"Before I get a kiss or after I get a kiss?" Kelley asked with a grin, deliberately teasing his bride in front of their guest.

"Kelley!" She scolded, her face its reddest, pulling away from him.

"You are right Bill, wives are bossy. Immediately after I said 'I do', Dar began giving orders." He teased as he slipped his work boots off.

"I tried to warn you." Bill sided, with a chuckle.

"Excuse me, Baby doll, while I shower." Said Kelley, giving his wife a light kiss.

"Kelley." Spoke Darla, pointing to his boots.

"Yes, ma'am." Replied Kelley, picking up his boots."

"It only gets worse, Kelley." Informed Bill.

"I'm sure it does." Agreed Kelley, as he left the kitchen.

"How has my big brother been?" Asked Darla pleasantly, as she set a place for him at the table.

"Okay." Answered Bill, avoiding eye contact with his sister, removing Heaven from her walker. "Boy, you are getting big, Heaven." Said Bill, avoiding conversing with his sister.

"Did you have time to visit with Sonja?" Asked Darla politely.

"Yes, last night, I had dinner at mom's and dad's. That girl will never change."

"Did she give you a hard time, dear brother?" Asked Darla, with an understanding smile.

"I could have slapped her." He answered bluntly, bringing a tickled laugh from his sister.

"Do you already know how she embarrassed me?" Questioned Bill with a weak smile.

"No, I just know Sonja, so I am sure she did a good job at embarrassing you." She answered still laughing, as Kelley returned from his shower.

"Married life is making my sister crazy." Informed Bill, as Kelley took Heaven from his brother-in-law, putting her in her highchair, as Darla continued in her tickled state, bringing smiles to both men's faces.

"Wife, may we eat?" Asked Kelley, pulling her chair out for her.

"Yes." Answered Darla, putting her hand over her mouth to conceal the laughter that wanted to escape her, as she stared at her empty plate, while Bill and Kelley sat down.

"Darla." Spoke Kelley, holding his hand out for hers.

"Excuse me." She apologized, quickly glancing at Kelley, putting her hand in his.

With the completion of Kelley's prayer, Bill put salad on his plate, then passed the salad bowl to his sister. As their eyes met, Bill grinned at Darla, knowing she would laugh as did Kelley.

"Excuse me for laughing, but I must know Bill how Sonja embarrassed you?" Apologized Darla, her face flushed.

Bill looked at his sister with a serious face as though she had told a secret. He then looked at Kelley, then his sister again.

"Why not tell Kelley also?" He asked, as though he disapproved of her question, bringing a smile to Kelley's face, causing Darla to continue in her laughter.

"Sis, it really isn't funny." Bill assured, with a half-grin.

"I'm sure it was not funny." Darla agreed looking down at her plate slowly picking at her food, getting her laughter under control once again.

"I was at home minding my own business when Sonja calls and says mom wanted me to come for dinner. I gave Sonja some excuse why I could not make it. Sonja refused to take no for an answer. She had me on the telephone for at least an hour, so I agreed. We each sit down at the table, Dad asks the blessing and no sooner than Dad says 'Amen', she looks me right in the eye and says, 'Bill, I have been looking for a victim all day.' I looked at her as if she was crazy, which she is. Then she said, 'and here you sit right before me.' Then she explains, 'I hate to go through one day without sharing salvation with someone.'" He informed, and both Kelley and Darla became tickled.

"Yet, you didn't slap her?" Darla asked, as she ceased her laughter.

"No, I told her she should mind her own business." He answered with a chuckle.

"What was Mother's and Dad's response when you were rude to Sonja?" Darla asked, surprised at her brother's comment.

"Mom went into shock and Dad tried desperately not to laugh."

"What was Sonja's comeback?" Kelley asked.

"Surely she had one." He added.

"She said you are a lost soul, so you are my business." Bill answered, sending both Darla and Kelley into hysterical laughter.

"Dad lost it. Here I am angry as all get out at Sonja, and Dad is cracking up laughing."

"Relax, Bill, Sonja won't be home again until Christmas break." Darla informed with a comforting smile.

"That girl is bold." Bill remarked, shaking his head as though still surprised with her actions.

"Kelley, you should have Sonja as a guest speaker for the youth sometime." Darla suggested, as she fed Heaven her dinner.

"Darla, I want to keep my job as youth pastor." Kelley replied with a smile.

"I am serious, Kelley, she does have a sense of humor." Darla defended looking into her husband's eyes.

"I am serious also." Kelley replied, ending the subject of Sonja.

"Babe, I must go. Bill if you will excuse me." Kelley said, getting up from the table.

"Of course." Bill replied.

"I will be home as soon as I am finished at the park, Babe." Kelley informed, leaning down giving her a kiss.

"If you get tired, don't wait up, you have to work tomorrow." He added.

"Okay. Be careful and I will be in prayer." Darla assured supportively.

Darla enjoyed her brother's company with Kelley away ministering to drug addicts, alcoholics, prostitutes and gang members, giving his time, love and the powerful ways to live a life free of bondage, with sharing scriptures from the Bible.

With Bill returning to his own home, Darla made herself comfortable on the loveseat in the den with her Bible. She prayed for some time that the Lord would protect Kelley, while busy in the Lord's work. She prayed the Holy Spirit would guide him, for souls to be saved and new converts fed.

It was after midnight when Kelley's car lights reflected on the window as he returned. Putting her Bible aside, Darla quickly went to the back door, unlocking the door for her husband.

"Hi, Preacher Kel." She greeted, happily.

"Hi, Babe." He greeted, laying his Bible down on the counter and then relocking the back door.

"I thought you would be sleeping by now."

"I wanted to wait for my husband and be assured you were okay. Now, I am ready to call it a night." She explained pleasantly.

"I was given a telephone number to call." Kelley started, hesitantly.

"Jose wants me to explain some Bible scriptures to him." Kelley looked into his wife's eyes for her approval, not wanting to disappoint her.

"If you will give me a goodnight kiss, I will see you in the morning, Preacher."

"Hmm, I can handle a kiss." Kelley replied with a grin, appreciating his wife's understanding.

Up extra early Wednesday morning, Darla kindly cared for her horse Princess and her Irish Setter Sam, relieving her hard working husband of his morning chores. She allowed him an extra forty-five minutes of sleep. With her shower taken and dressed in her nursing uniform, she woke her husband.

"You look tired Kelley, how late were you up?" Darla asked sympathetic, as she had breakfast with her groom.

"I was up until three." Kelley replied.

"Do you often have nights as late as last night?"

"More often than not." He answered with a smile, as he got up from the table. Picking up his empty plate and coffee cup, Darla gently put her hand on Kelley's.

"Kelley, leave your dishes, I will take care of them." Darla offered kindly.

"No, thank you, I have managed to carry my own dishes since I was a young lad." Bending down, he gave his bride a light kiss then placed his dishes in the sink.

"I didn't realize the time." He said suddenly, then started toward the back door.

"Kelley, I took care of Sam and Princess."

"Why?" He asked with disapproval on his face.

"So you could sleep later."

"Darla, don't do this again. I will carry my load." Darla's face turned red with Kelley's scolding.

"Okay." With flushed cheeks, Darla silently got up from the table, taking her dishes to the sink.

"Darla." Kelley spoke, tenderness in his voice and putting his arms around her.

"I didn't intend to hurt your feelings, I assure you. I sincerely appreciate your kindness. This is one of your traits I admire." He said with a gentle smile, quickly comforting his compassionate bride.

"I am a prideful husband and I will fulfill my responsibilities whether I am tired or not. I will not burden my wife, okay?" Kelley added with a comforting smile.

"Okay." Darla agreed with an understanding smile.

"I promised to take care of you, not overburden you." He reminded, looking into her eyes, and then gently kissed her lips.

"I have to get to work, you have a good day. I love you, Babe." He added before giving her another kiss.

"I love you, bye." Darla replied with a tender smile.

Heaven secure in her car seat, Darla began her drive to her hometown of her youth. With each trip to Dunes for her nursing job, Darla would be reminded of times in her childhood when her father had pastored the church in Dunes, where Kelley's family still attended. They were happy times filled with joy, love and play.

Standing on her in-law's porch at their front door with Heaven in her arms, she happily kissed her daughter.

"Good morning, Miss Darla." Dad Peterson greeted, in his cheerful manner.

"Good morning." Darla greeted pleasantly.

"Good morning, honey." Mom Peterson greeted.

"How is Heaven this morning?" She asked.

"She was fine yesterday." Darla replied.

"Good, I thought she missed her mother." Mom Peterson replied, taking Heaven into her arms.

Darla felt relieved to leave her daughter without her crying. Her work went more quickly and she was able to feel good about herself and her work without having to feel guilty for leaving her daughter for the day.

Her workday completed and her daughter in her arms, Darla hurried from her in-law's home to her car. Putting Heaven's diaper bag in the backseat, she started to put Heaven in her car seat when Heaven began to fuss, objecting to the car seat.

"Heaven please don't do this." Darla said with a sigh, as she put her daughter in the car seat regardless of her protesting. Heaven began to cry, kicking her feet and holding her arms up to her mother to take her, as though heartbroken.

"Is there a problem, honey?" Kelley's father asked approaching, he hearing Heaven's crying as he picked up the evening newspaper from the drive.

"Heaven is trying my patience." Darla answered with a weak smile.

"She wants me to hold her, but I can't drive and fulfill her wishes." She explained, wearily. Opening her car door, with Heaven crying her hardest and reaching for her as she started her car, she looked at her daughter feeling defeated, her heart aching to hold and comfort her, as she shifted her car into gear.

"Bye, Dad Peterson." Darla said wearily.

"Bye, honey." Her father-in-law replied with compassion on his face.

Darla patted and talked to Heaven the entire twenty mile drive home. Even Darla's singing to her did not soothe her.

"Sweetheart, please stop this crying." Darla said feeling near tears herself.

Pulling into her drive, Kelley came from the corral to greet his wife.

"What is wrong?" Kelley asked, noting his wife's troubled face with hearing Heaven's heartbroken cry. Kelley quickly took Heaven from her car seat into his arms, comforting and soothing her.

"Hey, Princess, Shhh." Kelley said as he held her close, loving her until her crying ceased. Heaven lay against her daddy's chest with her head against him as though exhausted.

Darla silently removed her purse and her daughter's diaper bag from the car. She could feel her husband's eyes on her silently questioning Heaven's upset. Leaving her car, entering the house, Kelley followed behind her.

"Dar?" Kelley questioned as he stood leaning against the counter with his daughter content in his arms.

"Heaven didn't want in her car seat. She wanted me to hold her. She cried the entire drive home." Darla answered feeling badly, looking at her precious baby.

"You couldn't do both." Kelley defended, to comfort his wife.

"She is getting to me, Kelley." Darla shared with watery eyes, looking into her husband's strong yet gentle face.

"In what way, Babe?" Kelley asked compassionately, as Darla began removing Heaven's bottles from her diaper bag.

"Excuse me for just a moment, Dar." He added then picked up the ringing telephone.

"Peterson's." Kelley spoke, observing his wife as she now washed her hands to begin their dinner preparations.

"Dad, I told some of the street people my new telephone number last night." Kelley spoke.

"Dar," Kelley whispered, putting his hand over the receiver so his father could not hear him.

"Did Mom give you telephone messages for me?"

"Yes, Monday, I am sorry Kelley." Darla answered, her face flushed.

"Don't worry about it." He whispered. Darla quickly removed the messages from the diaper bag, handing them to Kelley.

"Yes, Dad, Darla gave me the messages." Kelley spoke winking at his upset wife, bringing a weak smile to her face.

"I will try to put a stop to the disturbing calls, Dad."

"Dad, both Heaven and Darla are fine." Kelley said his face now flushed.

"I won't do what you are suggesting."

"Dar, don't prepare dinner." Kelley spoke with his hand over the receiver again.

"I hear you, Dad. I assure you, I will do what is best for my family. No, Dad, I will not." Kelley said his face stern.

Darla silently went to Kelley's aid to at least relieve him of Heaven.

"She is fine, Babe."

"Dad, my wife is presently upset, we have to be at church in an hour, so I honestly don't have time for this now. Sure, bye." Kelley said, and then put the telephone down.

"Dad intends to call me after church." Kelley informed with a weary laugh, his face flushed.

"You do recall me telling you both our parents gave me a list of rules?" He asked, putting his arm lovingly around his wife.

"Yes."

"I just threw both lists out the window." Kelley informed with a chuckle.

"Are you warning me that you have declared war?" Darla asked with a weak smile.

"No, Ma'am, I would never do that. I will honor our parents and respect their wishes. Your parents as well as mine, must learn Kelley and Darla Peterson run this home."

"In our parents' eyes, you are declaring war, Kelley." Darla replied with a nervous laugh.

"They will adjust, Babe. You best get dressed for church. We will stop after church to have dinner. We will also discuss what is bothering you."

"Okay." Darla agreed, giving her husband a smile.

Darla hurried to have both herself and Heaven ready on time for the Wednesday night service.

Entering the sanctuary only moments before the service was to begin, Kelley politely escorted Darla to a pew near the front where the young couple most often sat.

"You're almost late, Preacher." Cindy spoke as she and Dan sat in the pew behind them, like most services.

"Dar, tell your cousin to mind her own business." Kelley said, bringing a laugh from Cindy and a smile to his wife's face.

"Let us all stand please." Pastor Finks said through the microphone.

"Dar how was your honeymoon?" Cindy asked in a whisper.

"Girls, talk later." Kelley said quickly, hushing the intended talk, causing both Cindy and Darla to blush.

"Darla has a telephone, Cindy." Dan whispered scolding her. Overhearing Dan's comment, Kelley glanced at his wife and winked at her.

At the close of the pastor opening in prayer and greeting the congregation, he turned the service over to the song leader, as the congregation was seated.

Heaven sat on Kelley's lap while Darla held the hymnal for them to share. Pastor Finks silently motioned for Kelley to join him on the platform.

"Babe, take Heaven, please." Kelley whispered and then left his seat, sitting down on the platform next to Pastor Finks. Darla observing as the pastor whispered to Kelley and Kelley nodded his head as in agreement, then the two men joined in the song service.

The song leader left the platform with Pastor Finks returning to the pulpit.

"I have asked our youth pastor to lead us in testimony. When I asked Kelley if he was willing to lead us, his reply was 'Pastor, I am always prepared, I am a yielded vessel.'" He shared his face serious yet held pride.

"My heart is rejoicing for like Kelley, I see others learning to be yielded vessels obeying the Holy Spirit. This pleases me for this pleases my Father in Heaven."

"Amen." Kelley spoke as well as several in the congregation.

"Kelley." Pastor Finks spoke.

Kelley obediently joined the senior pastor at the pulpit. The pastor proudly put his hand on Kelley's back.

"About five years ago this young man, just completing high school attended a youth rally which was held here in our church. Some of us old timers put him on the spot, at this very pulpit announcing to all his intentions to attend Bible college to be a minister. He obeyed the Lord."

"Yes, Amen, Amen."

"Kelley stood before us a couple of weeks ago and he said 'I am not a pleaser of man, but of my Father which is in Heaven.' I see a unique Christian man here. Yes, he has his style as we each do, but his style speaks the will of our Father first. Amen?" Pastor Finks asked, looking at his congregation.

"Amen, Amen."

"Kelley, share with us in testimony." Pastor Finks said then returned to his seat on the platform.

"Thank you, Pastor. It strikes me funny, Pastor, that you should say I am unique and we each have our own style." Kelley said with a grin.

"I received a telephone call this evening from my biological father; this is why Darla and I were nearly late arriving. For those of you who do not know my father, he is a Godly man."

"Yes. Amen." Pastor Finks agreed.

"My father lives by many of his customs and standards taught him in his youth in Ireland. He is extremely strong-willed. When my dad said, 'Kelley, jump!' I did not ignore his order or say, 'In a minute, Dad' or 'Okay, Dad, I will tomorrow.' My response was 'Yes, Sir, I will jump as high as you say.'" Kelley shared, his face flushed.

"That's right." Darla's father agreed.

"My father-in-law knows my dad." Kelley explained.

"My biological father taught me a lot. I could never repay him if I lived to be a hundred, yet my father is my father and I am who I am. My father must obey the leading of the Holy Spirit as I must. The Lord has separate works for my father and me. My dad and I have an understanding in the ways of the Lord. As individual men, we have some opinions that differ. My father called me this evening to tell why I should do what I will not do." Kelley said, bringing laughter from the congregation.

"I assure you, my father being the true Irishman he is, temper and all, my telephone will be ringing when I return home because I refuse to apply his way to my way of life." Kelley informed with a grin and flushed cheeks, as the congregation laughed.

"Yet I say to my Heavenly Father, how high do I jump, Sir?" He added.

"Yes. Amen." The congregation agreed.

"Moms and Dads, we have some eager teenagers here tonight. They are learning to seek not your way of life or my way of life, but their Heavenly Father's way of life for them as individuals. They have learned how to pray, to seek the Lord's will so they will be used as vessels. They wish to share with you what the Lord is doing in their lives as they obey our Heavenly Father." Kelley informed.

"Kim." Kelley spoke, for the young fifteen-year-old girl to give her testimony first.

As the teenagers eagerly testified, Darla's heart was stirred. Their eagerness and sincerity reminded her of her and Kelley's teen years. She longed to become personally involved with teenagers again.

With the close of the testimony service, Kelley returned to the pew sitting next to his wife. Glancing at Heaven sleeping soundly on the pew, Kelley put his arm around his wife's shoulders, pulling her close to his side.

"Kelley, why not go home and I will make us a sandwich?" Darla asked as the service ended, she feeling tired.

"Because my dad will be calling and I would like for us to eat in peace."

"May we please leave now and not tarry? This has been a long day."

"Sure we can, Babe." He agreed, as though suddenly noting his wife's tiredness.

"Excuse me" Allowing Darla to step into the aisle, Kelley picked up Heaven with her blanket tucked around her from the pew.

"Kelley." Spoke two teenagers excitedly arriving at Kelley's side as he stood with Heaven in his arms.

"We want the youth group to have a cookout Saturday." The teenagers informed.

"Then have a cookout Saturday." Kelley replied.

"Pastor Finks says you have to approve it and you have to be present for it to be considered a church activity." Kim explained.

"Ask my partner." Kelley said, looking at his wife.

"Please, please, please, Darla." The girls begged excitedly.

"How could I possibly say no?" Darla asked with a soft laugh.

"Thank you, Darla, we love you." The girls said happily, each giving her a hug.

"Kelley, will you borrow your dad's truck? We intend to invite lots of kids."

"Have you no end to your wants?" Kelley asked teasing the teenagers.

"Ask and ye shall receive, Kelley." Kim answered, confident he would grant her wish.

"Call Darla tomorrow evening in regards to planning this spur of the moment cookout." Kelley instructed.

"Okay." Kim agreed, excitedly.

"Do I hear volunteers for chaperones?" Kelley asked looking at Dan and Cindy as they prepared to leave.

"Sure." The young couple answered, as they walked from the church with Darla and Kelley.

With their meals ordered, Darla looked at her husband with a pleasant smile and pride in her eyes.

"You look great behind a pulpit." She said.

"Thank you."

"You have a special way with people. Your ability to relate to others is superb." Darla continued happily, bringing a smile to her husband's face.

"Thank you, Babe." Leaning close to the table, Kelley took his wife's hand into his.

"What is the problem with my beautiful wife and daughter?" He inquired.

"Today Heaven did well until I picked her up from your mother. I put her in her car seat and she acted as though I had broken her heart. She kept holding her hands up for me to hold her while I was driving home. I felt so guilty that I couldn't comfort her. Monday was much worse, she cried for me when I left her. She was unpleasant for your mother most of the day. When I picked her up, she threw a fit nearly the entire drive home. I honestly don't understand. She has never acted in this manner. I have either worked or was attending classes since her birth, unless she simply missed me so terribly when we were away for our honeymoon." Darla answered her concern once again on her face.

Darla and Kelley were silent now, as the waitress returned with their meals. With the blessing asked, Kelley looked at his young bride in silence as they began their meal.

"I shared my upset, what is your upset with your dad?" Darla asked considerately.

"Nothing important, Babe. As for Heaven, I am sure, given a few more days, she will realize you're not leaving her all day and night. As you said, she did better today than Monday."

"I hope you're right, I do enjoy my work, Kelley."

"I know you do."

Heaven tucked in bed for the night, Darla dressed for bed. Kelley in the den on the telephone with his father, as he had predicted would happen. Entering the den in her night clothes, Darla silently brought Kelley's attention to the time. Putting his hand over the receiver, he looked to his wife's eyes.

"Go on to bed, Babe, you look tired." Kelley whispered.

"So do you." Darla replied, concerned.

"I will be fine." He assured her, so she kissed his lips lightly then gladly did as he suggested.

Thursday brought another full day for Darla to be with Heaven. Heaven excitedly crawled behind her mother, while Darla dusted and vacuumed her large three bedroom home. As noon arrived, with the completion of Heaven's lunch, Darla put her in her crib for her nap. Leaving home and going to the corral, she put Princess's bridle on her then hopped onto her horse's bare back. She kicked Princess, making her gallop. Darla enjoyed the thrill and excitement she felt from the swiftness of her horse. Returning to the corral, she enjoyed the freedom of the outdoors as she brushed her horse.

Entering her home, she quietly checked on Heaven, finding she was still sleeping. After her shower, Darla touched up her light blue eye shadow and mascara. She brushed her long dark hair, allowing her hair to hang freely the way Kelley liked her hairstyle most. Then she slipped into a nice slacks outfit, wanting to look her best when her husband returned from his long day of carpentry work.

Changing Heaven's diaper and taking her from her crib as she woke, Darla hugged her tight, making her laugh.

Excitement rose in Darla as she glanced through the kitchen window with the sound of a car engine, finding it to be Kelley.

"Hi." Darla greeted happily, meeting her husband at the back door and quickly bringing a smile to his tired, dusty face. Taking his lunchbox from him and sitting it on the nearest counter, she put her arms around her husband, kissing his lips lightly.

"I missed you." She informed with sparkles in her eyes.

"I missed you too, Babe." Kelley said, looking into his bride's eyes then kissing her lips long and gentle. Removing his lips from hers, he looked into his wife's eyes with a tender smile.

"I really should take a shower, I have sawdust covering me and you probably do also, now." He said, though still holding her.

"I am madly in love with you, so I don't care." Darla replied with an excited laugh, blushing with her forwardness, impatiently looking into her husband's eyes waiting for another kiss. Bringing a boyish grin to his face with her play, he then granting her silent wish.

With Kelley in the shower, Darla set dinner on the table then put Heaven in her highchair.

"The table looks nice, Dar." Kelley said as he assisted his wife with her chair.

"Thank you."

"Da, da, da." Heaven said happily, holding her arms up for Kelley to take her, her acknowledgement bringing a proud look to Kelley's face and a smile to Darla's face.

"Hi, Princess." Kelley greeted, giving her a kiss.

"I always knew you would be a daddy's girl." He added proudly, giving her another kiss.

"Mom is always trying to keep you all to herself." Kelley picked Heaven's highchair up, setting her chair between his chair and his wife's.

"I'm sure you will quickly win my daughter from me." Darla voiced with approval clearly in her voice, bringing a pleased smile to her husband's face.

"What is this?" Kelley questioned as he picked up a paper near his place setting, as they enjoyed their dinner.

"My secretarial duties for the day. Your mother invited us for dinner tomorrow evening, my mother invited us for Sunday dinner, the plans for the cookout for the teens Saturday, and your telephone messages both from your mother today and a few I received here."

"Perhaps I should put your on my payroll." Kelley said approvingly.

"What did you tell our mothers about dinner?" Kelley asked.

"That I had to check with you." Darla informed.

"What would you like to do?"

"It doesn't matter to me, whatever you wish."

"Tell them both, yes. I realize we both being out of our parents' homes has left at least our mothers with a void to deal with, perhaps this will bring some comfort to them."

"You are a dear." Complimented Darla pleased with his thoughtfulness.

"Husband, may we trade cars in the morning?" Darla asked, as she put a dish of dessert before him.

"Sure, why?"

"When I pick Heaven up from your mother after work tomorrow, I would like to be prepared if our princess here decides to scream while I attempt to drive. Your car not being a stick would be a lot easier for me to drive and tend to her if need be."

Kelley played with heaven until she tired while Darla cleaned the kitchen from dinner. Heaven dressed for bed, Darla gave her nighttime bottle to her as she rocked and sang to her until she fell asleep. Kelley attempted to prepare his sermon for his Friday night park ministry at his desk in the den between telephone calls.

"Kelley, it's late." Darla whispered leaning against her husband's desk as he busily searched through his Bible, relaying scriptures to whoever was on the telephone with him.

Kelley glanced at the clock on the wall, which showed the hour to be near midnight. He briefly glanced at his wife, and then began to turn the pages in his Bible again.

"Kelley, please, enough for tonight."

"Give me just a few more minutes." Kelley replied, clearly expressing his involvement in his present doings.

"This is what you said an hour ago, I'm going to bed." She informed, barely above a whisper, disappointed.

"Dar..." Kelley spoke, taking hold of his wife's arm preventing her from leaving his side.

"Please wait." He said with tenderness on his face, quickly calming her from her disappointment.

"Slim, we must call an end to this study for tonight. My wife is growing impatient with me." Kelley informed bringing a smile to Darla's face.

"Good luck with witnessing salvation to your family this weekend, you will be in my prayers." Kelley put the telephone down then looked at his wife, pulling her toward him and onto his lap.

"Slim said to tell you hi and you are dearly needed ministering in the park." Kelley shared holding his wife, looking into her eyes.

"Slim is visiting his family in L.A. this weekend. This will be his first visit home to his old neighborhood since you led him to the Lord a few years ago. He has been off drugs, but he will be in serious need of our prayers to endure the temptations while he attempts to lead his family to salvation."

"Then he will receive our prayers." Darla replied, her face serious, filled with concern.

"Most certainly." Kelley said.

"Hang on Wife." Kelley ordered as he tightened his arms around her, standing up and carrying his wife to their room.

Awake early again; Darla was glad it was Friday. Kelley looked so tired. Darla quickly found it impossible for her to keep his pace of awaking early and remaining up half the night. Though they were married, it seemed their time alone together was extremely limited. Pushing her Bible aside from her early morning devotions, she reached for the ringing telephone. Picking the telephone up, she heard Kelley's voice on the extension as though he was half asleep.

"Peterson's."

"Preacher Kel?" A hysterical girl questioned.

"Yes, who is this?"

"Joy, you gotta come preach to my Charlie, so he don't go to hell. The doctors, they say my Charlie is dying." The young street gang girl cried.

"Is Charlie at the hospital?" Kelley asked, now sounding fully awake. Darla's hands began to tremble as tears streamed down her face, hearing the young girl's desperate cry for help as she silently listened.

"Yes, at community, hurry preacher, they stabbed my Charlie five times. He told me tonight he would change his life when you came to the park to preach, but Charlie can't wait until tonight, please save him now." The young girl begged.

"Joy, I'm on my way, but listen to me. You know how to pray and you know how to lead Charlie to salvation. Get busy with Charlie now, I will see you shortly." He instructed.

Darla remained at the table, desperately praying for Charlie's soul and comfort for his girlfriend.

"Darla?" Kelley questioned as though in shock finding his wife sobbing.

"I'm praying; go to the hospital, Sweetheart." Darla explained, quickly relieving her already burdened husband from more burdens.

"I will tend to the animals and bring your lunch to you later."

"Thank you." Kelley quickly gave his wife a kiss and then hurried from the house.

Leaving her home with Heaven for her half day of work, Kelley pulled into the drive.

"I hoped I would catch you before you left for work." Kelley said getting out of his car.

"Charlie is gone and Joy led him to the Lord." He informed.

"Thanks for the prayers, Babe. Joy asked me to hold funeral services. I'm not ready to do funerals, so I asked your dad and he accepted."

"My dad? Is this the same father who forbid me returning to such type of people to witness?"

"Yes." Kelley answered with a weak smile.

"Your dad may not understand the ways of the hippies and people that live on the street, but he definitely understands lost souls and salvation."

"I know he does."

"In my haste, I forgot to drive your car. Would you still like to trade?"

"Yes, please. Kelley, there is a blanket in the trunk of my car. If you would put it over the seat before driving home from work, I would appreciate it." Darla instructed, as she now threw a blanket over Kelley's seat to prevent her white nursing uniform from becoming dirty from sawdust.

Darla drove as fast as the speed would allow her, fearing she would be late for work. Leaving Heaven with her mother-in-law, she was once again thankful for a pleasant departure. Only working until one, like most Fridays, Darla's work morning went by quickly.

"Hi, Dad Peterson." Darla greeted pleasantly, as she parked her car behind her father-in-law's truck.

"Hello, Miss Darla, how are you this fine day?" He asked, as he politely opened the front door for his daughter-in-law.

"Fine, thank you."

"Will you join Mama and me for lunch?"

"No, thank you, I need to do some grocery shopping." Darla answered, as she approached Heaven sitting on the floor playing with a toy.

"Mama." Heaven said excitedly as Darla picked her up, giving her a kiss.

"Hi, Sweetheart, Mommy missed you." Darla said happily, hugging Heaven playfully.

"Heaven was as good as gold this morning, honey. I am sure she will be fine now." Mom Peterson informed, pleased.

"You don't know how relieved this makes me feel." Darla happily confessed.

"I think my boy is making a big mistake." Dad Peterson stated, his face becoming stern, quickly bringing silence to Darla.

"Honey, please, it is lunchtime and Darla has things she needs to do." Mom Peterson said, desperately wanting to quiet her husband.

"Did Kelley not speak to you about you not working away from home and your child?" Dad Peterson asked. Darla's face turned its reddest, as she looked at her terribly concerned father-in-law.

"Miss Darla?" He asked as though growing impatient for her answer.

"No, Sir." Darla answered slowly, now realizing the disagreement between her father-in-law and her husband. Dad Peterson's face turned as red as Darla's, yet he bit his tongue not saying anymore.

"Honey, we will see you and Kelley at dinner this evening." Mom Peterson said, escorting Darla politely to the front door.

"Thank you for caring for Heaven, bye."

To Darla's surprise, Heaven cooperated with her mother when

put in her car seat. Arriving at the grocery store, Heaven chattered away as Darla pushed her in the shopping cart.

"Are you planning a party?" Darla asked, as she stopped near her brother putting liquor in his shopping cart.

"Hi, Sis." Bill greeted, his face turning red.

"I'm throwing a small party tonight. I would invite you, but you would probably slap me." He teased, trying to cover his embarrassment, bringing a smile to his sister's face.

"Don't over indulge tonight; I need your assistance tomorrow evening. I will expect you at five. You are in charge of two grills." Darla informed pleasantly. She kindly gave her older brother a kiss on his cheek, and then left his side.

"Darla, wait, who said I could show?" Bill asked surprised with her manner.

"I did. I am becoming bossier by the day." Darla answered with a gentle smile, bringing a grin to her brother's face.

"I will see you at five tomorrow evening." Bill replied.

"Thank you."

Arriving at home, Darla put Heaven down for her nap then tended to the groceries. As the time grew closer to Kelley's return from work, she left her sewing machine to prepare Heaven and herself for dinner with her in-laws.

When Kelley arrived from work, he quickly showered then left with his family for dinner at his parents, with having the park ministry to attend directly following dinner.

Kelley politely put Heaven in her highchair, and then assisted his wife with her chair. With the entire Peterson family seated, Dad Peterson asked the blessing. Darla felt tension present in Kelley's family members. She also was sure Kelley noticed the same. He seemed to glance at different family members as though silently questioning the problem.

"Dad, have I or my family offended someone?" Kelley finally asked.

"Your wife didn't tell you I spoke briefly with her today?" He asked letting out a sigh.

"No." Kelley answered, he now looking at Darla, as she returned her husband's look, yet remained silent. Kelley returned his eyes back to his father, politely waiting an explanation.

"I apologize to your wife and you, Son. I overstepped my boundaries with Miss Darla. I voiced my opinion to your wife in the matter you and I disagree on in regards to your wife working. I do apologize, Son." Dad Peterson said, as though ashamed of his actions.

Kelley looked at his father in silence for several long moments with his face flushed, clearly showing all present his disapproval of his father interfering.

"Let's go for a walk, Son." Dad Peterson suggested.

"Mama, Miss Darla, excuse us." The two men left the table in silence.

"My husband is sorry honey for upsetting you earlier today." Mom Peterson assured.

"I know he is." Darla replied with an understanding smile, her comment seeming to set her mother-in-law and the two younger brothers-in-law at ease.

"What are you doing tomorrow, Aaron?" Darla answered pleasantly.

"Nothing in particular." The young teenager answered.

"The youth group from our church is having a cookout tomorrow evening. You and your friends are welcome to come." Darla invited.

"What time?"

"At five."

"Will there be any pretty girls there?" Aaron asked with a big grin, surprising the women at the table.

"As a matter of fact, yes." Darla answered with a tickled laugh.

"I will be there." He assured, excited.

"I'm telling Dad you only want to go to see girls." Matt said.

"You will mind your own business, Matthew." His mother scolded.

"Aaron, clear the table please."

"Yes, Ma'am." Aaron spoke politely. Aaron and Matt cleared the table while Darla and her mother-in-law visited and Heaven played on the floor.

Kelley returned with his father, both men appearing to have settled their differences.

"Darla, I will walk you to the car, Dad is loaning me his truck for tomorrow. I have fifteen minutes to get to the park." Kelley explained, picking Heaven's toys up from the floor, then his daughter.

"Dad, thanks for having us." Kelley said shaking his father's hand.

"Mom, dinner was great, thank you." He informed, and then gave his mother a kiss.

"Matt, Aaron, have fun washing dishes." He teased, as his brothers did their evening duty.

"Thank you both for having us." Darla said pleasantly, giving both her in-laws a kiss, setting them completely at ease by her gesture.

CHAPTER TWO

Heaven re-adjusted to her new schedule, which came with her mother's marriage. Darla was again able to enjoy her hours at work, doing the work she loved. Kelley seemed to be away from home more and more. It seemed Darla spent more empty nights alone then not.

"Hello, dearest cousin." Cindy greeted, as she entered through the back door followed by her husband Dan.

"Hi." Darla greeted pleasantly, as she busily set the table.

"Kelley should be home soon, will you join us for dinner?"

"No, thank you, we already ate." Cindy answered, removing a tomato slice from her cousin's salad.

"Are you sure, Cindy?" Darla asked with a smile, catching her cousin in her salad.

"Yes, I am sure." She answered with a laugh.

"May I keep you company tonight? Dan is going with Kelley to the park ministry."

"Yes, please, I welcome your company. Kelley is gone more than he is home. I'm growing tired of looking at these walls." She shared with a smile.

"Speak of the devil, here he is." Dan said as Kelley arrived from work.

"Your wife says you are seldom home." He informed, causing Darla's cheeks to flush, as her husband glanced at her.

"My wife speaks the truth." Kelley replied, removing his work boots inside the back door.

"On the other hand Dan, I am no devil." He added, bringing a laugh from Dan.

"Just a figure of speech, brother, I take my remark back."

"Hi, Babe." Kelley greeted, giving his wife a kiss.

"How was your day?" He asked, remaining at her side.

"I had a good day." Darla answered with a loving smile, hoping to set her husband at ease from Dan's remark.

"Good." Kelley gave her another kiss.

"Da, da, da, da." Heaven said excitedly, as she stood hanging onto the cabinet, slowly trying to make her way to her father. Kelley went to her and picking her up, he gave her a tight hug then a kiss before he stood her back up on the floor. Heaven raised her arms to him again.

"Daddy has to take a shower, Princess." Kelley informed.

"Daddy had better hurry." Darla suggested, as she began setting dinner on the table.

"Yes, Ma'am. Dan, Cindy, excuse me." Kelley said as he left the kitchen for his shower.

"Dan, please don't repeat what I say in my moments of weakness." Darla pleaded with flushed cheeks.

"Darla, you are trying to be the 'perfect wife' having the 'perfect marriage', but it isn't going to happen. There are no perfect people; therefore, there are no perfect marriages. If you don't tell Kelley his absences are getting to you, you will begin to build resentment. I know you well enough to know you don't want this to happen." Dan said.

"No, I don't." Darla agreed, letting out a sigh.

"Dan, do allow me to be the one who tells Kelley how I feel." Darla stated.

"I won't say anymore." Dan assured.

With Heaven already in her highchair and Darla seated at the table with her guests, Kelley returned taking his place at the table. With everyone holding hands, he asked the blessing.

"You two are not eating?" Kelley asked, as he prepared his plate.

"We already ate." Dan answered, as the telephone began to ring.

"I will get it, Babe." Kelley offered, getting up from the table.

Darla picked at her meal, knowing from Kelley's conversation the caller would take her husband from their home. Darla could feel Cindy's and Dan's eyes on her, so she deliberately avoided eye contact with them.

"Babe, I need to go to the hospital...." Kelley started, as he intended to explain.

"I heard enough to know you must leave." Darla interrupted, feeding her daughter, avoiding eye contact with her husband also, while she secretly, desperately tried to hide her hurt feelings.

"I will be home after the park ministry." Kelley said, bending to kiss his wife goodbye and looking into her face, seeing her upset.

"Darla, what is wrong?" Kelley asked, his face bearing his concern.

"This isn't the time for questions, Kelley, you are needed." Darla answered, forcing a weak smile to relieve her husband of his concerns for her.

"We will talk when I get back."

Dan went with Kelley and Darla remained silent as she fed Heaven, her eyes watery. She tried to hold back the tears, but found her attempts were no use.

"Darla, you can't go on like this." Cindy said, putting her arm around her cousin, trying to comfort her.

"I'm being silly." Darla said wiping her tears away with her napkin, forcing a weak smile.

"Why do you say this? I would have slapped Dan if he left without completing a meal I had worked hard at preparing. You do have rights as a wife, even if Kelley is a minister." Cindy defended.

"Generally, I do well sharing Kelley with everyone; then at

times, I feel like this evening. I want to be selfish and say, 'No, he is my husband; I am having him all to myself.'" Darla shared with a nervous laugh, blushing as her tears continued.

"So, what is so terrible about wanting your husband?"

"It's horrible of me, Cindy, if I come between Kelley and the Lord's work." Darla answered, looking into her cousin's eyes for her to understand her position.

"I see your point." Cindy agreed, letting out a defeated sigh.

"It's not a matter of Kelley out goofing off, he is out working for the Lord, and I am fresh out of suggestions." She confessed with a tender smile.

"Have you talked about this with your mother?" She asked.

"No, you are the first to hear my complaining." She answered with a soft laugh, blushing as she wiped her tears away.

"I don't believe I would make a good minister's wife." Cindy confessed, bringing a smile to Darla's face.

Darla enjoyed her cousin's company. Her empty time filled with her husband's absence was good for her.

"Darla it is near midnight, is Kelley always this late?" Cindy questioned, concerned.

"Sometimes he comes home at midnight and sometimes much later." Darla answered with a weary smile.

"I would go crazy if I were you."

"Who is to say I'm not already crazy?" Darla asked with a soft laugh.

"Hello, girls." Kelley greeted as he and Dan entered the den, both appearing exhausted as they wearily sat down.

"What happened to you two?" Darla asked concerned, as did Cindy.

"I forgot to replace my spare tire. I had a flat, so the car is about four miles down the road." Kelley answered wearily.

"Kelly, I told..." Darla started when Kelley interrupted her.

"I know, Darla, you warned me several times." Kelley stated short with his wife, bringing immediate silence to her, surprising each present with his manner. Darla's eyes quickly filled with tears. She slowly turned her head, so no one could see her tears.

"Dan, I think we should leave." Cindy suggested, feeling uncomfortable.

"As soon as I help Kelley get his car, Honey."

"Dar..." Kelley started, slowly standing up, rubbing his head wearily.

"Yes?" She asked, avoiding eye contact.

"I need to borrow your spare to get my car home, where are your car keys?"

"I will get them." She informed, vacating from her chair.

"I will get the keys, Babe." Kelley said, now noting his wife's upset. Darla ignored him, starting past him with her tears still streaming.

"Darla please, I didn't intend to make you cry." He assured, taking hold of his wife's arm.

"You never intend to Kelley, it just seems to happen a lot lately." She replied sternly, looking into her husband's eyes, knowing her spite hurt her husband's feelings. She bit her lip as his pain was clearly on his face. Kelley stepped close to her, putting his arms around her.

"I'm sorry I have hurt you, Darla." He assured, holding her close to him.

"Dan, thanks, I will manage the car later. I apologize for all of this." Kelley said, filled with shame.

It seemed Darla cried forever with Kelley standing patiently calming and soothing her.

"Babe, Dan told me what you asked him not to tell me. I deliberately snapped at you for this reason because I allowed my pride to consume me. It seems I'm getting good at messing up and hurting you."

"Why did Dan tell you? He assured me he wouldn't. I knew my spur of the moment comment would bruise your pride if hearing from another before me."

"Dan isn't to blame, he volunteered nothing, and I knew you

were upset when I left. I had to work overtime to pull it out of Dan, believe me. You and I are hurt, sorry, and extremely tired. I suggest we take the telephone off the hook; we go to bed and sleep until we wake up with no alarm. When we wake, we hash all upsets out, openly and honestly. I am sincerely ashamed of my actions tonight. I had no right to speak to you as I did, regardless."

Darla fell asleep in her husband's strong arms, feeling comforted, loved and protected.

Awaking, Darla noted the brightness of the sun shining through the window. Noting her husband's absence, she glanced at the clock, 10 o'clock. Getting out of bed, she slipped her robe on. She noted the telephone was still off the hook and she smiled to herself at her husband keeping his word.

Entering the bathroom, she freshened up then began her search for her husband. Finding Kelley sitting at the kitchen table and Heaven attempting to walk, hanging onto the cabinets, she stood in the kitchen doorway dressed in her robe, leaning her head against the door casing with a happy smile, silently waiting to be noticed.

"Mama." Heaven said excitedly.

"Good morning, Sweetheart." Darla happily greeted, she now looking toward her husband.

"Good morning, Babe." Kelley greeted, pleased with his wife's calm happy nature with their upsets last evening.

"Good morning, Preacher Kel." She greeted with sparkles in her eyes and her face aglow. Darla went to her husband, sitting down on his lap.

"Would you please tell me the sudden change of heart? I have only been in the marriage business for four months." Kelley reminded with a pleased smile.

"Several things, how much of your time do I get this morning? You know I'm a slow talker."

"As much time as you need, Babe." Kelley answered sincerely.

"Would you like a cup of coffee?" He asked.

"Yes, please." Darla got up from her husband's lap. She went near his side as he poured her coffee.

"I did a lot of silent praying last night while in bed. My praying brought me to serious soul searching. I have been so worried that I wanted to be too selfish with you. I feared I would come between you and you obeying the leading of the Holy Spirit. I realized my confusion that I'm not number one in your life, the Lord is and I am second best." She shared with a soft laugh, bringing an understanding smile to her husband's face as he busily prepared his wife breakfast.

"I have been terribly bored while you are out doing the Lord's work He has assigned you. I know better than to have idol time. I preached this to the youth group just before we married. I am seeking out the Lord's work for me, Kelley. I believe my time has expired in just learning how to be married."

"I agree." Kelley said pleased, setting his wife's breakfast and medicine on the table, followed by assisting her with her chair. Refilling both their coffee cups, Kelley sat down at the table with his wife.

"I am ready to join you in the park ministry. I need and must join you. I can't wait to accompany you." Darla shared excitedly, her excitement bringing a laugh from her husband.

"Oh, Baby doll, you don't know how long I've waited to hear you say this." Kelley said happily.

"Would you like to take our daughter and me for a ride?"

"Sure, where would you like to go?"

"To visit my parents, unless you would like to go alone and confront my mother with my news." Darla answered with a nervous laugh.

"Whichever way you wish, Babe. I don't allow people to intimidate me as easily as you." Kelley replied with understanding.

"Thank you, however, I know it's my place to inform Mother. I would like your presence for moral support if you are comfortable with this."

"I'm more than comfortable with being at your side, Babe. We are partners working for the Lord, we must be partners or we will have strife between us."

"Honey, as far as my comment made to Dan and Cindy last evening..." Darla started, taking her husband's hand into her hand lovingly.

"I truly wasn't speaking against you, I only spoke one sentence. When you went to shower, I begged Dan not to repeat what I may say in my times of weakness. I simply expressed how I felt which is, I miss my husband. I wouldn't belittle you, Kelley." She explained compassionately, looking into her husband's eyes.

"Dan stressed this, Babe. As I said, I got my feelings hurt. Occasionally, I forget to be the strong man the Lord requires me to be and allow, as you said, 'my pride to be bruised.' Please tell me how you feel when my ways are neglectful or upsetting to you. I do not like others knowing more about my wife than me. It is my place to know, understand and correct."

"Yes, dear, I will hasten to Dan's warning, that it is impossible for one to be a perfect wife, having a perfect marriage. I will be obedient unto the scriptures which command me to be a help mate unto my husband. I will, thus forth, tell you when I am upset, believe me." Darla replied with a gentle smile, bringing laughter from her husband.

"I always knew the honeymoon would end and this day would come." Kelley confessed with laughter, his cheeks flushed.

"Come here, you." He instructed. With her hand still in his, he brought her to him as she stood.

"Sit, Wife." Darla sat down on her husband's lap, putting her arms around his neck, as the young couple looked into one another's eyes.

"I love you Mrs. Peterson and I am honestly sorry I have hurt you. This does break my heart when you hurt." Kelley shared, looking into her eyes.

"I know. I love you, Kelley and I need you and want as much of you as I can get." Darla replied sincerely, looking up into his eyes.

"How long has it been since I really kissed you?" Kelley asked with a tender smile.

"It has been much too long."

Kelley kissed his wife long and gently several times, and then held her in his arms reassuring her of her importance in his life.

"One more kiss, I hear a car in the drive." Darla suggested, eagerly.

"Sure, it's Bill and Dan. They took care of my flat tire problem." Kelley informed and then granted his wife her wish, kissing her once again.

"Babe, look towards the back door." Instructed Kelley with a grin his face flushed. As Darla looked she broke into a tickled laugh, quickly getting up from her husband's lap. Bill and Dan stood with their faces to the glass, appearing to be in shock.

"Send them away, Husband." Darla laughed embarrassed, sitting down at the table with her back towards the back door, as Kelley got up from his chair.

"That would be rude to send our visitors away." Kelley stated.

"They're the ones being rude." She replied with a soft laugh.

"True, but then, you know Bill and Dan enjoy seeing my beautiful wife blush." With a chuckle, Kelley opened the back door for their visitors.

"You're welcome to come in, I warn you, that you are entering at your own risk because my lovely wife says you both are rude." Kelley informed embarrassing his wife more, sending her into laughter as she put her face in her hands to hide her embarrassment.

"We are rude? I didn't see a do not disturb sign hanging on the door." Remarked Bill as he eagerly picked his niece up.

"My husband is becoming negligent. We have a no trespassing sign that he forgot to put out, apparently." Darla voiced with a soft laugh, bringing laughter from the three men.

"Quarrels can be a blessing because making up is lots of fun." Dan stated as he helped himself to a cup of coffee, bringing laughter from the others.

"The perfect marriage had their first quarrel?" Bill teased.

"We didn't quarrel. We each only made one stern comment to one another. I hardly call that a quarrel." Darla corrected.

"Sis, your one comment can be very bluntly to the point when tested."

Darla laughed now for several long minutes; her cheeks flushed knowing her brother spoke the truth, as did Dan and Kelley.

"Nor..." Darla continued between laughter.

"Nor, do I claim to have the 'perfect marriage'. I have just learned I'm not the 'perfect wife'."

"Allow me to be the first to congratulate you." Dan said, springing to his feet and extending his hand to his wife's cousin.

"A miracle has been performed." Bill sided, the men enjoying their teasing and laughter.

"Kelley, what is your calendar like this evening?" Darla asked, as she ceased her laughter.

"Considering the telephone is still off the hook, it is empty."

"I would like to have a cookout if you agree and invite our families. I would like to celebrate our obeying the Lord as we serve Him in His ministry as a united team." Darla suggested, excitedly.

"I say we leave the telephone off the hook for the day and celebrate." Kelley agreed with a pleased smile.

"Would you like to begin by sharing with Bill and Dan what you have decided?" Kelley asked his face now serious.

"Yes, thank you." She silently knowing her husband was making available the opportunity to share with her non-Christian brother, also knowing Dan's secret yearning to become involved in the ministry, due to her husband confiding in her. Kelley, obeying the leading of the Holy Spirit, made a way for Darla to allow the Holy Spirit to work through her to deal with their guests separate needs, this realization excited her even more.

"Sis, I don't have all day." Bill teased with a grin, often impatient with his sister's slow passive ways.

"Then I will be blunt, dear brother. I have had too much idol time on my hands and the Lord has answered my prayers in solving this problem. I will be returning to the park ministry as a partner with my husband, working for the Lord starting Tuesday." Darla shared, happily.

"Amen, it is about time." Dan remarked, sensing Darla's excitement.

"I am next in receiving my answer." With eagerness, he looked at Kelley.

"I believe you are right, Dan." Kelley encouraged wholeheartedly.

"I can't believe you are allowing Darla to return to the city park, Kelley." Bill scolded.

"It is Darla's choice to make. It is not my will for Darla's calling, yours or your parents will. It's the Lord's will she has chosen to obey. This is pleasing unto God; do you wish to question God in His judgment?" Kelley asked calmly, looking into his brother-in-law's face.

"I may not be a Christian, but I am no fool." Bill answered his concerns for his sister's safety apparent.

"Bill, Darla will never attend the park without me, this I assure you." Kelley informed, well aware of his brother-in-law's fears for his sister.

"I also, assure you this, Bill." Darla sided.

"I don't intend to be foolish either." She added with compassion, patting her brother's hand.

"Now, if you each will excuse me, I will make myself presentable to go share my news with my not-so-understanding mother."

Taking a quick shower, Darla dressed in a slacks outfit for the cool, winter Saturday. Leaving her room, returning to the kitchen, Darla quietly prepared her daughter's diaper bag. Dan sat at the table with his head bowed in earnest prayer seeking guidance in his life. Kelley stood at his side with his hand on his shoulder as he prayed aloud. Glancing through the kitchen window, Darla noted her brother's car was gone. Removing Heaven from her walker where her daddy apparently put her, she left the kitchen.

With Heaven bathed and dressed for their outing, returning to the kitchen, Darla found the men absent. Glancing through the window, she observed her husband seeing Dan to his car.

"I am blessed." Kelley stated happily, as he entered the house.

"I have two beautiful girls." He kissed first Heaven, then Darla.

"You may hear your dad shout, Heaven." Kelley said.

"If you feel the need to shout Husband, it is allowed as long as the shout is unto the Lord." Darla said with a soft laugh, excited for her husband's excitement.

"I feel bold enough to even deal with Mom Roberts." He shared with a pleased grin.

"Shall we go?" He asked anxious to be busy about the Lord's work, bringing an excited laugh from his wife.

"Yes, Preacher Kel, I am ready." Darla answered.

Kelley sang praise choruses during their drive from their country home to his in-law's home on the opposite side of town. Darla silently enjoyed the sweet presence of the Holy Spirit that seemed to flow from both she and her husband.

Parking his car near the patio doors of his in-law's home, the young couple could see Darla's parents having lunch.

"At least your parents are already sitting down." Kelley said with a comforting smile, bringing a smile to his wife's face.

"Hi, kids." Dad Roberts greeted as he opened the patio door.

"Hi, Daddy." Greeted Darla pleasantly, giving her father a kiss.

"Hi, Mother." She greeted, giving her a kiss as she sat at the table.

"Hi, dear, this is a nice surprise." Her mother stated.

"Babe, Kelley, can I get you kids a plate?" Dad Roberts questioned.

"Not for me, Daddy, thank you."

"Kelley? You must be getting hungry." Darla stated.

"No, thank you, Dan and I had a sandwich."

"I tried to call you earlier. I have since learned you have your telephone off the hook." Mom Roberts informed.

"I used to threaten Dad that I was having our telephone taken out during our years in the ministry." She shared with a gentle smile.

"This wasn't Mom's only threat." Dad Roberts informed with a chuckle, making his wife blush.

"Mark, don't be funny." Warned his wife with a soft laugh, bringing understanding smiles to the young couple's faces.

"I hear you, Mom. She has always ruled me with an iron fist." He teased.

"As time goes by lookout Kelley, wives can become unbearable." He warned.

"Dad, you had better be careful before you have Mother and me both upset with you." Darla suggested pleasantly.

"Thank you, dear." Her mother replied with a loving smile.

"What are you kids up to today, Kelley?" Dad Roberts asked as he pushed his empty plate aside, leaning back against his chair.

"My beautiful wife has some exciting news she can't wait to share with you and your wife."

"Papa." Heaven said, holding her arms toward her grandpa.

"Let me have her, Babe." Dad Roberts insisted eager to take Heaven into his arms.

"What is your exciting news, Babe?" He asked.

"I'm joining Kelley in the park ministry." Informed Darla pleased.

"Congratulations, Babe." Dad Roberts replied yet his face held his opinion on reserve, as he glanced at his wife's shocked expression.

"Darla Roberts, you can't be serious." Her mother scolded.

"Mother, I am Darla Peterson now and yes, I am quite serious." Darla assured with tenderness on her face, as her mother's face clearly expressed her disapproval for her daughter's comeback.

"Darla, you promised me you would never enter that park again."

"Mother, you made me promise. I was barely sixteen and I had to obey your orders. I belong in the park ministry, I feel empty inside. I have longed to return for four long years."

"Are you saying I was wrong to forbid your returning after what happened to you?" Mom Roberts questioned, as though daring her talk against her.

"No, Mother, I would never speak against your or Dad's rules set for me during my youth. You did what you had to do as my mother, protecting me. I was wrong and I am to blame for that horrible night and all my problems resulting from that night. I should have explained to you and Dad the importance of my returning. I am to blame, Mother."

"Kelley, have you encouraged Darla to return to the park, after you know the pain we each went through?"

"Mary, be careful what you say." Dad Roberts stated his voice was gentle for he understood her heartache, yet his voice held the sound of wisdom.

"I have encouraged Darla to seek the leading of the Holy Spirit. This is Darla's own conclusion as a result of her seeking. I do back her one-hundred percent. The Lord gave Darla and me this ministry as partners. I do not wish to now, or ever question the Lord's orders. I assure you Darla will never enter the park without me at her side. I trust and pray this will bring you some comfort." Kelley answered respectfully.

"Mother, please understand, I must obey the Lord." Darla pleaded kindly.

"I have never been able to put what happened to you out of my mind, Darla." Mom Roberts shared with moist eyes, her face bearing her pain, as she grew silent as though defeated.

"I know this, Mother. I don't pretend to understand the depth of your pain as a mother. If it is any consolation, I have never been able to put that night out of my mind either. I recall each painful detail of being beaten, but I have learned to answer the questions 'why me?' I too have learned to eliminate the anger from my heart. Do remember, Mother, please, the person who attacked me in the park wasn't one who hangs out in the park. He was an escaped convict, passing through town, please?" Darla asked, with her own eyes watery with seeing her mother's pain, as she looked into her devoted mother's eyes.

"I will try, dear." Mom Roberts answered forcing a weak gentle smile, as her tears escaped. "Excuse me, please." Mom Roberts left the kitchen to shed her tears in private.

Darla sat a moment, her heart aching for her mother's pain.

"Excuse me." Suddenly breaking their silence, leaving the table, Darla went to her mother's aid, she finding her weeping.

"Mother…" Darla started, surprised to see her mother so upset.

"Darla, please wait in the other room." Mom Roberts said her back to her daughter.

"I will not." She refused, going to her mother's side putting her arm around her and comforting her.

"You are becoming too big for your britches, disobeying me." She spoke, forcing a weary smile through her crying.

"It must come with age. Kelley is beginning to form the same opinion of me as you are." Darla shared with a tender smile, making her mother laugh.

"Mother, I love you dearly. I caused you and dad pain in the past. Trust me when I say the pain is over, be happy with me, and rejoice with Kelley and me as we obey the Lord as a team, as you and dad have always done. I need your prayers and your support. It can be a lonely life being a minister's wife."

"You learn quickly, dear." Mom Roberts complimented, with a pleased smile.

"Then you understand I need you to always back me?" Darla asked with tenderness in her eyes and sincerity on her young devoted face.

"Yes, Sweetheart, I understand your needs." Her mother answered hugging her daughter.

"I'm proud of you, dear. No matter how upset I may become with my concerns for you, stay united with your husband in his ministry, this is vital, sweetheart."

"Yes, Ma'am." Darla replied politely with a loving smile.

"Now, take your husband and leave, so I don't have to face him in my present embarrassing state." Mom Roberts ordered blushing, followed by a kiss for her daughter.

"Okay." With an understanding smile, giving her mother a tight hug followed by a kiss, she politely left her mother to her privacy. Returning to the kitchen to her father, husband and daughter, the men ceased their conversing with Darla's arrival, with looks of concern on their faces.

"Dad, we need to leave." Darla informed, taking her daughter from her father.

"Thanks for your approval; it means a lot to me." She assured with a loving smile, giving her father a tight hug and a kiss.

"You're welcome Babe. I am behind you and Kelley all the way."

"I know, Daddy"

"How is Mom, Babe?" Her father inquired, as he walked the young couple to the door.

"She will be okay." Darla answered with a reassuring smile.

"She is a Roberts." Darla reminded bringing a pleased grin to her father's face.

"You're right, Mom will be fine." Her father agreed.

"We will see you this evening, Sir?" Kelley asked, as he held his hand out to shake his father-in-law's hand.

"If my wife feels up to it, yes."

Kelley assisted his wife inside the car. With Heaven on her mother's lap, Darla gave her daughter her bottle, as she grew tired with their outing interrupting her naptime.

"Your dad is sincerely pleased you will be working in the park ministry." Kelley shared, as he started the car engine.

"I knew Dad would understand. He talked with me just before we married. In fact, he apologized for not allowing me to return to the ministry after my accident."

"Then you have one Roberts support." Kelley voiced with a comforting smile.

"One and a half, Mother will come around." Darla corrected confident.

Darla enjoyed entertaining. She loved the sound of laughter and her home being filled with voices. She enjoyed going from guest to guest waiting on them. She secretly wished her guests would stay forever. With her husband's busy schedule, she found it more often difficult than not to make plans for entertaining.

"Babe, would you like to go in separate cars this morning?" Kelley asked as he slipped his suit coat on.

"I will have to stay after the services for a Sunday school meeting." He added.

"No, attending services are the only time I am positive I get to be accompanied by you."

Darla enjoyed having Kelley sitting at her side in the young adult class during Sunday school. She had missed him even more than she had thought with his free time being so limited.

"Kelley." Pastor Finks spoke in a whisper, as he called Kelley from the classroom.

"Excuse me, Babe." Kelley whispered, handing Heaven to his wife.

Kelley was absent the remainder of class time. Darla secretly had wished for this time together. With class dismissal, she left the classroom, briefly visiting with the young adults. The time slipping by quickly, she hurried to the nursery. Checking, and then changing Heaven's diaper, she tiptoed down the aisle to her usual pew, finding her pew empty of her husband as the service began. She glanced at the platform, yet he was not there. Glancing at the middle section of pews, she spotted her parents, giving them a warm smile as they both did for her. Cindy soon joined her.

"It looks like the Pastor drafted both our husbands." Cindy whispered.

"Why?" Darla asked.

"To be ushers, it looks like I'm going to grow to be an old lonely wife also. Dan is talking about going into the ministry."

"We will grow old together." Darla replied with a comforting smile.

"Come have Sunday dinner with us." She added.

"I was supposed to invite you and Kel."

"We will discuss this after service. Kelley's pet peeve is visiting during service time." Darla suggested with a gentle smile.

The two young women were silent now, as they sat attentive,

joining in the song service. Kelley and Dan along with two other ushers approached the front of the sanctuary.

"They do look handsome." Darla whispered, with a loving smile.

"Yes, the handsomest." Cindy agreed, pleased.

Cindy and Darla listened attentively to the sermon without their spouses. Dan and Kelley sat in the back pews. At the close of the service the men greeted visitors, inviting them to visit again and shaking hands with each present as they left the sanctuary.

With Grandpa Roberts proudly taking Heaven from her mother, Darla was able to mingle greeting friends.

"Darla." Glenda spoke, a fourteen-year-old.

"May I speak with you?" She asked, her face appearing troubled.

"Yes, Ma'am, you may." Darla answered with a gentle smile.

"Excuse me." Darla said to the young woman she had been visiting with. Darla put her arm around the young teenager's waist, walking away from others to give them privacy.

"I need to apologize to you." Glenda began, her cheeks flushed as she looked at the floor.

"I don't know why you feel this need. I don't feel offended by you." Darla assured compassionately, comforting the troubled youth.

"For what I said about you when you were engaged to Kelley." She replied, her cheeks reddening even more.

"Oh." Darla said with a sigh, now recalling why the youth felt burdened.

"You only said, 'Kelley was marrying one who already had a child.' You spoke the truth."

"Yes, but I didn't say it as nice as you just did. I didn't intend for you or Kelley to hear me. I was gossiping. I've wanted to tell you I'm sorry for talking about you for a long time."

"You're forgiven and it is forgotten." Darla assured.

"Thank you for thinking enough about my feelings though to apologize." She added pleased, giving Glenda a tight loving hug.

"I told you Darla is a softy." Kelley spoke with a pleased grin, as he joined his wife.

"She is pretty too." Glenda said, now relaxed.

"She is beautiful." Kelley corrected, bringing a laugh from the teenager, as his remark made his wife blush.

"Dar, I have to attend the Sunday school meeting now. Dan and Cindy are joining us for dinner. If you girls would like to go home, I will ride out with Dan."

"Are you sure about the dinner arrangements? Cindy invited us to their home."

"I assumed..." Kelley started, his face flushed.

"Dear, you men must learn to talk to your wife's, do not assume anything." Darla instructed.

"She is also bossy." Kelley informed winking at Glenda, bringing a smile to her face as well as Darla's.

"Cindy and I will wait. We will work out dinner plans." Darla informed, kindly.

"Yes, Ma'am, I will see you in a bit."

Cindy and Darla visited while the Sunday school meeting was in progress. Heaven lay on the pew between the young women, drinking her bottle as she began to fall asleep. Cindy shared her fears of being a minister's wife. "A specter for all to observe and judge," was the words Cindy used to describe the role. This brought a tickled laugh from Darla. She hadn't thought of her present position in her cousin's manner.

Deciding to eat out with the lateness of the hour, the couples enjoyed one another's fellowship over dinner. Returning to their separate homes, Darla put Heaven in her crib. Kelley went to his desk in the den to study his prepared message for the six-thirty youth service. With her Sunday dress changed and her robe around her, Darla went to her husband's side.

"Honey, I'm going to take a nap, will you wake me if I don't hear Heaven?"

"Sure." Kelley agreed as he took his eyes from his study Bible.

"You do look tired, do you feel okay?" He asked.

"I am just tired. I will feel rested with a short nap." Darla answered giving her husband a light kiss.

Waking two hours later by her husband, Darla prepared a salad.

"You still look tired." Kelley said as they enjoyed their salad together.

"I am a little. I have had a full weekend."

"You still have a full night ahead of you with church and you work tomorrow." Kelley reminded, his face expressing his concern.

"True, but I will be off work all day Tuesday. I'm not ill, Kelley, I'm simply a little tired." She assured.

"You are leveling with me?"

"Yes, Sir." Darla answered with a pleasant smile.

Darla was pleased Kelley was able to sit with her during the evening service. With the close of the service, she sat back down on the pew, while Kelley remained standing, visiting with several that approached. She couldn't wait to return home and go to bed, ending her rewarding and exciting, yet tiring weekend.

"Darla, would you like to join your parents for a taco? Your dad is buying." Kelley informed, as her parents stood near her husband. Darla wanted to take a rain check, yet seeing the eagerness of her parents wishing for their company, she decided against her thought.

Darla was pleasant as she and Kelley joined her parents at the Mexican restaurant, yet she was quiet, secretly trying to conceal her overwhelming tiredness, as not wanting to alarm her family.

"Darla, could I talk you into teaching the high-teen girls class on Sunday mornings?" Her father asked.

"Do the parents of these teens know you are asking me to teach their daughters? Kelley has received unfavorable remarks of his choice in taking me as his bride with me having a child before marriage." Darla asked her cheeks flushed as her question seemed to bring a cloud over their table, silencing the happy excitement that was felt by all.

"I don't know, Babe." Her father answered, his face saddened as was her mother's and her husband's.

"If the parents approve, I would like to teach the class." She informed, with a loving smile, hoping to quickly cheer her family.

"You look tired, dear." Mom Roberts spoke concern in her eyes.

"Have you been taking your medicine, Babe?" Dad Roberts asked, as their eyes were each on her now.

"Yes, I have, faithfully. I have simply had a busy weekend. Tuesday I intend to sleep until noon." Darla answered with a soft laugh, hoping to relieve her parents and husband of their concerns.

"Kelley, you make sure she does this." Her Mother instructed, in her often-protecting way.

"Yes, Ma'am." Kelley agreed, he glancing at his wife as to say, 'you didn't level with me'.

"If you will excuse us, I believe I will get my wife home and to bed." Kelley added.

"Kelly, you haven't finished eating." She objected.

"Please finish eating, a few more minutes one way or the other isn't a big deal."

"I'm finished and it is late." Kelley replied, getting up from their table.

"He is as bad as you two were when I was growing up." Darla said with a gentle smile.

"Good, we are counting on this." Mom Roberts replied with a pleased smile.

"I'm doomed." Darla complained lightly, as she pushed her chair up to the table, bringing smiles to her parents' and Kelley's faces.

Kelley started his car then looked at his wife with both worry and disapproval on his face.

"Darla, why did you accept your parents' invitation with you being this wore out?"

"They seemed eager to have us join them. Kelley, I'm not ill, please quit worrying. I will be fine by morning." She assured. Kelley silently looked away from his wife then pulled out of the parking lot, as though in deep thought.

Arriving at their home, Kelley opened the car door for his wife. He handed her his house key.

"I will get Heaven and her things while you get ready for bed."

He instructed. Darla silently carried out her husband's wishes, knowing he was annoyed with her.

Dressed for bed, Darla entered the nursery where Kelley sat rocking Heaven, as she drank her bedtime bottle.

"May I give our daughter a goodnight kiss?" Darla asked with an understanding smile.

"Of course you can." Kelley answered with gentleness in his eyes as Darla kissed the top of her daughters head.

"And my husband?" She inquired with a loving smile.

"Most definitely." He answered and then kissed his wife's lips.

"Goodnight, Babe."

"Goodnight." Darla replied.

When waking the following morning to the alarm and quickly turning it off as not to wake her husband, Darla felt better. As she had predicted, her overwhelming tiredness had lifted. She knew this experience was a warning to her body. As much as she disliked her solution, she knew she had to stop her late nights waiting her husband's return. This meant any number of nights could pass without saying goodnight to one another. This saddened her heart, for she already felt they saw too little of one another.

"Oh, Lord, help me be more patient with both Kelley and myself as we be your servants." She silently prayed.

"Kelley, it is time to get up." She said as she woke him.

"Call your dad and tell him I'm taking the day off." Kelley replied, rubbing his head.

"Is this what you would like?" Darla questioned not sure, if her husband was serious.

"Yes, but don't call him." Kelley said, as he got out of bed.

"You look better this morning." He noted, relieved.

"And you doubted my honesty?" She asked, as she quickly made their bed.

"Your brother is right. You do have a way with words." Kelley said with a grin.

"You didn't answer my question."

"Nor will I answer your question." Kelley informed with a chuckle, bringing a smile to his wife's face.

"Your breakfast will be ready when you return from caring for our horse and dog, Husband." Darla informed pleasantly, as she started to leave the bedroom.

"Your horse and your dog that I inherited." Kelley mumbled teasing, bringing a laugh from his wife.

Darla's workday was busy. Having a terrible case of the flu going around, the doctor's office was full of unscheduled appointments. When closing time arrived, the waiting room still had patients that hadn't seen the doctor. Picking the telephone up, Darla called her mother-in-law explaining she would be late to pick Heaven up. Darla did her job quickly to get the patients in and out, yet it seemed the doctor was content working in slow gear.

"Darla, you are to call Kelley when you have a minute." The secretary informed.

"Thank you." Darla replied kindly as she went to the telephone to call home.

"Hi, Honey." She greeted pleasantly.

"Hi, Babe, I understand the flu bug has hit our area."

"Yes, it has been hectic all day. If Dr. Paul doesn't shift into high gear, I'm leaving him to fend for himself."

"Do I hear irritation in my gentle wife's voice?"

"Yes, Kelley, I don't know when I will be finished here." She answered with a sigh, disliking her family time being interrupted.

"I will meet you at my parents' house. Mom invited us for dinner, so you will not be concerned with dinner preparations." Kelley said.

"Your mother is a life saver. Honey, will you drop off some clothes for me? I would like to change my uniform here. I certainly don't want my family catching this flu."

"Sure, I'll be by shortly."

Darla felt relieved when the doctor saw the last patient; she quickly tended to her duties.

"Darla, would you finish up and lock up for me? I'm late meeting my wife for dinner." Dr. Paul informed. Before Darla could answer, he started toward the back door with his briefcase.

"I will help you, Darla." The secretary Gloria offered, sympathetically.

"Thank you." Darla accepted forcing a weak smile.

"Dr. Paul sometimes forgets we have families also." Gloria complained.

With everything in order, Darla quickly washed up and changed her clothing. Glancing at her watch, she locked the office doors then hurried toward her car. She secretly hoped Kelley's family had started dinner without her, for she knew it was way past their dinner hour.

"Where are you going, beautiful?" Kelley asked as he pulled up by his wife.

"Crazy." Darla answered with a weak smile.

"I bet. It's eight o'clock." Kelley said.

"I know, I'm sorry, Honey." Darla apologized, feeling guilty for being late.

"It couldn't be helped. Mom sent a plate of dinner for you, I will follow you home."

It was eight-thirty when arriving home and near nine when Darla had Heaven settled in bed.

"Babe, Gloria wants you to call her." Kelley informed.

"Gloria?" Darla questioned slowly, as she quietly left her daughter's room.

"If she asks you to work tomorrow, remind her you are off on Tuesdays." Kelley reminded before returning to the den.

Entering the bathroom, Darla began her bath water. Going to her bedroom, she gathered fresh clothing. Sitting down on the edge of her bed, she returned Gloria's call. "This is Darla, Gloria, Kelley said you called."

"Yes, Eunice called and she is sick with the flu. Dr. Paul will need you to fill in for her tomorrow."

"Gloria, Kelley has already voiced his opinion on my working tomorrow. To be honest with you, I'm exhausted." Darla replied slowly.

"This is too short of notice for me to get a temporary nurse for tomorrow. Dr. Paul will need you, Darla."

"I know." She agreed with a sigh.

"I will see you in the morning." Darla agreed after moments of hesitating.

Slowly leaving her room, she returned to the bathroom. She felt like her stomach was in knots. She had not been faced with going against Kelley's wishes since they had married. She knew she did need to rest tomorrow for her long day had exhausted her. Tomorrow night was to be her first night with her husband in the work her heart longed to return to, yet she was employed by Dr. Paul. It would not be fair to him to leave him in such a spot.

Dressed for bed feeling drained from her exhausting day and her problem at hand, she returned to her room. Feeling defeated, she picked up the telephone on the night stand.

"Cindy?"

"Yes. Hi, Dar."

"Hi, I have a major problem." Darla began nervously, feeling like a trader.

"What's wrong?" Cindy asked concerned.

"I need a sitter for Heaven tomorrow, are you free?"

"Yes, I will sit Heaven Darla, but what is your problem?" Cindy asked.

"Darla." Kelley spoke standing in the doorway with his hands on his hips, appearing most annoyed. Darla suddenly felt like a small child caught with her hand in the cookie jar. She knew her face must be its reddest.

"Darla, Darla?" Cindy called.

"I'm sorry, I'm okay. I will explain in the morning." Putting the telephone down slowly, Darla didn't return her eyes to her husband.

Kelley silently left the doorway standing in front of his wife, leaning against the dresser.

"Are you going to ignore me?" He questioned, thoroughly irritated.

"No." Darla answered letting out a long sigh, looking up into her husband's face.

"Kelley, I didn't have a choice, Eunice is sick with the flu. I couldn't allow Dr. Paul to be without a nurse tomorrow, please understand." She explained feeling too tired to bicker.

"Have you looked in the mirror tonight? You're exhausted, Darla." Kelley scolded.

"Kelley, I can't walk in and out of my job as I please, I do have an employer to answer to. I truly don't want us to quarrel. I simply don't have a choice."

"What about the park ministry tomorrow evening?" Kelley asked.

"I want to attend, of course."

"Darla, listen to me and hear me. You will not be in any condition to attend. You will be more tired tomorrow than you are now."

"I'm really tired, honey, please, can we hash this out in the morning?" She asked, feeling weak, as she slowly began removing her robe.

"Kelley, would you pull the covers back?" She asked putting her hand to her head as it began to ache.

"Darla." Spoke Kelley worried, as he quickly pulled the covers back.

"I just need to rest." She explained, lying down on the bed, appearing drowsy.

"Dar, what do I do?" Kelley questioned nervously.

"Hold my hand until I fall asleep." She answered with a weak smile.

"I will be a new person in the morning." She assured.

"You crazy girl, you're one person, not five." He scolded with tenderness in his voice. Taking Darla's hand in his, he kissed her lips gently.

"Mm, I feel better already." With her eyes closed, she gave her husband a loving smile and within moments, she was sleeping soundly.

Filled with worry, Kelley called Dr. Paul, questioning him in detail of his wife's condition.

"Let her sleep. Plenty of rest along with her medicine and proper diet, she will bounce back. You tell Darla I won't allow her to work for at least two weeks. I'm disappointed in her for allowing this to happen, she knows better, Son. She knows when she needs to slow down before reaching exhaustion." Dr. Paul informed.

Kelley sat for a few moments looking at his sleeping wife. Feeling helpless, he called his parents' home. "Dad, is Mom still awake?"

"No, Son, Mama had a long day. Maybe I can assist you?" Dad Peterson questioned.

"Maybe you can. Do you know any details about Darla's iron deficiency? You and Mom have been good friends with Darla's parents since we were kids."

"I know little, I only know of the time you and she were teenagers and Miss Darla spent some days in the hospital for this problem."

"This is what I keep recalling." Kelley replied rubbing his head wearily.

"Your Missy's ill?" Dad Peterson asked concern in his voice.

"I called her doctor, he calls her state exhaustion. Darla says she will be okay by morning, yet her doctor tells me she is not to work for at least two weeks. The doctor says with proper rest, diet and her medicine, she will bounce back." Kelley explained, yet still not finding comfort with his information.

"Son, I'm going to say something that I have on my heart. I don't wish any misunderstanding between myself and my boy. You, I'm proud to be your father. Son, does your Bible command you to have your house in order?"

"Yes, Dad." Kelley answered closing his eyes rubbing his head as though defeated.

"Miss Darla is a wonderful person and a true Christian. She is like my son and me at times, prideful. If your wife fails to listen to the signs that tell her to stop, be her signal, Son. It is your place to care for her in every way. Do you understand your old-fashioned father?"

"I understand, Sir." Kelley answered with a weak smile with his father's ways.

"Thanks, Dad, I should allow you to turn in for the night."

"The hour is never too late or too early when one is in need." He assured.

"We will be praying. You call if you have need of us." He added.

"I will, thanks again, Dad."

Kelley quietly removed the alarm clock from the nightstand near his wife's side of the bed. Leaving the bedroom, he closed the door. Opening the closet door in the hall, he removed a blanket. Entering the den, he set the alarm then made his bed on the sofa. Kelley lay awake for some time thinking on his wife's illness and her wishes as an individual. He thought about her role as a wife, mother, and his as her husband and the head of his family.

Awakened by the alarm, Kelley looked at the time as he turned the alarm off.

"Four-thirty, why does she get up so early?" He questioned, resetting the alarm for six. Kelley lay awake, unable to return to sleep with the matter of his wife's health tugging at him. With the passing of several long moments, repeating his questions over and over in his head, he got up from the sofa.

Quietly entering the bedroom, he went to his wife's side silently observing her as she slept. He recalled assisting her brother when Darla collapsed at school when she was a sophomore in high school. He recalled as he drove her to the hospital while her brother held her in his arms. He recalled the hours at the hospital waiting, wondering when she would awake.

"I will not allow you to do this to yourself again, Babe. Not for me or for any other reason." Removing fresh clothing from his room, he reclosed the bedroom door as he departed.

Showered and dressed for the day, Kelley entered the kitchen starting a pot of coffee. He stood near the sink staring out the kitchen window, waiting for the coffee to make. The telephone began to ring. Kelley quickly snatched the receiver from the hook hoping the incomplete ring had not waked his wife.

"Who on earth is calling at this hour?" He thought as he glanced at the clock.

"Peterson's." He spoke.

"Kelley, I'm sorry, did I wake you?" Cindy questioned apologetic.

"No, you have called before I have had my coffee though."

"I'm sorry. Darla is usually by the telephone at this hour." She explained.

"Are you telling me this is a morning ritual?" He asked surprised.

"Only on Tuesdays and Thursdays, Darla's days off work."

"Does everyone get up before I do in my wife's family?" Kelley questioned.

"Darla had the alarm set for four-thirty. It's now five-thirty and you are up and going." He added, bringing a laugh from Cindy.

"I may be awake, but I'm not my cousin. I haven't lifted a finger except to drink my coffee. Where is my cousin?" Cindy asked.

"She is sleeping." Kelley replied as he poured himself a cup of coffee.

"I'm sorry Kelley, I will call back later." Cindy replied quickly.

"Wait Cindy, please. Did Darla call you last night to sit Heaven today?"

"Kelley, I don't know what is going on. I don't want in the middle of anything." Cindy answered hesitant.

"My wife is under the weather from exhaustion. I'm merely trying to establish a lasting solution before she wakes." Kelley explained his concern present in his voice.

"I wasn't aware Darla felt poorly. She didn't mention this, but then she wouldn't want to worry anyone." Cindy voiced with a sigh.

"I have a feeling she has voiced herself more to you than anyone. I need some help in understanding my wife, Cindy. Trust me when I say I am at your mercy."

"I will help however I am able. I honestly don't know how I could help." She replied, feeling his desperation.

"For example, I had no idea she gets up at four-thirty in the morning. She wakes me at six, you knew this. She should be sleeping later than four-thirty."

"This I am able to answer. May I come out and have coffee with you?" Cindy asked, compassionately.

"Please do." Kelley answered feeling a sense of relief.

"I will be right out." Cindy informed.

Sitting his coffee cup on the counter, Kelley went outside to feed and water their horse and dog. He lingered in the yard when finished with the animals, hoping to catch sight of Cindy's car in hopes she held his answers within her.

As Cindy drove into the drive Kelley approached her, politely assisting her from her car.

"Good morning." He greeted his young face tense with worry for his wife.

"Good morning." Cindy greeted now seeing the depth of Kelley's upset, her heart quickly going out to him.

"Like I said, I'm not Darla, at six in the morning I'm half here. The other half of me is at home in my cosmetic bag." She shared with a comforting smile, bringing a relaxed smile to Kelley's face.

"I need more coffee at this hour also." She added.

"Coffee, I'm able to assist you with. Let's go inside." Kelley suggested.

Kelley sat a cup of coffee on the table for Cindy then a cup for himself. Sitting down at the table across from Cindy, Kelley's face showed his deep concern once again as he looked at his wife's cousin.

"You keep saying you are not your cousin, are you trying to tell me something?"

"Yes. Kelley, Darla not only wants to be the best wife like most of us, she has to be the best. In her eyes, to fall short of her expectations of herself, she has failed you. Darla gets up much earlier than you to ensure her the proper amount of time to look her best when she wakes you."

"I don't believe this." Kelley said releasing a long sigh.

"Darla wants to be the best wife, mother, nurse and Christian.

Kelley, look around your home, everything is perfectly in its place, and everything is spotless. If Darla had to get up at two in the morning and go to bed at midnight to fulfill her obligations, she would. She isn't capable of doing a task half way. You are the same way to a degree, you both are perfectionists."

"I feel everyone should always do their best. I never thought of either of us as perfectionists."

"Well, you are." Cindy informed.

"With Darla it is obligation. She has to always look her best for you, prepare you the special breakfast, the special dinner. If she thinks she will be five minutes late with your dinner, she worries she has let you down. If Heaven cries and she isn't right there to hasten to her need that second, she feels she has let her down. Everyone and their needs come first. You know Kelley, as kids, Darla would give me her priceless doll if I requested it. She will give of herself until she has nothing left to give if you allow her to. She is too sensitive and too compassionate most of the time for this crazy world. You know this, Kelley." Cindy added.

"What I'm about to tell you, Kelley, you must keep to yourself. You must find a way to reassure Darla without telling her I have spoken with you.

"As I said earlier, I'm at your mercy. I will keep our conversation between you and me." Kelley assured, sincerely.

"You recall the Friday night I spent the evening with Darla while Dan joined you in the park ministry?" Cindy asked.

"I recall this." Kelley replied.

"Darla shared with me her fears of not being enough for you." Cindy informed.

"Why, have I done something to make her have such questions?" Kelley questioned.

"No. She is still punishing herself for her brief time of straying from the Lord. She said at times she feels unworthy of your love. She is terribly sorry that others have offended you and embarrassed you by her past. She said you have always remained true to the Lord, that perhaps she deserves to be condemned, but not you."

"I was afraid this might happen." Kelley confessed rubbing his head wearily.

"I had hoped my taking a stand when Darla and I were engaged when speaking in church in my defense of our engagement would be enough to prove us equally worthy of one another. I stressed to her on our honeymoon the importance of her forgiving herself. If anyone deserves the treatment of royalty it is Darla. She harbors no bitterness toward the few passing judgment on her. Instead, she prays that she not be a stumbling block by the past that she is unable to erase."

"This is our Darla, strong, patient, loving, forgiving, yet very tender and sensitive. She needs a protector. She needs you Kelley. She needs your love, reassurance, and your strength. I have no doubt you are capable of getting her past her insecurities, nor do I doubt my cousin's will to overcome whatever is a hindrance in her marriage or her relationship with the Lord."

"Excuse me, Cindy." Getting up from the table, Kelley picked up the telephone, calling his father-in-law.

"Good morning." Kelley greeted.

"I dislike informing you of this, but I must stay home today. Darla isn't feeling well. No, please do not send her mother I believe I am needed today. Perhaps tomorrow her mother could come. Yes, I spoke with Dr. Paul last night and he ordered rest and no working for two weeks. Thank you, Sir. I will call you this evening." Kelley put the telephone down then politely refilled Cindy's coffee cup.

"Kel, would you like for me to sit Heaven today? Darla did call me last night asking me."

"No, thank you, I will be here, so this isn't necessary." Kelley answered.

"I appreciate you driving out, Cindy. You have helped me to understand in areas I wasn't aware of. I assure you, I will do right by Darla."

"This I know. You and Darla will get through this. Thanks for the coffee. If you or Darla need me, call Kelley." Cindy offered, as she got up from the table then placed her coffee cup in the sink.

Kelley cared for Heaven when she woke. He kept busy, yet his mind was on his wife, waiting for her to wake to be reassured that she would be okay again.

It was afternoon when Darla woke. Her head ached terribly, when she sat up on the side of her bed. Discovering the alarm missing from her nightstand, she slowly went to her dresser, finding her body felt weak and tired. Picking up her watch from her dresser top, learning it was after one, her heart seemed to skip a beat, she had let both her family and her employer down.

Slowly slipping into her robe, she made her way down the hall to the bathroom. As she washed her face she looked in the mirror. Her face was pale and her head pained her. In her present state there would be no concealing from her husband or anyone how terrible she felt.

"Darla." Spoke Kelley, tapping on the bathroom door.

"Yes?" Questioned Darla, leaning against the sink to support her body as she dried her face and Kelley opened the door slowly.

"Are you okay, Babe?" He asked, his expression quickly changing from concern to worry as he noted his wife's weakened state.

"No, I'm not okay." She answered, forcing a weak smile.

"I'm a bit lightheaded." She informed, holding her hand out to her husband. Kelley took her hand in his, assisting her through the doorway. As she neared his side, he let go of her hand, putting his arm around her thin waist, allowing her to lean against him for support as he walked her to the kitchen table.

"That was a long walk." She shared with a weary smile as she sat at the table appearing terribly weak.

"And you wanted to work today." Kelley reminded, with gentleness in his voice.

"I don't claim to be the wisest person." She answered, blushing.

"Perhaps you are not the wisest, but definitely the most beautiful and loving person." Kelley replied, giving her a light kiss.

"Thank you."

"What would you like to eat, Babe, breakfast or lunch?" Kelley asked.

"Actually, I would like to know where Heaven is." Darla said with concern on her face.

"In her crib napping, she and I had a full morning. I wore her out." Kelley informed with a comforting smile, setting his wife quickly at ease.

"Now, what would you like to eat?" He asked.

"A sandwich will be fine please." Darla leaned her head on her hand as she tired from sitting up and her head pained more.

"You may eat in bed, Dar, I won't object."

"Perhaps this would be wise." She agreed feeling drained.

"Perhaps my kind husband will spare me the walk?" She asked, closing her eyes and rubbing her aching head with her weak hand.

"Sure, Sweetheart." Kelley replied, his face expressing his fear with her weakened state. He picked his wife up, carrying her in his arms to their bedroom, putting her on the bed and pulling the covers over her.

"Honey, would you get my medicine and a pain pill, please? My head feels like it's going to explode."

"Yes, I will be right back with your medicine."

Darla kept her eyes closed as she gently rubbed her head until Kelley returned. Propping pillows behind his wife, he assisted her to a sitting position. Her pills taken, she handed her husband her water glass.

"Thank you." She said with a weak smile.

"You're welcome. I will make your lunch, Babe." Kelley kissed the top of his wife's head then departed from their bedroom.

Sitting up with her head leaning against the pillows, Darla's eyes grew moist. She was thoroughly disappointed in herself for allowing herself to become worn out. Her foolishness caused Dr. Paul to be left shorthanded on a day he needed her most. Even if Heaven would cry out for her now, she was too weak to care for her and Kelley, she thought, he must be scared to death.

She had not only cost Kelley a day's pay, but also let her father down by Kelley's absence from work. Tonight was to be her first night in four years to return to the park ministry. The work the

Lord had chosen for her. She had even let the Lord down, she thought, as her tears escaped.

"Babe?" Kelley questioned, as he returned to his wife's side with her lunch tray.

"I'm punishing myself for my failures." She explained, wiping her tears away.

"I can't believe how I have disrupted so many people's day by me being ill."

"We will work together, sweetheart, so this doesn't happen again." Kelley comforted, placing the tray before his wife.

"What is done is done, so eat your lunch. I want you to hurry and get your strength back." He instructed, sitting down beside the bed.

"I can tell by the size of my lunch." She agreed with a tender smile.

"Dr. Paul said you are to eat three balanced meals."

"You spoke with Dr. Paul?" Questioned Darla, looking into her husband's eyes, seeing the depth of his fear as she slowly began eating her lunch.

"Yes, I called him last night to learn how to help you get better. I was scared, honey. I kept thinking about your visit to the hospital when we were teenagers. I'm not fond of the idea my wife could be lying in the hospital." He shared, his face bearing his heartache.

"Sweetheart, when I went to the hospital I had missed taking my medicine for several days. My present medicine is working. I didn't do my part." Darla explained, compassionately.

"I'm sure Dr. Paul told you with rest, eating properly and my medicine, I will bounce back." She said.

"This is what he said. He also said you have warning signs before reaching this stage." Kelley shared, his expression now showing his disapproval as well as his concern. Darla's face flushed, as she was now silent, slowly eating her lunch, avoiding her husband's eyes.

"Did you have these warning signs, Darla?" Kelley asked.

"Yes." She answered, glancing at her husband's face briefly.

"I honestly thought Kelley, if I could hang in until today to really rest, I would be okay. I didn't realize I was this exhausted until last night." She assured, now looking into her husband's eyes hoping to comfort him. Kelley's face was now expressionless, he not allowing his wife to read his thoughts, he remaining silent.

Darla forced herself to eat all that she could.

"Are you full, Babe?" Kelley questioned, breaking their silence.

"Yes." She answered, once again rubbing her aching head. Kelley got up from the chair kindly removing the tray.

"Rest, Babe." He said, gently kissing her lips.

Darla slept soundly until late in the evening. When she woke, Kelley was sitting near the bed reading a book.

"Hi, sleepy head."

"Hi, what time is it?"

"A little after eight." Kelley answered, laying his book aside.

"Then Heaven is already in bed?" Darla asked with disappointment on her young face.

"She has been asleep for about fifteen minutes."

"How did Heaven do today?" She questioned, as she slowly sat up on the side of the bed.

"Finc." Kelley assured.

"I believe I will go give her a goodnight kiss." Darla replied feeling terrible for neglecting her daughter.

"Do you feel up to the walk?" Kelley asked as his wife slowly stood, holding onto the nightstand to steady herself.

"I must feel up to it, I'm her mother." Darla answered with determination on her face. Kelley silently walked with his wife, once again allowing her to lean against him. Arriving at her daughter's crib, Darla gently patted her on her back, and then gave her a kiss on her cheek. Looking up into her husband's eyes with a tender smile, Darla spoke. "She appears fine."

"I told you this." Kelley whispered with an understanding smile.

"I'm a terrific dad." He added.

"I know you are. My daughter and I are most lucky to have you." Darla replied pleased.

Assisted to the bathroom then back to bed, Darla ate her dinner in bed. Sleeping soundly until mid-morning the following day, Darla was wakened by the telephone.

Picking the telephone extension up, Darla heard her mother's voice before she could speak.

"It's Kelley, has Darla woke up?" He questioned, his voice sounding troubled.

"No, dear, I'm sorry I'm not able to offer you some good news as of yet." Mom Roberts answered.

"Good morning." Darla greeted as she lay in bed on the extension.

"I'm eavesdropping." She informed, hoping to comfort her husband.

"Mom Roberts, would you please visit my wife and inform me how she is?"

"Yes, Kelley."

"I feel better, Honey." Darla informed pleasantly.

"Good, your voice sounds stronger. How is your headache?" Kelley asked.

"It's gone." Darla gave her mother a smile as she entered her bedroom. "Here is Mother, Kelley." Darla handed her mother the telephone.

"Mother, please tell Kelley I feel better." Darla said, as she slowly sat up then got out of bed.

Slipping into her robe, Darla slowly left her bedroom for the bathroom. Although she still felt tired and weak, she did feel stronger. Her headache and lightheadedness was entirely gone.

"How are you getting along, Darla?" Mom Roberts asked outside the bathroom door.

"Fine, Mother, thank you." Darla replied as she slowly freshened up.

"I will start your breakfast, dear."

"Thank you." Leaving the bathroom, Darla slowly went to the kitchen.

"Mama Mama!" Heaven exclaimed excitedly, charging toward her mother in her walker, bringing a happy smile to Darla.

"Heaven has been saying your name all morning."

"Whoa, slow down Sweetheart." Darla said, grabbing hold of the walker so her daughter did not bang into her legs. Going to the table, Darla sat down.

"Heaven, come here." She said, holding her arms out toward her. Heaven excitedly went to her mother holding her arms up.

"Oh, Heaven, you must weigh a ton." Darla said, finding she could barely lift her daughter, as she sat her on her lap, hugging her happily.

"Darla, be careful." Her Mother cautioned, noting her weakened state.

Heaven was too excited to sit still with seeing her mother. She tried to stand on Darla's lap.

"Sweetheart, you must sit." Spoke Darla, finding it difficult to hold her active excited baby.

"I will take her, dear." Mom Roberts suggested, quickly removing Heaven from her mother's lap. Heaven began to fuss, reaching for her mother.

"Mother..." Started Darla, her heart going out to her daughter as her mother put her back in her walker.

"Darla." Spoke her mother sternly, causing her to blush and be silent. Darla sat silently looking away from her mother. Her heart ached to hold her daughter and grant her, her wishes.

"Mommy can't handle you until she gets stronger, dear." Spoke Mom Roberts, giving her granddaughter a kiss. Returned to her walker, Heaven quickly returned to her mother calling her name and holding her arms up to her.

"Mother, this is unbearable." Darla said with watery eyes, as she looked at her daughter wanting her.

"You being ill is unbearable to each of us, Darla. The sooner you get better, the sooner we each will feel better." She placed her daughter's breakfast on the table before her.

"Clear your plate. I assure you, I'm a much tougher nurse than your husband." Mom Roberts said with a comforting smile.

Darla silently began her breakfast. Sitting Heaven's highchair near her mother, Mom Roberts handed Heaven a cracker, as she sat her in her highchair.

"Here is your daughter, dear."

"Thank you, Mother." Darla replied, her eyes still watery for letting her daughter down. Darla took Heaven's tiny hand in hers, talking to her as she ate.

Mom Roberts tidied the kitchen, allowing her daughter and granddaughter to enjoy one another.

Completing her meal, Darla pushed her plate aside, leaning back in her chair wearily.

"Mama." Heaven said happily, once again holding her hands up to her mother.

"Mommy can't hold you, sweetheart." Darla said, giving her daughter a kiss, her eyes quickly growing moist.

"Dear, you really need to go lay down, Heaven will be fine."

Darla silently got up from the table and as she kissed her daughter her tears escaped. Ignoring her daughter calling her, she started for her room, her tears streaming.

Returning to her room and lying down, she cried for her daughter for some time before drifting off to sleep.

It was after four when Darla woke up. Slipping out from under the covers, she removed a pair of faded blue jeans from her dresser and a baggie sweatshirt. Leaving her room, she entered the bathroom starting her bathwater. It seemed to take her forever to bathe, tiring her, yet the warm water felt good. Removing the stopper from the tub, she slipped into her faded bell-bottom jeans, blue sweatshirt and blue socks. She sat down on the stool for a few minutes, catching her breath from her tiring activity. Slowly reaching for her brush, she brushed her long dark hair, allowing it to hang freely. Laying her brush down, she slowly stood up.

"Darla." Spoke Kelley, tapping on the door.

"Enter." She replied, putting her hairbrush away.

"Hi, am I keeping you from washing up?" She inquired with a weak smile.

"No, your mother said you have been in here for some time, I was concerned.

"I'm moving a bit slow."

"Do you feel better than yesterday?"

"Yes."

"Good, you look better. Your mother has dinner ready."

"May I talk you into picking up after me first?" Darla asked, appearing weak as she leaned against the sink.

"Sure." Kelley quickly tidied the bathroom.

"May we have dinner now?" He asked, putting his arm around her waist.

"Yes."

Entering the kitchen, Darla was surprised to learn her parents were having dinner with them.

"Hi, Dad." She greeted, as Kelley assisted her with her chair.

"Hi, Babe, how do you feel?"

"I feel better today than I felt yesterday."

"Darla." Spoke Kelley, holding his hand out toward his wife. Putting her hand in his, Kelley began asking the blessing.

"Mama, Mama!" Heaven exclaimed.

"Shhh." Darla said quickly, yet found her hushing to no avail.

"I'm sorry, Kelley." Darla apologized with the close of his prayer.

"For what? She is a baby and she has missed her mother." Kelley replied.

"Mama!" Heaven continued. Darla slowly got up from her chair.

"I will just hold Heaven for a few minutes, Mother." Darla said, removing her daughter from her highchair, as her mother remained silent. Dad Roberts and Kelley looked at the two women with questions in their eyes. As Darla took her baby into her arms, it was apparent Heaven was too heavy for her weakened state, though she returned to her chair with her daughter regardless.

Heaven excited wanting her mother after two days without her, pulled on Darla's sweatshirt trying to pull herself up to stand on her mother's lap. Darla's face quickly expressed the strain she was enduring, attempting to handle her active ten month old. Kelley got up from the table, gently taking Heaven from her. Heaven began to fuss, reaching and calling "Mama."

"Kelley, she misses me." Protested Darla as Heaven continued to fuss. Kelley silently returned to his chair with Heaven on his lap.

"You really should eat your dinner, Dar. Your mother is a good cook." Kelley said, breaking their silence. Kelley shared his dinner with Heaven, quickly bringing contentment to his daughter.

Slowly picking up her fork, Darla began her dinner feeling defeated, avoiding her family's eyes.

"Kelley, would you like me to stay with Heaven and Darla this evening so you can attend the midweek church service?" Mom Roberts asked.

"No, thank you. I am sure you are tired. I would like to be the one to be here."

"Who filled in for you at the park ministry last night?" Darla asked, suddenly realizing her illness was also interrupting Kelley's ministerial duties.

"Dan and I hear he did a fine job." Kelley answered.

"I'm sure he did." Darla replied approvingly.

"Last night was to be your big night back to the park, right?" Dad Roberts questioned.

"Yes, I have disappointed several people the past couple of days." Darla answered, her face flushed as she picked at her food.

"You can't undo what is already done, Babe. However, if you do this to yourself again, I may forget you are an adult and turn you over my knee. You have no reason to be in your present state. Kelley provides well for you."

"I know this, Dad." Darla answered pushing her half-eaten meal aside and letting out a sigh, her face its reddest.

"Darla, you have to eat." Kelley reminded, pushing her plate back toward her secretly winking at her, bringing a weak smile to her tired face. He always seemed to know when and how to comfort her.

Darla finally managed to complete her dinner by the completion of her family having their dessert.

Kelley got up from the table with Heaven in his arms. He washed her face then put her in her highchair, sitting her next to her mother. Kelley looked at his wife, putting his hand on her shoulder to comfort her.

"You, wife, let Heaven be." He ordered, and then gave his wife a light kiss.

Mom Roberts began to clear the table.

"Please leave the dishes you have done more than enough for us today." Kelley assured politely, as he refilled everyone's glass with tea.

"Besides, I'm just starting to get the hang of it." He added with a grin, bringing smiles to each ones face.

Going to the cabinet, Kelley removed a small plastic bowl putting pudding in it. Putting a spoon in Heaven's hand, he sat the pudding on her tray.

"Kelley, she will have pudding everywhere." Darla said, surprised at her husband.

"I will clean up after her; she has to learn some time." He insisted, enjoying watching Heaven.

"She has been attempting to master the spoon since you have been out of commission, Babe." Kelley assured, bringing approving smiles to each.

"I hear my bed calling me." Darla informed, slowly getting up from her chair.

"Mother, thanks for everything." Darla added giving her mother a kiss.

"You're welcome, dear."

"Daddy, love you." Darla said, giving her father a kiss.

"I love you, Babe."

"Yuck, Heaven." Darla said with a happy smile, looking at her daughter with pudding all over her face, hands and in her hair.

"Mama." Heaven said, grinning at her mother.

"Oh, no, it's Daddy you want." Darla said, bringing laughter from her family, as she managed to find a spot to kiss her daughter.

"Excuse me while I walk with Darla." Kelley said politely.

"Sure." Dad Roberts replied.

"Do I have to walk, Kel?" Darla asked, smiling at her parents.

"No." Kelley answered, sweeping his wife off her feet.

"Maybe I will take my time getting well." She informed, bringing tickled laughter from her parents and a grin from her husband. As Kelley neared their bedroom, carrying his wife, Darla looked into her husband's eyes.

"I love you, Kelley."

"I love you, Babe." He replied with a tender smile, giving her a kiss then standing her to her feet, he kindly straightened the covers for her.

"I will be in to check on you after I put Heaven to bed." Kelley informed as his wife anxiously got on her bed, beginning to feel drowsy.

"Please do." Darla said with a weary smile, as she lay on her side facing her husband.

"Honey..." She spoke as he started to leave.

"Thanks for being the best and for being mine."

"You're welcome, Baby doll." Kelley replied, and then gave his wife a kiss.

"Rest, you don't look as well as before dinner."

"Aye aye, Sir." She said with a weak smile, as she closed her drowsy eyes.

Darla slept through each of Kelley's visits to check on her. Waking near midnight, noting her bed was empty of her husband, she became alarmed. Getting up from her bed, still wearing her jeans and sweatshirt, she left her room. Noting a light on in the den at the end of the hall, Darla went to the den. Upon entering, she was immediately relieved seeing her husband at his desk with the telephone to his ear and his Bible open before him.

Kelley raised his head noting his wife, as she began walking toward him.

"It's late Preacher." Darla reminded, in a whisper. Kelley took his wife's hand in his, pulling her down on his lap. Putting his arm around her shoulders, he held her close to him, allowing her to rest her head on his shoulder.

"Slim, we are going to have to call a halt to our study for tonight, my wife caught me breaking curfew again."

"No, Angel will not be able to attend the park ministry Friday." Kelley stated.

"No, she will not be able to attend next week either." Darla raised her head up looking into her husband's eyes with disapproval on her face.

"I will be able to attend next week." Darla voiced in a whisper. Kelley looked at his wife, yet did not respond to her.

"The doctor said two weeks, so I intend to see to it she follows the doctor's orders." Kelley said, looking into his wife's eyes, his mind made up.

"Bye, Slim." He concluded.

"How do you feel, Babe?" Kelley asked, putting both his arms around her.

"More rested then dinner time. I woke finding you not in bed and this concerned me."

"My bed is over there until you have recuperated." Kelley informed, pointing to the sofa.

"Surely you are not serious."

"I'm quite serious. I have been sleeping there since Monday."

"Why?" She asked as though shocked.

"So you are not disturbed by my getting in and out of bed and not having the alarm wake you."

"You surely aren't able to sleep well on the sofa. I don't want you to continue this. It's not fair or right that you be forced from your bed." Darla said sympathetically.

"Nonetheless Dar, it's necessary until you are well." He insisted, even though he knew this saddened his wife's heart, making her feel guiltier.

"Is Mother coming tomorrow?" She asked, leaning back against her husband resting her head once again on his shoulder.

"No, you get my mother tomorrow, Cindy on Friday and yours truly on Saturday and Sunday." Kelley informed.

"You seem to have everything under control." Darla said, giving her husband a loving smile.

"Remember this when you are well, Babe. I'm capable of assisting you. It isn't necessary for you to become overburdened."

The following morning, Darla again slept until midmorning. When she woke, she felt even stronger. She knew she was now nearing the end of days in bed recuperating and this made her feel better mentally as well. She couldn't wait to regain all of her strength, being in full charge of herself, her home, her family, her job and whatever additional tasks the Lord may have in store for her.

Although her bath went more quickly this morning, she still found it a chore, tiring from the activity quickly. Leaving the bathroom, she sought out her daughter and mother-in-law. Locating them in the front room, she eagerly joined them.

"Good morning, Mom Peterson." Darla greeted with a pleasant smile.

"Good morning, Honey."

"Mama." Heaven began happily, as she sat on the carpet with her toys, Darla immediately going to her.

"Honey, I have been instructed by both Kelley and your mother that you are not to lift Heaven." Mom Peterson informed, her comment quickly causing Darla's smile to fade.

"This is for your own good, Sweetheart. After you have your strength back, you will have all the time you both need to make up to her." She added with a loving smile.

Darla sat down on the floor leaning her weak body against the sofa.

"Come to Mommy, Sweetheart." Darla said, holding her hands out toward her daughter with a weak smile. Heaven quickly crawled to her mother. Darla refrained from picking her baby up, but she hugged and kissed her several times.

"Is anybody home?" Bill questioned from just inside the back door.

"We are in the front room." Mom Peterson answered.

"Hello, Sister Peterson." Bill greeted politely, sitting down on the sofa near his sister, as she remained sitting Indian fashion on the floor.

"Hello, Bill." Mom Peterson greeted.

"How have you been?" She asked.

"Much better than my sister, I hear." Bill replied.

"How are you, Sis?" Bill asked, compassionately.

"I'm better. I feel stronger each day." She answered with a kind smile.

"You don't appear too peppy to be feeling better. I guess you gave Mom, Dad and Kelley a legitimate reason to be scared over you." He voiced with disapproval in his voice.

Darla now took her eyes from her brother, as her face flushed, detecting another lecture. She picked up one of Heaven's toys handing it to her daughter, smiling as Heaven eagerly took the toy from her.

"Bill, I need to prepare Darla's breakfast. Would you like to join her?" Sister Peterson asked getting up from the chair she was sitting in.

"Due to my sister standing me up for our luncheon date, I accept."

"I forgot, Bill." Darla said, quickly looking at her brother.

"I should have called you." She added.

"I'm not complaining, I get home cooking." He confessed with a chuckle.

"Join me for coffee, I haven't had mine as of yet." Darla suggested pleasantly, holding her hand out for her brother to assist her up from the floor and Bill assisting her to her feet.

"Are you going back to your hippie days?" Bill questioned, as Mom Peterson picked Heaven up from the floor.

"I don't understand your question." Darla replied, looking into her brother's eyes.

"Your dress, faded bellbottom jeans, socks with no shoes and a sloppy shirt." Bill explained bringing a smile to the two women's face, knowing how Bill enjoyed teasing his sister.

"I'm being comfortable and bumming, okay? I assure you, I won't embarrass you or my husband by leaving my home dressed in my present attire." She said with a gentle smile, as she sat down at the kitchen table, glancing at her mother-in-law.

"Remember the time you wanted to wear jeans out to dinner with Mom and Dad?" Bill questioned with a chuckle, as he sat her cup of coffee before her.

"Yes, Bill, I remember." Darla answered, leaning her head on her hand, as she grew tired.

"You remember I have a guest present." She warned, hoping to hush her brother.

"Sister Peterson is not a guest, she is family." Bill replied with a mysterious grin.

"My brother has always enjoyed embarrassing me." Darla shared with a weak smile.

"How old were you, Sis?"

"Sixteen. I remember the age quite well." Darla answered with a soft laugh, her face flushed from embarrassment recalling her rebellious time.

"The four of us were going out for dinner, Sister Peterson. Mom never approved of girls wearing jeans. Darla had her hippie jeans on. Mom told Darla to change her way of dress. Darla responds by saying she is already dressed. This aggravated both our parents by her rudeness. Mom gave her speech about Dar's dress then told her to change. Darla silently refused by not budging. Dad came unglued, informing her she would change. Dar said, 'Yes, Sir' and flew out of the room to change." Bill shared laughing, bringing laughter from both women.

With the completion of her meal, Darla excused herself, growing terribly tired. Returning to her bedroom, she made her bed, lying down on top of her covers. Though her brother's teasing always made her blush, she had enjoyed both, his visit and his sense of humor.

"Darla." Kelley spoke.

"Hi, Honey." Darla greeted with a loving smile.

"How was your day?" She asked.

"I had a good day." Kelley answered, sitting down on the edge of the bed.

"How was your day?"

"Bill visited, wearing me out and embarrassing me by sharing my embarrassing teen years with your mother. But besides that, I had a better day." Darla answered pleasantly.

"Good, Mom said you have only eaten one meal today. We have to start getting you up at meal times. You are to eat three meals a day, not one or two." Kelley informed, deeply concerned.

"Okay, is it dinner time?" Darla asked.

"Yes."

"Do we have guests for dinner? I'm bumming today." She explained, pointing to her dress.

"No, Mom just left. You look fine, regardless. Come have dinner." Kelley instructed, standing up then quickly assisting his wife.

"You are walking much better."

"I'm on my way to a complete recovery, Husband." Darla assured, with a comforting smile.

"I hope so, Babe. This has been a long four days." He replied concern on his young, tired face.

It was nice having the dinner hour alone together.

"Kelley, are you aware the telephone is off the hook?" Darla asked as she pushed her dinner plate aside.

"It is one of my solutions to one of several of our problems. The telephone comes off the hook during mealtime. This way no one will be allowed to call your husband away from eating your fantastic meals again." He explained, bringing a pleased smile to his wife's face, his idea touching her heart.

"I really appreciate this, Kelley."

"Dar, I will do whatever is necessary to keep you both well and happy. I'm not always able to read your mind. If something I do upsets you or if there is not enough of you to go around, please tell me." Kelley requested, sincerely.

"If this is the way you wish." Darla agreed, leaning back in her chair, taking Heaven's tiny hand in hers.

"You said we have several problems." Darla said, looking into her husband's eyes, questioning him with her eyes.

"The major problem is your health. Every area of our lives has been affected by your illness. I have some suggestions to help ensure you do not become exhausted again."

"Share your suggestions with me. I can use some fresh ideas."

"No more getting up at four-thirty in the morning. Babe, I do not care if you are in your robe when you wake me at six or how you are dressed. You look beautiful to me, regardless. No more waiting up for me to return home, you go to bed when you are tired. I assure you, I will always return. My body doesn't require the amount of rest that yours does. I'm beat by the end of each week and I'm healthy. You have been putting in more hours than I have."

"Kelley, if I don't wait up for you, there will be times when several days pass without even a goodnight said. There are more times than not that I see too little of you."

"I have a solution for this problem also. Dan is working with me now in the park ministry. He will take half of my calls that take me away until late at night, so I will be home more for my family and for my family's needs. I have been neglectful and I sincerely apologize to you for this, Babe." Kelley replied his cheeks flushed for failing his wife's needs.

"I'm extremely thankful to Dan for this. I don't see Cindy going for Dan leaving her sitting at home until all hours of the night." Darla said surprised.

"Believe me, when I say Dan is already in the dog house." Kelley informed with a chuckle. "Since you've been ill, Dan is receiving all the calls. Cindy is ready to murder her husband. Dan hasn't been blessed with a wife as patient as I have. You see Babe, you must hurry and get well before I lose my helper I just acquired." He added laughing, bringing an understanding smile to Darla's face.

Kelley got up from the table, removing his fussing daughter from her highchair. With her face and hands washed, Kelley stood Heaven up on the kitchen floor.

"Do we have any other problems?" Darla questioned, leaning her head on her hand. Kelley glanced at his wife, his face growing serious. Letting go of his daughter's hands, he went to the kitchen counter. Putting the telephone back on the hook, he then removed the pitcher of tea from the counter.

"Would you like more ice, Babe?" He asked, as he refilled their glasses with tea.

"No, thank you." She replied patiently waiting for her husband to answer her question. Kelley added ice to his glass, and then returned to his chair at the table.

"Your dad discussed you becoming the teen girls Sunday school teacher with the board members and several parents. You have the job if you want the job."

"Really? This is great." Darla replied, impressed.

"Dar, don't agree to this until you hear me out. After you hear me out, please take the time to pray and search out the Lord's will, please." He advised compassionately.

"Okay." She answered, sensing her husband was troubled.

"There is one mother throwing a fit over you teaching her daughter because you had Heaven before you married. She could give you a hard time." Kelley warned, knowing this was embarrassing to his tenderhearted wife.

"Joy Timmons' mother?" She inquired, her face flushed, her eyes watery.

"How did you know?"

"She makes it very clear she can't stand me, Kelley."

"You've never mentioned this."

"What good would it do? She is entitled to her opinion. I most certainly did mess up. No matter how one looks at this, I'm to blame. You can't protect me from everyone, dearest husband." Darla said with a smile, taking Kelley's hand in hers.

"Do pray about this Dar, before you decide." Kelley suggested sincerely.

"I will."

"You're intending to join me in the park ministry too. You have your nursing job, church services, besides a family and a home that you manage to keep spotless, and now perhaps, becoming a Sunday school teacher. You have proven by you becoming ill, you aren't able to handle all of this. Something must be eliminated." Kelley said wisely, looking into his wife's eyes with gentleness in his eyes.

"Kelley, there is nothing I want to eliminate." Darla informed, as though shocked by his suggestion.

"We are not discussing wants. We are discussing solutions to existing problems. You must re-evaluate your priorities. You don't have a choice because your health is at stake. Our bodies are the temple of the Holy Spirit and He commands us to take care of ourselves. God receives no glory when we abuse our bodies."

"Kelley, I have never suggested that you give up any of your activities." Darla defended.

"Dar, have you not been listening to me? You have no choice. You are not able to do the work of five people. The amount of work means nothing without quality. This is not being fair to yourself, Dr. Paul, to me, to your daughter, to each family member we have called on to help us out, and yet you want to add more activities. If you intend to be a part of the park ministry, your job has to go in addition to you ceasing the early rising hours and late to bed hours." Kelley informed.

"You're ordering me to quit my job?" Darla questioned, shocked.

"No, Babe, I'm saying you can't do both. I assumed you would obey the Lord by returning to the ministry. Your nursing is a want that you chose. You must decide where the Lord wants you. I will promise you this, I will not allow you to be in this condition again regardless how upset you become with me, nor will I allow you to do both the nursing and the park ministry."

"Kelley, I worked hard to become a nurse." She shared with watery eyes.

"I know you did, Babe." Kelley sympathized, as his wife's tears released.

"This isn't fair. Kelley, I have worked so hard since we married to fulfill each of my obligations."

"Darla, please, you have done a superb job with everything. I know how hard you have worked. You are still missing my point." Going to her side, Kelley put his arms around her.

"The point is, you have worked much too hard. You now must learn your limitations and accept them. This is all I'm requesting. You are everything to Heaven and me. I just want my wife to be well and happy." He assured, hugging her.

"Mama, Dada." Heaven said, as she pulled herself up standing, holding her daddy's pant leg, smiling happily.

"How can you look at this sweet face and not smile, Babe?" Kelley asked, with tenderness in his voice.

"It's difficult." Darla answered, smiling through her tears as she looked at her daughter.

Kelley picked Heaven up, sitting her on her mother's lap, and then looked into his wife's eyes with a loving smile.

"We need you, Mom." Kelley spoke, bringing a happy smile to his wife as her tears quickly came again.

"Good. I need you both to need me." She replied with a happy smile, Kelley's ways touching her tender heart.

"Here, Babe." Kelley informed, handing his wife his handkerchief.

"I told you before we married I would keep you well supplied with handkerchiefs."

"I remember." Darla replied with a soft laugh, as she wiped her tears away and blew her nose.

"Give Mommy a kiss, Princess." Kelley said, as he held Heaven up to her mother.

Darla kissed Heaven then Kelley put Heaven in her highchair. Darla silently observed her husband's intentions. He repeated his steps from the night before, giving Heaven a spoon and a small dish of pudding.

"Honestly, Kelley." Darla scolded lightly as her daughter quickly had pudding covering her face as Kelley cleared the dinner table.

"Baby doll, it is the perfect solution to keep our daughter out of my hair while I do dishes. She is learning at the same time." He replied with a grin, finding Heaven's appearance amusing.

"Your daddy is silly, Heaven." Darla said, smiling at her daughter. Darla pulled her legs up on the kitchen chair. She wrapped her arms around her legs resting her head on her knees as she watched her daughter working on her pudding, while her husband washed the dinner dishes.

Kelley picked up the ringing telephone. He held the telephone with his shoulder as he continued the dishes.

"Petersons." He answered.

"Hi, Cindy." He greeted.

"I'm washing dishes, smarty pants. No, washing dishes is not my favorite pastime." He replied with a chuckle.

"Darla is better." He answered.

"I do appreciate you giving up your day tomorrow to help out, Cindy. Absolutely nothing, don't allow her to lift a finger. I am aware my wife can be stubborn." Kelley replied with a chuckle, turning from the sink glancing at his wife.

"You are both in trouble." Darla said, with a weak smile as she grew tired from being up.

"Thank you, Cindy. We will see you in the morning."

"Darla, let us get you to bed before you fall asleep in the chair." Kelley said politely, assisting her to her feet.

By Sunday, Darla felt much better. She found she couldn't go the entire day without a nap yet. She was able to care for her daughter, so this alone brought satisfaction.

"Darla." Kelley said as he stood near the side of her bed, dressed in a suit, waking her.

"Will you be able to manage Heaven while I attend youth service?" I will not stay for the evening service."

"Sure." She agreed kindly, as she sat up on the side of her bed.

"I intended to be awake before now. Where is Heaven?" She questioned, appearing sleepy.

"She is in her playpen. She should be fine until I return." Kelley remained hesitant, observing his wife as she remained sitting on the bed.

"Honey, you best go or you will be late." Darla instructed, looking up into her husband's eyes, seeing his concerns.

"Kel, I will be okay." She assured as she stood.

"I'm fully awake now." Darla gave her husband a kiss goodbye then walked him to the back door.

With her husband's departure, Darla poured herself a glass of orange juice, taking it to the den where her daughter played.

"Mama, Mama." Heaven said, holding her arms up for her mother to take her.

"Hi, Sweetheart." Darla gave Heaven a kiss.

"Mommy can't hold you now." Leaving the playpen, she turned the stereo on, choosing her favorite gospel albums. Heaven soon found contentment again with her toys and the soothing music.

Sitting down on the sofa, sipping her orange juice, Darla's thoughts went to the conversation between her and her husband a few days earlier. 'You must eliminate your wants. Obey the leading of the Holy Spirit in your eliminating.' She picked up a Christian magazine from the end table, apparently her husband had been reading. 'Unless your work is for the Lord and chosen by the Lord, your works are in vain.'

"Mama, Mama." Heaven said again as she pulled herself up, standing in her playpen.

"Wait for Daddy, Angel, he will be home soon." Darla said, as she lay down on the sofa.

By the end of the second week with being off work, Darla was well. Once again in full charge of herself, her daughter, her husband and her home. It felt great being on top again.

Kelley assisted his wife with the dinner dishes. Picking up the ringing telephone, he laid the receiver down.

"It's for you, Babe."

"Hello." Darla greeted, as she leaned against the counter.

"Hi, Candy." She greeted, excitedly.

"Your invitation sounds tempting, perhaps another time? I'm still grounded until next week." Darla said with a soft laugh, bringing a smile to her husband's face.

"You know my husband, he doesn't bend any rules. Thank you for inviting me, have fun. Bye."

Darla went to her husband's side. Removing the dishtowel from his hands she laid it on the counter. Putting his arms around her waist, she then put her arms around his.

"You are a wonderful husband." Darla said, and then kissed her husband's lips, several times.

"You are a wonderful wife, Babe." Kelley assured, looking into his wife's sparkling eyes and happy face.

"I did as you asked. I searched myself and have spent much time in prayer in regards to my activities. I believe I better be obedient to the Lord. I will join you next week in the park ministry and I will accept the Sunday school class. Perhaps when Heaven begins school, the Lord will allow me my desire of my heart, returning to nursing."

"He promises us the desires of our heart." Kelley ensured, most pleased with her decisions.

Darla enjoyed teaching the teen girls class, though her patience were tried at times, she found the girls to be eager, interesting and challenging.

The park ministry truly was Darla's first love. With her four-year absence, she had forgotten the depth of her yearning being used by God to witness salvation and the comfort of the Holy Spirit to those with desperate needs, as the people who sought refuge in the city park. Though she witnessed to both sexes and every age, her heart seemed drawn more toward the younger teen girls. She wanted to offer them their solution before their young lives were destroyed.

CHAPTER THREE

Darla dressed for her busy day while Kelley dressed for work.

"You look nice, Babe. Where are you off to this morning?"

"To the juvenile center, Katie is incarcerated." Darla answered sadly.

"Katie? What has she done? She isn't a tough kid."

"I don't know, she had a friend call asking if I would come. I wish there was something we could do for her, as you say 'she isn't a tough kid', not yet anyway."

"There is something we are able to do." Kelley said taking his wife's hands in his.

"Let us pray." He added.

As the young couple reverently closed their eyes, Kelley prayed aloud. He asked their Heavenly Father to lead and guide Darla as she visited Katie. He requested protection over Katie during her stay at the juvenile center, as well as for her salvation.

With Kelley's departure for his workday, Darla quickly tidied the bedrooms and the kitchen. Her mind was full of questions regarding the barely fifteen-year-old teenager who called out for her. Darla had seen her often at the park ministry, yet Katie had kept her distance, not allowing Darla or anyone who worked in the ministry to the street people to become close to her. She seemed to harbor loneliness and fear, more than a hard, tough street kid's ways.

Arriving at the juvenile center, Darla entered the huge heavy doors with Heaven. "I would like to see Katie Dobbs, please." She informed.

"Are you related to her?" A rather large, rough appearing woman asked.

"No, my husband is her minister and she has asked to see me. Please, I will not stay long."

"What is your husband's name?"

"Kelley Peterson." Darla answered nervously.

"Preacher Kel?" The woman questioned with a half grin.

"Yes, Ma'am." Darla answered.

"You have some identification?"

"Yes." Sitting her purse on the counter with Heaven on her hip, Darla removed her driver's license. The woman looked at Darla's driver's license then at Darla.

"So, you're the gal a lot of these kids in here call Angel?"

"Yes, Ma'am. May I see Katie? She is expecting me."

"Sure, it is a pleasure to meet you. You and your husband are fine people to care about these kids."

"Thank you Ma'am." Darla replied with a kind smile.

"Unlock the doors for Preacher Kel's wife. She is here to see Katie Dobbs." The woman informed, speaking into an intercom.

Though nervous, Darla walked through the doorway as the huge door opened. Escorted to a small room, Darla waited nearly an hour with Heaven growing restless on her lap.

"Shhh, Sweetheart." Darla spoke growing impatient herself.

"Katie, hi." Darla spoke, as the battered teenager entered the room.

"Hi." She greeted. She sat down at the small table across from Darla.

"May I ask what happened to you?" Darla concealed her own heartache not wanting to express pity, causing Katie to withdraw.

"Yep, my ole man decided to use my face for a punching bag." Katie's face turned red from embarrassment.

"By 'ole man', do you mean your father or a boyfriend?"

"My dad, I don't have a boyfriend." She answered with a shy smile.

"My mistake." Darla replied with a gentle smile.

"This your baby?"

"Yes, my one and only, her name is Heaven."

"Heaven, that is far out." Katie repeated with a smile.

"I got your message you wanted to see me." Darla stated.

"Yes, I didn't think you would come." Katie replied.

"Why would I not come if a friend asks for me?"

"I didn't think you would come to a place like this, you're too nice." Katie answered.

"The only difference between you and me, Katie, is that I have asked the Lord into my heart and you are holding out on Him." Darla assured.

"You have a pretty baby, Angel." Katie said, touching her tiny hand.

"Would you like to hold her?"

"Sure." She answered, excitedly. Darla silently observed while Katie played with Heaven.

"Katie, why are you here?" Darla questioned after several long silent moments.

"Because I got scared, so I called the cops on my ole man. I guess that was a dumb move on my part." Katie answered, her face flushed again.

"Why do you say it is dumb, you calling for help?"

"I'm locked up, I didn't break the law, but I'm not free. I heard they let my dad out of jail as soon as he was sober, but I have to stay here now. At least until they find a foster home for me."

"You have no idea how long you will be here?" Darla questioned eager to understand Katie's position.

"No." Katie sighed as though bored with Darla's questions.

Darla was silent now, respecting Katie's privacy. She hoped she hadn't overstepped her boundaries, appearing too pushy. She didn't want Katie to shut her out now. This was the most Darla had heard Katie speak.

"I'll probably be here forever since I'm not a little kid. Nobody wants kids my age unless it is to their advantage." Katie spoke, suddenly breaking their silence.

"Explain, 'to their advantage'." Darla suggested.

"You know, live-in housekeeper, babysitter, whatever the adults have need of, is what you become. Some adults don't care what you do; they just want the extra money the state pays them for keeping a foster kid."

"You are sure this information is correct?" Darla questioned, feeling this unbelievable.

"I have been there, I know." Katie handed Heaven back to her mother.

"Thanks for coming, Angel. I heard Preacher Kel stops in on his lunch hour twice a week. The kids did not mention your visits. I just wanted to see you once more. I think you're a nice person."

"Good, this is the way Heaven and I feel about you. May we come visit you tomorrow?"

"Sure." Katie answered, as though surprised by Darla's request.

"Have you been given ice for your swelling?" Darla inquired, checking Katie's face closely.

"At first, it doesn't hurt much, anyway." Katie answered, concealing her true feelings.

"Mrs. Peterson, I must take Katie now, she has classes to attend." A female guard informed.

"Yes, of course." Darla agreed, politely.

"Katie, there is a good foster home waiting for you." Darla assured.

"Keep your chin up, Kel and I will be praying." She added.

"Thanks."

Darla silently watched Katie until the doors at the end of the hall closed, separating them. She wanted to run after her, removing her from the institution back to freedom, yet where could Katie go to truly be free? She was a victim, all alone in a hard, cruel world.

Leaving the juvenile center, Darla was near tears. Driving past the construction site where Kelley and her father were busy at work, she decided to stop. It was unlike her to interrupt Kelley on his job with a personal problem, but she had to see Kelley about Katie's problem.

Kelley, seeing his wife drive in, walked toward her approaching car.

"What's wrong, Babe?" He questioned, noting her upset.

"I'm worried about Katie. Kelley, her dad beat her up, her face looks terrible. She has to stay at the juvenile center unless she is able to be placed in a foster home. Kelley, if they are not able to find her a home, the juvenile center will be her home." Darla shared with watery eyes.

"Is there anything we can do for her?"

"I don't know, Babe." Kelley answered, as though in deep thought.

"I will stop by the juvenile center on my lunch break and see what I may learn about Katie's case. I will do what I am able to do for Katie."

"Thank you. Surely there is an alternative to living in that horrible center."

"I'm sure there is. I best get back to work or your dad will dock me my lunch hour. I will see you at home." Kelley said, giving his wife a kiss.

"Bye." Darla replied feeling some relief.

Darla met her cousin for lunch and they spent the afternoon shopping. Though Darla appeared pleasant, her heart was not into shopping. She continued to worry for Katie's well-being.

"Dar, what is bothering you?" Cindy asked.

"You are a million miles away." She added.

"I apologize, Cindy. I'm concerned about a young teenager. She is at the juvenile center. She needs a good home with lots of love. I keep trying to rack my brain for a home for her." Darla explained, deeply saddened.

"Why not your home, you have plenty of room. You and Kelley have an abundance of love. Besides, you are best at mothering." Cindy suggested.

"I would love to share our home with Katie, but Kelley and I are not foster parents, Cindy."

"Become foster parents."

"Perhaps we will." Darla replied, becoming excited with her cousin's suggestion.

Returning home from her day away, Darla became more and more excited over Cindy's suggestion. With Heaven cared for and content, Darla went to the telephone inquiring how to become foster parents. With her information gathered, she began her preparations for a special dinner for her husband. She intended to have him in the right mood before sharing her wishes with him.

"Hi, Babe." Kelley greeted as he arrived from work.

"Hi." Darla greeted happily, giving her husband a kiss as he placed his lunchbox on the counter.

"What's the special occasion? The table looks nice."

"Our love for one another." Darla answered, looking into her husband's eyes.

"And I thought the honeymoon was over." Kelley stated.

"You told me the honeymoon would never end."

"So I did. I will take my shower, so you may continue to win me over when I return, to whatever it is you are wanting." Kelley's wisdom brought flushed cheeks and a smile to his wife's face.

"You are terrible. Go take your shower." Darla said.

"May I remove my dusty work boots first?" Kelley asked.

"You had better remove them unless you find pushing a vacuum cleaner interesting." Darla answered, bringing a chuckle from her husband.

"Dada." Heaven said excitedly, as she clumsily walked to Kelley, working hard to master the skill of walking.

"Come here, Princess." Kelley said, as he backed up making Heaven walk farther to reach him.

"Kelley, quit teasing her." Darla ordered, though smiling at his play.

"The fun is over, Mom is present." Kelley said, picking Heaven up. He gave his daughter a hug and a kiss. Going to the telephone with his daughter in his arms, he removed the telephone from its cradle then stood his daughter back on the floor.

"I will take my shower, Babe." He informed, followed by a quick kiss for his wife.

Darla was silent as they began their meal. She had no idea what Kelley's response would be to her wishes regarding Katie.

"I saw Katie briefly." Kelley informed, breaking their silence.

"She doesn't look good. Vera informed me she is not adjusting at the center. She fears Katie may begin to develop the ways of the hardened kids." He shared, with sadness in his eyes.

"Did this Vera mention how soon they could get her out of that mini prison and into a foster home?"

"Yes, Vera said maybe never. No present foster parents want to deal with teenagers."

"What do you suggest we do now?" Darla asked, searching her husband's eyes with hers.

"I don't know, Babe." Kelley answered, looking at his wife.

"We certainly need to continue to pray for her."

"I have heard you say many times, Kelley, that prayer is nothing without works."

"What are you driving at, Dar?"

"I think we should allow Katie to have you and me as foster parents. As Cindy says, we have an abundance of love. We do have an extra bedroom. I don't see why we would not qualify as acceptable foster parents. Cindy also pointed out my best quality is mothering."

"Cindy is correct on all of the above." Kelley agreed, yet his voice expressed hesitation.

"But?" Darla questioned, patiently.

"We agreed we wouldn't bring the street kids into our home. We do have a baby to think about." Kelley reminded.

"I still feel this is wise, Honey. Katie isn't your average hardened street kid. She isn't a drug addict or prostitute. She is simply a young girl with no one to love her. She is scared and all alone in this world and this breaks my heart. You and I always knew we were wanted and loved. I honestly cannot imagine the depth of her pain. I only know this isn't right for her to continue unloved, nor am I able to bear knowing of her needs and doing nothing when the Lord continuously blesses us." Darla shared with watery eyes.

"I will speak with Vera tomorrow and see what we need to do to give Katie a home." Kelley said compassionately.

"Thank you, Sweetheart. I am forever indebted to you."

"This I know, you best always remember this, when I eventually learn to say no to you." Kelley warned, bringing a soft happy laugh from his wife.

"By the way Husband, I was never told by you that you donate two of your lunch hours each week to visit the kids at the juvenile center. How long has this been going on?" Darla asked, pleased.

"I have been going there since I graduated from college." Kelley said.

"Good, I used your name to get past the oversized guard at the front desk; otherwise I wouldn't have been allowed to see Katie."

"The oversized guard is Vera." Kelley informed, with a grin.

"She is the one who pulls the strings in our community when by-passing red tape is necessary. Therefore, if you want Katie out quickly, be nice to her. She is quite capable of being difficult if she chooses." He added.

"Trust me, I believe you." Darla confessed with a soft laugh.

"I have no intentions of ever crossing her."

"When do you plan to see Katie again?" Kelley asked.

"Tomorrow."

"I suggest you not speak of our wishes to Katie in case our plan doesn't work out. She doesn't need this kind of a letdown." Kelley advised.

"I agree."

"You realize, Dar, considering Katie's age and she being a girl, she would mainly be your responsibility."

"I realize this. I do not believe I have left out any area while going over and over this idea today. I know I know very little about Katie and what problems may be locked away inside of her. I do not believe for a minute she is unreachable though."

"I do not believe this either, Babe." Kelley replied, getting up from the table.

"If you will excuse me, I would like to mow the lawn before it becomes too dark."

Two weeks had passed since Darla's first visit with Katie. Though Darla was faithful to visit daily, Katie seemed to withdraw more with each passing day. Darla could see the anger beginning to build within her with being held behind locked doors against her will.

Busy making her grocery list for her planned morning outing, Darla was interrupted by the telephone.

"Good morning." She greeted pleasantly.

"Hi, Babe, if you will meet me at the juvenile center in an hour we may pick Katie up."

"Oh, Kelley, this is terrific!" Darla exclaimed, happily.

"I take it you will meet me?" He asked with a chuckle.

"Of course I will meet you!" She answered, smiling at herself with her expressed excitement.

Kelley was waiting in his car as Darla parked in the parking lot at the detention center. Kelley took Heaven from her car seat, carrying her as he escorted his wife inside the center.

"Hello, Miss Vera." Kelley greeted politely.

"Hi, Preacher, Katie has been waiting. She doesn't appear too excited with her new home, but I assure you this is a cover until she checks you and your wife out. I hope she never enters our doors again because she doesn't belong here." Vera informed.

"I agree." Darla sided, sympathetically.

"Send Katie Dobbs out, please." Vera spoke into the intercom.

As Katie entered through the huge locked door, she was completely expressionless, sad, lonely and withdrawn. She approached carrying a large paper bag in each arm, which contained her clothing.

"Hi." Darla greeted Katie, with a tender smile.

"Hi." Katie greeted, with a shy smile.

"Allow me to assist you with your heavy load." Darla offered kindly, starting to remove one of the bags from Katie.

"I will carry them." Katie insisted, stepping back from Darla, her actions surprising Darla, Kelley and Vera, bringing expressions of concern to each.

"Moody teenagers." Darla said, bringing a half smile to Katie's face.

"Preacher, you need to sign Miss Katie out." Vera informed, winking at Darla approving of her style.

"You are a glutton for punishment, three moody females." Vera teased.

"You are reading my thoughts." Kelley confessed, with a laugh.

"My parents do not live far. I have a feeling I will be visiting them often." He added, bringing a smile also from Katie.

"You probably will." Vera agreed, with a laugh

"Let us go, moody teenager." Kelley said, winking at Katie. Katie blushed, yet she also smiled.

"Thank you, Vera." Darla spoke kindly.

"You're welcome, good luck."

Once outside the building, Darla looked at her husband. "I believe Vera has a heart after all." Darla said, with a soft laugh.

"Darla." Kelley scolded, with Darla being catty. Katie smiled at the young couple's ways.

Arriving at Darla's car Kelley removed Heaven's car seat from the front seat, putting it in the backseat and then fastened his daughter in her seat.

Darla unlocked the trunk of her car.

"Katie, put your things in here, dear." She instructed and Katie silently placed her bags in the trunk.

"Kelley, where is my spare tire?" Darla asked.

"I will get it, Wife. Be patient. I have only had it for a few weeks." He replied with a chuckle.

Going to his car, Kelley removed the spare from the trunk returning it to his wife's car.

"Are you happy now?" He asked, closing the trunk of her car.

"Very happy, thank you."

"I must get back to work. You girls have a nice day." Kelley said, and then kissed his wife goodbye.

"Katie, welcome to our family."

"Thanks." Katie replied blushing.

"Do you enjoy grocery shopping?" Darla asked as she started her car.

"I don't mind. I always shop for me and my dad." She answered.

"I am glad to hear this because today is my grocery day."

Katie kindly pushed the shopping cart with Heaven while Darla placed her choice items in the cart. She was terribly shy. It seemed Darla was continuously causing her to blush at the simplest question or the slightest compliment.

"What are teenagers eating for snacks these days?" Darla asked giving Katie a tender smile.

Katie shrugged her shoulders as to answer, 'I don't know.'

"Now I understand why my mother would become annoyed when I gave her the silent treatment. It is irritating." Darla said, taking hold of the shopping cart, preventing Katie from walking with the cart.

"Katie, please answer my questions. Trust me when I say I truly want an honest answer. I do not know what you like to eat. You do intend to eat, right?" She asked, looking into her green eyes with tenderness in her eyes and gentleness in her voice. Katie did not respond, but her face turned red.

"I will guess then." Darla decided with a comforting smile, withdrawing her question.

With the grocery shopping completed, Darla was as silent as Katie was during their drive home.

"Where are we going?" Katie asked suddenly, breaking their silence.

"We are going home." Darla answered with a kind smile.

"I thought you lived in town."

"No, we live in the country. Kelley and I like our home. I trust you will also."

"Will I share Heaven's room?" Katie asked slowly, as though she was unsure if she had the right to ask her question.

"No, you will have your own room. It would be difficult for you to study with a baby in your room."

"I would not mind." Katie assured quickly.

"I would. It is difficult to receive good grades if you do not have a quiet place to study."

"No one bothered to tell my dad this." Katie said with a smile.

"He likes to play poker at his house. He and his friends get somewhat loud. He thinks I should be able to study while they are acting stupid."

"Are you a good student?" Darla asked.

"I'm not bad. I got my report card a couple of weeks ago. It was not good enough for my dad, but then nothing I do is."

"What were your grades?"

"Two B's and the rest A's."

"Your dad gave you a hard time with grades like that? My brother would have thrilled my parents to death with those grades." Darla shared with a soft laugh, bringing a relaxed expression to Katie's face.

"Then you are on my side and not my Dad's side?" Katie asked as though desperate for an answer.

"Are you referring to your report card or do you mean your present situation between you and your father?"

"I guess I mean both."

"As for your grades, I give you an A+ considering the noisy poker parties." Katie smiled her biggest smile yet.

"I am presently on your side. If you break rules deliberately, I guarantee you a punishment; but Katie, I would still be on your side. Love should not be measured by how perfect one is. If this were the case, I would be an unloved daughter, sister, mother, wife, and friend, which I am not. I am very loved by all the above."

"Is your family happy like you and Kelley?" Katie asked.

"You have noticed a thing or two about your foster parents. Here I thought you have been turning us off, especially me." Darla said, glancing at Katie with a tender smile.

"I have never turned you or Preacher Kel off. I would never do this to hurt you. Sometimes I find it difficult to fit in with people because I get scared I might mess up." Katie shared with flushed cheeks.

"What do you say Kelley and I teach you not to be scared?"

"This would be great. Do you really think I could feel like normal people some day?" Katie asked as though eager to begin learning immediately.

"Yes, Deary. I believe you may accomplish anything you set your mind to accomplish." Darla answered confident, bringing a pleased look to Katie's face.

"I am going to be somebody special someday." Katie replied with a shy smile.

"Oh, Sweetheart, you are special. You are very special. You have simply needed someone to tell you this." Darla assured sincerely, her heart going out to the young, unloved girl.

"You have a horse?" Katie asked, her face lighting up.

"I have a horse and a dog. There comes Sam." Darla said pointing to the approaching Irish Setter.

"Oh, I have always wanted a dog and a cat. Does he bite?"

"No, he is very gentle." Darla answered as she parked her car.

"Go meet Sam." She instructed.

"Thanks." Katie replied, quickly getting out of the car.

Darla showed Katie the house and then the barn, the corral, and Princess her horse. Katie asked questions about everything around her, yet when Darla asked Katie questions, Katie answered as briefly as possible or not at all.

Though Katie had her moments of silence, Darla thought her

first week went well. As the hour arrived for Katie to return from school on the bus, Darla patiently waited the sound of the school bus as she prepared dinner. Glancing at the clock, noting the bus was fifteen minutes late, Darla had a sick feeling in her stomach. She allowed another ten minutes to pass.

"Oh, Katie, where are you?" She questioned aloud, frightened for the teenager.

As it neared Kelley's arrival time from work, Darla sat on the step stool near the telephone, hoping it would ring giving her news of Katie's whereabouts.

"Katie." Darla spoke surprised as she entered the back door with Kelley.

"I have been worried sick about you." Darla informed. Katie's face was flushed as she silently stood avoiding eye contact.

"Kelley, what is going on?" She asked, letting out a long weary sigh.

"I picked her up down the road. She will not talk to me." Kelley answered, rubbing his head. He was also weary as he pulled out a chair from the table, sitting down and looking at his wife, silently giving her the floor.

"Katie, you will answer me." Darla ordered sternly.

"Why were you not on the bus?" Katie stared at the floor.

"Katie, look at me. I am speaking to you."

Katie looked at Darla as ordered. Her face clearly expressed she was scared.

"Honey, please answer my question." Darla repeated, now seeing her pain.

"I went to my dad's house after school. I didn't intend to miss the bus, honest Angel."

"Why did you go to your dad's? You are not to see him and you know this." Darla reminded, surprised with her doings.

"I needed him to sign a paper for school. I have to turn the paper in Monday." She answered nervously.

"Your dad is not to sign anything for you. You are in Kelley and my custody."

"The office said my dad had to sign."

"I am not disputing your word, you simply misunderstood. Kelley is the only dad that can sign for you now. Give Kelley the paper." Darla instructed patiently. Katie slowly opened her notebook. Removing the paper, she handed it to Kelley.

"I'm sorry, Kel. I really did not do anything wrong." Katie defended with watery eyes.

"Katie, this says you have refused to dress for gym all week. You do not see anything wrong with disobeying by not dressing?" Kelley asked, looking at the frightened girl.

"No, because I have an excuse."

"You did not give your teacher an excuse."

"I couldn't tell her." Katie defended, tears now streaming down her young face.

"Yet, you sincerely have a legitimate reason?" Kelley asked. Katie nodded her head yes.

"Produce your reason Babe, and I assure you I will go to school Monday and straighten this out."

"I am supposed to wear a swimsuit 'cause I have swimming this semester." Katie stated.

"I can't wear a swimsuit yet." Katie turned her back toward Kelley and Darla. She lifted her sweater exposing the lower part of her back. Her back was covered with cuts and bruises from being beaten. Darla put her hand over her mouth as her tears were quickly released. Kelley too looked as though he was near tears.

"Katie." Kelley spoke, quickly going to her.

"I will take care of your gym teacher, Sweetheart." He assured, looking into her eyes.

"Your dad could not have done this. These wounds are fresh. Did this happen while you were at the detention center?" Katie nodded her head yes.

"You poor kid." Kelley said, putting his arms around her. Katie began to cry, and then sobbed while Kelley held her for some time.

"Dar..." Kelley spoke, motioning for his wife.

"Take her, Babe. I have a call to make." Darla hugged and comforted Katie while she continued to cry.

Kelley went to the counter and flipped through the telephone book. Picking up the telephone, he dialed the telephone quickly.

"Vera, this is Kelley Peterson. I would rather you not call me Preacher. At the moment, I am about as angry as I can get. The problem? The problem is a young girl is taken from her father so she will be protected from another beating and while she is locked up, mind you for her safety, she received the same treatment. What kind of place are you running?" Kelley angrily asked.

Kelley was silent now, but his face still bearing his anger as he remained on the telephone.

"I didn't intend to cause more trouble." Katie whispered, as she ceased her sobbing.

"You have done nothing of the sort. Kel is doing his fatherly duties, dear." Darla assured with a loving smile.

"Come, sit down." She offered, pulling a chair out for Katie, she too sitting down at the table.

"Katie, did you report this?" Kelley asked, putting his hand over the receiver.

"No, but Shirley, one of the guards, saw it happen. I didn't know who I could trust."

"When did this happen?"

"Monday, just before you and Angel picked me up." Katie answered.

"Vera, she couldn't tell you because one of your own people watched her get beat." Kelley informed.

"Shirley." He answered.

"I have always been straight with you. I guarantee you if you do not get this Shirley out of that center and away from innocent kids, I am pressing charges on Katie's behalf."

"You do that. I will be in first thing Monday morning for a look at Shirley's termination form, thank you." Kelley spoke and then put the telephone down.

"This world has surely gone mad." Kelley voiced, as he desperately tried to calm himself.

"I agree, Honey." Darla said. She looked at Katie, giving her a weary smile.

"Mama." Heaven said, holding her arms up, becoming fussy.

"Are you getting hungry, Sweetheart?" Darla asked as she picked her daughter up.

"Katie, I promise you, Babe, as long as you are living in this home no one will dare to lay a hand on you again." Kelley informed her.

"Thanks Kel." Katie replied, deeply touched by his caring.

"Honey, maybe if you take a shower it will help relax you, so you will be able to eat." Darla suggested, looking at her husband with compassion.

"This is Angel's polite way of telling me I need to cool off." Kelley explained winking at Katie, bringing a smile to her face. Kelley left the kitchen for his shower.

Darla put Heaven in her highchair, and then went to Katie where she remained silently sitting at the table. Putting her arm around Katie's shoulders lovingly, she looked into her eyes.

"Perhaps this gives you more insight to just how special you are, Sweetheart. I have never seen Kelley this upset. Welcome to our family. We believe a family sticks together regardless." She shared.

"We love you, Sweetheart." Darla assured her as she gave her a tight hug and a gentle smile.

Darla began setting dinner on the table and Katie got up from her chair to assist.

"Honey, go put your books away and wash your face. Then come assist me." Darla suggested.

Within a few weeks, Katie had adjusted to Darla and Kelley's ways. She began to take notice in her speech, using proper English with Darla's coaching. She began to understand the meaning of the word respect toward others and even toward herself. She did not offer hugs or kisses to anyone except baby Heaven, although, she was learning that touching is okay, if expressed in the proper manner. Perhaps, even necessary to make one feel complete. Both the Roberts and Peterson family had adopted Katie as though she were a blood relative.

Darla busily prepared dinner as every evening. Heaven played with her toys on the kitchen floor.

"Hi, Angel." Katie greeted as she returned from school, placing her books on the kitchen counter.

"Hi. How was your day?" Darla asked pleasantly.

"Okay, except I have tons of homework." She answered as she removed a glass from the cabinet. Going to the refrigerator, she removed the jug of orange juice, pouring herself a glass.

"Kay, Kay." Heaven said excitedly, walking toward Katie happily.

"Heaven." Katie spoke with a pleased smile as she lovingly picked up the toddler.

"Angel..." Katie spoke as she sat down on the counter with Heaven on her lap, near Darla's workspace.

"May I go to the show with my friend Valarie Friday night and spend the night with her?"

"You may have Valarie spend the night with you if you would like." Darla answered kindly.

"Really?" Katie asked, as though surprised.

"Yes, really. I do not know Valarie. If you would begin bringing your friends home I would appreciate this, so I will know your friends."

"How would we get to the show? You and Kel have the park ministry Friday night." She questioned in her shy manner.

"I do not like disappointing you and I know it must seem to you that Kel and I are continuously introducing you to rules and our strict ways. Shows are off limits. We do not attend shows. Therefore, neither do you." Darla answered in her gentle way.

"Angel, all of my friends attend the show and I have always gone also."

"Again I say welcome to our family, full of rules and restrictions, but endless love." Darla said with an understanding smile. Katie forced a weak smile, ceasing her talk. Darla knew she was not pleased and her smile was merely to be polite.

"If I ask Preacher Kel, would he allow me to attend the show?" Katie asked slowly.

"You know Kelley and I do not have separate sets of rules, Katie, but if you would like to ask him and be told no twice, be my guest."

"I need to study." Katie said, letting out a disapproving sigh. Katie got down from the counter. She carefully stood Heaven on the floor. Removing her books from the counter, she silently left the kitchen.

Katie was overly quiet during dinner.

"Is something bothering you, Katie?" Kelley questioned.

"I am not very hungry. May I be excused, I have tons of homework." Katie spoke, avoiding her foster dad's question.

"Not until you have eaten your dinner and helped with the dishes. You may answer my question now, please." He reminded looking at the saddened teenager with gentleness on his strong face.

"I do not understand why I cannot attend the show with my friends." Katie answered, looking into her foster dad's eyes.

"Because we are Christians." Kelley answered in his calm manner. Katie returned her eyes to her plate as she continued to pick at her food.

"Babe, we do not promote pornography, R rated, or X rated movies. You may be innocent of this as many others are. When you pay to watch a G rated movie, your money also goes to support the improper movies. This is the main reason. Secondly, I would not care to have my daughter or son sitting in a darkened room filled with strangers. Nor would I want this type of environment for a teenager dating. This is not wise." Kelley explained patiently.

"You know Katie, it could be worse. Darla and I could say yes all the time and not care where you are or what you are doing."

"Eat your dinner kiddo. It is getting late and we have church tonight." Darla reminded, attempting to cheer up her foster daughter. Darla got up from the table to start the dishwater.

"Kel, I have a lot of homework. I would rather stay home."

"Do you enjoy hearing me say no?" Kelley asked, glancing at his wife for help to understand Katie's mood.

"Katie knows we each attend church as a family. She is upset with our movie rule; therefore, she is testing our patience." Katie's face turned its reddest, as though clearly expressing guilty as charged.

"I know, I tried these little 'get even' numbers on my parents also." Darla confessed with a soft laugh, she blushing with her confession.

"Women, I will never understand them." Kelley said with a grin, bringing a smile to both Katie and Darla's face.

Katie remained somewhat distance. As the Petersons met at the breakfast table Friday morning, Katie appeared irritable.

"Is there something special you would like me to prepare for your dinner guest this evening?" Darla asked pleasantly looking at Katie.

"No." Katie answered, followed by a sigh.

"Valarie is not spending the night." She answered looking at Darla, clearly expressing her irritation.

"Why? Have I done something?" Darla asked as she sipped her coffee.

"You will not allow us to have fun." She answered as though blaming Darla for her unhappiness.

"You had best watch your tone." Kelley advised his face stern. Katie's face turned it reddest.

"Valarie does not want to keep your company simply because we will not allow you to attend the show?" Darla asked.

"Yeah." Katie answered sadly.

"The word is yes." Darla corrected.

"Yes." Katie replied, getting up from the table.

"Where are you going?" Darla questioned looking at Katie, her face now expressing her irritation.

"To school." She answered, avoiding her foster parents' eyes as she removed her schoolbooks from the counter.

"Put your books down, Katie." Darla instructed in her sternest tone.

"Sit down. You have not been excused. Furthermore, for future knowledge, do not ever consider walking away from me when I am speaking with you."

"Yes, Ma'am." Katie replied as she returned to the table, she surprising both Kelley and Darla with her rudeness.

"I will not apologize for my beliefs or any decisions made on your behalf. Either you will accept this in a mature manner, or you may continue to feel sorry for yourself. You will not give me a hard time, regardless. I simply will not tolerate it." Darla scolded.

"If your friend is a true friend, it would not matter to her whether you attend the show this evening or not. Perhaps you should take notice of your acquaintances and learn who your true friends are and who are not."

"Yes, Ma'am." Katie agreed.

"May I please be excused now? The bus will be coming." She explained her tone gentler.

"You may be excused." Katie gave Darla a kiss goodbye.

"I am sorry." She apologized with flushed cheeks.

"Your apology is accepted. Do have a good day, Sweetheart." Darla replied, giving her a kiss goodbye.

"Thanks." Katie said with humbleness.

With the back door closed behind Katie, Darla let out a long sigh and then looked at her husband.

"Teen years, I recall how at times, the tiniest thing was so important, my poor parents." Darla shared with a soft weary laugh.

"Girls are definitely much different than boys. Maybe you could tell Katie it is acceptable to tell me goodbye, also."

"Sure." Darla agreed with a smile.

"She has come a long way and learned a lot in the couple of months she has been with us, so be thankful, Honey. We seldom receive the silent treatment anymore."

"True, that was irritating." Kelley confessed with a laugh, as he got up from the table placing his dishes in the sink.

"Have a good day, Babe." Kelley said and then kissed his wife goodbye.

Busy with her household chores and Heaven, Darla entered

Katie's room with a basket of clean clothing. Opening the drawers to Katie's dresser, Darla straightened her clothing to make room for her clean clothes. In doing so, she discovered a stack of notes neatly tucked away, bound by a rubber band. She started to ignore the notes, yet she was concerned with Katie's sudden moodiness. Perhaps the notes contained answers to Darla's questions in fully understanding Katie's needs. Finally, she removed the stack of notes and then left Katie's room.

Heaven in her crib for her nap, Darla returned to Katie's room, sitting down at her desk. Placing the stack of notes on the desktop, she silently read note after note.

Katie,

Why do you keep hurting me? Why won't you visit me? What have I done that is so terrible? I kept you. I am not like your mother. I have never left you. I need you Katie. You are all I have since your mother left us. Please come visit me.

Love, Dad

Katie,

Why did you call the cops on me? I would never hurt you on purpose. I am sorry if I hurt you. You belong to me, not anyone else. It is not right you living with strangers. They do not love you. People do not love people that are not blood. Call me Katie, so we can discuss seeing each other.

Love, Dad

Katie,

I will give notes to Jim's daughter Valarie to give to you since those people will not allow you to see me. Those people you live with are not right, Katie. Do not trust them. It is not natural to keep someone's kid from him or her. Write me.

Love, Dad

Katie,

Why won't you visit me? You know I love you and I need your
help. I cannot make it without you. You always took care of
everything for me. Meet me at the show Friday night. Please,
so I will really know you are okay. You are breaking my heart
by ignoring me. I have never ignored you. I will be waiting.
Love, Dad

"Poor Katie." Darla whispered, as she continued to read numerous letters, her heart aching for the confused teenager.

"Dar." Her brother called from the kitchen. Darla quickly got up from Katie's desk beckoning to her brother's call.

"Hi, Bill." She greeted, giving her brother a kiss.

"What brings you out my way?"

"I had a client to visit in this area. I thought I would stop and check on you." He answered, removing his suit coat, hanging it on a kitchen chair.

"Have you had lunch?"

"Not yet, I am meeting Paula in an hour. We are having lunch together."

"Then the two of you are speaking to one another, this is good." Darla said with a pleased smile.

"We are barely speaking. Do not get your hopes up. I am just getting used to being a bachelor again."

"You are not a bachelor, dear brother. You are a married man. Remember this." His sister warned kindly.

"Sis, it is fair play, trust me. Paula has not been sitting at home for the past four months. I do not know why I even agreed to meet her."

"Perhaps it is because underneath the pain you have both caused one another, you love her and she loves you." Darla suggested with tenderness in her eyes.

"I do not know. Maybe you are right. I do know I am past the age of game playing."

"I will pray you both grew past this stage." Darla offered with a gentle smile.

"I am sure you will." Bill replied with a chuckle.

"Would you like a glass of iced tea?"

"Yes, please. I saw Katie this morning. I thought she was supposed to stay away from her father."

"She is." Darla informed, her young pretty face quickly expressing her concerns for Katie.

"She was at Tommy's restaurant this morning with him."

"You are sure, Bill?" Darla questioned, sitting his glass of tea before him.

"Darla, I spoke to her. I should have called you, right?"

"Yes, Bill or made her leave with you one." Darla answered quickly going to the telephone.

"I am sorry, Sis. Katie seemed fine."

"It is not your fault." Darla comforted, as she quickly dialed the telephone.

"Yes, I am Darla Peterson. I am checking to see if Katie Dobbs arrived at school on time this morning." Darla informed, nervously.

"If she should arrive later, please have her call home."

"What can I do to help, Darla? I am sorry about this."

"Go with Kelley to get Katie." Darla answered with watery eyes.

"Where?"

"My guess is her father's home. Please hurry, Bill. They have been together for several hours already."

"You stay put, Sis. Kelley or I one will call as soon as we have Katie."

"Please hurry, Bill." Darla coached, as she saw him to his car.

Darla prayed consistently for Katie's well-being. Bill broke all speed limits as he hurried to his brother-in-law's work site. Bill sounded his horn as he pulled in the drive. Both Kelley and Mr. Roberts came outside of the partial built home they were building.

"Dad, I need Kelley. I will bring him back." Bill informed.

Both Kelley and Dad Roberts looked at one another. Kelley

removed his carpenter's belt laying it down and then quickly getting into his brother-in-law's car.

"What is going on?" Kelley asked.

"Katie did not go to school." Bill answered as he quickly pulled out of the drive.

"I saw her this morning at Tommy's restaurant with her father. She seemed okay. Darla called the school to see if Katie was there. They have her marked absent. Darla says to check at her father's house first." Bill explained as he drove.

"Take a right here." Kelley instructed, concealing his emotions and opinions.

"You realize we do not have a search warrant." Bill reminded, glancing at his brother-in-law.

"I do not feel that I need one. Are you with me on this?" He asked, looking at Bill.

"All the way."

"If Katie is there I just want to get in, take her, and get out."

"Even if it means going through locked doors?" Bill asked.

"You bet." Kelley answered.

"It's the third house on the right, Bill. His truck is there, block it in." Bill parked his car inches from the truck.

"I hear him yelling." Bill said as they approached the front door.

"Katie is in there." He added, looking at Kelley with concern on his face.

"I know." Kelley replied as he knocked on the door.

"Go away. We don't want nothing from nobody." Mr. Dobbs yelled, followed by profanity.

"He is drunk." Kelley voiced as he carefully turned the doorknob. Finding the door unlocked, Kelley looked at Bill.

"Dumb move on his part, I am going in."

"I am right behind you." Bill assured.

"Let's go." Kelley thrust the door open. Both men jumped to separate sides of the doorway as they entered, not knowing what they might be met with.

"Bill!" Kelley yelled, as Mr. Dobbs came at Bill with a baseball bat. Bill ducked just in time, as Mr. Dobbs swung the bat. Kelley circled around behind the man, grabbing him from behind. Kelley squeezed his ribs until he dropped the bat.

"Where is Katie?" Kelley questioned, still squeezing him.

"I, I don't know." The drunken man answered in pain from Kelley's hold on him.

"I have him, Kel. Go find Katie." Bill ordered.

"You leave my Katie be, she is mine." Mr. Dobbs threatened.

"Shut up." Bill ordered.

"Katie." Kelley called, going from room to room.

"It is okay, Sweetheart. Where are you, Babe?"

"Kelley." Katie called, barely above a whisper from the front room where Bill stood holding her father.

"Kelley, she is in here." Bill called. Kelley quickly re-appeared.

"I believe she is behind the sofa."

"Katie." Kelley called as he neared the sofa.

"Kelley." Katie answered in her softest voice.

"Oh, Babe." Kelley said as though he was about to cry.

"You leave my Katie be!" Mr. Dobbs angrily yelled.

"Make him go away Kel, please." Katie begged as she lie curled up in a ball as though protecting herself, with her face buried in the carpet and a cushion over her head.

"Katie, come on, Babe, get up." Kelley coached, leaning over the sofa to reach her.

Katie remained, as she was too scared to move. Kelley pulled the sofa away from Katie. Kneeling down next to her, he slowly removed the cushion finding her face, hands and sweater had blood on them.

"Katie, where are you hurt?" He asked as he slowly turned her face sideways.

"Oh, Babe." He said with a sigh as he saw her lip split open.

"Kelley?" Bill questioned.

"We will have to take her to emergency. Her lip needs stitched." Kelley explained, leaving Katie's side, going to the kitchen. Kelley opened the freezer, removing ice cubes. He opened and slammed drawers until he found a dishtowel. Wrapping the ice in the towel, he returned to Katie's side.

"Katie, help me out. Come on, get up." Kelley instructed.

"No more pain, Babe. You are coming home." With still no response, Kelley picked her up as though she were a toddler.

"Here, put this ice on your lip." With trembling hands, Katie did as instructed.

"You are not going anywhere, Katie!" Mr. Dobbs yelled.

Katie turned her head toward Kelley's chest, closing her eyes tight. She allowed the towel of ice to fall from her hands, as she quickly covered her ears with trembling hands.

Kelley quickly walked past Mr. Dobbs and out of the house. Kelley opened the back door of Bill's car. Attempting to sit Katie on the seat, she tightly held on to Kelley's shirt.

"I am right here, Katie. I am not leaving you. Let go of my shirt." Katie finally released Kelley's shirt.

"Lie down, Babe." Again, Katie did as her foster father instructed.

"Let's get out of here." Kelley said, as Bill quickly came from the house.

"I smell whiskey." Bill said glancing at Kelley, as he backed out of the drive.

"Her sweater is soaked with it."

"It is on your shirt also, Preacher." Bill said with a chuckle.

"I cannot wait to see my sister's face when you attempt to explain why you smell like booze." He added bringing a smile to Kelley's face.

"Kel." Katie spoke.

"What, Sweetheart?" Kelley asked, turning around in his seat.

"May I sit up, please? It hurts to lie on my shoulder."

"Sure, Honey." Kelley answered sympathetically.

Bill pulled up near the emergency room doors.

"I will park the car and then I will be in." Bill informed.

Kelley got out of the car. He went to Bill's window, leaning close to Bill's ear.

"Call Dar, but please spare all details. Call the police. I am pressing charges.

"Okay."

"Katie, come with me, Babe." Kelley instructed.

Katie slowly got out of Bill's car.

"Are you going to send me back to juvy?" Katie asked, still trembling from her ordeal.

"Of course not." Kelley answered, surprised with her question.

"We are stuck with each other."

Putting his arm around her shoulders, they entered the hospital. Katie looked up into her foster father's eyes with watery eyes, and then leaned her head against him as they walked.

Reaching the desk, Kelley pulled Katie closer to his side, comforting her. She remained silent at his side with her head against him.

"May I help you, Sir?" A nurse asked.

"Please. I have a young lady here who has not learned to avoid flying objects." He winked at Katie.

Kelley stayed at Katie's side, holding her hand. He soothed and comforted her, helping her to relax and be less frightened. With the departure of the doctor, two police officers entered the room. Katie looked up at Kelley.

"Are they taking me away?" She asked, as tears began streaming down her confused, frightened face.

"No, Babe. You need to tell the policeman what happened and then we will go home." Kelley answered.

Katie told her story to the police officer.

"We thank you, Katie. Stay away from your biological father and do yourself a big favor. It appears this guy here is not too bad of a father." The officer advised.

"Yes, Sir." Katie replied, giving Kelley a pleased smile.

Bill drove Kelley back to his worksite.

"If I were you Kel, I would tell my Dad as little as possible." Bill suggested.

"This is my intent." Kelley replied, opening the car door.

"Katie, you take care, Honey."

"Okay, Uncle Bill." She replied as she got out of her foster uncle's car.

"Kelley, tell Bill to wait." Dad Roberts instructed as he approached.

"Bill, your Dad wishes to speak with you."

Bill politely got out of his car.

"Son, did you stand your wife up for lunch?" Dad Roberts questioned with disapproval on his face.

"Not intentionally, but I guess I did."

"She was by. I do not have to tell you she is not happy with you."

"I will take care of the problem." Bill assured, returning to his car. He pulled out of the drive, returning to his busy, daily schedule.

"What happened?" Dad Roberts questioned, glancing at Katie and then his son-in-law.

"Katie felt sorry for her father because he wanted to see her. She had breakfast with him and then one thing led to another. Our Katie got the short end of the stick." Kelley explained.

"I thought Katie is supposed to stay away from her father."

"She is. Her head is about as thick as her foster mom's head at times." Kelley said, putting his arm around Katie's waist, comforting her.

"They both have too much heart. They seem to see everyone's needs except their own." Kelley added.

"I hear you." Dad Roberts replied letting out a sigh, concern on his face.

"You might as well call it quits for the day."

"Thank you Sir." Kelley replied sincerely.

"Babe..." Dad Roberts spoke, putting his hand on Katie's chin, turning her face toward him.

"Mind your foster mom and dad, they will never hurt you." He advised and then kissed her forehead.

"Yes, Sir." Katie replied with tenderness in her voice.

"We best get you home. Mom is waiting and wondering." Kelley said.

"Bye, Grandpa." Katie said respectfully.

"Bye, Babe." Dad Roberts replied compassionately.

Kelley politely opened his car door for Katie and then closed the door for her. Starting the car engine, he pulled his car out of the drive, starting for home.

"My wife will be quite upset with all of this, especially since you have been hurt. Be prepared for the lecture of your life. She will worry every time you leave the house now and worry until you return safely." Kelley informed, glancing at Katie as he drove.

"Kel, I promise I will not go with my dad again." Katie assured, her face flushed from embarrassment with the upsets created.

"I know you won't. I do not beat children, but I do believe in paddling. You dare to break this vital rule again; I will give you a paddling." Kelley informed, looking at his foster daughter.

Katie's face turned its reddest. She had brought shame to herself. She hung her head, staring at the floorboard.

"Katie..." Kelley spoke, more gentle.

"I told you I would protect you. This I want to do more than anything. When you go places you are not to be, I am unable to fulfill this." He explained, gently patting her on her shoulder.

"You must help me out. You must also assist Darla by proving she may trust you when you come and go from home. You are fifteen. We will not do for you what you should be responsible enough to do for yourself."

Katie leaned her head back against the seat. Her face beginning to bare the pain her body felt from her biological father punching on her. She silently went over her day from her actions at the breakfast table with her foster parents to the present moment. She thought on Bill's kindness, Grandpa Roberts' kindness, Angel's kindness and Preacher Kel's kindness. How could her foster family possibly love her more than her own father could? Yet, Kel was right; her foster family inflicted no pain on her in any manner. They offered her more love then she could ever contain.

"How do I learn to love them back?" She silently questioned.

"Is your shoulder bothering you, Babe?" Kelley questioned, noting her flinching with driving on the bumpy country road.

"Yes, Sir." Katie answered barely above a whisper.

"Mom will make you feel better." Kelley assured with compassion.

"You know she is a nurse, right?"

"Yes, I saw her college graduation picture in the den. Angel knows how to do so many things."

"True, she is a smart lady and sweet and kind and loving and beautiful." Kelley replied with a grin, bringing a brief smile to Katie's face.

"She is also good at giving lectures." Katie stated, bringing a laugh from her foster dad.

"I would keep this bit of knowledge between you and me, kiddo."

"Being respectful to your elders, this much I have learned."

"You have learned a lot. Dar and I are proud of you."

"There is so much to learn, though. Sometimes I get so nervous I am going to mess up and embarrass you and Angel." Katie said.

"Babe, no matter how old we become one never stops learning, nor does one ever quit having moments of fear. If you always do your best, you will conquer all that you wish. Just for the record, you have not embarrassed me or Darla since you have become our foster daughter."

Turning into their drive, Katie now had butterflies in her stomach. She hoped Darla would not yell and scream at her or strike her for disobeying and causing her hours of worries. Whatever Darla's ways of getting even with her, she truly felt she deserved it for expressing ungratefulness to her foster parents by being with her father.

Entering the kitchen through the back door, Katie heard the stereo playing her foster mother's favorite hymns.

"My guess is Mom is in the den, ladies first." Kelley instructed, allowing Katie to lead the way.

Darla sat on the sofa with her back to the doorway. The

telephone was next to her along with a box of Kleenex. Heaven sat in her playpen busy with her toys.

"Angel." Katie spoke barely above a whisper as she neared Darla. Katie, in her petite size, looked frightened and alone. Her medium length blond hair was tangled. Her new white sweater reeked of whiskey. Her right arm was in a sling. Her upper lip was bruised.

"Oh, Katie." Darla said as her tears fell.

"Come and sit down, Honey." She instructed in her most gentle tone. Katie sat down next to her foster mother. Darla put her arm around her, pulling her close to her and hugging her.

"I am sorry that I disobeyed, Angel." Katie said as she began to cry.

"I know you are, Sweetheart. Darla soothed, leaning Katie's head on her shoulder while they both shed their tears. I understand your feelings of obligations to see your father. These are natural feelings, but Katie, he is not deserving of your love. He continues to hurt you physically and break your heart. I fear with one too many beatings there will not be a Katie. I simply could not bear to see this happen to you. We love you so much, Sweetheart. We just want the best for you. You so deserve to have the best in every way. You have lived with fifteen years of pain. The pain must end. It is past time for you to be filled with joy and happiness, security and safety. Kelley and I are willing to give you our all, so please freely take and be happy and content." She instructed sincerely.

Katie raised her head from her foster mother's shoulder. Removing Kleenex from the box, she blew her nose.

"If I clean the corral for Kel, may I have a new sweater? This was my favorite." Katie said with a shy smile as she looked into her foster mother's eyes, bringing a soft laugh from her. She requesting from Darla for the first time, her shy way of choosing her foster family as her very own family.

"You may have a sweater." Darla answered happily as her tears continued, she realizing Katie was silently choosing her family, now willing to accept being loved and accepted by others. Darla also knowing that Katie requesting a material item from her foster family was a big step for her.

"After she cleans the corral and burns that sweater." Kelley voiced.

"Your foster dad drives a hard bargain." Darla said with a loving smile.

"Kel is easy, this is a hard bargain." Katie replied, pointing to her dislocated shoulder and stitched lip.

"You remember this the next time your dad makes you feel guilty for not seeing him, Deary." Darla advised.

"Yes, Ma'am." Katie agreed politely.

"Perhaps you should get cleaned up. I do not care for the odor of whiskey. I will be in shortly to assist you and then we will get some ice for your lip." Darla suggested as she carefully inspected Katie's lip.

"Who stitched your lip?" She asked with her completion of her examination. Katie shrugged her shoulders.

"Dr. Martin." Kelley informed.

"We will have to remember this. He did an excellent job." Darla voiced, impressed.

"Go start your bathwater, Deary." With Katie's departure, Darla looked at her husband wearily.

"How much static are we going to receive with Katie taking off like she did?" Darla questioned, concerned.

"I believe we are fine this time. I called the police on her father. If she would continue to take off like this, the state will definitely remove her from our home."

"I will tell her this, so she fully understands each of our positions." Darla said, getting up from the sofa. Going to her husband, she gave him a kiss.

"Excuse me while I assist our troubled teen." Darla spoke with a weary smile.

"While you are relaxing, you might find the stack of notes on your desk I discovered in Katie's dresser interesting." Kelley looked at his wife and then got up from his chair, going to his desk.

With Katie freshened up, Darla kindly brushed her snow-white hair for her.

"How are you going to manage your studies next week? You are right handed."

"I will manage. Next week we have semester exams. I am trying to eliminate the two B's from my next report card." Katie answered, determined.

"I will agree to you keeping your studies up, but that will be your limit until your shoulder heals, Missy."

"No dishes or housework?"

"I know, lucky you." Darla said with a laugh.

"There." She said, laying Katie's brush aside.

"Now you look beautiful again." Katie looked at Darla, her face flushed.

"You must know you are very attractive." Darla said searching Katie's eyes with hers. Katie silently looked away from her foster mother.

"Turn around and look in the mirror." She instructed. Katie did as she was told.

"You have the prettiest green eyes. They sparkle as if they were made with glass, even when you are sad. My eyes only sparkle when I am happy. You have the prettiest complexion. Lucky you, you do not have to worry with acne. You have beautiful blonde hair and you are short, this is a big plus. Your boyfriend may be any height and you will not be taller than he will."

"My real mom has green eyes. She was really pretty." Katie shared.

"Then I assume you take after her. You are very pretty, Katie. What is more important, you have a pretty heart. You are gentle and kind and you care deeply for others. You are simply pretty inside and out." Darla complimented, giving her a hug.

"I love you, Sweetheart."

"I love you and Kel too, Angel." Katie replied.

Katie returned to the den as ordered with the television on, holding ice to her swollen lip. Kelley was outside getting a head start on his weekend yard duties. Heaven walked around the kitchen calling for her daddy while Darla prepared dinner. Drying her hands, Darla answered the ringing telephone.

"May I speak to Katie please?"

"Who is calling?"

"This is Valarie."

"One second please." Darla replied.

Entering the den, Darla placed the extension near Katie.

"You have a telephone call, dear."

"Thank you." Katie said, picking up the telephone.

Arriving back in the kitchen, Darla carefully put her hand over the receiver, listening.

"Katie, your dad truly misses you." Valarie said.

"Valarie, I should not be talking with you." Katie said, letting out an irritated sigh.

"Why? We have known one another forever."

"We have never been friends and we never will be." Katie informed.

"Fine, but this does not change the fact that your dad needs you." Valarie continued.

"Really? You know everything about my dad and me, right?" Katie asked, becoming annoyed.

"Sort of, I know what my dad tells me."

"Which are probably a bunch of lies. You go to my dad's home during one of his poker parties. You wait on those drunken slobs until two or three in the morning. You let them put their filthy hands all over you and clean up their vomit. I hate your dad. He makes me sick. You are not my friend. Do not ever give me another note, speak to me or call my real parents' home again." Katie ordered angrily, slamming the telephone down.

"Easy on the ear tiger." Darla thought, thrilled with Katie's speech.

"Hi, Dar." Kelley's younger brother Aaron greeted as he entered through the back door.

"Hi." Darla greeted happily, giving him a hug.

"How does it feel to be a college man?"

"Free and I like it." He answered picking Heaven up.

"You are getting big, Pumpkin, and walking even."

"Do you have any good news from the big city of L.A.?"

"Are you kidding? There is no good news in Los Angeles, although I am the bearer of some good news. Your favorite brother-in-law is having dinner with you and attending the park ministry." Aaron informed in his usual cheery way.

"This is great. We welcome your company."

"Wouldn't anyone?" He asked, bringing a tickled laugh from his sister-in-law.

"Da." Heaven said, excited by her mother's laughter.

"Whoa, I am not your Da. I do not intend to be anyone's Da. Kids are more trouble than they are worth." Aaron expressed.

Katie entered the kitchen to empty her melted ice from its bag.

"Hi, Aaron." She greeted politely.

"Speaking of trouble, double-trouble has arrived." Aaron teased.

"Why must you always be annoying?" Katie asked, bringing a laugh from Darla and a grin to Aaron's face.

"My, are we not spunky. Who got ahold of you?"

"My dad." Katie answered, pouring two glasses of orange juice.

"Are one of those for me?" He questioned as though eager for something to drink.

"Yes, Aaron."

"My brother actually abused you?" Aaron asked.

"No, not Kel. My biological dad."

"Personally, I have always found it difficult to tolerate one father, let alone two. I suggest you scratch the dad off that makes you look like this. Do yourself a BIG favor." Aaron advised his face now serious.

"Hmm, you have finally said something intelligent." Katie voiced, bringing a tickled laugh from both Aaron and Darla.

"So much for the shy Katie that used to live here." Aaron remarked.

"That Katie is gone forever. This Katie is going places." Katie replied, blushing at her forwardness.

"She is right, Aaron. Do not dispute her word." Darla sided, winking at Katie.

"I never doubted the shy Katie was going places. Good luck Kay in all you tackle, including the other person." Aaron said laughing.

"Aaron." Katie scolded, her face turning its reddest.

"Did Kay tell you she decked me the last time I visited?" Aaron asked.

Darla's mouth flew open with surprise, as Darla looked at Katie.

"Aaron if you tell Kel, I will deck you again." Katie warned, setting her glass in the sink.

"Katie." Darla scolded lightly, disbelieving their talk.

"Excuse me, please." Katie said quickly leaving the kitchen.

Kelley opened the back door.

"I will explain later, Dar." He whispered.

"Hi, big brother." Aaron greeted.

"Hi. Did you come for dinner?" Kelley asked as he removed his work boots.

"As a matter of fact, yes." He answered, bringing a smile to his brother's face.

"Aaron is going with us tonight to the park ministry." Darla informed, pleased.

"We could sure use you, buddy." Kelley assured, sitting down on the step stool near the counter.

"I have a report due. I need four people with different personalities I am supposed to psychoanalyze by Monday. I figure I will kill two birds with one stone tonight. Help you out and help my report out."

"I see no problem with this." Kelley agreed.

"Maybe I will get Katie to be one of my clients." Aaron teased.

"You forget you had that thought, guy. You leave Katie alone." Kelley warned sternly. Darla's face turned red as she felt for her brother-in-law's awkward situation as she silently tended to dinner.

"I will." Aaron assured respectfully.

"I was joking, Kel."

"Do not joke about her in this manner." Kelley said calmer.

"Poor kid has been through enough head games to last her a lifetime."

"I know." Aaron agreed his face now solemn.

"I did not mean to jump at you. It has been a bad day." Kelley apologized, his voice gentle once again.

"I assumed as much. I saw Kay."

"Then you understand?"

"I understand. I understand her father should be shot." Aaron answered.

"I best not comment. I would rather not see my wife go into shock." Kelley replied, bringing a smile to Aaron and Darla's face. Kelley reached for the telephone as it began to ring.

"Wait." Darla ordered.

"If it is for Katie, ask who it is."

"Peterson's." Kelley answered.

"Sure, who is calling please? Hang on while I get her."

"Dar, a girl named Valarie."

"I will tell Katie. Listen to the conversation. She has already called once." Darla found Katie in the den, reading a book.

"Telephone, Sweetheart." Darla said pleasantly and then returned to the kitchen.

Kelley held his hand over the receiver.

"Valarie's dad is getting on the telephone." Kelley informed, looking at his wife puzzled.

"Oh, Kelley, they will not leave Katie alone." Darla said, frightened for the innocent teenager.

Kelley's face turned red as anger filled him. He quickly stood up as though ready for a fight.

"Get off the phone, Katie." Kelley angrily ordered.

"Now!" He ordered louder.

"What are you, some kind of a nut?" Kelley asked.

"Hey, jerk, I heard every word you said. You ever call or go near Katie and I will have child molestation charges brought against you along with harassment, after I personally break every bone in your body."

"Kelley, watch what you say, please." Darla warned nervously.

"He hung up. Darla, go get Katie. She heard an ear full of filth." Kelley ordered still angry. Darla quickly left the kitchen.

"Kelley, I cannot find her." Darla informed, panic-stricken.

"She has to be here. Did you check the closets?"

"What?" Darla questioned, looking at her husband as though he had lost his mind.

"She hides when she is scared, Babe. Come on. Aaron, help us and look in everything."

The three young people checked every closet. They looked under each piece of furniture in every room.

"Where could she be?" Darla asked, heartbroken for Katie.

"Dar, did you take Heaven's toys out of her toy box and put them in her crib?" Kelley whispered.

"No."

"She is in the toy box then."

"How could she fit?"

"Trust me she will make herself fit if she is scared enough. You and Aaron go to her. She might be frightened of me. I raised my voice to her on the telephone." Kelley instructed, rubbing his head nervously, feeling as though he had failed Katie. Kelley impatiently waited in the hallway outside Heaven's room.

"Kay." Aaron called as he and Darla approached the toy box. There was no response.

"Katie." Darla spoke.

"I am scared, Angel." Katie responded.

Darla opened the lid to the toy box. Katie was shaking from head to toe as though she was having a seizure.

"Sweetheart, it is okay. Come out of the toy box."

"I am scared, Angel." She repeated not budging, still trembling without a tear in her eyes.

"Aaron." Kelley whispered motioning for his brother.

"Take her out of the toy box. She will not begin to feel safe until she is in your arms. Darla cannot lift her."

"Okay." Aaron agreed, shaking himself.

"Kay, I am going to help you out. Dar is not strong enough to lift you." He informed as he slowly took hold of Katie's arm.

"Aaron, be careful of her arm." Darla reminded.

"I do not know any other way to get her out. She is packed in."

"Ask her if I may help her." Kelley whispered, now standing in the doorway, yet out of Katie's sight.

"Katie, may I get Kelley to get you out Sweetheart, please?" Darla asked, desperately working hard to keep her tears back.

"Is Kelley going to punish me?"

"For what, Sweetheart? You have done nothing wrong." Darla answered her heart breaking.

"Kelley knows." She answered, tears now beginning down her cheeks.

"Katie, I cannot bear this, to think you have been violated, Sweetheart. I am sorry." Darla said, hurrying from the room.

"Great." Aaron whispered with Darla's departure. Kelley slowly approached Katie.

"Angel is crying Katie because she understands the pain the man on the telephone has put you through. I am crying inside because you have been hurt so terribly so many times. Never once has it been your fault." Kelley spoke gently, slowly taking hold of her hand. Katie did not pull away from him. Slowly she tightened her grip on his hand.

"I promised you Sweetheart, no more pain. I stopped your dad today. I will stop Valarie's dad too. These men are mentally sick, Katie. You are fine, good, normal and scared. Please allow me to make the pain stop and the fear to go away. Please, Katie." He pleaded with tears in his eyes. Katie took hold of Kelley's shirt, holding on tightly.

"Kay, you have to help Kel. He cannot pull on your arm." Aaron explained desperately attempting to help his brother free her.

"This is impossible, Kel."

"Difficult yes, nothing is impossible, little brother." Kelley replied, as they both worked to free her.

"I have her. When I say now, pull the toy box to the left."

"I am ready." Aaron informed.

"Now." Kelley said.

"Oh, Katie." He sighed, holding her close to him. Katie continued to hold steadfast to his shirt. Aaron looked at his brother with disbelief in her behavior.

"You are the psychology major. I was counting on you to help me out." Kelley said with a smile, as he comforted his foster daughter.

"Reading a book is no comprehension to seeing with the naked eye." Aaron confessed, appearing to be in shock himself.

"Do you think you are capable of locating my wife?"

"Smarty aleck." Aaron mumbled as he left the nursery.

"What am I to do with three moody emotional girls?" Kelley asked smiling at Katie. Katie turned her head against Kelley's chest so he could not look at her face. He was silent now. Carrying Katie from the nursery, he took her to the den. Sitting her on the sofa, she held tight to his shirt, refusing to let go.

"I'm scared, Kel." She informed with tears once again streaming down her cheeks. Kelley sat down next to Katie. Putting his arm around her shoulders, he leaned her head against his side.

"I am right here, Babe. I will not leave you, Sweetheart." Kelley assured comforting her. Katie kept her eyes open as her tears continued appearing as though she was in a daze.

Aaron entered the den with Heaven.

"Dar went to freshen up. She will be in in a minute." Aaron informed.

Kelley rolled his eyes up and shook his head as though not believing his wife, bringing a smile to Aaron's face.

"Da Da." Heaven said, holding her arms out toward her father.

"Ka." Heaven said, touching Katie's soft blonde hair.

"Ka needs some loving. Give Ka a kiss." Kelley said. Heaven put her mouth on her daddy's cheek, giving him a kiss.

"You are a silly girl." Kelley said as Heaven giggled at her daddy's play.

"Ka." Heaven said again, patting Katie's head.

"You love Katie, Princess?"

"Mama."

"Hi, Mom." Kelley said, looking into his wife's reddened eyes.

"I see you have your hands full." Darla said, sitting down next to her husband.

"Better full then empty and if I had another arm, I would put it around your shoulder."

"I am fine, Kelley." Darla replied with a weak smile.

"Are you leveling with me, Babe?" Kelley questioned, looking into her eyes, his face most serious.

"I am okay now. I had a flashback. I could not bear to think....." Darla started, her eyes quickly feeling with tears.

"I realize what happened, Babe." Kelley interrupted, allowing her to be silent before she lost her composure again.

"I am about to stir up some trouble. I do not know what all will come out. Would you rather go to Cindy's or your parents?" He asked compassionately.

"No, my place is here with you and being available for Katie." Darla answered, blinking hard to control her tears.

"Would you take Heaven then, please?" Darla kindly took her daughter.

"Katie, I know you hear me, Babe. I am going to tell on Valarie's father." Kelley informed.

Katie tightened her grip on Kelley's shirt.

"He will not be able to scare you if we tell. Instead, he will be punished and no more punishing you for wanting to be good, happy, and safe. The sooner you deal with your fears, the sooner you will be able to put them in the past for good." Kelley kissed the top of Katie's head.

"We love you, Babe."

Kelley sat in silence for several moments silently praying.

"Aaron, would you please bring me the telephone from my desk?" Kelley asked.

"Sure." Aaron answered.

"I am scared, Kel." Katie said, looking into Kelley's eyes as she remained with her head against him.

"I know, Sweetheart." Kelley replied, kissing the top of her head. Kelley dialed the telephone.

"Dan, I will not be able to make it tonight to the park ministry. Will you be able to handle it?" He asked.

"Good. No, Darla is not ill. We have a family emergency with our eldest daughter." Kelley shared, tightening his arm around her shoulders, comforting her.

Pushing the disconnect button, Kelley dialed another number.

"Bill, this is Kelley. Are you busy?"

"Forget going to the club for one Friday night."

"Yes, I need a big favor. I know you have friends in the right places. I would like to give you some names and then you see if there have ever been charges filed or complaints of molestation, possible rape." Katie brought her feet up on the sofa. Still clinging to Kelley's shirt, she laid her head on his leg, turning her face toward the sofa with her eyes still open and a faraway look in her eyes. Kelley patted her on her back.

"How soon? Yesterday."

"Thanks Bill."

"Yes, I will be home." Kelley concluded.

"Katie, I need names, Babe." Kelley informed with the telephone to his ear, soothing her blonde hair.

"Tom Sanders is Valarie's dad." Katie said, tears starting down her cheeks.

"Some other names are Sam Finks, Billy Sonders, and Harold Long." Kelley, Darla and Aaron looked at one another with disbelief. They each had looks as though having ill stomachs. Kelley slowly relayed the names to Bill.

"Is there anyone else, Sweetheart?" Kelley questioned hesitant, he now fearing what all Katie's unknown held.

"Brian Tanner." Katie began again. Katie named several more names. When she finished, she was trembling from head to toe.

"Katie, you must fight the fear. You are safe." Kelley encouraged.

Picking up the telephone again, Kelley rubbed his head. He now looked tired and drained.

"Good evening, Vera. This is your favorite Preacher."

"Yes, the troublemaker. Brace yourself; I am knee high in more trouble. I need a reputable witness and you are the best I know."

"For Katie's behalf. Would you please drive out to my house?"

"I told you I am knee high in trouble. I intend to call the police also."

"No, Vera, there will be no trouble for you. I need you on my side. Katie's father worked her over today. She is a wreck emotionally. I need you to bear witness of her emotional state. I will answer all your questions when you arrive without hesitation." Putting the telephone down, Kelley leaned his head back, closing his eyes.

"Honey, I am going to get Heaven ready for bed." Darla informed.

"Okay, Babe. Goodnight Princess." Kelley said.

"Kel, I am going to take off. I should not be here." Aaron said standing up.

"On the contrary, you are my second witness. You witnessed Katie go from fine to hiding in a toy box. For you, this is a valuable lesson in how cruel our world has become for our children. I would appreciate you staying."

"Sure." Aaron agreed.

"Kel, will Aaron not like me anymore?" Katie asked.

"Aaron?" Aaron went to Katie's side.

"Kay, you know better. You are terrific and you are deserving of the name Angel as Darla is. Trust me Kay, if I was not a Christian, I would take all those names and spend the night busting heads. You and I are friends forever." He answered sincerely. Katie closed her eyes with hearing Aaron's response.

Aaron went to the window staring outside. Kelley picked up the telephone again.

"I need an officer sent out to my home. I need to file a complaint in regards to telephone harassment."

Once again, Kelley sat with his eyes closed, silently praying for comfort for his family, protection, guidance and peace within his foster daughter.

"Aaron, may I offer you some dinner?" Darla asked as she returned to the den.

"I am not sure I will be able to keep it down." Aaron answered, turning from the window.

"Kel?"

"No, thank you. You and Aaron eat."

"Katie, will you eat something, Sweetheart." Darla asked, leaning her head against hers.

"No, thank you, Angel."

"We need to get some more ice for your lip, kiddo." Darla said lovingly.

"It is okay." Katie assured.

"Who is the nurse in our home, you or me?" Darla asked with a gentle smile.

"You."

"I will get some ice, Honey." She informed followed by a kiss.

"We love you."

"Love you too." Katie replied.

"Husband, may I interest you in some iced tea?" Darla asked kindly.

"You may interest me in a kiss."

"In front of Aaron and Katie?" Darla asked blushing.

"We will pretend they are not present." Kelley answered, bringing a soft laugh from his wife though she lightly kissed his lips.

Though Kelley was unable to have any of the men prosecuted, he had put a fear in them. Valarie, her father and even Katie's father left Katie alone.

It was nearly a month before Katie truly relaxed, learning to be Katie and building her self-confidence. Kelley had won Katie's respect and admiration by standing up to everyone for her. She was beginning to believe she truly was special, just because she was Katie. She felt comfortable bringing friends home, often staying the entire weekend. She still was not sure about God, Jesus, Heaven, Hell, and salvation, yet it was necessary she attend services faithfully. She had made some close friends at church. She often referred to Kelley and Darla as mom and dad when speaking to them when she felt extra confident or extra happy. When speaking to others in regards to them, she referred to them as her parents.

Darla was brushing Princess as Heaven sat in the swing when Katie's school bus arrived. Exiting the bus, Katie had an unexpected guest with here, which happened more often than not. Darla did not mind, at least this way she was able to know Katie's friends. As the girls approached, Darla was surprised to see that her guest was Joy Timmons from church, whose mother was not fond of Darla.

"Hi, girls." Darla greeted pleasantly, as Katie and Joy arrived at the corral, Darla meeting them at the fence.

"Hi." Katie greeted happily, giving Darla a kiss.

"Hi." Joy greeted.

"Does your mother know you are here?" Darla asked.

"Not yet. I need to call her." Joy answered.

"Make sure you do this, kiddo." Darla instructed with a gentle smile.

"Mom, if Joy's mom says it is okay, may Joy spend the night?" Katie asked hopeful.

"I see no problem with tonight, but we would need to take her home early in the morning. We have plans tomorrow."

"Thanks." Katie said.

"Let's go call your mom." Katie suggested excitedly. The girls started toward the house.

"Angel, may I take Heaven in with us?"

"You may." Darla smiled with Katie happily taking Heaven from the swing, hugging her.

"Do you always have to babysit for them?" Joy questioned.

"I do not have to, I like to. Heaven is my sister." Katie answered.

"You tell it like it is kiddo." Darla thought with a pleased smile.

Finished brushing Princess, Darla started for the house. As she opened the back door, she could hear Joy's voice, angry and loud. Opening the door, she quickly entered for fear the girls were quarreling.

"This is really dumb, Mother. I do not want to come home." Joy protested on the telephone.

Darla was surprised to hear the teenager speaking so hateful to her mother. Katie silently looked at her foster mother with flushed cheeks knowing she disapproved.

"Mother, I am at Pastor Kel's home. What could possibly go wrong? You are so narrow-minded." Joy accused.

"Joy, be careful how you speak to your mother." Darla scolded, embarrassing the teenager. Joy's face turned red as she spoke calmer.

"You do not know what you are talking about." Joy said, appearing frustrated.

"Dad would allow me to stay."

"Perhaps you may stay until seven. I will be going into town then." Darla said as she washed her hands at the kitchen sink.

There was more bickering back and forth. Joy finally hung the telephone up and then sat down at the table, annoyed.

"Who won?" Darla asked with a tender smile.

"My mother won. She is so irritating."

"Is your mother allowing you to stay until seven?" Katie asked hopeful.

"She said I have to come home now. Would you give me a ride home, Darla?"

"Yes, at seven." Darla answered.

"But my mom said I have to leave now."

"Joy, my mom should not drop everything. She and my dad have plans tonight." Katie defended, rescuing her foster mother.

"Besides, I told you to call your mother from school to see if you could come."

"Honey, call your mother back. She is more than welcome to

drive out and pick you up. Otherwise, I will take you home at seven."

"I am not calling her back." Joy snapped. Darla's face was now flushed by Joy's rudeness. Katie glanced at Darla growing nervous with Joy's actions.

"You will call your mother now. You are a guest in our home. I will tolerate no disrespect from you." Darla ordered sternly. Joy got up from the table and called her mother.

"I am to go home at seven." Joy informed, avoiding eye contact with Darla.

"Do you want to do something?" She asked, looking at Katie.

"Sure, but you owe my mom an apology, Joy." Katie answered; disbelieving her guest could be so hateful.

"For what?" Joy asked, annoyed. Katie got up from the table becoming just as annoyed with Joy as Joy was with her.

"For what? For being rude and hateful." Katie accused.

"Katie, sit down." Darla ordered sternly.

"Get your books, Joy. I will take you home now."

"Fine." Joy remarked sarcastically.

"If my Mom was not here, I would slap you." Katie informed, glaring at Joy.

"Katie, I have heard enough and you will be still. Watch Heaven and make a salad."

"What about Kel?"

"I will deal with Dad. You do not allow this to happen at dinner hour again." Darla ordered, hurriedly removing the extra keys from the key hook.

"Yes, Ma'am." Katie replied with flushed cheeks.

Heaven in her high chair, Katie and Kelley patiently sat at the dinner table awaiting Darla's return.

"I am getting hungry. How about you?" Kelley asked.

"Yes, Sir." Katie answered, sipping her iced tea.

"Mom should be coming." Katie assured, glancing at her watch.

"Here comes Mom." Kelley informed in his relaxed, calm way. Darla entered through the back door appearing aggravated.

"Hi, Honey." She greeted with a weak smile as she quickly washed her hands at the kitchen sink and then joined her family at the table.

The young family members each held hands as Kelley asked the blessing.

"Did you have a bad day, Babe?" Kelley asked as he prepared his plate, passing his wife the plate of dinner rolls.

"No. I had a great day. This evening my patience has definitely been tried." She answered, attempting to calm herself.

"What errand did you have to tend to?"

"Katie, you did not tell Dad about your wonderful guest?" Darla questioned as though disappointed in her.

"No. You said you would deal with Dad."

"I was referring to our disrupted dinner hour, not to the actions of you and your guest."

"I am sorry. I did not understand." Katie apologized.

"You understand now." Darla informed patiently, looking at her foster daughter as did Kelley.

"I invited a guest home. I did not do anything, she did. She was terribly rude to Mom. I defended Mom as you said, Dad. You said a family sticks together. Then Mom got upset with me for defending her and took her home." Katie explained.

"Who was your guest?" Kelley asked.

"Joy Timmons, from church."

"Her mother allowed her to come to our home?" Kelley questioned, surprised.

"No, she came then called her mother." Darla answered.

"Good ole Sister Timmons would not allow Joy to stay?"

"Correct." Darla answered.

"Of all the friends Katie has, she has to bring Joy home. I was willing to accept this, hoping and praying it would work out. Joy becomes rude to me; Katie jumps in for my defense and this I will accept. Our daughter, in a very unlady-like manner, proceeds to tell Joy if I was not present, she would slap her." Darla explained her face flushed as she expressed her disapproval.

"This will surely give Sister Timmons some fresh gossip about me and now Katie."

"Babe, Sister Timmons will gossip whether she has facts or no facts. Personally, Katie responded as most would. The point is she did not slap her."

"It is not proper for fifteen and a half year-old girls to be threatening to slap another." Darla scolded.

"Joy is as impossible as her mother most of the time. It may help her attitude if someone would slap her." Kelley said with a chuckle, attempting to lift his wife's spirits.

"So much for supporting your spouse." Darla said as she fed Heaven.

"Babe, you are not being fair. Lighten up please. I had a crummy day."

Darla grew silent, attempting to calm herself and put the upset aside.

"Katie, as far as the comment in regards to slapping, all joking aside, Mom is right. Use your head to work things out, not violence." Kelley instructed.

"Yes, Sir."

"Mom, I did not know Joy would act as she did, or I never would have invited her."

"I know." Darla assured letting out a deep sigh.

Kelley winked at his foster daughter, secretly congratulating her for learning how to set her foster mother at ease so bygones could become bygones more quickly.

"Katie, you are as much in the spotlight as Dad and me by becoming our daughter. It is very difficult at times, yet necessary to bite your tongue and acquire self-control when you are a member of a minister's family. Some people watch for us to make a mistake. We are supposed to be perfect in some people's eyes. Just be the best you are capable of being, dear, regardless of others actions and others provoking." Darla instructed with gentleness once again in her voice.

"Okay." Katie agreed compassionately, not wanting to hurt her special family, she had been granted.

"If you will excuse me, I need to take a quick shower. Katie will you take over for me?" Darla asked.

"Yes." Katie finished feeding Heaven.

"You have thirty minutes, Babe." Kelley reminded as he began clearing the table.

"I will hurry." Darla replied, then hurried from the kitchen.

"Kel, why does Joy's mother not want her to come to our home?" Katie asked.

"She has a vendetta against Mom." Kelley answered as he began the dishwater.

"Against Mom? I thought everyone liked Angel." Katie said as though shocked.

"Most do, but no matter how hard you try to get along with others Katie, there will be someone you clash with. The best solution I am able to give is to avoid the person's company as much as possible."

"I guess I should avoid Joy then. She does not have but a couple of friends. She is not well liked at school. It seems the kids at church tolerate her, but I do not believe they care for her either. I was trying to be nice to her when I invited her over. She has started sitting at my lunch table. My friends have really been rude to her." Katie shared.

"She does tend to purposely rub people the wrong way. I would say she is old enough to know better. If you are able to be her friend, perhaps you will be able to help her see why others do not care for her. Regardless, I would not bring her home again without checking with Mom." Kelley advised with a grin.

"I understand." Katie replied with a smile.

"Hello." Mom Roberts greeted as she let herself in through the back door.

"Hi, Mom." Kelley greeted.

"Hi, Grandma." Katie greeted with a tender smile.

"It appears my daughter has put you both to work."

"It is sort of my fault. I messed Angel's schedule up." Katie explained, blushing.

"Darla messed a few of my schedules up in her days, so I would not worry about it." Mom Roberts replied with a gentle smile.

"Allow me to take Heaven over Deary while you give Dad a hand."

"Yes, Ma'am." Katie answered politely.

"I will finish Kel." Katie offered.

"Good. I gladly resign. I believe I will hurry Mom up before my schedule is demolished."

Katie finished the kitchen then turned the kitchen light out. She entered the den where her foster grandma and Heaven were.

"All finished dear?" Mom Roberts asked.

"Yes." Katie answered pleasantly, sitting down on the sofa Indian fashion.

"Does Darla allow you to put your shoes on the furniture?"

"No, Ma'am, but Kel does." Katie answered with a sly smile as she slipped her shoes off.

"Katie, shame on you." Grandma Roberts said with a soft laugh.

"Darla says you are excited over our shopping outing in San Diego tomorrow."

"Yes, I have lived this close to San Diego my entire life. Tomorrow I will see a real city for the first time." Katie replied excitedly.

"Then you have never seen the ocean?" Grandma questioned.

"No, but I would love to."

"You tell my daughter I said she best take you. She loves the ocean."

"I could not do this." Katie said blushing.

"Dar and Kel are too busy. Besides, I could not ask this for me."

"Why not? Darla had no problem begging and pleading with Grandpa and me to go to the ocean or whatever idea popped into her head."

"That is different. I am not Kel and Angel's blood daughter. I do not have the right to ask these things." Katie said slowly, disliking being reminded that she was only a foster child.

"Grandma, I have homework I should do. May I be excused?" Katie asked, quickly changing the subject with feeling uncomfortable.

"If you feel you must spend your Friday night studying." Grandma answered looking into Katie's eyes as though reading her hidden thoughts.

Katie's face flushed. She was unsure whether her foster grandmother wished she stay or if she thought her rude if, she did not stay.

"Go study, Sweetheart. I do not mind." Grandma said as though she did know her foster granddaughter's thoughts, as Darla often did.

"Thank you."

"You are welcome." Grandma replied with a comforting smile.

Katie entered her bedroom closing her door behind her. She put her favorite forty-five records on her record player and then lay down on her bed releasing her tears. She wished the terrible lonely feeling that had suddenly consumed her would leave. It made her feel out of place and begin to question her security with Angel and Preacher Kel as a family. It was as if her mind would play tricks on her, reminding her of each of her imperfections. Mainly, reminding her she was not a blood relative. At any time or any day, she could be jerked out of the only family she had ever had, being forced to tough out whatever the hard cruel world forced on her. For the honest facts were, she belonged to the state.

"Katie." Grandma spoke, knocking on her door. Katie quickly wiped her eyes.

"Yes." Katie replied, remaining on her bed. Grandma slowly opened her bedroom door.

"Katie, are you ill?" Grandma questioned concerned.

"No, I am tired." Katie answered as she lay in the dark, with a faraway look in her eyes. Grandma sat down on the edge of her bed as she gently soothed Katie's hair.

"You have been in here for two hours with no light on. I guess you decided against homework."

"Yes, Ma'am." Katie answered, appearing both sad and distant.

"I did not intend to make you feel bad. I am truly sorry."

"You did not do anything, Grandma." Katie assured quickly.

"You and I both know better. I triggered a sore spot in you. An area you have not had enough time living here to heal. I often forget your last name is not Peterson, like my daughter's and Kelley's. I forget Katie because to me, a name in writing does not mean much. In my heart from the moment I met you, you became my granddaughter. You automatically inherited both Kelley's and Darla's families when you moved into this house, as we each inherited you. Sweetheart, trust me, not a one of us are made to offer our love and support to you and then take it back as if we never knew you. Genuine love lasts forever. It does not matter whether or not you are blood to develop a relationship or a bond of love." Grandma Roberts spoke, her heart going out to the saddened, confused teen.

"I have been doing okay most of the time now. Grandma, it is not anyone's fault, but mine. When this crummy feeling hits me, I cannot always make it go away. I get scared that this is all a dream and I am going to wake up and have no one again. I do not want to be alone ever again." Katie shared as tears began down her cheeks.

"Honey, I truly understand this. Darla has made sure we each understand your feelings, so we are careful not to provoke this feeling within you."

"Really?" Katie asked, surprised.

"Yes, really, now I will have to tell her and Kelley that I goofed tonight. Do you think Darla and Kelley will forgive me or cross me off their list?"

"Grandma, they would always forgive you."

"You are right and the same goes for you. Darla and Kelley are always yours, dear; always a home, always parents, and always love. No matter what, you will never be alone unless you choose to shut yourself away from them or us. Do you understand?"

"Yes, Grandma." Katie answered with a shy smile.

"I will come out of my dungeon." She added, bringing a soft laugh from her Grandma.

"Good. I made you some popcorn."

"Thank you." Katie said, forcing a smile. Removing her nightclothes from her drawer, Katie left her room. Taking a quick shower, she desperately fought the feeling of loneliness, truly wanting to get back on top.

"I believe this is one of your favorite programs, dear." Grandma Roberts informed as Katie entered the den.

"Yes, it is." Katie answered, sitting down by her Grandma, sharing a bowl of popcorn together. Katie began to feel somewhat better with having company to keep her mind busy.

"Grandma, you may go home if you would like. It is after eleven and you look tired." Katie suggested kindly.

"I will stay. I would not rest knowing you and Heaven were here in the country alone."

"Mother..." Darla spoke, entering the den.

"I am sorry we are later than usual." She apologized, sitting on the arm of the sofa.

"It is okay, dear. Be a dear and walk me out." Grandma Roberts said.

"Bye, Katie. I will see you in the morning." Kisses exchanged, Katie turned the television off.

"Sweetheart, we have company in the kitchen if you would like to join Dad and me." Darla invited.

"No, thank you." With the lights turned out, Katie went to her room, turning her radio on and slipping under her covers.

"Katie." Darla spoke as she entered her bedroom.

"Yes, Angel?" Darla went to Katie's side turning her lamp on.

"Mother said she made you feel uncomfortable. Are you okay?"

"I am fine. Grandma did not do anything. It was my doing to myself. I am okay now." Katie answered, feeling almost completely on top of her insecurities.

"Good. You are going to overcome every single fear. I have faith in you." Darla said, with a loving smile.

"Goodnight, Honey."

"Goodnight." Katie replied.

Katie felt as she belonged by morning. She disliked herself terribly when she let her guard down, allowing her past fears to haunt her. She fell in love with San Diego. She had a blast shopping with Darla, Grandma Roberts and Aunt Cindy. Grandma even insisted Cindy drive to the beach so Katie could see the ocean. To Katie, her day was a dream come true. At the end of her long wonderful day, as Katie drifted off to sleep, she still had a smile on her face. Her heart was overflowing with excitement and happiness.

Awaking Sunday morning filled with happiness from her day in San Diego Katie chose her new outfit Darla had bought her to wear to Sunday services. Dressed for Sunday school, Katie entered the kitchen.

"Whew, you look pretty." Complimented Darla pleased.

"Beautiful is more like it, Mom." Kelley sided.

Katie blushed with her foster parents' compliments. She was not yet able to see herself as pretty or beautiful, yet she was able to feel she looked nice. This step alone was a big accomplishment.

"Thank you." Katie said, as she poured milk in her bowl of cereal.

Katie almost felt like a princess. Her foster parents' ways made her feel as though she was special.

Lingering outside the church building with several of the teens visiting before Sunday school began, Katie felt as content and carefree as any well-adjusted teen her age. Joy Timmons approached the group along with her mother.

"Katie." Sister Timmons spoke in a sharp tone, causing Katie's cheeks to flush.

"Yes, Ma'am?" She questioned nervously.

"My daughter is never to go home with you again." She ordered, pointing her finger in Katie's face, humiliating her in front of the other teenagers.

"Okay." Katie agreed, barely above a whisper. Katie stood in silence as Sister Timmons and Joy went inside the church. Katie did not feel the least bit special now, not in her dress or in her heart. She felt as an outcast and all alone. She no longer belonged and she was shamed in front of her friends.

"Katie, what happened at your home?" Jessica asked.

"Nothing happened." Katie answered, feeling defenseless and defeated.

"Why is Sister Timmons so angry?" Another girl questioned.

"I honestly do not know. Joy was at my home for only an hour Friday after school and then my mom took her home because she was being terribly rude to my mom." Katie shared as though devastated.

"That sounds like Joy. My mom almost slapped her once. I am not allowed to open the front door to her." Shelby shared.

"But I did not do anything." Katie insisted, still stunned by being scolded by a stranger.

"Don't worry about it, Katie. My dad says Sister Timmons is nothing but a troublemaker." Gary said.

Katie was so humiliated that she felt awkward and out of place. As she entered the teen girl's class with her friends, she withdrew. She began to feel angry, that she had been stripped of her happiness. She could feel Darla's eyes on her as she began to teach the class.

Joy turned around in her seat, looking at Katie.

"My mom told you." Joy whispered.

"Why?" Katie asked.

"Joy and Katie." Darla spoke.

"I would appreciate you saving your chit chat for later." Katie's face turned red. She stared at the floor avoiding everyone's eyes. She wanted to leave and never return to the church.

As soon as Darla dismissed class, Katie was out the door before Darla could speak with her. With the morning worship service beginning, Katie slipped in the back pew although she knew it was her foster parents' wishes that she set with them for the morning services. She felt her old ways of being a loner pulling strongly at her. It is painful to love and feel rejection. On top of the mountain one moment and then so low, she could barely cope the next. It was simply too much to deal with. She felt as though her mind was ready to explode as she had both her old ways of surviving pulling at her and her new way.

"Kelley." Darla whispered as they stood up along with the congregation.

"I do not know where Katie is." She whispered concern on her face and in her voice.

"Is she upset?" Kelley asked rubbing his head wearily.

"Yes, but I do not know why."

"These interruptions must stop." Kelley replied looking at his wife irritated.

Darla's face flushed as she became silent. She was not clear about her husband's comment.

"I do not believe this." Kelley sighed after several long moments. Darla was now concerned for her husband's upset as well as Katie's. Without another word, Kelley slipped out into the aisle, heading for the back of the church.

Locating Katie in the side section on the last pew, Kelley sat down beside her.

"What are you hoping to prove?" He asked, clearly expressing his irritation.

Katie's face flushed. She looked into her foster dad's face and then quickly looked away.

"Mom is concerned with your absence. I am fully irritated. Now get up and go where you are expected to be, quietly. There is a service already in progress." He spoke sternly.

"Kel...."

"Do you understand when I say my patience is gone?" Kelley questioned quickly.

"Yes, Sir." Katie answered slowly standing up.

Kelley got up, standing in the aisle to allow Katie to lead the way. Reaching her foster parents' pew, Katie started to slip behind Darla where she stood to sit on the opposite side of her as most Sunday mornings. Kelley took hold of her arm firmly stopping her.

"Right here." He ordered and then let go of her arm, forcing

Katie to stand between he and Darla. With her face its reddest and feeling ashamed that her foster parents were upset with her, she stared at the floor.

Darla's heart went out to Katie. She wanted to put her arm around her, telling her everything would be okay. She looked at her husband, questioning his harshness and impatience. Kelley glanced at his wife as to say 'do not even question me'. Therefore, she silently prayed for the Lord to bring comfort to both her husband and daughter.

"Mama." Heaven said as she stood near Darla with her tiny hand in hers. Darla picked Heaven up.

"Kay." She said, reaching for Katie wanting to play.

"No, Shhh." Darla said, taking the tiny hand that reached for her older sister into her hand, kissing it.

"Mama, Kay." Heaven said beginning to fuss with not getting her way. Darla quickly sat down, reaching for Heaven's bottle to quiet her.

The congregation was instructed to sit. Katie looked at Heaven, feeling badly for her not being allowed to comfort her as she often did during the service when Heaven requested her. She briefly looked at Darla, seeing her young gentle face baring her unhappiness from concerns. She knowing Heaven was quieted by her bottle instead of Katie, so Katie would not be intruded upon with her present upsets. Darla looked at Katie giving her a warm smile.

"Katie." Kelley spoke in a whisper.

"Pay attention to the speaker. We are here to learn and this is not a social hour." He ordered with sternness. Katie's face turned its reddest. She obediently kept her eyes on the speaker, silently wondering why Kel was so upset with her.

With dismissal of the service, Kelley politely collected Heaven's things, returning them to her diaper bag.

"Kelley, I need a word with you." Pastor Finks informed.

"We have dinner guests coming." Kelley informed hesitant.

"I will only keep you a few minutes."

Kelley set the diaper bag on the pew. He silently went with the pastor. The two men neared the platform out of earshot of others. Darla and Katie observed as they patiently waited. Both men's faces were tense. Kelley put one hand on his hip as though he was thoroughly annoyed, yet remained silent as Pastor Finks spoke. Kelley then shook his head as in disagreement, speaking briefly. The pastor spoke again, patted Kelley on his shoulder and then walked away. Kelley stood a few minutes as though in shock by their conversation.

"Please dear, be on your best behavior." Darla whispered, looking into Katie's eyes.

"I believe Dad has had his share of upsets as well as you have this morning." Darla warned, with gentleness in her eyes.

"Yes, Ma'am." Katie agreed, looking at her foster dad, her heart going out to him.

It was as though Kelley suddenly snapped back to reality. He glanced at his family patiently awaiting him. His face flushed, finding their eyes on him along with their looks of concern. His face seemed to relax, as he started toward his family, as though it was necessary he not burden them, concealing his upset. Kelley silently took his sleeping toddler from Darla's lap. Katie kindly took the diaper bag.

The Peterson family was silent on their drive from church to their country home. Parking his wife's car, which was used as the family car, Kelley took Heaven from his wife. Unlocking the back door, he patiently allowed his wife and daughter to enter their home first. Katie placed the diaper bag on the counter unpacking the necessary refrigerator items. Kelley held Heaven with one arm as he answered the ringing telephone. Darla slipped her heels off and then checked the roast baking in the oven.

"Peterson's." Kelley spoke in the telephone.

"Yes, I heard." He answered.

"I am not in the position to make any comments. I do not have this right because I am merely the youth pastor; I am not the associate pastor." Kelley hung the telephone up.

Katie left the kitchen. Entering the nursery, she placed Heaven's diaper bag on her dresser. Going to her room, Katie removed her favorite faded blue jeans from her dresser and a sweatshirt. Dressed for a casual Sunday afternoon, Katie tied her white tennis shoes. Picking up her new outfit Darla had picked out special for her in San Diego, she hung it with great care in her closet.

"Katie, I could use your help, dear." Darla informed outside her closed door.

"I am coming." Katie answered quickly closing her closet door. Arriving in the kitchen, Katie silently assisted her foster mother with dinner preparations.

"Are you silently getting your upsets under control?" Darla asked, appearing tired and drained.

"Yes." Katie answered giving Darla a weak smile, hoping she would worry less. She looked so tired and sad.

"Good. Remember Sweetheart, there is always a tomorrow. Things will be brighter." Darla said with a weary smile.

The telephone rang once and then was silent.

"Speaking of tomorrow, I believe I will call the telephone company demanding they remove our telephones." She complained lightly, bringing a smile to Katie's face.

"Da." Heaven said as Kelley entered the kitchen, hurrying to him.

"Not now, Heaven." Kelley spoke. Katie and Darla both looked at Kelley with his irritated tone, with puzzled expressions.

"Katie, did you have words with Sister Timmons this morning?"

"Kelley, Katie..." Darla started.

"Darla, please." Kelley snapped immediately hushing his wife. Darla was silent, yet her expression clearly told Kelley he would receive her opinion of his tone later in private.

"Did you smart off to Sister Timmons this morning, Katie?" Kelley questioned.

"No, Kel, I do not smart off to adults." Katie answered with flushed cheeks.

"Katie, she is on the telephone right now. She says you did. She also says you threatened Joy in Sunday school class."

"I did not. Please believe me, Kel. I did not bother anyone. I wanted too, but I didn't so no one could talk against us." Katie assured with watery eyes.

"Did anything happen between you and the Timmons?" Kelley questioned his voice calmer.

"Yes. Before class, Sister Timmons jumped on me when I was with my friends. She told me Joy was never to come to my home again. I said okay. In class, Joy laughed at me because her mother jumped on me. I asked Joy why her mother did what she did and then Angel told us to quit talking. I did not do anything wrong, Kel. If you do not believe me, ask my friends." Katie assured, working hard to hold her tears back.

"I believe you." Kelley replied, picking up the extension.

"Sister Timmons, I find your accusations hard to believe." Kelley spoke.

"I could have told you this." Darla remarked, looking at her husband clearly disapproving of his manner. Kelley held his wife's stare with his eyes, as he continued on the telephone.

"I do not care to discuss any of this any further, Ma'am. Good day."

"Dar..." Kelley began.

"Kel, either you or I one best go for a walk before you and I converse." Darla interrupted, now irritated. She removed the telephone from the hook to prevent any further calls.

"I best go for a walk." Kelley said, secretly winking at Katie.

"I would ask you to join me Katie, but Mom needs you." He informed as he picked Heaven up to take her with him.

"She may go." Darla informed, avoiding eye contact with her husband. Kelley silently motioned for Katie.

Kelley and the girls stayed outside until Kelley's family arrived for dinner. Kelley explained both his and Darla's moods to Katie. He listened as she shared her upsets with him. With time, Katie learned everyone has bad days and she learned how to deal with such upsets without feeling as though her world was falling apart, or that she was all alone. She became stronger and wiser. Like Grandma Roberts said, she did not need a paper or certain name to know she belonged. She belonged forever. Her head learned this as well as her heart.

Katie had become a sweet young lady over the months spent in the Peterson home. She had asked the Lord into her heart and was a walking testimony to everyone she met. A loving family of security and Jesus was everything in the world to Katie.

CHAPTER FOUR

Katie excitedly assisted Darla and her Aunt Cindy preparing their picnic for their day away at the beach in San Diego. This would only be her second visit and first visit to swim.

"Are you bringing your bikini Katie, so you will receive a nice tan?" Cindy questioned purposely to tease Darla.

"Yes." Katie answered, smiling at her aunt.

"Katie, you best be teasing, otherwise you will be stuck on the beach while we are swimming." Darla warned with a smile.

"I am teasing, Mom." Katie quickly said with an excited laugh.

"Have you seen my swimsuit, Cindy?" Katie asked.

"No."

"You will love it. Angel picked it out. It is a pretty lavender and goes to my ankles."

"Oh, you." Cindy replied laughing.

"Dar, we will have to do this again soon and have Kelley and Dan go." Cindy suggested.

"Kel never has time to take Mom to town, let alone San Diego." Katie voiced.

"Deary, you are trespassing." Darla cautioned.

"Excuse me." Katie apologized quickly.

"Where is Kel?" Cindy asked.

"He is at the hospital. He received a call early."

"One of the street kids?"

"Yes, it usually is. They snap their fingers and Kel runs to their beckon call." Darla answered.

"May we please change the subject? I want to have a nice day." Darla said blushing before she complained more.

Katie had a blast in the ocean along with her two best friends, Jessica and Shelby from church. As the sun began to set, Darla calling an end to their play, Katie briefly hesitated to admire the beauty of the sunset against the water. Darla went to Katie's side putting her arm around her waist.

"Is not our Heavenly Father the greatest of artists?" Darla asked, she too impressed by the beauty of the sunset.

"Yes." Katie answered happily.

"I wish we could stay forever."

"You and me both. Dad and I used to come here often when we were dating. There really was a time in Dad's life when he made time for fun." Darla shared, bringing a smile to Katie's already happy face.

"Maybe Kel will bring you soon, Angel." Katie suggested, hopeful for her kind sensitive mother.

"This would be nice." Darla replied as they started toward Cindy and Katie's friends.

It was near nine when Darla and Katie returned from their outing. Kelley kindly met the girls, assisting them unloading the car.

"Did you have a good time Katie?" Kelley inquired.

"I had the greatest time in my entire life." Katie answered happily.

"Dad, you should take Mom next weekend. I will care for Heaven." Katie suggested excitedly.

"Thank you for your offer, Katie." Darla said.

Darla put her arms around her husband's waist happily, looking up into his eyes.

"May we go? I would love to have one entire day all alone with no interruptions. As Katie says, please, please, please."

"Sure." Kelley answered, looking into his wife's eyes.

"Really?" Darla asked both excited and surprised.

"Yes, really. Perhaps I could interest you in having breakfast with me also at a certain restaurant on top of a certain mountain?"

"Yes, yes, yes." Darla answered with an excited laugh.

"Thank you, Honey." She added.

"You are welcome." Kelley started to kiss Darla when Darla quickly put her hand on her husband's lips.

"Goodbye, Katie." Kelley said, reading his wife's thought.

"Katie is gone, Dad." Katie said as she made her exit.

"You are terrible." Darla said with a soft laugh, blushing.

"Hmm, where was I?" He asked playfully, as he gently pulled his wife closer kissing her several times.

Katie was excited all week with summer break beginning at the end of the week.

"Angel, guess what?" Katie asked excitedly as she entered the back door from school with her friend Jessica.

"I give. What?" Darla questioned pleasantly, giving Katie her full attention.

"I have a job for the summer if you and Dad say it is okay." She answered thrilled as she hopped up, sitting on the kitchen counter.

"Where?"

"At the Christian bookstore with Jessica. If you say yes, I may begin Monday."

"I think it sounds great."

"Thank you." Katie replied happily, giving her mother an excited hug.

"You are welcome, Sweetheart, but slow down. You still have to ask Dad."

"I know." Katie agreed.

"May Jessica stay until church time?" She asked politely.

"Yes, she may."

"May I ride with her to church?"

"Probably, but do ask Dad." Darla reminded.

"Is there anything else you would like to have, Miss Katie?"

"A car like Jessica's." Katie answered, bringing a laugh from her foster mother.

"I told you how Dad and I received our cars."

"I know working and saving. This is why I want this job, so I can do the same."

"Sweetheart, answer the telephone please." Darla instructed as she finished icing a cake.

"Peterson's." Katie spoke.

"Hi, Dad." She greeted excitedly.

"Dad may I..." Katie started happily then her silence brought the disappearance of her excitement.

"Yes, Sir. Bye." Katie put the telephone down.

"Mm, Jessica there is icing left." Katie said, picking up the icing bowl delaying delivering her mother saddened news.

"Mom, you want some?" She asked sticking her finger in the bowl and then licking her finger, as did Jessica.

"No, thank you, silly." Darla answered, surprised with the girl's actions at their ages.

"Enough trying to spare me. What is dad's message?" She asked, looking into her daughter's eyes.

"He will not be home for dinner. He will be home in time for a shower and church. He is at the hospital with Jose. He got stabbed in a fight." Katie answered, feeling for her mother, knowing she missed his too often hours of absences.

"We must say a prayer for Jose then." Darla replied as though she was not disappointed.

"I will Angel." Katie agreed sincerely.

"Excuse us."

"You are excused, dear."

Returning home from the midweek service, Katie decided to wait to ask her foster dad about her job. He appeared terribly tired. She excused herself, giving her parents their far-in-between time together.

Katie set the table for dinner and then began making a salad.

"Dad is home." Katie informed, noting his arrival from the window above the sink.

"He is out of his car. Now he is going to the corral." Katie said, giving her foster mother a smile.

"He is now putting water in Sam's pan."

"Katie, you are spying." Darla scolded with a surprised smile at her forward play, her expression bringing a tickled laugh from Katie. Darla lovingly put her arm around Katie's waist as she now observed her husband's doings through the window.

"Dad looks terribly tired." Darla said, with concern on her face and in her voice.

Kelley now put the water hose in the horse's troth. He stood leaning against the fence petting his wife's horse.

"Mom, if Dad would allow me, I could make his work load lighter by doing the yard work and caring for Sam and Princess." Katie suggested compassionately.

"This is kind of you, but Dad would not allow you. I tried doing what he considers a 'man's' responsibilities once for this reason. You would have thought I offended him. He will not have his wife or daughter burdened by him being too tired. He and his pride can be irritating at times." Darla shared with a gentle smile.

"Like Grandpa Peterson." Katie said with a pleased smile.

"Yes, like his father." Darla agreed.

"Go ask Dad about your job."

"Okay." Katie agreed, excited.

Katie seemed to mature so much over the summer. She loved her job and was full of excitement with life. It seemed Kelley was seldom home, running to and from at the first sign of someone in need of prayer, comfort, and Bible study. Darla was running low on patience with his absence. At times, she felt she did not have a husband.

Kelley had received a call that a young kid he and Dan had been witnessing to was near death in the hospital. Both Kelley and Dan had left their separate homes, staying at his side. Darla waited up until midnight for her husband. With no news of when he might return, she finally went to bed.

"Kelley?" Darla questioned, waking suddenly.

"It is me, Babe." He answered slipping under the covers.

"Kelley, it is four in the morning."

"I know. We best get to sleep." He replied. Kelley was sleeping soundly within minutes.

"Kelley Peterson, you are crazy." Darla whispered lightly kissing her sleeping husband's forehead. Within a couple of hours, Darla hesitantly awoke her husband to prepare for work. Kelley wearily got out of bed with no complaining of being tired. Darla observed her husband with saddened eyes. Katie was right; Kelley seemed to do nothing these days, but work.

"Lord, how much more may he possibly give before there is nothing left of him to give?" She silently questioned.

Kelley in the shower, Darla awoke Katie to prepare for her job and then started breakfast.

"Good morning, Mom." Katie greeted pleasantly.

"Good morning, Sweetheart." Darla greeted, placing her breakfast on the table.

"Did Dad come home?" She asked slowly, not wanting to intrude.

"What is left of Dad arrived at four this morning." Darla answered, concerned for her husband.

"Did Dad get hurt?" Katie questioned quickly.

"No, Honey, scratch my remark." Darla answered forcing a weak smile.

"Good morning, girls." Kelley greeted, taking his place at the breakfast table.

"Good morning." Darla greeted.

"It is nice to see you." She added.

"Thank you. I am sorry I was so late, Babe." Darla smiled as though politely accepting his apology, yet she remained silent.

"Dad, you look terribly tired." Katie voiced sympathetically.

"Have you been talking with Mom about dear ole Dad?" Kelley

questioned with a smile, sensing his wife's disapproval of his endless schedule.

"Dad, I am able to see for myself. We barely see you." Katie answered.

Kelley's face flushed as he grew silent, keeping his daughter's stare for several moments.

"I am sorry. Apparently I am trespassing." Katie said slowly. Kelley remained silent, sipping his hot coffee.

"Kelley, why not allow me to call Dad telling him you will not be in for work today. He will understand. You do need to rest." Darla suggested compassionately.

"No, Darla." Kelley spoke firmly, his tone making both his wife's and daughter's faces flush, bringing silence to his wife.

Kelley rubbed his head wearily as he quickly calmed himself. Looking now at his wife with tenderness in his eyes, he gently took her hand in his.

"I appreciate your intentions. Babe, I am not going to take advantage of my employer because I am married to his daughter. I have never missed a day of work for myself and I will not start now. Okay?" He questioned with tenderness in his voice and on his face.

"You are the boss." Darla answered as though defeated.

"I am not trying to be a boss." He assured.

"I know this." Darla agreed.

"I, along with you and others will probably be forced to close this ministry shortly. The violence is running people away now. I feel I must do what I am capable of to reach all possible before we are forced out of the park with our ministry." Kelley shared, his heart saddened and heavily burdened.

"I best pray for more patience then." Darla confessed with flushed cheeks.

"And you, Katie, be patient please, Babe. I do not like being away from my family any more than you and mom do. Where the Lord leads, I must follow. Where He sends, I must go. I am His servant."

"Yes, Sir." Katie agreed with a tender smile.

"You are the greatest, Dad." She added.

"I second this." Darla said with a comforting smile, as she looked into her husband's eyes.

"I have not forgotten how special my family is either." Kelley assured, deeply touched by their support.

Darla could feel the tension as Kelley had voiced, among the street kids at their meetings in the park twice weekly. It was becoming difficult to conduct a service with the violence around them seeming to get closer to their group.

Dressed in her usual Friday evening attire, faded blue jeans, sweatshirt and tennis shoes, Darla was dressed for the park ministry; simple dress for these special people. They seemed to shy away from the Sunday go to meeting appearance. She softly sang as Heaven played nearby and she prepared dinner. Darla picked up the ringing telephone.

"Good afternoon." She greeted.

"Hello, Darla. This is Pastor Finks. How are you?"

"Fine, thank you. How is my favorite pastor?" Darla asked pleasantly.

"Since you were brought up in a minister's home knowing first hand we preachers have had days also, I have had a terrible day." He answered.

"I'm sorry to hear this. Is there anything I could do to brighten your day?"

"You have already by you offering your assistance. Thank you. What I need is for Kelley to give me a call before he makes plans to attend the park this evening. Darla, this is extremely important. He is not to enter the park before he speaks with me. You, young lady, stay home tonight. I will be near my telephone waiting Kelley's call." Pastor Finks informed concern in his voice.

"I will do as you have advised." Darla assured.

Darla was filled with questions and sadness. She loved being a part of the ministry to the street people more than any task she had ever undertaken. Although she had felt for several weeks, the violence would push their ministry out of the park, perhaps not indefinitely, yet for some time.

Darla's thoughts were soon interrupted by a knock on her back door. Setting the dinner plates down intending to set the table, she went to the door.

"Pastor Finks, come in, please." Darla offered kindly.

"Kelley should be home any minute."

"Good. Darla, I received shocking news immediately after my call to you. Slim has been shot."

"Oh, no." Darla said, her eyes filling with tears.

"I know, Honey. You led him to the Lord when you were sixteen, I was there and I remember. He was a true Christian and servant unto the Lord all these years." Pastor Finks said, with his arms around Darla comforting her.

"Is he..."

"He is at complete peace now, Honey." Pastor Finks informed. Darla cried hard.

"Mama, Mama." Heaven said, bothered by her mother crying, as she hit on her leg, attempting to get her attention.

"Mom." Katie said as she and Kelley returned from their jobs. Darla continued to cry her hardest in her pastor's arms.

"Pastor?" Kelley questioned his face as white as a sheet, as he went to his wife.

"Slim is at peace now, Son." Pastor Finks informed, allowing Kelley to take his wife in his arms.

"Oh, Babe." Kelley said, appearing as though he was in shock himself as he held and comforted his wife.

"Mommy." Heaven said again beginning to fuss. Katie quickly picked up her baby sister as she too had watery eyes.

"Ka-tee." She said, hugging Katie's neck.

"The ministry is closed, for a season anyway." Pastor Finks informed.

"What?" Kelley questioned, hoping he would never hear this.

"Son, it is over. No more stepping a foot inside that park. It is a war zone. The Lord has warned each of us. Slim was warned. He had to return once more to attempt to lead one more to salvation. Do not be foolish, Kelley. Heed to the Lord's warnings always. He has already opened another door for you and you know this. Do not allow emotions to sidetrack you. Obey without questioning the leading of the Holy Spirit." Pastor Finks advised with wisdom.

Kelley was silent. He silently comforted his wife, silently praying and searching his heart. Pastor Finks had spoken wisely. Obey the leading of the Holy Spirit. He and Darla lived by this vital must.

"Mom?" Katie spoke, barely above a whisper.

"Yes, dear?" Darla questioned as she desperately tried to get ahold of herself, avoiding her daughter seeing her face.

Katie silently placed Kleenex in her mother's hands.

"Thank you." Darla said as she wiped her face, looking up into her husband's solemn, expressionless, and tearless strong face.

"Oh, Kelley, you have done a wonderful job, Honey. You have worn yourself out to do the best job. The Lord knows you truly need a rest. He also knows your family needs and misses you terribly." Darla spoke, giving him a tight hug to comfort him, for the losses he felt.

"Your wife is right, Preacher Kel." Pastor Finks voiced. He patted Kelley on his shoulder.

"I know, Sir, she usually is." Kelley replied looking down into his wife's saddened eyes as they comforted one another with tenderness in his eyes, he kissed her forehead then gently laid her head against his chest as he silently continued to comfort her and receive comfort.

Pastor Finks quietly motioned goodbye to Katie and then let himself out. Katie quietly left the kitchen with Heaven, allowing her parents their time needed in private.

"How long has it been since your husband has had time to go for a walk with you?" Kelley asked looking into his wife's eyes.

"I do not recall the last time." Darla answered in her gentle way.

"Too long, right?"

"Yes." Darla answered honestly.

"Let us do this now." He suggested in his most sensitive manner.

The young couple spent some time outside alone, together comforting one another and together discussing losses and gains.

Together planning, not looking back, least tempted to turn back disrupting the Lord's plan for their tomorrow.

With Heaven tucked in for the night and her bath taken and dressed for bed, Darla sat down in the den. With her Bible and Sunday school quarterly before her, she studied her lesson for her teen class the following morning. Kelley sat at his desk studying over his talk for youth service the following evening.

"Babe, where is Katie?" Kelley asked from his desk.

"She is in her room finishing her homework."

"Would you mind getting her? I have put off talking with her long enough."

"No, I do not mind."

Returning to the den with Katie, Kelley left his desk sitting down on a chair as Katie and Darla sat down on the sofa.

"Katie, I will be accepting a pastoral position in Tucson, Arizona in six weeks." Kelley started as he observed his foster daughter's face quickly change from curious to sad.

"Do I have to return to juvy?" Katie questioned slowly, barely above a whisper. Kelley and Darla both looked at Katie as though they were heartbroken with her question.

"Katie, I thought you had finally eliminated that fear." Darla said quickly.

"The state owns me. I cannot move to Arizona." Katie explained, her eyes quickly filling with tears.

"Kelley?" Darla questioned suddenly feeling sick at her stomach.

"She is right." Kelley answered sitting back in his chair, suddenly feeling like the biggest heel of the century for not remembering Katie as a foster daughter instead of a biological daughter.

"I apologize, Sweetheart. I honestly forgot. I have not thought of you as a foster daughter for months." Kelley explained as Katie's tears started down her cheeks.

"Nor I, Honey. We both should of thought of this before Dad spoke with you." Darla comforted putting her arm around Katie's shoulders.

"I promise you, Katie, I will work something out. We would

never give you up." Kelley assured, his heart going out to the sixteen-year-old. Katie's tears continued as Darla attempted to sooth her.

"I am sorry, Darla." Kelley said standing up, wanting to go to Katie, yet feeling like a trader at the same moment.

"I know, Honey. We are both guilty for this upset." Darla soothed, feeling badly for her husband also.

Kelley stood for the longest time staring out the den window while his foster daughter continued to cry in his wife's arms.

"May I be excused please?" Katie asked with tears still streaming.

"Yes, dear." Darla answered.

With Katie's departure, Darla went to her husband's side, putting her arm around his waist to comfort him.

"What do we do now, dear?" She questioned letting out a sigh.

"I do not know." Kelley answered.

"I cannot believe I have allowed this to happen. I just opened up the door to all of Katie's old fears that has taken a year of hard work from everyone to close. Everything involving our future is at stake also." Kelley voiced nervously.

"I am perfectly aware of this." Darla agreed looking drained.

"Honey, it will all work out somehow." She encouraged.

"I believe I will clean the barn."

"At nine-thirty at night?" Darla questioned, sympathetic.

"I will re-stack the hay. It will give me an excuse to throw something." Kelley answered, shaking his head at himself as he left the room.

Darla went to the ringing telephone. Picking up the receiver, she sat down at her husband's desk.

"Hello."

"Hi, Dar, this is Cindy." Her cousin greeted. Katie started to enter the den then stopped in the hall at hearing her foster mother on the telephone.

"How did you know I needed my dearest friend to talk to?"

"What is wrong?" Cindy asked.

"Everything possible, but Katie's heartbreak is our number one concern."

Katie stood against the wall in the hallway deciding to listen to her mother's telephone conversation.

"Kelley is in the barn re-stacking the hay. He said it would give him an excuse to throw something. He is simply kicking himself senseless. Kelley started to tell Katie of our move to Tucson. Katie reminded us we do not have the legal right to take her out of the state. Cindy, everything is at stake. We could never lose Katie. She is our daughter, yet Kelley only has work here for six more weeks with Dad. He already informed the board of his resigning as youth pastor, therefore this job is promised to another. Kelley has a job in Tucson. Everything seemed so perfect. The most Kelley and I worried about was Katie being upset having to change high schools and leaving her friends. Katie asked if she had to return to juvy. It was all Kelley and I both could do to hold our tears back." Darla shared as her tears began down her cheeks.

"If it means washing dishes twenty-four hours a day to stay here so we can keep Katie, so be it."

Katie quietly sat down in the hallway releasing her tears again.

"They really do love me as a real daughter." She thought her heart deeply touched.

"Cindy, I know Kel and I believed his taking the church in Tucson was the Lord's will for us. I am not questioning this, yet I will not allow Katie to be without the only family she has. No way could I believe for a minute the Lord would expect us to do such a thing."

"This is kind of you to offer Katie your home. I am also sure my parents, Kelley's parents and Bill would offer. I do sincerely appreciate your offer, but Katie has a family with Kel and me. I realize Tucson is not the other side of the world, Cindy." Darla spoke, feeling defeated.

Katie wiped her tears away and then quietly stood up. She slipped out the back door. Going to the side door of the barn, Katie saw her foster dad kneeling, silently praying. She glanced at the bales of hay, noting they had not been moved. She smiled to think her foster dad would actually throw something would be a first for him. She quietly went to his side. Kneeling down next to her foster dad, she took his hand in hers.

"Dad we will work everything out, right?" Katie asked looking up into his sad, yet gentle eyes.

"We must, Babe. We are a family." Kelley answered putting his arm around his foster daughter's shoulders.

"I certainly am sorry I have placed doubt in your mind in regards to your place in this family. I would not purposely hurt you, Princess." He assured his voice cracking and his eyes watery.

"I really know this. I kind of freaked momentarily. Dad, you always say you respect people more when they level with you. I heard Mom talking to Aunt Cindy on the telephone. I am willing to bargain if you are game."

"I do not understand. What did you hear Mom say?" Kelley asked.

"That your jobs end here in six weeks. Dad, you have to go to Tucson. You and Mom know the Lord is sending you there. On the other hand, I only have one year of high school after this year. I really want to finish school with my friends. Maybe, if you and Mom will agree, I could stay with Aunt Cindy during the school year and go home with you and Mom for the summer. When I really get lonesome for you, I could run Aunt Cindy's telephone bill up." Katie suggested with a gentle smile.

"This is more than kind of you, Katie. I do not know about this, Babe." He said, looking at Katie in deep thought.

"Dad, Cindy made this offer to Mom. This is where I got this idea. I am not yet this wise on my own." She shared bringing a smile to her foster dad's face.

"Angel turned Cindy down, but if you, I, and Aunt Cindy stick together, we could change her mind. It would probably take all three of us."

"Are you suggesting Mom is stubborn?"

"Yes." Katie answered with a laugh.

"A bit possessive also." She added.

"You had better hope Mom does not overhear you." Kelley said with a grin, glancing toward the door. Katie's face turned red as she quickly glanced toward the doorway, expecting to see her foster mother, but there was no one there.

"Dad, that was not funny." Katie said laughing.

"Come on." Kelley said standing up, holding his hand out to his daughter, assisting her to her feet.

"It is getting late, kiddo. Mom is probably worrying."

"I noticed you did not throw the bales of hay." She teased, causing her foster dad to blush with laughter.

"I believe you more than overheard Mom's conversation. You deliberately listened to her entire conversation." Kelley accused.

"I listened to the entire conversation only because it was about us. Dad, neither you nor Mom would have leveled with me about your job situation, so it was necessary."

"You better make sure it is not necessary again." He warned.

"Yes, Sir." Katie answered with a shy smile, blushing.

Kelley did not burden his wife with Katie's suggestion. First thing Monday morning, he and Darla applied for legal guardianship of Katie. Katie appeared to be her usual happy, content, carefree self. This surprised Darla.

"Katie." Darla spoke as they had dinner.

"Aunt Cindy tells me you do not want to go to Tucson even if Dad and I receive legal guardianship of you. Is this the way you feel?"

"Yes, Ma'am." Katie answered slowly, unsure of her foster mother's opinion.

"Mom, I have attended school here my entire life. It would mean a lot to me if I were allowed to graduate with my class. I could go home on school breaks and summer vacation. Aunt Cindy..."

"I am aware of each idea your Aunt Cindy has." Darla interrupted, clearly disapproving of the idea.

"Mom, please?" Katie questioned.

"I belong in this school with my friends."

Darla said no more. Though it bothered her terribly to grant Katie her wishes, she remembered how it upset her as a teen to move, leaving her friends behind.

Kelley and Darla had four weeks remaining in their present home. Darla carefully began packing her china. She felt excited Kelley would be pastoring, yet she had emptiness. Though Katie had not been granted consent to stay at Cindy's home to finish school where she wished, Darla felt she would not be leaving for Tucson with them and this saddened her.

"Hi." Darla greeted pleasantly as Kelley and Katie arrived home.

"Hi, Babe." Kelley greeted giving his wife a kiss.

"Are you okay?" Kelley asked concern in his eyes.

"Oh, I suppose I will be." Darla answered with watery eyes.

"I am going to miss our Katie terribly." Darla said with a smile.

"I may stay?" Katie questioned, surprised with her change of heart.

"I seem to be the only one giving you a hard time about staying. If you will be happier, dear, you may stay."

"Thanks, Mom." Katie said, giving her a hug.

Darla worried Katie would miss out having a mother and father example daily. Her Aunt Cindy was more a sister image than a mother image, yet Darla could not bear to uproot her either, with all the disruptions she had endured throughout her young years.

"Why did you ride the bus home this evening, Deary?" Darla asked as Katie arrived from school.

"I called Sam at the Christian bookstore. He gave me permission to miss work this evening." Katie assured quickly as she sat down on the kitchen counter.

"I want to share a note I received today with you." Katie informed her face troubled.

"Okay." Darla agreed, setting her dinner preparations aside, giving Katie her undivided attention.

"It is from my biological mother." She informed slowly, handing the paper to her foster mother. Darla silently took the paper, reading the words to herself.

Dearest Kate,

I am aware you have celebrated your sixteenth birthday. I do think of you and hope you are happy. I hear you have a nice family and this pleases me. Your dad and I were not made to be parents. I would like to see you. If you would also like this, I will be at El Taco Saturday at noon. We may have lunch together and I have a special gift for you. I do love you.

Love, Kay

"I always called my mom Kay. She preferred this because she said she was too young to be a mother."

"Would you like to see your mother?"

"Yes. I have not seen her since I was five. I have a special gift for my mother. I do not know if she will accept it."

"Why would you question her accepting your gift?"

"It may not mean anything to her. I actually have two gifts for her. My first gift is forgiving her for not wanting me and not hating her for this anymore. My second gift is telling her the way to salvation that she may have eternal life. I do not know if she will understand that gifts of love are priceless." Katie answered her young face tender and sincere.

"Oh, Katie, you are a very unique young lady. If your mother chooses to refuse your gifts, I pity her." Darla replied giving Katie a tight hug.

"I am so proud of you."

Katie had butterflies in her stomach as she prepared for her luncheon date with her biological mother.

"Katie." Kelley spoke, entering Katie's room.

"Yes?"

"Here are my car keys, Babe. I have some errands to run. Mom is busy packing with your two grandmas. Enjoy your luncheon date."

"Dad, I cannot take your car." Katie spoke slowly, her cheeks flushed.

"Why? You cannot take Mom's car until you allow me to

teach you to drive a stick." He reminded looking at his daughter, questioning.

"Your car, it is an expensive item. I cannot borrow a car."

"Katie, you must. I am already late to meet Pastor Finks for a meeting. Forget your Dad's ways and rules, please? We share in our family. Take my car and have a good time."

"Yes, Sir." Katie replied though hesitant.

Katie waited for two hours at the restaurant for her mother. She felt such a letdown. She wanted to cry, yet no tears came. Slowly getting up from her table, she saw a woman resembling her mother hurry out of the restaurant. Katie was momentarily stunned. Surely, it was not her mother. Picking up her purse, she went to the cash register to pay for her coke.

"Miss Katie Dobbs?" The cashier asked.

"Yes, Ma'am?"

"Your mother left your birthday gift in the parking lot. It is the pretty red car with the ribbon around it." The cashier informed her with a big smile.

Katie stared through the window with disbelief.

"Where is my mother?" Katie asked with watery eyes.

"All I was told is to give you this birthday card and car keys."

"Thank you, Ma'am."

Katie went outside the restaurant, looking all around hoping to catch a glimpse of her mother. With tears streaming down her face, her heart broken from missing her mother's arrival, she slowly went to the car. She ran her fingers over the new shiny red paint.

"I did not want a car, Kay. I just wanted to see you once more." She whispered.

"Hi, stranger." Aaron spoke with a big grin as he got out of his car. Katie quickly wiped her tears.

"Darla sent me to check on you." He informed as he approached. Reaching her side seeing her tears of sadness, Aaron's face quickly saddened.

"Kay, what happened?" He questioned compassionately.

"Please, give me a minute." Katie said still crying.

"Sure Kay." He agreed considerately.

"It looks like someone has received one swell gift." He remarked glancing at the car they both stood next to. Katie silently held her car keys out to Aaron. Aaron appeared as though he was in shock.

"This is your car?"

"Yes. Please take the keys." Katie answered as she got herself under control.

"Yes, Ma'am. I gladly accept these keys." He replied in his humorous way, bringing a smile to Katie's face. Aaron unlocked the door getting inside and examining the sports car.

"A five speed even. Boy, could I have fun with this car, Kay." He remarked with eagerness on his face, he got out of the driver's seat and closed the door.

"I cannot drive a stick." Katie shared, smiling at Aaron's eagerness.

"Sure you can. I would love to teach you. May I?"

"Yes." Katie answered with a soft laugh over his excitement.

"Now that you are laughing, I have a question for you." Aaron informed putting his arm around Katie's shoulders in a brotherly manner.

"Are you okay, Kay?" He asked, looking into her eyes, her tears quickly coming again.

"I only wanted to see my mother once. I waited two hours, Aaron. I get an expensive car and a card telling me she is getting married and her fiancé is never to know I exist." She shared beginning to cry again. Aaron pulled Katie close to him allowing her to cry on his shoulder.

"Forget her, Kay. She does not deserve your tears or your love." He advised compassionately.

"I guess I really knew she would not show. I almost did not come myself, so I could avoid the disappointment if she did not show." Katie said, opening her purse for a Kleenex.

"But then, you are not a coward." Aaron defended with an understanding smile.

"Thanks for your support."

"You will always have my support, Kay. This is a promise." He said.

Katie silently dealt with her upsets from her biological mother disappointing her. She quickly mastered the knowledge of driving a five speed also.

With only three days remaining before the Peterson's departure date, Darla woke extra early. She was glad it was Saturday. This would be Kelley's first chance to assist her with their packing since deciding on their move. Kelley was always busy elsewhere and Katie was busy with school, her part-time job, studies and friends. Darla worked hard at concealing her resentment toward both her husband and daughter, yet it seemed it was becoming difficult for her to bite her tongue, as the two seemed to go on their merry ways offering little if any assistance in preparing for their move.

Putting a load of laundry in the washer, getting a head start on her morning, still dressed in her robe with the earliness of the hour, Darla felt tired. Going to the kitchen and starting the coffee, she wearily sat down at the table rubbing her head, feeling a headache beginning.

"Please, no headache today. I have no patience or time for such delays." She thought.

The coffee pot finished perking; she poured herself a cup of coffee. Removing her medicine from the cabinet along with a pain pill, she hoped both pills improved the way she felt. Picking up the last empty box that sat on the kitchen floor, she packed the remainder of the dishes she could do without using their few days remaining. Returning to the laundry room, she tended to the laundry. Quietly setting a basket of Katie's clothes outside her room, she then made herself presentable for her family and busy day.

"Darla." Kelley spoke, sitting up in bed.

"I am sorry, Honey, I did not intend to disturb you." She apologized as she removed her shoes from the closet.

"Why are you already dressed at this hour?"

"Because there is a lot to be done between today and Tuesday." Darla answered in her gentle way.

"Go back to sleep." She ordered, kissing his lips lightly.

Going outside and checking Katie's car for the boxes she promised to bring from work the evening before, Darla was met with disappointment.

"Oh, Deary, how could you forget?"

Returning inside the house, she refilled her coffee cup. Sitting down at the table, she went over her list of duties.

"Good morning, beautiful." Kelley greeted, giving his wife a kiss.

"Mm, good morning." Darla greeted pleased with his greeting.

"I will gladly accept another kiss." She said.

"May I have my coffee first?"

"No, you may not. I am tired of waiting. My need comes before your coffee." Darla answered, looking up into his eyes as though scolding.

"Of course it does." Kelley agreed, giving his wife a kiss.

"You look tired, Babe."

"I am. Perhaps you will understand me today if I have little patience."

"I understand." Kelley answered with concern on his face.

"You have a headache?"

"A bit of one." Darla said.

Kelley stood looking at his wife in silence for several moments.

"We have guests coming this evening." Kelley said suddenly remembering.

"Yes, and lots more packing to be done today. You and Katie have both been too busy elsewhere. I am not capable of doing all that is needed to be completed in the next three days alone."

"This should not be expected of you." Kelley replied with flushed cheeks, feeling guilty with his neglect.

Kelley removed a coffee cup from the counter. With his cup of coffee, he sat down at the table, picking up his wife's list.

"I asked Katie to bring boxes home last night. I checked her car and apparently, she forgot. We are completely out of them." Darla informed her voice beginning to sound tired.

"She has not even packed her things as of yet."

"I thought you told her last week to pack and take her things to Cindy's."

"I told her. Something always seems to come up, changing plans."

"I am not in a position to give her a lecture in this matter. I am guilty of this myself." Kelley confessed, his expression bearing his guilt.

"I agree." Darla replied though with tenderness on her face.

"Katie and I will simply have to work overtime to finish up. You are not lifting a finger today. You give the orders and we will carry them out." Kelley instructed.

"I love it when you take charge." Darla said with a soft laugh, bringing a smile to her husband's face.

"I will wake Katie." Kelley said.

Kelley returned to the kitchen picking up the telephone inviting his brother Aaron to come give them a hand. Removing a bowl from the cabinet, he began making pancake batter.

"Good morning." Katie greeted, appearing half-asleep as she sat down at the table.

"Good morning, dear." Darla greeted.

"Dad, it is only seven-thirty." Katie informed after looking at the clock.

"You and I have a lot to do today." Kelley informed busy with his breakfast preparations.

"Will we be finished by noon? I have plans to go to the beach if it is okay." Katie said, resting her head on her hand.

"I am not in the position to answer you." Kelley said smiling at his wife.

"No beach today, Deary. Remember to ask before you make plans."

"Yes, Ma'am." Katie politely answered though her face expressed her disappointment.

"Katie, I checked your car, but I did not find any boxes."

"I forgot, I am sorry."

"Have you managed time to pack your things yet?" Darla asked politely reminding her.

"No, Ma'am." Katie answered slowly with flushed cheeks.

"Katie, I believe I just heard strike three called on you." Kelley spoke, looking at his foster daughter. His comment making her blush more.

"I believe you and I both have been taking Mom for granted. When Mom says do something, get it done."

"Yes, Sir. I am sorry for being irresponsible, Mom." Katie apologized.

"Your apology is accepted."

Kelley placed their breakfast on the table.

"Dar, lie down after you eat. Katie and I will manage Heaven and your list."

"Thank you, I believe I will."

"You are not feeling well?" Katie asked compassionately.

"I am just a little tired from exceeding my limits, dear. I will be fine."

"Grandma Roberts said this is how you become ill and why you must take medicine." Katie said, now realizing why her father was taking charge.

"This is how she begins becoming ill. If she gets past this stage, she and I are going to tangle big time." Kelley informed looking at his wife with concern on his face.

"If you two will pull your weight and I rest today, I will not get past this point." Darla assured, clearly getting her message across to both her husband and daughter.

"Yes, Ma'am." Kelley replied.

By mid-afternoon, Darla felt much better. She was surprised at all her husband, Katie and Aaron had accomplished. Relaxing in the den with a book, Heaven played near her mother.

"Darla, Bill is on the telephone. He wants to know if you will be offended if he brings Paula to the cookout this evening." Kelley asked.

"Why would I mind? I have been praying for a year that they would work things out."

"Bill thought you might be upset with Paula for her rude remarks she made to you when we were engaged." Kelley explained.

"No, I do not hold grudges." Darla replied, laying her book aside.

"I will tell my brother." She decided, getting up from the sofa.

Katie and Kelley had everything ready when their families arrived for the cookout. Darla was both pleased and grateful. There was excitement in each family member. This was Darla's and Kelley's farewell evening to both their families before they moved out of state, putting miles between their homes and their lives.

"Kelley said after dinner he will show the film he took on your honeymoon." Cindy shared, as she and Darla leisurely walked through the yard visiting and Bill tended the grill.

"This should be interesting. He and I have never taken the time to see the film." Darla replied breaking into a tickled laugh, blushing.

"What?" Cindy questioned smiling with her cousin's laughter.

"Kelley will be as surprised as everyone else with the film." She answered, still laughing.

"Darla, maybe you should warn him not to show the film."

"Oh, no, I am glad he is willing to share this special time with our families. He deserves being embarrassed. He thinks he is clever, but you will see."

Darla slipped away from her guest, seeing Katie alone at the corral petting Princess.

"A penny for your thoughts." Darla said, lovingly putting her arm around Katie's waist.

"I am going to miss you, Dad and Heaven. It just hit me that you are really leaving." Katie shared with flushed cheeks.

"Sweetheart, come with us. You know this is what I want. You do not have to stay." Darla assured.

"I would not fit in, in a new school. I am not outgoing like you, Mom. I would feel out of place. When I feel out of place, I get that terrible lonely feeling. I do not want to go back to all of those feelings. I guess I want both, my school here and you and Dad. Does this sound childish to you?" Katie asked with watery eyes.

"Not at all." Darla answered, giving Katie a tight hug.

"Why is it, Deary, we never seem to have our cake and eat it too?" She asked bringing a smile to Katie's face.

"Kay, Aaron says to tell you we need you on our volleyball team. He says you are able to hit hard." Matt, Kelley's youngest brother informed.

Katie and Darla both laughed, knowing Aaron sent sarcasm in his message.

"May I be excused?"

"Yes, have fun." Darla answered.

"Katie." She said.

"Yes?"

"Did you meet Uncle Bill's wife?"

"Yes." Katie answered, wrinkling her nose and expressing her disapproval.

"Go." Darla instructed with a disapproving smile.

Darla turned toward her horse petting her soft nose.

"I am going to miss you also, Princess." Darla said as her heart, as Katie's was already missing all and everyone she would be leaving behind. Kelley approached from behind Darla, slipping his arms around her waist.

"Hi, Baby doll." He greeted, pulling her close to him.

"Are we all alone or do we not still have guests?" Darla questioned, blushing with her husband's embrace.

"We are married, Baby doll." Kelley reminded, Darla leaning back, allowing her husband to hold her.

"I am going to miss living here." She shared looking up into her husband's eyes.

"I will be a full-time pastor with our move. There will be many days you will have me all to yourself." Kelley reminded with a tender smile, and then kissed the top of her head.

"For this reason, I cannot wait to move. I have missed you so terribly, Kelley with your hectic schedules here." Darla informed, turning around, facing her husband.

"I will feel like a new bride again." She shared. Looking into her husband's eyes, she kissed his lips.

"I have missed you also, Babe. I was too busy and preoccupied to notice the depth I have missed you. I have seen the light and I like what I see." He assured, taking his wife into his arms, gently kissing her.

"You know, Brother Peterson, I did teach my daughter to be a good hostess." Dad Roberts spoke as the two men approached, embarrassing the young couple.

"Aye, my son too, knows better." Dad Peterson agreed as the two laughed enjoying their teasing.

"I do not believe these two are our Dads. Kelley said with a chuckle, removing his arms from around his wife.

"It is our fatherly duty to interrupt." Dad Roberts insisted with a teasing grin.

"No, Sir. You lost that right a year ago when your daughter became my wife." Kelley informed with flushed cheeks.

"I suppose you are right." He agreed with a chuckle.

"We have some good kids, Pastor." Dad Peterson said with pride on his face.

"Two of the best." Dad Roberts agreed sincerely.

"This is because we have great dads." Darla assured. She kindly gave both men a kiss and then left the men fold to visit.

It was exciting for Darla and Kelley having their families sharing past experiences along with the joy of Kelley receiving his first pastoral position.

Joining her older brother at the grill, Darla politely assisted him.

"How is your reconciliation with your wife going?"

"Trust me, Sis; my marriage is the pits compared to you and Cindy's marriages. I do not know why I agreed to try to make this marriage work again. I honestly believe it is a waste of both our time."

"Bill, you know what the problem is. The Lord will mend your marriage if you would allow this. Cindy and I are fortunate we have Christian spouses. With Kelley and I both serving the Lord, we still manage to have our share of difficulties. The Lord helps make our down times more bearable. If you would only turn back to the Lord, Bill, then lead your wife to salvation you then, will be able to salvage your marriage."

"Sis, you sound like a preacher's wife." Bill said with a chuckle.

"And Mom and Dad." He added.

"So? When are you really going to do something about your situation with Paula?" Darla questioned bluntly.

"I..." Bill started, growing silent and tending to the grill as his wife joined them.

"What is so amusing?" Paula asked as she sampled one of her husband's hamburgers.

"My kid sister is attempting to turn me religious." Bill answered, making light of her usual manner of questions and possessiveness over him. Paula looked at her husband as though shocked with the idea.

"You, religious?" Paula questioned.

Bill avoided his wife's question, keeping his eyes on the grill.

"Darla, if you are able to get your brother into church, you will have performed a miracle." Paula said sarcastically as though mocking the idea.

"Actually Paula, I suggested to Bill that you both attend church as a united team." Darla shared in her gentle way, as she looked into Paula's eyes.

"Are you suggesting if Bill and I attend church, we will live happily ever after?" Paula questioned sarcastically, as though challenging an argument.

"No, I am not saying this." Darla sensed eagerness in Paula to learn underneath her sarcasm.

"Mommy." Heaven said, pulling on her mother's pant leg. Darla picked her daughter up and then returned her eyes on Paula.

"Paula, I say if both you and Bill would receive salvation by asking Jesus to forgive you of everything, pray, read your Bible daily, attend church and do these things living your lives for the Lord, according to the Bible, then and only then will you and my brother be happy." Darla explained in her slow patient way.

"What is your opinion about this religious talk, Bill?" Paula asked, her tone bearing even more sarcasm.

Detecting an argument about to surface as usual from his wife, he remained silent. Bill kept his eyes on the grill, not looking at either his wife or sister.

"Papa." Heaven said, holding her arms out as Kelley and his father passed by.

"Daddy." She added, giggling, reaching for both her father and grandfather.

"Allow me my granddaughter, Darla." Dad Peterson instructed taking Heaven into his arms lovingly. Dad Peterson continued his private conversation with his son nearby.

"Mr. Peterson actually calls Heaven his granddaughter?" Paula questioned surprised.

Bill threw the spatula down as his anger flared over his wife's ridiculous ways of creating friction. Bill's sudden loudness had brought everyone's eyes to the commotion and silence to everyone.

"Why do you insist on causing problems?" Bill questioned with his tone rising.

"Bill, please do not say anymore." Darla requested with pleading eyes.

"I am a big girl and I am capable of defending myself. Paula asked me the question. She is family, so I will answer her so she will have more understanding." Darla spoke gently calming her brother.

"This is a perfect example, Paula of how loving our God truly is. Yes, Kelley's parents love Heaven as their biological granddaughter. Because of their Christian walk with the Lord, they have the ability to love and forgive mistakes." Darla shared, her face flushed as her families heard of their talk.

"But, surely you have shame by having Heaven?" Paula questioned, her voice softer and without sarcasm. She truly appeared to be longing for this special love.

"Paula..." Bill started, angrier.

"Bill, be patient. She is not condemning; she wants to understand about Godly love. If I have to stand before the world and be embarrassed repeatedly of my mistake by answering questions that might lead your wife to salvation, so be it. Please do not interrupt." Darla scolded, shocking her brother into silence with her orders.

"Yes, Paula, I have shame. I cannot undo the mistake, therefore I am reminded daily of this. I was not a Christian then; I was a young college kid. I carried Heaven for all those months while I attended college. I saw the stares and I heard the whispers, but I had to go on with my life. I was so ashamed I did not tell my parents until it was time to come home. Heaven was several months old. I gave birth to Heaven with no one at my side because of my love for my family, I could not bring shame to them. The only good I saw was when I was handed a tiny innocent baby who needed only love to make her feel wanted. She was so innocent it was to me as though she was sent from heaven. She was the only good I saw and this is why I named her Heaven. God forgave me and most Christians forgive. I know some will never forgive, so this makes my shame lasting, but Heaven is completely innocent. I would say the Lord has provided her every need." Darla answered in her slow gentle way.

"Everything does seem perfect for Heaven." Paula agreed thoughtfully.

"What happens if Heaven learns Kelley is not her biological father? Are you not living a lie before her?"

"I do not know what the future holds for Heaven or any of us. I do know Heaven's present life is good and right. As far as a lie, there is no lying. Kelley adopted Heaven, so he is her father. He is the one caring for her." Darla answered hesitating, her eyes growing moist.

"Bill, you really should have explained most of this to your wife already. No wonder she feels as an outsider. You have been married for three years and she does not know your family." Bill looked at his sister, silently questioning her attack on him.

"As you and Bill have found, Paula, a piece of paper representing a marriage license does not guarantee love between husband and wife. It takes more than a biological parent to be loving and devoted to a child. Because a child is born does not guarantee a parent or a loving parent. God guarantees love. No paper, nothing biological, just simply genuine love. Love comes only from the heart. I have been told my entire life how much I look like my mother and that I have the Roberts' patience, but I am adopted." Darla informed, looking into Paula's eyes.

"You what?" Paula questioned, disbelieving her ears.

"I do not feel adopted. I do not wish to learn anything about my adoption. I am sure my parents have a paper some place that says I am adopted. The way I see it, God gave my parents the daughter they needed and me the parents I needed. I do not relate well to blood relationships automatically producing love or families. If that were true, Katie would be with her biological parents. My love for Katie is the same amount of love I have for Heaven. Paula, we do each love you and we are heartbroken that you and Bill are so miserable when it is all so senseless. God's love makes a world of difference in your life." Darla explained.

"Bill, you have been a loving and devoted brother and son. You always were so sensitive to my feelings and my needs, as well as Mother's and Dad's. Why is it you are not able to give this to your wife for both your sakes?" Darla asked.

Bill looked at his sister in silence, feeling ashamed.

Paula looked at Darla with tenderness in her eyes for the first time since they became acquainted.

"I had no idea why Bill thinks of you in such a special way, but now I do understand. You are full of love and understanding. Perhaps you each are very special, but I could not see past my jealousness over the bond Bill has between each of you. I did not see the bond as love. This is something my parents never taught me." Paula shared with tears streaming down her cheeks.

"Bill, am I jealous of the love and happiness your family possess? Will you teach me their kind of love, so you and I will be happy? I mean happy like your sister and loving?" Paula shared with tears streaming down her face.

"You know the way to salvation, Bill. It is time you teach Paula and take charge of yourself and your wife." Darla instructed.

"But..."

"But what? If you surrender your all to the Lord, you will have to give up your style of parties and some of your old friends and old ways. Your wife is pleading for you to show her the way. She should never have to wait for you to respond to her needs." Darla coached with firmness.

Bill looked at his sister with flushed cheeks. She seemed to understand his wife much more than he did. He looked at his wife gentle and tender yielded, as she had been when he first fell in love with her. He glanced at his audience who awaited his response. Suddenly, as though all his self-pride broke, he lovingly took his wife into his arms, comforting and soothing her.

"Dad, I think we could use a preacher." Bill spoke with moist eyes.

"You think or you know, Son?" Dad Roberts questioned, going to his son's side.

"I know and I am ready." Bill answered sincerely.

Both Darla and Kelley's families went to Bill and Paula's side, praying silently. Dad Roberts prayed aloud a simple sinner's prayer. Darla stood with Heaven held by one arm and her other arm around Katie. She was so happy for her brother and sister-in-law that she felt like shouting.

"Mom, I didn't know you are adopted or that Dad adopted Heaven." Katie whispered.

"Perhaps now you will be able to understand one doesn't have to be a blood relative to have a family. God truly is in the business of restoring the family, regardless of one's mistakes or misfortunes."

"Yes, Ma'am." Katie's eyes grew moist, as her heart seemed to know she did not need a legal paper to tell her, her place nor did she have to be blood related.

It was a glorious evening; each family member seemed to have a special sparkle in his or her eye and a song in his or her heart with the conversion of Paula and Bill.

As the Peterson and Roberts families made themselves comfortable in the front room, Kelley prepared the movie projector as Darla tucked Heaven in for the night.

Joining her family in the front room, Darla wearily, yet happily sat down on the carpet, leaning against her husband's legs.

"You do remember what is on this film right Babe?" Kelley asked with a boyish grin.

"Yes, Kelley I remember." Darla answered pleasantly, her face already flushed.

"I was your victim." She accused, bringing curious smiles to her families' faces as Katie, Aaron and Matt returned from outside sitting on the carpet.

"On your honeymoon?" Aaron questioned the most curious.

"This was my reaction." Darla confessed with a soft laugh, looking up at her husband, her face its reddest.

"It was all in fun, Babe." Kelley voiced with a grin, eager to flash his wife's embarrassing moments upon the screen.

"You remember this as I get even with you."

"Sure." Kelley agreed.

"I am a good sport."

Darla glanced at Cindy, they secretly exchanging smiles. Bill turned the lights out as Kelley started the projector.

The film running, the beautiful mountain scenery appeared on the screen. Each silently admired the beauty Kelley had captured on film. The film now showed Darla in her robe at the breakfast table appearing half-asleep with her hands over her face, attempting to hide from Kelley's filming, bringing laughter from the observers.

"Cindy, I thought Darla was elected best dressed in high school." Bill questioned with a chuckle.

"She was. I do not know what happened to her there." Cindy sided, smiling at her cousin.

"You will not believe her outfit she chose for the day." Kelley shared laughing, bringing a tickled laugh from his wife her face its reddest. Darla appeared on screen dressed in Kelley's big sloppy flannel shirt and rolled up baggy jeans. She left their cabin for her fishing outing and the group roared with laughter.

"I would have slapped him, Darla." Paula voiced.

"I would have slapped him twice." Mom Peterson defended, surprised at her son for embarrassing his bride.

"Did you slap Dad, Mom?" Katie asked smiling at her mother.

"Not yet." Darla answered with a soft laugh.

"Remember our deal, Bill?" Kelley asked with a pleased grin.

"In regards to Darla fishing?" Bill questioned.

"That is the one."

"You cannot be serious?" He questioned.

Kelley pointed to the screen. Darla picked up a worm as though both frightened by it and disgusted, shivering as she stuck her hook through the worm.

"How did you manage to have her bait her own hook?" Bill questioned laughing, almost hysterically.

"I told her if she did not bait her own hook and help catch fish; she would not have any dinner." Kelley answered laughing.

"Honey, I apologize for my son's conduct. I no longer claim him." Dad Peterson said bringing more laughter, as Kelley's face reddened.

The group grew quiet now as they admired scenes of their nature walk. Darla looked up into Kelley's eyes, her heartwarming toward him as the log church appeared on screen. Kelley lovingly put his arms around his wife's neck as he gave her a kiss on top of her head. The film showed Darla and Kelley kneeling at the alter with Kelley's special words to his bride recorded for all to hear.

"Now I know why you did not slap Dad, Mom." Katie said proudly, deeply touched as everyone was by Kelley's expressed love to his wife.

"This is beautiful, Kelley." Mom Roberts complimented.

Kelley now appeared on screen in his apron, hurrying around the kitchen as though a nervous scatterbrain, elderly lady bringing laughter from all.

"Dar, you did not do this." Kelley remarked, he now embarrassed, laughing with flushed cheeks.

Laughing, Darla started to crawl away from her husband's reach.

"Get back here." He ordered, pulling on her sweater, bringing her back to him.

"I believe your wife is quite clever, Son." Dad Peterson said laughing, finding his daughter-in-laws getting even method, most amusing, as did everyone.

"There is much more." Darla assured with a tickled laugh.

"I am so glad you are such a good sport." She added with uncontrollable laughter.

"You silly girl." Kelley mumbled, surprised by her play.

On screen, Kelley left the cabin. He appeared as though just awaking. His hair was tousled, his flannel shirt was unbuttoned, his tennis shoes untied, with a bath towel over his shoulder. The couple's guests now laughed at Kelley's appearance.

"Dar, how much did you film?" Kelley questioned with a nervous laugh, prepared to turn the projector off.

"Just enough to get even. Relax dear and enjoy. I think you look cute." Darla answered bringing laughter from each present, including her husband.

Kelley walked from the cabin to the lake. He slipped his shirt and shoes off, dropping them to the ground along with his towel. Kelley was now in the water.

"Darla, turn the camera off." Kelley ordered on film.

"This is not funny."

"You thought I looked funny wearing your baggie clothes yesterday. It is my turn to have fun." Their families laughed at Darla's feistiness.

"Come on, Dar, the water is cold. Please turn the camera off." He pleaded between laughs as he began to shiver in the water.

"You may have the towel, catch." Darla offered, tossing the towel toward him, the towel landing in the water.

"Whoops, I am a bad shot." She said laughing.

"Darla, turn off the camera." Kelley ordered annoyed. The film was momentarily blank.

"Darla Roberts, you were terrible." Mom Roberts scolded, shocked with her daughter's doings.

"She will probably be a Roberts again by the end of this film." Kelley teased.

"My son deserves this and probably much more." Dad Peterson defended.

The film showed Kelley now standing with the water soaked towel around his waist, buttoning his shirt. Everyone laughed at the sight of him.

"I would never cross my sister again, Kelley." Bill suggested.

"I do not believe this; I thought you left the lake, Dar." Kelley said sitting back against the sofa with his hand on his face, embarrassed.

Kelley reappeared on screen with his shirt and jeans on. He felt in his back pants pocket, finding it empty, he searched briefly on the ground.

"Dad, what were you looking for?" Katie asked.

"His comb." Darla answered.

"Watch." She instructed with a tickled laugh. On screen, Kelley attempted to comb his hair with his fingers.

"I bet that crazy girl took my comb." Kelley spoke aloud on tape, as he tucked his shirt in.

"My shoes." He spoke as though becoming putout with his wife. The film went blank.

"I returned Kelley's shoes and comb." Darla explained, giving her husband a tender smile.

"I do not believe my wife did this to me." Kelley said looking into her eyes with a gentle smile, shaking his head as though amazed at her capabilities.

"You do plan to go home with your parents tonight, right?" He asked, bringing a tickled laugh from her causing her to blush over her play. Kelley put his arms lovingly around her neck again, she continuing to lean against his legs as their eyes looked once again at the screen. The film showed their preparations to leave their honeymoon cabin and then it cut off.

"We did have a wonderful time." Darla said pleased, as Kelley turned the lights on.

"With many more years of wonderfulness to come." Kelley agreed sincerely.

Tuesday morning came all too soon for Darla. She silently watched as the men loaded their belongings. Her heart was deeply saddened that she was saying goodbye to her family, friends and Katie. The home she and Kelley had redecorated together, they were leaving behind for the job the Lord had chosen.

Staring out the car window as Kelley drove across the state line leaving California and entering Arizona, Darla released her tears. She thought of all she was leaving behind. Kelley had been silent thus far. She knew his heart was also aching. They were leaving all the years of their young lives behind. They were going to an area where they would be strangers, only having one another as family and for some time, most likely, only one another's friendship. Though her heart was terribly saddened, she was not sorry, for she knew the Lord was leading them.

After several long hours of driving, Kelley pulled up in front of the parsonage. Darla silently and patiently waited for her husband to get out of the car first and open her car door for her. They sat several minutes not speaking and not vacating the car, each in his and her separate thoughts.

Within a few weeks, Kelley had established a busy work schedule, yet not an overloaded schedule, allowing proper family time and time to give to his congregation as they had need of him. He worked hard for the Lord. He visited the sick in the hospital. He made regular weekly visits to the elderly members of the church, ensuring their needs were met. He spent a couple hours daily knocking on doors inviting strangers to church and to salvation.

The congregation, though small in number were kind and devoted to the Lord, their church and the pastor and his family.

Katie spent every other weekend with her God given parents

and school breaks for holidays. She appeared more grown up with each visit. Katie had been on summer break for nearly a week. Darla's heart was full with her home with her, Kelley and Heaven.

Darla and Kelley silently had their separate devotions at the breakfast table, enjoying their morning coffee.

"Good morning." Katie greeted pleasantly as she entered the kitchen with Heaven, giving both her parents a kiss as did two and a half-year-old Heaven with Katie holding her.

"Good morning." Her parents greeted.

"What would you like for breakfast, Katie?" Darla asked.

"Heaven wan Twix." Heaven said happily.

"Come here, Miss Heaven." Kelley said, holding his hands out to take her from Katie. Kelley sat Heaven on his lap.

"Mommy asked Katie her wishes. You wait until Mommy asks Heaven." Kelley instructed.

"Right?" He asked Heaven.

Heaven shook her head yes, smiling at her daddy as she looked into his strong, yet gentle face.

"Katie, you have the floor."

"I will help myself to a bowl of 'Twix' with my sister, if this is acceptable." Katie answered mocking Heaven with a tender smile.

"Is this the type of breakfast you have when not under my supervision?" Darla asked.

"Yes." Katie answered smiling, glancing at her father, the two knowing Darla was a firm believer in a hot breakfast.

"Your Aunt Cindy and I are likely to tangle yet."

"Uncle Dan and Aunt Cindy do not eat breakfast, only yours truly. Occasionally when I feel energetic, I cook."

"I feel energetic." Darla informed kindly, getting up from the table to prepare breakfast.

"Pastor Finks says perhaps soon we will be able to have a park ministry again." Katie informed excited.

"I am glad to hear this." Kelley replied, pleased.

"Who are you referring to when you say 'we'?"

"It would be the church ministry as before. By us, I am referring to Uncle Dan, Aaron and I. Possibly Shelby, she is undecided."

"When this happens, I would want to speak to Uncle Dan before you become a part of this ministry." Kelley said.

"May I ask why?" Katie questioned.

"No." Kelley answered. Katie looked at her father, silently questioning him not giving her an explanation.

"Katie, what is Aaron doing for the summer?" Darla asked breaking the silence Kelley's negative answer had brought, she knowing Kelley's concern was for her safety and her protection. Her husband as well as Darla's thoughts quickly going back to the attack on Darla when visiting the city park when Darla was a teenager. Kelley would take whatever measures necessary to protect his family.

"I seldom see him. He only calls Uncle Dan to inquire of the park ministry. I do not know." Katie answered as she politely assisted her mother with breakfast.

"I have some literature I brought with me in regards to different colleges. I would like you and Dad to help me choose a good Christian college when it is convenient for both of you. I really need to decide. I am sure I will receive a scholarship. My counselor seems confident anyway."

"With your grades, I am sure you will, Sweetheart. Dad is the one who keeps up on the Christian colleges. He has made it a point to do so, since you expressed this over Christmas vacation."

"Thanks, Dad." Katie said, impressed.

"I cannot believe I will be attending college in one more year."

"You are growing up so quickly and we get so little of you. Before we know it, you will be graduating from college and wanting to marry." Darla voiced proudly.

"Maybe marriage about ten years after I graduate from college, if I ever marry. I want to do a lot of things and see places first."

Darla enjoyed hearing Kelley minister. She enjoyed sitting in the congregation admiring his handsome appearance, his style of preaching and observing his sincere dedication to the Lord. This pleased her very much and she enjoyed their quality family time.

The men in the congregation backed Kelley. They soon worked with him witnessing to the lost, bringing them to church. It was a slow process, but the small congregation was steadily increasing by the joining of new converts. The women also began to be more involved in soul winning, not hiding their salvation under a bush, rather allowing their lights to shine. Kelley spent much time with special Bible studies with the new Christians teaching them the importance of growing spirituality that they would grow strong in the ways of the Lord, secure and steadfast.

Darla busily packed her family's suitcases for their first visit home since moving to Arizona. She was consumed with excitement and happiness. Though she and Kelley's families had been faithful to visit the young couple in their home and visit the services hearing Kelley preach, they had not been granted the opportunity to visit their hometown.

"Mommy, is Katie coming home with us?" Three and a half-year-old Heaven asked as she entered her mother's bedroom.

"For the summer, but after the summer Katie will be leaving for college."

"I wish she would stay forever." Heaven said her blue eyes growing sad.

"Me too, Sweetheart." Darla replied, giving her daughter a kiss on her cheek.

"Are you about ready, Babe?" Kelley asked as he now entered the bedroom.

"It is getting late." He informed, growing impatient to begin their week vacation.

"I am ready, Daddy." Heaven informed, quickly forgetting her sadness, excited over her first vacation.

"Good." Kelley replied gently pulling both of her long dark ponytails, making her giggle with his play.

"I am ready, Husband." Darla answered with a happy smile, closing the suitcase.

With their suitcases loaded in their station wagon, Kelley opened the back car door for Heaven and then the front car door for his wife.

"Did you remember your movie camera to film Katie's graduation?" Darla asked, hesitating before getting in the car.

"Yes, Babe. May we please go?"

"Yes." Darla answered with an understanding smile with his impatience.

After only a couple hours of riding in the car, Heaven grew sleepy. Lying down on the backseat, she was soon sleeping soundly. Darla moved from the passenger door, sitting close to her husband looking up into his eyes with happiness on her face.

Removing Kelley's right hand from the steering wheel, she put his arm around her shoulders. Kelley glanced in his rearview mirror, attempting to check on his daughter's doings.

"Relax, Heaven is sleeping." Darla informed, reading his thoughts as she snuggled up close to him, followed by a light kiss on his lips.

"Perhaps she will sleep the entire ride." Kelley said with a tender smile, tightening his arm around his wife followed by a kiss.

"Perhaps, but do remember you are driving." Darla said, her remark bringing a smile to Kelley's face.

Darla and Kelley enjoyed visiting with both of their families, spending time at each one's home. Katie was so much as an adult. She had matured even more since her visit home on spring break. Darla and Kelley both were most pleased for her, with all she had accomplished. She was a lovely young lady and a dedicated Christian.

"When did you get a new car?" Katie asked as Kelley drove toward San Diego.

"Last month. Do you like it?"

"It is nice. I for myself prefer small sporty cars, but then I only have Katie to please."

"Dad said we needed a family size car." Darla explained, pleased with her husband's reasoning.

"Surely Dad does not intend to fill this huge car." Katie teased.

"He best not." Darla answered quickly, her face growing serious. Kelley laughed with his wife's response. Katie smiled at her mother's gentle, yet at times, determined ways.

"Mommy, I am hungry." Heaven informed as she sat next to her older sister with her head leaning against Katie.

"It is not lunchtime, Sweetheart. What did you have for breakfast at Uncle Bill's home?"

"Nothing." Heaven answered.

"Apparently Kelley, we are the only family that still eat three meals." Darla said, with a sigh.

"So it seems." Kelley agreed with a sigh.

"She will have to wait at least an hour. There is no place to stop."

"I know." Darla replied kindly, though her voice held her concern to fulfill her daughter's need.

"Have you had breakfast, Katie?" Darla asked.

"No, Ma'am. I stand guilty of being an anti-breakfast eater." Katie answered with a shy smile, blushing. Darla released a long weary sigh, as she grew silent.

"Daddy, I am hungry." Heaven informed, now leaning against the front seat, looking up at her father as though he could instantly supply her with a meal.

"I know, Princess. As soon as I see a restaurant, we will stop so you may eat, be patient." Kelley replied in his calm manner.

"I do not want to be patient." Heaven said pouting, sitting back against the seat with her arms folded, stubbornly, surprising both of her parents.

"Heaven!" Darla scolded, sternly.

"You will be patient and you will speak nicely." Darla ordered.

Heaven was silent as she unfolded her arms, looking at her mother's threatening and disapproving face, deciding it best for her sake to obey.

"I am telling you, Darla, Heaven is seeing too much of Ellen." Kelley advised.

"What do I do? Tell Ellen's mother she may visit our home but not her daughter?" Darla questioned defensive.

"No, Babe."

"Heaven will simply learn as you and I had to, that she does not act like others if their actions are improper." Darla insisted.

Heaven's mood changed quickly. Darla and Katie enjoyed shopping for Katie's graduation dress. With Katie's choice dress and shoes purchased, the Peterson's spent the remainder of the day at the beach, enjoying a time of family togetherness.

With Katie in school for the remainder of the week, the Peterson couple spent their days visiting with friends and family. By Friday, Darla was weary from their busy active pace.

Awaking early, in the comfort of her husband's arms by Heaven climbing on the bed calling her mother with impatience in her voice, Darla slowly turned her head toward her daughter.

"Good morning to you too." Darla said, annoyed with Heaven's manner.

"I want you to get up." Heaven ordered.

"I want you to hush." Darla ordered in her sternest tone, bringing immediate silence to Heaven. Heaven silently sat on the bed, looking at her mother with flushed cheeks.

"Honestly, Heaven, you will stop acting like a baby or I am going to spank you. I have heard enough of you bossing others."

"So much for sleeping in." Kelley mumbled glancing at the early hour on the clock.

"Grandpa did not get angry when I woke him up." Heaven said.

Both Darla and Kelley looked at one another with disbelief, then at their daughter.

"Why did you disturb Grandpa?" Darla questioned with fury on her face.

"I just wanted to." Heaven answered, hanging her head, knowing she was in serious trouble.

"I will straighten this out, Babe." Kelley offered, getting out from under the covers.

"You look terribly tired. Rest." He instructed giving her a kiss.

"I do not know if this is possible with Miss Heaven in this home." Darla responded looking at her daughter sternly. Heaven looked at her mother with flushed cheeks and then her father.

"Are you going to spank me, Daddy?" Heaven asked, looking at her father with saddened, watery eyes.

"We will talk about this in the other room. Mommy needs to rest." Kelley answered as he dressed for the day.

"Heaven, your clothes are on the dresser, so get dressed please." Darla instructed calmer, rubbing her slightly aching head.

Darla returned to sleep, sleeping until mid-morning. Awaking, she felt rested. She took a leisurely bath. Dressed in a cool shorts outfit and sandals for the warm June desert climate, she tidied the bedroom she and her husband had occupied and then left the room locating her parents and Kelley visiting in the family room.

"Good morning." Darla greeted pleasantly as she joined her family with a cup of coffee in her hands.

"Since when do preacher's wives wear shorts?" Dad Roberts inquired, causing Darla to blush.

"Since this preacher's wife went on vacation." Darla answered pleasantly, quickly bringing approval to her father's face.

"Where is our ill-mannered daughter?" Darla asked looking into her husband's eyes as she sat down next to him.

"She is playing on the patio." Kelley answered, pointing toward the window where Heaven was playing.

"Kelley told us of Heaven's new playmate." Mom Roberts informed.

"Ellen..." Darla said with a weary sigh.

"She is a year older then Heaven, yet she throws tantrums whenever she does not get her way. Her mother allows her to tear through our home and she gets into Kelley's desk even if I tell her not to. Her mother is a sweet person, so I do not know how to deal with this. Heaven is quickly picking up bad habits from Ellen. I am at your mercy, Mother. Do you have any suggestions?" Darla asked, as though desperate.

"Yes. If the mother will not take charge of her child, you take charge while she is in your home. I know this is difficult, but it is necessary, dear. Being a pastor's family, many people will enter your home. You and Kelley establish your rules and ways for your home. Whoever enters your home, enforce your rules. You will soon find your home in total confusion if you do not do this. If Heaven is not allowed in her father's desk, then why should a child that does not live in your home be allowed to do this? You will allow Heaven to feel intruded upon in her own home. If you will recall, I scolded your friends when they did wrong as well as you. Trust me, dear, when I say others would love to run the pastor's home. Your home is, and must always remain, a private refuge for your entire family, regardless of age." Mom Roberts advised.

"Is this what you have been trying to tell me, Husband?" Darla asked with flushed cheeks as she looked into Kelley's eyes.

"Babe, you know I am not one to say 'I told you so', but I told you this." He answered with a grin, embarrassing his wife with his honesty, bringing a soft laugh from her.

"Darla is a bit stubborn like her mother." Dad Roberts said with a chuckle, he now causing his wife to blush.

Darla and Kelley learned a lot from their visit with Darla's parents. They had many questions answered in regards to their position in the leadership of others. The Roberts' years of experience and wisdom was welcomed by the young couple. It was important that they perform their jobs to the best of their ability and their work be pleasing unto the Lord and not in vain.

Along with both, the Roberts and Peterson families, Kelley, Darla and Heaven each dressed in their best, were present as Katie received her high school diploma. Following the ceremony, Bill and Paula held a celebration dinner for the families with Katie as the guest of honor at the country club. The entire event was breathtaking to Katie. She had never experienced the amount of joy and specialness shown to her as her God given parents and their families showed her on her special day. She shed many happy tears.

"Do you realize now dear, just how special you are?" Darla

asked, slipping her arm around Katie's waist as they left the country club.

"Yes, Ma'am." Katie answered happily, giving her mother a tight hug.

Katie spent the summer with her parents. Her days were spent working at a grocery store and her evenings with her family. Saturdays, she went on outings with her friends she had acquired in Tucson learning and seeing all there was to see in their area.

"I want to see a lot and do a lot before I settle down." As she once shared with Darla, she was busily achieving her goals.

"It is terribly quiet with Katie away at college." Kelley voiced as they sat on the porch of the parsonage, watching Heaven riding her bike with training wheels.

"Too quiet." Darla replied. Kelley put his arm around his wife's shoulders, pulling her close to his side.

"We have never discussed our having children." Kelley said looking into his wife's eyes.

"You would like to discuss this?" Darla asked slowly, not knowing of her husband's wants.

"Then you have the floor, Honey." She said.

"Heaven will be five soon. I would say five years is spacing quite well between her and her brother." Kelley shared with excitement in his voice.

"A brother." Darla repeated with a tickled laugh.

"Kelley, you know there is no picking and choosing the gender. What happens if we should have a daughter?"

"Then we wait a couple of years and try for a son again." He answered his face serious.

"May I ask how many daughters you are more than willing for me to carry before stopping?"

"At least a half dozen." He answered with a boyish grin.

"Kelley, I am being serious and you are joking. If you are not joking, my response is no deals." Darla replied quickly, as Heaven approached ceasing their talk.

"I want a son, Wife." Kelley whispered as he got up to assist his daughter putting her bike away and bringing a smile from Darla.

Kelley making known his wishes to have a son, seemed to open Darla's eyes. Kelley had made no real demands of her with the exception she not become overworked or overburdened. He asked for nothing from anyone for himself. Now, after four years of marriage, he has one request. Darla secretly took more notice of Kelley's possible wants. With doing so, she often noticed a faraway look in his eyes. She felt he was searching. Perhaps the Holy Spirit was dealing with him, preparing another task for him. Whatever it was, she would be patient, allowing him to choose the right moment for himself to share his yearning with her.

Heaven sleeping soundly, dressed for bed, Darla relaxed on the sofa with her Bible reading.

"Darla." Kelley spoke as he entered the front room, returning from a counseling session with a young couple, his face troubled.

"Yes?" Darla questioned as he sat down next to her.

"I have been rather restless for several months, with pastoring the church. I have spent hours in prayer searching and seeking to fill this area, yet to no avail. I began to take a good look at the church body and myself as the pastor. The church attendance has more than doubled since we first arrived here three years ago. It was a lot of hard work to build the congregation the first two years. This past year, the congregation has more than pulled their weight to teach new converts the way of the Lord. I almost feel useless. I have too much empty time on my hands." Kelley shared.

"Is my husband's work finished in Tucson, Arizona?" Darla questioned patiently.

"Yes, Babe." He answered, unsure of her feelings to his news.

"Surely you must know I would not question this decision. I know which master you serve. I also know you do not make important decisions without ample time to search out the correct decision or without conversing with our Heavenly Father. I am a helpmate, Sweetheart." Darla assured with a tender sincere smile.

"I sincerely appreciate your vote of confidence." Kelley replied his face relaxed.

"Where do we go from here?" She asked in her slow gentle manner.

"Home." Kelley answered, noting the excitement arise in his wife, as she attempted to conceal it, until hearing him out.

"Your uncle has made me a fantastic offer on the country home we rented from him when we married. It is the perfect place to carry out our next work." He shared, hesitating, looking away from his wife briefly.

"What, Honey?" Darla questioned, sensitive to his uncomfortableness, hoping her gentle tone set him at ease.

"You and I becoming full-time foster parents, taking in all the children the state will allow us. I feel if we could teach the very young about Jesus and offer a loving, safe Christian environment, perhaps a few more children will be spared the horror Katie was forced to endure for too many years." Kelley explained.

Darla's eyes grew moist, as she recalled what little Katie shared of her years of horror.

"Mm...so I may acquire mothering half a dozen kids after all." Darla remarked with a loving smile.

"You are a wonderful mother with the patience of Job." Kelley replied sincerely.

"I need your opinion, Babe." He added.

"I believe it to be an honor and a privilege to teach children of our Lord and mother those who are without a loving home. When do we move?"

"Is three months soon enough?" Kelley asked with a pleased smile.

"The end of May? Katie will be coming for summer break."

"I know. We will all go home together."

"You truly have thought of everything and everyone. I believe I may fall in love with you all over again." Darla said with an excited laugh.

"I do not mind in the least." Kelley assured, putting his arm around his wife's shoulders, giving her a hug.

"The Lord gave us these years of a more normal family schedule to give us time to grow stronger and wiser in our marriage. He never fails us. He has given you and I both, the desires of our heart when He gave us one another."

"This Kelley, I know. This, our love and you, I will always cherish." Darla shared sincerely, looking into her husband's eyes with great admiration.

Kelley and Darla busily decorated the dining room of the parsonage for Heaven's surprise birthday party. This would be her last birthday party with her many church friends in Tucson. Darla wanted her party to be extra special for this reason. With everything ready, including the special visit made by Grandma and Grandpa Roberts, also to surprise their five-year-old granddaughter, Kelley left his home to return with Heaven. With the children waiting in the dining room along with Darla and her parents, each grew silent as Kelley approached the front door with Heaven. Heaven entered the dining room, followed by her daddy.

"Surprise!" Her waiting guests yelled. Heaven put her hand over her mouth in disbelief, as her family and friends sang happy birthday to her.

"Grandma! Grandpa!" She exclaimed hugging her grandparents' necks tightly, giving them both a kiss excitedly.

"Thank you, Mommy." She remembered excitedly giving her mother a kiss and a hug. The group of four, five and six-year-olds hurried outside giggling and chattering noisily with excitement ready to play party games.

Darla happily observed as her husband took charge of the children and the games.

"Kelley is certainly a natural with kids." Dad Roberts said admiringly.

"I am surprised you and Kelley have not had a child yet, Babe." He added casually, his eyes remaining on Kelley's doings as he spoke.

Darla remained silent, yet her face flushed. She felt her mother's eyes on her, yet she pretended not to notice.

Heaven politely said goodbye to her last guest. She excitedly shared her gifts with her grandparents before taking them to her room. Returning to the front room, Heaven quietly stood by her grandpa while he and her daddy conversed. Her grandpa looked at her with his gentle wise way.

"What is on your mind, Babe?" He questioned.

"Since I am five now, am I too old to sit on your lap?" Heaven asked thoughtfully.

"Of course not." Grandpa answered with a pleased grin.

"Your mother sat on my lap when she was five." He assured gently assisting his granddaughter, fulfilling her wishes.

Busily cleaning up the party remnants, Mom Roberts kindly assisted her daughter.

"I have a hard question for you." Mom Roberts informed with gentleness in her voice.

"I will do my best to answer your question." Darla assured pleasantly, as she washed dishes.

"Have you and Kelley discussed having children?"

"Briefly, a few weeks ago." Darla answered.

"Why are you and Dad concerned with this matter?" Darla questioned, puzzled.

"You know Kelley's parents, and Dad and I have been friends for years, dear."

"Yes." Darla answered finding this fact had no bearing on the present subject.

"Apparently Kelley has expressed his wishes to have a child to his parents, preferably a son, I gather." Mom Roberts shared with a gentle smile, she knowing her daughter felt she was intruding. Darla's face turned its reddest.

"I honestly am surprised with Kelley's talk. This is a subject that should be kept between him and me."

"You are right to a certain point. On the other hand, it is perfectly natural for Kelley to want his own child when you are perfectly capable of granting him this wish. It is also natural for his parents to want their son's child for a grandchild."

"I do not believe this, Mother." Darla said feeling frustrated, taking her eyes from her mother, back to her dish washing to calm herself.

"Dar, would you make some coffee please?" Kelley asked.

"Your dad and I would like a cup."

"Yes." Darla answered, quickly drying her hands to prepare the percolator.

Kelley stood a few minutes in silence noting his wife was upset. He glanced at his mother-in-law whom avoided eye contact with him as she continued to dry the dishes.

"Kelley." Darla said forcing a weak smile.

"Mother and I are talking girl talk. The kitchen is presently off limits to men."

"Yes, Ma'am. I am gone."

"You handle your husband quite well." Mom Roberts complimented with a loving smile, bringing comfort to her frustrated daughter, as she returned her mother a smile.

"There is not a thing wrong with Kelley discussing whatever he wishes with his parents. This is just as natural as you and me having our present girl talk and you sending your husband from the room."

"You are right." Darla agreed her nature calmed.

"I do promote modesty, yet you have always found it difficult to even discuss the facts of life when you and I had our mother, daughter talks. You have always been too modest. Therefore, I advise, do not be hard on Kelley for freely speaking what is good, natural and his heart's desire with his family."

"Mums the word." Darla assured.

"You and Kelley married so quickly after you returned from college that I did not have time to fulfill all of my duties as your mother, preparing you for marriage. Please allow me to do so at this time. If I bruise your over-modest ways, forgive me. This is not my intention, okay?"

"Okay, Mother." Darla agreed with an understanding smile, tucking her defenses aside, allowing her mind to be open.

"It is as natural for a husband to want to father a child as it is for a wife to want to mother a child. I realize you have no problem understanding this, dear. I sense, knowing my daughter, that you do not understand a husband's need to have his very own biological child. The child represents the husband's deep love for his wife and his wife's love toward him. This child silently by the child's birth expresses to the world a couple's love. Do not deprive your husband or yourself of the wonderfulness the Lord has instilled within husband and wife. Allow you and your husband to experience and enjoy all the beauty the Lord has blessed you both with." Mom Roberts shared in her gentle way.

"Kelley and I have Heaven and Katie and will have foster children with in months. I truly have questioned Kelley's wish for he and I to have our own child for these reasons. I honestly did not look at Kelley's wishes in the manner you have described. You have made me feel guilty for not seeing the depth of his desire. I am his wife and I should know these things." Darla confessed her cheeks flushed.

"Join the crowd, Deary. Not a one of us, regardless of age and experience knows everything. There is no perfect one but Jesus." Mom Roberts reminded supportively.

"You are a good wife, Sweetheart. One can't help but see that you reverence your husband."

Mom and Dad Roberts's mini vacation to Tucson was educational, refreshing and exciting. Darla and Kelley welcomed visits from family members. Though the young couple had made many friends during their dwelling in Tucson, they quickly learned a pastor and his spouse are expected to be everyone's friend regardless. Yet, friendships toward the pastor and wife were often withdrawn at the drop of a hat. When family visited, the young couple would feel relieved. They could completely relax, letting their hair down. Their families accepted them just as they were flaws, imperfections and all.

"Mom, Dad." Katie called, letting herself inside the parsonage.

"Katie is home!" Heaven exclaimed excitedly running to her sister and giving her a tight hug.

"Hi, Heaven." Katie greeted excitedly. Picking up the five-year-old, Katie hugged Heaven.

"You are becoming all grown-up." Katie said.

"I start kindergarten after summertime." Heaven informed, agreeing with her sister.

"Where are Mom and Dad?"

"In my room, they are taking my bed apart. We are moving to California." Heaven answered excitedly.

"I know we are."

"We are going to live in the country and have animals and lots of kids." Heaven shared happily.

"Whew, this sounds exciting."

"Mmhuh." Heaven agreed.

"What do you say you and I sneak in your room and surprise Mom and Dad?" Katie asked, bringing a giggle from Heaven with her idea.

"Okay." She agreed,

Katie and Heaven quietly went to Heaven's room. Heaven held her hand tightly over her mouth, so her giggles could not be heard as she stood next to Katie in the bedroom doorway.

"Would you like some help?" Katie asked, quickly bringing her foster parents' eyes upon her.

"Katie. Hi, Sweetheart." Darla greeted, hurrying to her.

"We have missed you terribly."

"I have missed each of you also." Katie assured happily.

"Katie." Kelley spoke, giving her a tight hug.

"Welcome home, Babe."

"Thank you." She replied deeply touched by her family's affection.

"May we interest you in moving to Ragweed with us or would you prefer Tucson?" Kelley questioned teasing.

"To Ragweed, please." Katie answered, excited to see her high school friends and her hometown.

"Babe, let us take a break." Kelley suggested, looking at his wife.

The Peterson family was reunited. Katie assisted in packing their belongings. She could not wait to return to Ragweed, their favorite home and spend summer break as a family. Both Kelley and Darla were also excited that they were going home.

CHAPTER FIVE

The young Peterson family immediately began preparing their home and themselves for foster children. Their home in Ragweed, California would soon be full. Each was excited, as they busily went about their Father's work. Kelley prepared the outside of the home. He put his carpentry skills to work, making a nice play area as well as a playhouse. He planted a large garden to supply his family with daily fresh vegetables to be canned and frozen for the brisk, chilly desert months. He tended to the calf he purchased to fatten and butcher later. There were chickens to care for, supplying them and their families with fresh eggs as well as poultry for the freezer, a milk cow, Princess, Darla's horse, a pony, Sam their Irish Setter and Katie's cat, she had found along the roadside.

Darla made the nursery, which Heaven had once occupied, into an attractive, inviting, boyish look bedroom for possible foster sons. Katie and Heaven now shared the frilly, bright, attractive, feminine bedroom Katie had once occupied. She organized menus, recipes for a large family at budget price, yet with sufficient nutrition.

Heaven was filling with excitement daily as she impatiently waited the arrival of a foster brother or sister or both. She was thrilled she would not be an only child much longer. She soon would have a daily playmate.

Katie had returned to the Christian bookstore for employment while with her family on summer break. She was considerate to pull her weight with chores before running off with her friends. Each Friday night, she attended the park ministry with her Uncle Dan that was once again in operation, as did Kelley's brother Aaron. She admired her foster parents' plans to foster homeless or unwanted and unloved children. She understood their drive to give love, for she held a similar goal. Her goal was to achieve a degree in psychiatry to become a Christian counselor, counseling children of abuse and neglect. She wanted to give to others the same as her foster parents had freely and lovingly given to her. She intended to work in her hometown near her God-given family and continue in the park ministry to street kids upon completion of college.

"I love to touch the chicken's soft feathers, Mommy." Heaven said happily, as she took time from assisting collecting eggs to pet the chickens, bringing a smile to her mother's face.

"It is a lot of work living in the country." She shared with a sigh as she once again carefully collected eggs.

"Yes, it is, yet you are allowed the privilege of learning about animals and being able to enjoy them whenever you like. For example, touching the soft feathers of a chicken, or riding your pony. If we lived in town, you would miss so much. We could not have our animals in town. I believe we are fortunate." Darla reminded Heaven with an understanding smile.

"Honey, come see who is here." Kelley called.

Kelley stood outside the chicken pen, patiently waiting for his wife to join him. Removing his handkerchief from the back pocket of his jeans, he wiped his dirty hands from his gardening.

"Deary, collect the remainder of the eggs for me, please." Darla instructed, leaving her daughter beckoning to her husband's call. Leaving her daughter's side and exiting the small building, she noted a caseworker from the welfare department speaking with her husband. Two boys and a girl quietly sat several yards away at the Peterson's picnic table.

"Hello, Mrs. Jones." Darla greeted with a kind smile, as she joined the caseworker and her husband.

"Good evening, Darla. Your husband says you both are more than willing to tackle three children."

"My husband is the boss."

"I would like you to understand the children are presently frightened. The boys, Michael and Carlos are brothers. Michael is four and Carlos is two. Their mother is ill and they may need a home for as long as a year. Michael is very protective of his brother. He seldom leaves his side. I just removed these children from another foster home, due to abuse in the home. It may take some doing for you both to win their trust." Mrs. Jones explained. She grew silent as Heaven left the chicken pen, carrying the basket of eggs.

"Heaven, sit the basket down. Mrs. Jones has brought you two brothers and a sister." Kelley informed.

"Thank you, Mrs. Jones. I have been waiting forever!" Heaven exclaimed, eager to meet the children.

"May we play, Daddy?"

"You may." Kelley answered, pleased with her eagerness to welcome the children. Heaven excitedly ran toward the three children.

"Karry is five." Mrs. Jones continued.

"She has a history of severe child abuse from her mother. She may be adopted at some point, providing we find a couple interested enough. She does not trust women at all. She is extremely shy of all adults. She gets along well with children. She is not family oriented with her mistrust in adults. For this reason, she may never be adopted."

The couple's expressions bore the sorrow they felt for the three sad, lonely and frightened children. They, along with Mrs. Jones silently observed from their distance, Heaven inviting the children to play on her swing set. Michael held his arm tightly around his younger brother, not budging. Karry looked at Heaven as though she wanted to join Heaven in play, yet she too remained silent and still. Heaven, in her forward, friendly manner took hold of Karry's hand and Michael's hand.

"I will push you on the swings if you would like." Heaven suggested, as the children silently went with her to her swing set.

"Perhaps Heaven is a natural understanding their uncomfortableness." Mrs. Jones commented pleased with what she saw.

"She has been thoroughly briefed in her position as a foster sister." Kelley assured.

"I am glad to hear this. This is always better for the permanent child in the family. It is not easy for most, even well-adjusted children, to share their parents. You have my telephone number if there are any problems, call me."

"We will." Kelley agreed, picking up the basket of eggs from the ground. The young couple walked Mrs. Jones to her car. With her departure, they went to the picnic table, sitting down, observing the children.

"Karry looks like a miniature Katie." Kelley said with a tender smile.

"She is such a pretty child. How could her own mother dare to harm her?" Darla questioned, barely above a whisper, her heart aching for the curly blonde-haired, brown-eyed saddened five-year-old.

"My only answer, Babe is sin. Sin is hardening hearts all around us."

The first couple of weeks were the most difficult. Michael was afraid to allow Carlos out of his sight for fear he might be harmed or they might become separated. Karry barely spoke except to Heaven and Michael. Both Karry and Carlos spent several restless nights waking up crying from their past frightening them in their dreams. Kelley and Darla took turns spending late hours rocking and soothing their fears away. With much love, patience and reassurance, the nightmares finally ceased. Michael gradually slipped away from his brother, entrusting him in Darla's care, with both boys soon, happily adjusted. With their past growing dimmer and dimmer, love and trust for Darla and Kelley began to grow. Heaven seemed never to grow weary of sharing her home or her parents. Though Karry was distant with her foster parents, she and Heaven had become best friends. Katie often donated a few hours on Saturdays, taking the four children to the park, the small zoo, or for an ice cream.

With summer near an end, Darla began preparing Heaven's and Karry's wardrobes for the coming school year.

Her family still sleeping, Darla poured herself a cup of coffee. Slipping out the back door, she sat down at the picnic table with her coffee and Bible, enjoying the quietness of the early morning and fresh air. After spending some time with her devotions, she started toward her home with her empty coffee cup. Entering the back door, Kelley sat at the kitchen table holding Karry on his lap.

"Good morning." Darla greeted politely, though looking into her husband's eyes silently questioning Karry arising so early.

"Good morning, Babe." Kelley greeted, his voice calm and controlled, yet his eyes shared his heart was saddened.

"Is Karry ill?" Darla asked, gently putting her hand on Karry's chin, turning her face from against her foster dad's chest. Facing her, Darla's heart saddened as she found tears streaming down her young face.

"Kelley?" She questioned, as she gently wiped Karry's tears away.

"Karry woke finding you gone. She thought you had left us."

Darla's face now bore the pain her heart felt for the troubled, insecure child. Pulling out a chair from the table near her husband, Darla sat down as she gently took Karry's hand into hers.

"Sweetheart, come here." Darla instructed with tenderness in her eyes and voice.

Karry obeyed Darla, yet she kept her eyes staring at the floor. Gently, Darla put her hand on Karry's chin, lifting her head.

"Karry, look at me, please."

Karry looked into her foster mother's eyes with her saddened big brown eyes.

"If I should ever be away from home without you, Heaven or Kelley, I will always return. This is my home and each of you are my family. I do not know of any place I would rather be then here. I do not know of anyone I would rather be with then each of you. I love you too much to stay away forever." Darla assured with a gentle smile.

"Everyone always leaves me. I try to be good, but..." Karry spoke, her eyes quickly filling with tears. She became silent, staring at the floor again.

"I am not others." Darla informed picking Karry up, sitting her on her lap. Once again, Darla lifted Karry's head, looking into her foster daughter's eyes.

"I am Darla and I love you, Sweetheart. You are a very good girl and special. I will never take my love away from you nor will I do anything to hurt you or make you cry." She assured gently wiping Karry's tears away.

Darla hugged and comforted her petite five-year-old foster daughter, her own eyes filled with tears for the pain the child was forced to endure.

"Mommy, what is wrong with Karry?" Heaven asked, as she neared her mother rubbing her eyes sleepily.

"She felt lonesome for a mommy." Darla answered looking into Karry's eyes, giving her a loving smile, bringing a shy smile to Karry's face.

"Did Mommy make you feel better, Karry?" Heaven asked.

Karry, in her shy way, nodded her head yes, as she slowly got down from Darla's lap.

"Are you ready to get dressed?" Heaven asked, looking at Karry. Again, Karry nodded her head yes. Heaven took Karry's hand in hers as they left the kitchen.

"Karry has been with us almost three months. How long will it take her, Honey, to put her past behind her?" Darla asked looking into her husband's eyes saddened for Karry.

"No one is able to answer this, Babe, except time." Kelley answered as he refilled his wife's coffee cup.

"Three months is not much time compared to five years of neglect and rejection."

"I suppose not." Darla replied with a weak smile.

"I have a couple of requests from you also." Kelley informed, as he returned to the table. Darla gave her husband her full attention, temporarily putting her concerns for Karry on hold.

"I want to accept the assistant pastor position Pastor Finks has offered me."

"I assumed you would." Darla replied pleased.

"You have no objections then?"

"None, whatsoever."

"Thank you. This was easy enough." Kelley said with a grin.

"Your second request?"

"I want you to set an appointment with Dr. Paul for a thorough check-up. If he feels you are healthy enough, I want to have a child." Kelley answered, as he took his wife's hand into his.

"A son, I suppose?" Darla questioned with a tender smile.

"Of course." Kelley answered with a proud grin, bringing a tickled laugh from his wife.

"You have given this a lot of thought?"

"Darla, I told you in February I wanted you and me to have a child, this is August. How much thinking must I do?" Kelley questioned impatiently, causing Darla's face to flush.

"I was referring to the hospital and doctor expense and the fact we have four children at present." Darla answered gently, as not to offend her husband or deny him his wishes.

"Babe, we have been conservative since we married nearly six years ago. I too, will have the salary from assistant pastor position. It will not be much, but it will care for the added expense of a baby." Kelley assured sincerely.

"As far as you and I having four children, for the record, we have one child. Three children belong to the state. Heaven is my daughter through adoption. I do not believe I am requesting too much, wanting to have a child with my wife after six years of marriage. There is a limit to my patience."

"Honey, I did not intend to imply your wishes should not be granted. You have every right to experience this wonderfulness. I will call Dr. Paul's office today and schedule an appointment for a check-up." Darla assured quickly, comforting her husband.

"I am guilty of moving slow at times." She added with a soft laugh, her cheeks flushed.

"How true this is." Kelley replied with a relaxed smile, his comment bringing laughter from his wife.

Kelley tended to Michael and Carlos while Darla took the girls to town, shopping for school clothes. Though Karry's actions expressed she was as excited as Heaven to go shopping, once inside the clothing store, Karry withdrew. She would not tell Darla which dresses or shoes she liked. Her face would turn its reddest with each question Darla asked. She would silently stand, hanging her head and staring at the floor.

"How would you girls like to dress as twins?" Darla finally asked, hoping she had found a solution to set Karry at ease. Heaven became thrilled with the idea. Karry smiled her shy smile, expressing her approval, as she remained silent.

"I will be in the next aisle. You girls decide which dresses you like and when you have decided, come get me."

"We get to choose our own dresses just like grown-ups?" Heaven asked, surprised.

"You choose, and then we will see if I agree with your choices."

"Okay." Heaven agreed happily.

Karry waited until Darla was out of her sight. With the disappearance of her foster mother, her excitement was expressed to Heaven without hesitation. Darla was thrilled to see Karry respond so normal with just she and Heaven together. One would not know she possessed mistrust in adults or lacked security or love by her actions when alone with children. In fact, she could be quite forward with Heaven.

"Oh, Sweetheart, if only you would learn to trust adults again also." Darla thought, letting out a long sigh, expressing her concern.

"Hi, Darla." Paula greeted kindly, as she joined her sister-in-law.

"Hi. Whew, I like your taste." Darla complimented, observing the dress in Paula's hand.

"Thank you. Bill is taking me out for a special dinner." Paula explained pleased.

"I hope you have the time of your life." Darla wished happily.

"I intend to. Why is it you are spying on Heaven and Karry?" Paula asked in her often-curious way, her accusations bringing a laugh from Darla.

"I have been caught. Karry is too shy to express her wishes in school dresses to me; therefore, they are shopping like grown-ups so Karry will feel free to choose what she likes." Darla answered pleasantly as the two women observed the five-year-olds.

"Where do you get your ideas to figure that child out?" Paula asked impressed with Darla's solution.

"Everywhere. Kelley and I read a lot of material on abused children. Having Katie and dealing with her problems the past several years has given us insight, the Bible and observing Karry as an individual and lots of prayer."

"Apparently you and Kelley are gifted with understanding children. Katie is a wonderful person. Bill and I were discussing a few days ago the changes in Karry already."

"Thank you for your compliment. Katie does still have a few bridges to cross, though it has been five and a half years since we laid claim to her. Karry, I do not know the answer as of yet to teach her to trust adults. Do you have any suggestions?"

"I am at a total loss when it comes to understanding children." Paula answered.

"Mommy, Karry and I are ready to show you the dresses we like." Heaven informed excitedly.

"Heaven." Darla scolded lightly looking at her daughter patiently. Heave quickly put her hand over her mouth.

"Excuse me, Mommy." She said, remembering not to interrupt.

"You are excused. Now, would you be a dear and greet your aunt?"

"Yes, Ma'am." Heaven answered blushing.

"Hi, Aunt Paula." Heaven greeted with a smile as she comfortably corrected her forgetfulness.

"Hi, Heaven." Her aunt greeted, smiling at her well taught manners.

"Hi, Karry." She also greeted, smiling at the shy five-year-old.

"Hi, Aunt Paula." Karry greeted, barely above a whisper as though she was concerned she might make a mistake.

"Karry and Heaven are shopping as grown-ups, Aunt Paula." Darla informed, winking at Karry for her successful greeting quickly relaxing her foster daughter.

"Then I better be on my way and not delay their shopping."

Heaven showed her mother their choice of dresses as Karry silently stood next to Heaven.

"Karry, do you agree with Heaven?" Darla asked approving of the dresses.

"Yes, Ma'am." Karry answered with flushed cheeks, surprising Darla by speaking instead of nodding her head.

Reaching the shoe department, Darla suggested from three different shoes the girls could choose. She stepped a few feet away with her back to the girls, yet within hearing distance this time.

"I like these." Karry said.

"Which ones do you like?" She asked Heaven in a whisper.

"I like those." Heaven said, going to a different style of shoe.

"Mommy said we cannot get those." Karry reminded.

"I know. Heaven replied with a sigh.

"If Daddy were here, he would get us these." Heaven said.

Darla almost laughed at the girl's talk.

"But Daddy is not here. Please do not make Mommy mad at us, Heaven. She is nice to us." Karry said nervously, fearing Heaven would argue the shoe issue.

Darla walked away from the girls before she was forced to release the laughter that wanted to escape her. Observing now from a distance out of ear shot, Darla was sure Karry was working overtime on Heaven to forget about the shoes her mother previously expressed they could not have. Finally giving in, Heaven returned to the shoes her Mother had suggested. Darla noted the relief expressed on Karry's face.

Shopping completed, Darla took the girls out for a late lunch, making their day together more special.

Returning home, Heaven excitedly shared her new things with her daddy as he sat at his desk giving her his full attention. Karry silently observed Heaven's excitement and her foster dad's nice comments of approval. Darla sat on the edge of her husband's desk, observing each of their actions.

"Excuse me, Daddy. I have to hang my new dresses in my closet." Heaven informed.

"Hold on a minute, Princess." Kelley said.

"Wait until Karry shares what she has in her bags."

"We have the same." Karry said shyly as she stood with her bags on the floor near her.

"Really?" Kelley asked in his calm way.

"Yes, Sir." Karry answered.

Darla noticed her husband's expression as Karry surprised him by verbally answering his question.

"Show me." Kelley encouraged.

Karry picked up her shopping bag. She silently removed her items from her bags. Kelley repeated his comments of approval as he had with Heaven. With each compliment, Karry blushed.

"You girls will be the prettiest girls in kindergarten." Kelley assured, bringing smiles to both girl's faces.

"You may hang your dresses up now."

"Twins?" Kelley questioned with a grin, as the girls left the den.

"Grown-up shopping? Yes, Sir? Are you sure you did not major in psychology?" Kelley asked.

"Each day being a parent confirms this." Darla answered with a tender smile.

"Are you aware Karry refers to you and me as Mommy and Daddy?"

"No. I have yet to be called Kelley by her." Kelley answered, sensing his wife was concerned his face growing serious.

"I overheard Karry speaking to Heaven. She did not say Darla or Kelley. She said Mommy and Daddy. What is our Karry thinking, Kelley? She could be adopted any time. She has been forewarned of this fact." Darla shared her concerns for Karry's happiness clearly on her face.

"I do not know, Babe." He answered, now understanding his wife's fears.

"We must find a way to learn what she is thinking. She must not be allowed to live in a world of pretend or make believe."

"I agree." Kelley replied, rubbing his forehead as though in deep thought.

Karry began to relax more in her foster parents' presence within the next couple of weeks.

Waiting outside, Carlos' Sunday school classroom as the dismissal bell rang. Darla took his tiny hand in hers as they went to Michael's class. With both boys' hands in hers, they left the Sunday school section to enter the sanctuary for the morning worship service.

Approaching her pew in the front, she briefly greeted Cindy and Dan. Michael sat down on the pew. Darla assisted Carlos sitting next to his brother. Katie sat on the pew in front of her foster family with her girlfriend Jessica. Karry and Heaven soon arrived, sitting with Katie. Kelley sat on the platform with Pastor Finks. Bill and Paula soon arrived, joining Cindy and Dan on their pew. Carlos began calling Bill's name, noting his arrival. As Darla attempted to hush him, Bill stood and leaning over his sister's pew, he took Carlos from her side.

"I will hold him." Bill whispered.

With the announcements and song service completed, the musicians, song leader and Kelley quietly left the platform as the pastor began his sermon. Kelley sat down next to his wife.

"Hi, Baby doll." He whispered in his wife's ear, bringing a smile to her face. He lovingly put his arm around her shoulders as he turned the pages in his Bible. Michael got up from sitting next to Darla. Going to his foster dad's side, he sat down next to him leaning against his side. Karry soon left Heaven's side near Katie. Both her foster parents silently looked at her, curious to her wishes. Coming to her foster parents' pew, Karry sat down next to Darla, putting her head on Darla's lap. The young couple looked at one another with looks of approval. Karry had not freely touched or reached out for a hug or a kiss since becoming their foster daughter. Darla gently patted Karry on her back and then gently soothed her blond hair of curls.

Within a few more weeks, Karry would often linger behind Heaven, staying at either Kelley or Darla's side briefly as though silently enjoying her foster parents' company, having them all to herself.

"Here comes Kelley." Four and a half-year-old Michael said, as he and his two and a half-year-old brother came inside from their play on the swing set.

"Go wash your hands for lunch, boys." Darla instructed as she set lunch on the table.

"How was school, girls?" Darla asked pleasantly as they entered the kitchen with Kelley.

"Karry..." Heaven started. Karry quickly turned her back to her foster mother.

"Heaven." Kelley spoke, quieting his daughter.

"Karry may want to tell Mommy herself after we eat lunch." Her father suggested.

"Yes, Sir, Daddy." Heaven agreed looking at Karry, feeling badly for her upset.

"Girls, go change your dresses. Lunch is ready." Darla instructed.

Darla looked at her husband as the girls vacated the kitchen.

"Apparently, Karry was tapping her pencil on her table top. The teacher slapped her hand for disrupting. Karry spent the morning crying." Kelley informed. Michael and Carlos returned, sitting down at the table.

"Why did Mrs. Keel slap her? She could have told her to stop." Darla voiced, annoyed with the teacher's action.

"I dealt with Mrs. Keel. I informed her she is not to administer physical discipline with Karry again."

"Perhaps after lunch, I will call her and give her my opinion." Darla replied irritated.

"Babe, please do not call, she is an elderly woman. She is strict and stern. She gave me her word she would abide by our wishes. I explained to Karry striking her is severe punishment. Mrs. Keel had no idea Karry has a history of abuse. She truly felt bad that Karry became so upset. Let us eat, Babe." Kelley silenced as the girls returned for lunch. Kelley assisted his wife with her chair and with the blessing asked; Darla and Kelley prepared the children's plates.

"Daddy, why will you and Mommy not allow Karry to stay with us?" Heaven questioned, shocking her parents with her question.

"I do not understand your question. Karry is here." Kelley said, looking at his daughter.

"Karry said you and Mommy will get tired of her being here and send her away." Heaven explained.

"That is silly." Michael voiced, bringing smiles to his foster parents' faces.

"Heaven you tell all our secrets." Karry said blushing, as she now picked at her lunch.

Heaven was now quiet, she with flushed cheeks for her foster sister being displeased with her. Kelley smiled at his wife with each of their comments.

"Karry, it is okay to tell a secret if someone is upset and you need a mom or dad to help with the upset." Darla explained.

"Perhaps next time Heaven, you will tell Daddy in private though. This way neither you nor Karry hurt one another's feelings." Darla suggested.

"Okay." Heaven agreed.

"Karry, Kelley and I will not send you away. You are our foster daughter. We love you as a daughter. We do not send our children away because we are displeased with them for doing something they should not do, nor do we send our children away because they tire us." Darla assured.

"Okay?" She questioned.

"Okay." Karry agreed.

With Katie away at college, Karry seemed less content without Katie sharing the girl's room at nighttime. She had finally begun addressing her foster parents by their first names, yet she did not appear pleased with this, either.

Kelley, busy in the dining room with his tutoring lessons, Carlos still napping and the other children at play, Darla entered her tiny sewing room. Sitting down at her sewing machine, she worked on a new dress to add to the girl's wardrobe.

"Darla." Karry spoke, tapping her foster mother on her arm.

"Yes, Sweetheart?" Darla questioned, looking into Karry's eyes, sensing she was upset.

"You said I am like your daughter." Karry started hesitant.

"Yes, I did." Darla agreed with a gentle smile.

"Why do I call you Darla? Heaven does not have to call you Darla. I want a Mommy and a Daddy too. Why will God not give me a Mommy and a Daddy?" Karry questioned.

It was all Darla could do to hold her tears back as Karry's longing touched her heart.

"Karry, I am Heaven's biological mother. I have had her since she was a baby. I am your foster mother. I will be your foster mother until Mrs. Jones finds you your very own parents to adopt you. Do you understand what I am saying?" Darla questioned as gently as possible. Karry's eyes quickly filled with tears.

"Honey, please do not cry. Darla said, moving her chair out from her sewing machine. Karry was now sobbing. Darla picked her up, sitting her on her lap, holding and soothing her, hoping to bring some comfort.

"I thought you would not make me leave here." Karry reminded, as though desperate, sobbing her hardest.

"Karry, please do not do this to yourself. I will not make you leave nor will Kelley. This is true. I would never tell you a lie, Honey." Darla assured, her eyes growing moist from Karry's continuous crying.

"Surely you want your very own parents, right?" Darla asked, soothing her hair away from her wet face.

"I want you for my Mommy." Karry answered, putting her arms tightly around Darla's neck, as though afraid if she let go she would be taken from her.

"Oh, Karry." Darla comforted, holding and rocking her heart broken foster daughter. Darla's tears were now released also. She felt so helpless with not being able to tell Karry what her heart desired.

"Mommy." Heaven spoke; now saddened hearing Karry's sobbing and seeing her mother's tears.

"Sweetheart, have Daddy's students left?"

"Yes." Heaven answered slowly, concerned for her mother and foster sister.

"Please tell Daddy he is needed."

"Okay, Mommy." Heaven quickly left her mother's side. Darla continued rocking Karry and patting her on her back. Karry held steadfast to Darla's neck, not easing up with her crying.

Kelley entered the sewing room.

"Why are my pretty girls crying?" He questioned, putting his hand on his wife's shoulder.

"Karry wants you and me to be her parents permanently." Darla answered with her tears still streaming. Kelley's expression quickly shifted from concern to sadness.

"Have you reminded her how the system works?"

"Yes, but her wishes are not allowing her to accept the facts." Darla answered looking into her husband's eyes, hoping he had a solution.

"Karry." Kelley spoke, turning her head so he could see her face.

Karry kept her eyes closed as she cried her hardest, as though she had no control over her crying.

"I will take her, Babe." He decided.

Taking Karry from his wife, he left the sewing room. Entering the den, he sat down remaining silent as he held her, allowing her to get her crying out.

Darla pulled herself together. After checking on the other children, she began preparing dinner.

"Mommy." Heaven said, looking up into her mother's face.

"Are you okay now?"

"I will be fine, Sweetheart, but I could use a hug." Darla answered with a smile.

"Mm, thank you. I feel much better now." She assured returning her daughter's hug.

"Will Karry be okay?"

"I hope so, Honey." Darla answered, giving her daughter a kiss.

"Karry just wants you and Daddy to be her Mommy and Daddy forever. She does not want to be adopted by strangers. She and I have been praying. We are asking God to never let that Mrs. Jones come back here, so she will not be able to give Karry to people she does not even know." Heaven shared in her foster sister's defense.

"Oh, Sweetheart, you girls must not pray in this manner." Darla said, suddenly feeling drained with her daughter's information.

"You and Karry have both known from the moment Karry arrived in our home that she might be adopted. Daddy and I have been praying for special parents for Karry. I know if God sends adoptive parents it will be because Karry would be happier with them then she is here. You pray for God to choose her home and her parents. This way, if Karry remains here, not adopted, this is right. If Karry is adopted, that will be right. Sometimes Honey, what we think is right is not always the best. If God chooses, it is always the very best." Darla advised.

"Please pray that God chooses Karry's permanent home from now on."

"Yes, Ma'am." Heaven answered, half-heartedly.

"It would be great if both you and Karry would quit worrying and enjoy each day with one another. You are too young to be burdened with worries. Perhaps you could share this with Miss Karry when you and she are sharing secrets." Darla suggested with a gentle smile.

Karry and Heaven made no further mention of Karry's wishes to remain a permanent member of the Peterson family. Although it was apparent, Karry was terribly unhappy since making her wishes known of whom she wanted as parents. The Peterson couple did their best to make Karry happy, yet it seemed their efforts were in vain.

"Kelley." Darla spoke, as she and Carlos joined him and Michael outside where Kelley was busy trimming the hedges.

"I have a suggestion in regards to our foster daughter's unhappiness. Would you mind taking a break?"

"No, I do not mind. Michael, you and Carlos go play. You may help me in a few minutes."

The two boys went to the sandbox to play with their cars.

"Are we in a position to adopt Karry?" Darla asked her eagerness clearly in her eyes.

"I am not sure. I have been deeply concerned with this matter myself. I will check into this, Babe."

"Perhaps your friend Vera could pull some strings and hurry matters up. What progress Karry had made is quickly fading. She continues to withdraw from me."

"She is withdrawing from me also." Kelley shared.

The necessary paperwork done, Darla and Kelley anxiously awaited news in regards to Karry becoming their daughter.

Dad Roberts' workload had picked up. He requested Kelley's assistance. Kelley's carpentry employment took him away from home Monday, Wednesday and Friday. Kelley tutored students on Tuesday afternoons. Pastor Finks seemed to be having Kelley preach more and more. Kelley seemed to enjoy whatever task came his way.

Karry was so well behaved, yet she continued to hold her emotions back. The sparkle she once had for a brief time in her eyes, had not returned.

Kelley away working for the day, and the boys napping, Darla entered the den where the girls sat playing with their dolls.

"Would you girls join me for a walk? It is a pretty day out."

Heaven quickly took her mother's hand in hers as they walked. Karry silently walked near Heaven.

"Karry, I have two hands. May I hold your hand, also?" Darla asked with a tender smile. Karry nodded her head yes and then went to her foster mother's side.

"Perhaps you could spare me one of your beautiful smiles also?" Darla asked, giving Karry a smile. Though Karry blushed, she smiled at her foster mother.

"Mommy, when I begin piano lessons in the summer, may Karry go with me? She wants to learn also." Heaven shared hopeful.

"Perhaps, although I have never heard Karry say she would like to learn to play the piano." Darla answered kindly.

"Karry likes it better if I tell you and Daddy for her."

"I know this. Daddy and I like it better when Karry speaks for herself. You both will be six years old soon. This is too old to allow someone to speak for you. Do you girls agree?"

"Yes, Ma'am." Heaven answered.

"Karry?"

"Yes, Ma'am." She answered, her face flushed as though embarrassed.

"Would you please share your wishes with me of you taking piano lessons?"

"I want to, like Heaven."

"Just so you will be doing the same thing Heaven does or because Karry would enjoy playing the piano?"

"So, when I am a grown-up, I will get to play the piano at church." Karry answered.

"Sister Smith says she will be too old to play at church when I am a grown-up. She told Heaven she would teach me and Heaven."

"I like your reasoning." Darla approved. Karry smiled with her foster mother's approval.

"See Heaven, Karry knows how to talk."

The girls looked at one another, exchanging smiles over Darla's comment.

Darla began taking regular walks with the girls, encouraging Heaven to allow Karry to speak for herself and encouraging Karry not to rely on Heaven.

Michael and Carlos were continuously reminded of their mother. Darla had a picture of her sitting on the boys' dresser. Michael had no problem remembering, yet Carlos was only two and his remembrance was vague.

Kelley returned from work finding his family dressed in their Sunday best, visiting in the den.

"Each of you looks nice." He complimented, impressed.

"I noticed the table is not set. Are we having dinner out?"

"Yes, as soon as you are ready."

"Mommy said we are celebrating." Heaven informed happily.

"We are?" Kelley questioned, looking at his wife.

"Most definitely." Darla answered, happily.

"You will understand when you check the mail on your desk."

Kelley went to his desk. Silently, he opened the special envelope, his heart also filling with joy. Putting the letter down, Kelley went to his wife leaning down, kissing her lips lightly.

"Congratulations, Mom." He spoke with a pleased smile.

"Congratulations to you, Dad."

"I will shower and dress quickly."

The three older children were excited as they took their seats at the table in their Daddy's choice restaurant. They impatiently awaited Kelley to share with them what they were celebrating.

"Karry, have you continued to pray your way for parents? By this, I mean for Darla and me to be your parents forever?" Kelley asked.

Karry and Heaven's faces turned red, as though guilty. The girls looked at one another briefly.

"I assure you, Princess; I am not upset with you. Is this the way you have prayed?"

"Yes, Sir. It is my desire of my heart." Karry answered slowly with flushed cheeks.

"Do you know how to spell Peterson?"

Karry shook her head no.

"I will teach you. You are adopted. Your name is Karry Peterson now. Darla and I are your parents." Kelley informed with a pleased grin.

"Forever and ever?" Karry asked excited.

"Forever and ever, Babe." Kelley answered.

Karry got out of her seat quickly, giving Kelley's neck a tight hug. "You are my Daddy."

"Yes, Babe." Kelley answered with a chuckle, tickled with her happiness and excitement.

"Do I get a hug?" Darla asked happily with watery eyes.

"Yes, Mommy." Karry answered, quickly leaving Kelley, hugging Darla's neck tightly.

"Oh, Sweetheart, I love you. I am so proud you are my daughter."

"I love you too, Mommy." Karry said, giving Darla a kiss.

"I know you do, Sweetheart."

"Karry, we are sisters forever." Heaven said excitedly.

"Mmhuh, twin sisters like Mommy said." Karry agreed proudly, as she returned to her seat.

"Sweetheart, you must not cry. We do have a church service to attend after dinner." Kelley reminded with an understanding smile as he gently brushed a tear from her face.

"I know." She agreed, quickly removing a Kleenex from her purse.

"Happy tears." Michael said with a big grin.

"Yes, dear." Darla replied with a soft laugh as her tears began again. She desperately tried to stop them, but was unsuccessful, as she continuously blotted her eyes with Kleenex.

"I am sorry, Honey." She apologized, glancing at her husband.

"I understand, Babe. I am not sure others in this restaurant do though." Kelley said.

Darla's face flushed at the remembrance they were in public.

She kept her eyes down; looking at her plate in hopes others would not notice her tears.

Halfway through their meal, Michael leaned over as he sat next to his foster mother.

"Kelley, Darla is still crying. She is really happy." The five-year-old informed with a big grin, bringing a tickled laugh from Darla and smiles to each family member's face.

Her meal completed, Darla left her family at the table briefly. Entering the women's room, she quickly washed her face from her crying and then touched up her lightly applied make-up.

Arriving at church, the young couple briefly greeted others, conversing and shaking their hands as they slowly made their way to the front of the church to the pew they regularly occupied. The girls went ahead of their parents, greeting their grandparents Roberts, their Aunt Cindy, Uncle Bill and their spouses. With their greetings completed, they sat down on the assigned pew. Michael silently stayed at Kelley's side. Carlos held Darla's hand, as he stood at his foster mother's side to prevent him from his desire of running and playing in the sanctuary.

Kelley approached his wife as she now spoke with a widow lady. Gently putting his hand on his wife's shoulder, he politely excused her from her visit and then escorted her to her choice pew. Leaving his family seated together, he joined the senior pastor whom was now sitting on the platform nearing the service hour.

"Mommy, may I sit with Grandma and Grandpa?" Heaven asked, hopeful.

"If you hurry, the service is about to begin."

Heaven hurried to her grandparents' pew in the middle section. Carlos went to the far end of their pew lying down with his blanket, like most evening services. Karry sat on one side of Darla and Michael on the other side as the service began. With the completion of the song service and announcements, Michael growing sleepy, he looked up at his foster mother.

"Darla, may I lie down too?"

"Yes, you may."

Followed by a kiss on his cheek, Michael stretched out on the pew between Karry and his brother. Though tiring also, Karry remained sitting up. Scooting close to Darla, she leaned her head against her side.

Pastor Finks introduced Kelley to lead in testimonies as he did most Wednesday evenings.

"A day does not pass without me being faced with a testimony unto my Lord. Besides being a minister, I have a teaching degree. Dealing with the young ages my wife and I do in our home, I quickly learned my degree is of little assistance. Karry, our foster daughter of several months has been awaiting adoption. Darla and I have been granted the privilege of assisting the Lord in answering Karry's prayer request. She refused to accept the state would place her in another home due to adoption. Karry believed God would grant her the desire of her heart, regardless of me or my wife explaining to her the ways of the system. Her faith remained true to the Lord. She held onto a piece of scripture and stood steadfast by it. Tonight, my family and I are pleased and overjoyed to witness the answer of a five-year-old's prayer. Today Karry became our adopted daughter. This was the desire of her heart. She did not just want parents, she requested specific parents, believing God could do anything. He does daily for us all. I for one could never thank my Heavenly Father enough for His endless love." Kelley shared sincerely.

"Mommy." Karry whispered.

"Daddy told everyone I have you and Daddy for my parents." Karry said with a pleased smile.

"Daddy is proud you are our daughter." Darla replied, giving Karry a kiss and a hug. Karry smiled the biggest smile ever as Darla's reply touched her heart.

It seemed Kelley's testimony had stirred hearts. Each testimony thereafter was focused on the family and the importance of a family.

As the pastor began his sermon, Kelley joined his wife, sitting next to her and putting his arm around her shoulders. He winked at Karry bringing a smile to her face. Karry soon laid her head on her mother's lap, drifting off to sleep.

Karry quickly became as a happy-go-lucky child. Her personality was not as forward as Heaven's, yet she was just as happy and content.

Returning from a busy day, Darla laid next to her husband with her head on his chest and his arm around her.

"Why is it each one in our family is granted their hearts desire almost immediately except me?" Kelley questioned as he soothed his wife's hair.

"I do not understand this either, Sweetheart. I wish I had the news your heart hopes for." Darla answered compassionately, as she looked into her husband's gentle face.

"Apparently it is not in the Lord's plan for me to become pregnant just yet." She comforted.

"Are you aware wife, each desire of my heart involving you has taken me a great length of time to be granted?" Kelley asked looking into his wife's eyes.

"Knowing you has definitely taught me patience." He added with a laugh, bringing a tickled laugh from her, with his accusation.

It was a terribly warm summer desert day. Michael and Carlos would be reunited with their biological mother within the next few months.

"Mommy, may we play in the sprinkler after lunch?" Heaven asked.

"You may, after you and Karry return from your piano lessons." Darla answered as she and her family ate lunch together.

"If Daddy would allow us to have a swimming pool we each, regardless of age, could enjoy fun in the water." She added, glancing at her husband with a loving smile.

"Oh, Daddy, could we have a swimming pool? Please?" Heaven and Karry begged. Kelley looked at his wife knowing she deliberately wished the girls begging him for her wish.

"Katie has often suggested the backyard is more than large

enough for a nice size pool." Darla informed, looking into her husband's eyes as the girls continued their pleading.

"Girls, I get your message." Kelley informed, quieting their pleas.

"Honey, pools are expensive." Kelley reminded looking at his wife.

"Kelley, we never splurge. It does get boring being conservative all the time. This would be something, regardless of age, we could always enjoy as well as our friends and families." Darla suggested, looking into her husband's eyes hopeful.

"Katie is home for summer break, yet we barely see her. She is either at the beach on her days off from work or at a friend's house swimming."

Within a couple of weeks, the Peterson's in-ground pool was under construction.

"This is the extent of our splurging for the rest of our long lives." Kelley informed with a smile, as he and his wife observed the progress of the pool construction.

"Must you always remind me of limits?" Darla questioned with a gentle smile, putting her arm around her husband's waist.

"You bet I must." Kelley answered, quickly causing his wife to blush with her laughter.

Darla went to the front door beckoning to the doorbell.

"Good afternoon." She greeted pleasantly as a woman along with three boys stood on her front porch.

"Mrs. Peterson?" The woman questioned.

"Yes."

"I am Mrs. Ryan with the child welfare department. Mrs. Jones referred you and your husband to me."

"Come in, please." Darla invited.

"Please have a seat. What may I do for you?" Darla asked.

"I was informed you take emergency cases for foster children."

"This is correct." Darla answered, as she briefly glanced at the three boys, giving them a kind smile.

"I need a home for these three boys immediately."

Carlos ran in the front room returning from his errand with Kelley. He excitedly shared the gum in his mouth Kelley had given him and then quietly sat down on his foster mother's lap.

"Hello." Kelley greeted politely.

"Hi." Mrs. Ryan greeted pleasantly.

"Hi, boys."

"Hi." The three boys greeted their faces sad, lonely and uncomfortable.

"Honey, this is Mrs. Ryan. These boys need a home." Darla informed.

"We have the home." Kelley replied sitting down next to his wife.

"This is a big relief. Do you have room for three? They are brothers and I am desperately trying to keep them together."

"We will make room." Kelley assured.

"How long do the boys need a home?" Darla asked.

"Three years."

"What's the matter lady, three years too long for you?" The oldest boy questioned.

"Tom!" Mrs. Ryan scolded quickly hushing the child.

"I do not mind answering his question." Darla defended.

She silently sat a moment, sizing up the feisty youth. She knew she wanted him in her home. He needed a loving Christian environment. He was sad and hurting inside.

"How old are you, Tom?" Darla questioned in her slow gentle patient way.

"I am ten." Tom answered in a fearless tone.

"Pete is eight and Bobbie is seven." He added as though proud of his brothers.

"Just for the record Tom, neither my husband nor I turn any child away. I am not sure you will want to stay here." She challenged in her gentle way.

"How come?" Tom questioned, curious.

"It takes a lot of work to fit in our family. Kelley is a minister. You will have to attend church and be kind and considerate of other's feelings. We have animals and a huge yard. We each pull our share of the workload. Kelley is also a teacher. He is good to assist with homework. If you and your brothers stay, you will be the oldest. Therefore, you will be Kelley's right hand man. This is a big responsibility." Darla shared.

"Mrs. Ryan, my brothers and I wanna stay here. This place is a piece of cake." Tom informed, crossing his arms now leaning back against the chair as though perfectly relaxed, as though he could choose his home. The Peterson couple smiled at the ten-year-old's feistiness and bluntness.

"Mr. Peterson, I need to speak with you and your wife in private." Mrs. Ryan informed.

"Tom, Pete, Bobbie, there is a cookie jar in the kitchen. The kitchen is straight ahead through the doorway. Help yourself to some cookies and then go outside through the kitchen door and meet the other children." Kelley instructed.

"Pete, you and Bobbie go ahead, I want to hear what Mrs. Ryan has to say." Tom ordered.

Pete and Bobbie silently and obediently got up from their seats starting toward the kitchen.

"Tom, I did not hear anyone ask you to stay." Kelley spoke with sternness in his voice.

Tom's face turned red. He silently got up from the chair to join his brothers.

"Tom." Kelley spoke, his voice more gentle.

Tom stopped walking. He turned facing Kelley in silence.

"We also use manners in this family and show respect to our elders."

"I will not be rude." He respectfully agreed.

"Good. You and I should get along fine in this case." Kelley replied approvingly.

"I apologize for Tom's behavior. The boys are truly well mannered. They had a wonderful mother. She was killed in an auto accident a couple of weeks ago. Their father was a businessman. His work kept him away from home much of the time. He is presently in prison for income tax evasion. He will be released in nearly three years." Mrs. Ryan explained.

"The boys will be fine. They will receive lots of love and guidance and we will all work together." Kelley assured confidently.

Kelley had predicted accurately. The three brothers adjusted quickly to the Peterson's ways as a family. They had been loved and well taught. This made Kelley and Darla's role much easier to fulfill as their foster parents. They showed no signs of neglect nor did they appear to bear scars of abuse.

Darla prepared dinner with Karry and Heaven at her side learning to assist. Kelley enjoyed the Saturday evening playing football with the boys. Kelley and Darla felt it was important to work and play with the children besides their regular responsibilities as parents.

"Mommy are we getting any more kids?" Heaven asked appearing aggravated.

"No dear. Seven children at one time is plenty."

"Good. Karry and I are running out of plates and chairs."

"All the beds are taken too. I think we better stop." Karry said.

"Girls, I think you both are right." Darla agreed, giving both girls a kiss on top of their heads. The girls looked at one another, exchanging smiles, pleased their mother appreciated their opinions.

"Will you two please call Daddy and the boys for dinner?" Darla asked, as she began setting dinner on the table.

"Mommy! Mommy! Tom is hurt!" Heaven exclaimed as she ran through the back doorway with freight on her face.

Darla set the dish down she had in her hands to hurry to Tom's aid when the boys and Kelley entered through the back door.

"Tom, what happened?" Darla asked, guiding the ten-year-old to the sink with concern on her face.

"I got tackled." He answered flinching, as Darla carefully washed the large scrape on his arm.

"What happened to you, guy?" Katie asked sympathetic as she returned from her Saturday of activity with her friends.

"He got tackled and falled down." Three-year-old Carlos answered.

"Who tackled you, Dad?" Katie asked as she teasingly accused her father. Katie's comment quickly brought Darla's attention from Tom's arm to her husband.

"Kelley you should not play so rough with the boys. They are too young for tackle football." Darla scolded.

"You could play volleyball or baseball." She added.

"Volleyball is for sissies, Mom." Kelley replied, winking at Tom, ignoring his wife's scolding and often over-protective ways. Darla sighed at her husband's ignoring comment as she doctored Tom's arm.

"Kelley, did you see that pass Pete caught?" Tom questioned, he too ignoring his foster mother's over-protectiveness.

"I sure did." Kelley answered with a pleased grin as he washed his hands at the kitchen sink.

"You are alright Pete." Tom informed, putting his arm around his brother's neck.

"Would you rough and tough boys please go wash for dinner?" Darla asked.

"Yes, Ma'am." The boys replied, smiling at Darla's ways.

"You and your boys are going to make me old before my time." Darla warned, as her husband assisted her with her chair.

"The boys had a good time, Mom." Kelley replied followed by a light kiss on his tender compassionate wife's lips.

"You young lady got me in trouble." Kelley informed, as he passed by Katie, she taking her seat at the table.

"Sorry." Katie apologized, giving her father a smile.

"Kelley says Darla spends all her time worrying." Eight-year-old Pete informed with a grin, as the boys sat down at the table.

"What else does Kelley say about me, boys?" Darla questioned with a sly smile, glancing at her husband, noting his face turning red.

"Do not dare answer that question, boys." Kelley ordered quickly, bringing smiles and grins from his family.

"You never have played fair."

"May we please eat, Dad?" Darla question as though he alone was responsible for delaying their dinner, again bringing smiles to the children's faces with Darla's scolding play.

"Let us pray, kids." He instructed, holding his hands out toward the two children next to him.

His family followed his example, taking hold of hands with the ones next to them. With their heads lowered reverently, Kelley asked the blessing over their meal.

"Dad, may I have some friends over after church tomorrow for a swim?" Katie asked as the family prepared their plates.

"Whom would you like to invite?"

"Jessica, May, Shelby, Brian and Gary. I spoke with Aaron earlier and if you say yes, I thought I would invite him also."

"You may have the pool to yourself and you may invite the girls."

"The girls only?" Katie questioned not understanding.

"Yes, please. No mixed bathing other than family, Babe." Kelley answered.

"Okay." Katie agreed, though surprised with her father's rule.

Katie assisted her mother with the dinner dishes, Kelley and the boys attended to the animals and milking, and Karry and Heaven collected the eggs.

"Mom, since when does Dad believe it is a sin for guys and girls to swim together?" Katie questioned as they worked together.

"Never, it is one of those individual decisions". Darla answered.

"The church does not approve of mixed bathing. Dad and I are pro and con on this matter. As a teenager, I went swimming with my friends, as did Dad. It depends on the dress and the crowd whether I feel comfortable or not. Age makes a difference in one's opinion, conduct and thinking. With Dad being a minister, you know he must be careful in all his actions or he leaves himself open to ridicule. This would not be pleasing unto the Lord. Dad is associate pastor of the church, so if he promotes one way and Pastor Finks another way, divisions could begin. This is most displeasing to God. For the sake of any misunderstandings or upsets, Dad has made this rule." Darla explained.

"Remind me not to marry a minister. I intend to only have God to answer to." Katie said with an understanding smile.

"Sweetheart, simply being a Christian, we are commanded to have a good reproach before man. There is no escaping persecution at some point and time. Not even for you, Deary."

"I understand this. If I do not marry a minister, I believe I will receive less persecution." Katie replied honestly.

"Perhaps. My prayer for you dearest Katie, is you always serve the Lord and you obey the leading of the Holy Spirit. You do this and the Lord will see you through everything."

"This I promise I will do." Katie assured, sincerely.

"Mom, I have to return to college in two weeks. I know you have a lot to do with having all these kids. I have been wondering if you will have time to go to San Diego and shop with me. If you are not able to get away, I understand."

"Katie, how long have you been my daughter?" Darla questioned, giving Katie her full attention, looking into her eyes.

"Five years."

"Long enough to know I do not exclude one of my children to make room for another child, am I right?"

"Yes."

"Our shopping trip to San Diego for your school needs has been a tradition since I became your mother. It is our special day away together which I cherish. Will next Saturday be acceptable for you?" Darla asked.

"Yes, Ma'am, next Saturday will be perfect." Katie assured happily, giving her mother a hug. With her arms still around Katie, Darla looked into her happy eyes.

"Perhaps I will have a special secret to share with you while we are away. I hear mothers and daughters are allowed to share secrets regardless of how old they become in age." Darla said happily.

"You do not have to wait until next Saturday, tell me now."

Katie encouraged anxious, her impatience bringing a soft laugh from Darla.

"Saturday, Deary. I have my reasons for waiting. Now, if I may impose on you, would you give Dad a hand with the kids? I believe I need to lie down for a while. This has been a full week." She explained with a gentle smile.

Darla rested while Katie and Kelley took charge of the younger children's baths. When morning arrived, Darla did not feel as rested as she had hoped. Completing a warm relaxing bath, she slipped into her robe.

"Babe." Kelley spoke lightly tapping on the bathroom door.

"The door is unlocked." Darla replied in her pleasant manner.

Kelley opened the door and entered the bathroom with concern on his face.

"Good morning." Darla greeted with a loving smile, giving her husband a kiss.

"Good morning. You look pale. Are you feeling poorly?"

"I feel tired." She answered honestly.

"It has been some time since I have felt this tired. Honestly, I am surprised the way our family size has increased. If my husband will grant me a day of rest, I assure you I will be in full charge again."

"Sweetheart, you may have as many days as you wish to rest." Kelley assured, putting his arms around his wife's waist.

"I have truly been blessed with the most wonderful husband of all." Darla replied, slipping her arms around her husband's waist, giving him a tight hug.

"And I have always believed I am the luckiest husband."

"You may kiss me, Husband. I am never too tired for this." Darla instructed with a happy smile, bringing a smile to her husband's face.

Kelley kissed his wife long and gently.

"Tell me, Nurse Darla how is it possible for you and I to be madly in love, yet we do not have a child yet?"

"This is an easy question. We have requested for the Lord's timing, not ours."

"We both are guilty of this." Kelley confessed and then kissed his wife again.

Darla stayed home from the Sunday services, resting. Kelley took full charge of the children, managing quite nicely. She did not feel exhausted, which she was thankful. She intended never to allow herself to become exhausted as she had when she and Kelley first married. Her day off would allow the extra needed rest to prevent this from happening.

With the younger children resting after dinner to prevent them from tiring so quickly during the upcoming evening service, the older family members relaxed each in his or her way. Kelley relaxed in a recliner with a book. Awaking from a restful nap, Darla joined her husband in the den.

Picking up her electric guitar with the volume turned on low, she played her favorite praise choruses. Pete and Tom soon entered the den, sitting on the carpet and listening to their foster mother play for their first time.

"You boys are welcome to sing along if you would like." Darla suggested with a kind smile.

"No, thanks." Pete replied quickly with a big grin.

"Tom?" Darla questioned.

"No, I do not know many church songs yet."

"Tom sings best in the shower anyway, Babe." Kelley teased, bringing a smile to Tom's face.

"Do you allow kids to play your guitar, Darla?" Tom inquired.

"This depends. I do not allow anyone to play with it as a toy, but if you would like to play it and you are careful, I will gladly share." Darla answered, holding her guitar out towards Tom.

"Tom never let anyone touch his guitar." Pete shared in his often-forward way, causing Tom to blush.

"You play then?" Darla questioned, surprised.

"Yes, but I have never played church music. I am not real good yet. I would like to play in a band when I get older." Tom answered as he sat down on the sofa with the guitar in his hands.

"Play what you know." Kelley encouraged, laying his book down.

Darla and Kelley listened attentively as Tom's playing surprised them.

"I am impressed." Darla complimented.

"You play well, son." Kelley complimented.

"Thanks." Tom replied.

"Kelley, do you think you could get my guitar for me?"

"And my drums?" Pete questioned excitedly.

"You play drums?" Kelley asked.

"Yes, Sir, I play real well." Eight-year-old Pete answered proudly. Darla and Kelley laughed at his confidence.

"I am going to be in Tom's band."

"What other hidden talents do you boys have?" Kelley questioned.

"We are good roller skaters and pretty good kids." Pete answered in his humorous way with a big grin, bringing laughter from his audience.

"Does Bobbie also have a musical talent?" Darla inquired.

"No, but Mom said he has a good voice for a little kid. She would say he might be our lead singer in our band." Pete answered his face serious now as he thought of his deceased mother.

"Our mom played the piano. She was real good." He shared with a pleased grin.

"You remind us of our mom." Tom informed, looking at Darla.

"She was nice like you are." He added.

"I consider this a special compliment, Tom. Thank you." Darla replied, deeply touched.

"And pretty like you." Pete sided.

"You boys best be careful, with such nice compliments I may develop a big head." Darla said with a gentle smile.

"Nope, you will never be that way. Our mom was not that way either and everyone liked her except our dad. Tom says he is a playboy."

"Pete." Tom scolded, embarrassed.

"You said that he had lots of girlfriends and that was why he was never home." Pete reminded in his defense.

"You do not have to tell everybody what I say. I am just a kid and maybe I was wrong. Besides, we have to like Dad now." Tom replied slowly, looking away from his brother.

"Why?" Pete questioned as though aggravated with Tom's information.

Darla and Kelley silently glanced at one another with the boys talk.

"We have to live with him when he gets out of prison." Tom informed, staring at the floor as he answered his younger brother.

"Mom said we would never have to be with Dad when she was not around." Pete reminded as though determined to keep distance between him and his father.

"Pete, Mom is gone. Mrs. Ryan said when Dad gets out of prison and gets a job, we have to live with him." Tom explained.

Pete's eyes quickly filled with tears. He got up off the floor, hurrying from the room.

"Tom, what is the problem, Son?" Kelley questioned in his calm manner.

"My dad made our mom cry a lot. We did not see much of him. He was always away and we do not like him much." Tom answered.

"Your dad never mistreated you boys?"

"No, Sir."

"Did he mistreat your mother?" Kelley asked.

"I don't know. I do not think he hit her. Every time he would come home for a couple of days, Mom would cry and then he would leave again."

"What do you say you and I try to cheer Pete up?" Kelley questioned, getting up from the recliner.

"Okay." Tom agreed, setting the guitar down carefully.

"Kelley, do you think you could get some of our things for us from our home?" He asked as he left the den with his foster dad.

"I will try, Son." Kelley answered, putting his hand on the young boy's shoulder.

Kelley spent extra time with Pete and Tom, with the three of them often going on errands together. Bobbie and Michael seemed content spending most of their time together with Carlos often tagging along behind them.

"Hello, most beautiful girls." Aaron greeted as Darla, Katie, Heaven and Karry put the finishing touches on dinner.

"Hi." The girls greeted with smiles.

"Are you having dinner with us, Uncle Aaron?" Heaven asked.

"Yes, thank you for asking. Where is my brother?"

"He had some errands to run after work. He should be home soon." Darla answered.

"I thought I would see if he would like to attend the park ministry with us tonight."

"Aaron, your brother presently has his hands full in several doings now. Please do not tempt him." Darla suggested.

"You, Dan, Katie and the others are doing a terrific job with the park ministry without Kelley assisting."

"Yes, Ma'am." Aaron agreed politely.

Kelley appeared preoccupied during dinner. He was quiet and withdrawn. When the kids shared their doings at school with the completion of their first week of a new school year, Kelley seemed to half-hear them. They soon grew quiet, wondering why he appeared uninterested. Aaron attempted to make conversation with his brother in hopes to change his solemn mood. He glanced at Darla and shrugged his shoulders as though puzzled.

"Honey, did you have a bad day?" Darla questioned, near the completion of their meal.

"No, unusual, but not bad." Kelley answered, looking at his wife as though her question informed him of his preoccupied state, snapping him back to the attention of his family. Kelley was attentive through the remainder of his meal, yet exceptionally quiet.

Katie away at the park ministry and the children each sleeping, Darla found her husband in the den. Kelley sat at his desk reading his Bible as though in deep concentration and tremendous concern on his face. Darla neared his desk, sitting on the edge of it.

"Honey, what is troubling you?" She questioned compassionately.

Kelley looked up from his searching in his Bible, looking into his wife's eyes, remaining silent.

"What, Honey?"

"I am your helpmate." She reminded with tenderness.

Kelley rubbed his head as though weary as he often did when troubled. Closing his Bible, he leaned back against his chair as though relaxing some and then once again, looked into his wife's eyes.

"You recall I had to visit the welfare office to drop the forms off to the boy's caseworkers." Kelley started.

"Yes." Darla agreed in her patient way.

"Tom, Bob and Pete's caseworker wanted to speak with me. She asked me if we would be interested in adopting the boys."

"Why?" Darla asked, she just as surprised as her husband.

"The boys' father does not feel he would supply them with a proper home life without the aid of his wife. Apparently, in Tom's letters to his father, he has requested he and his brothers be allowed to live here indefinitely. The boys' father passed Tom's letter on to the caseworker." Kelley answered.

Darla released a long sigh as she continued to search her husband's thoughts by looking into his eyes and observing his expressions.

"What was your response to Mrs. Ryan's news?"

"I told her I could not respond at this time. I am stunned. We are not financially able to adopt every child that needs a home. Surely, God does not expect this of us." Kelley answered.

Though his response was a statement, his eyes and expression clearly expressed, he was questioning the Lord's will.

"Kelley, I know you will search and pray until you know the Lord's will in this matter. While you are doing this, remember this, the Lord has richly blessed you and me from birth. We have never lacked for love or a comfortable home. We have never been without a meal. We have always had sufficient clothing. You and I honestly do not know what it is like to truly call out by faith for the Lord to supply us. Mother says our generation is a spoiled generation. We must have everything right now, lest we fold under the pressures and desires of our material wants. I believe she is right. We have not had our faith ever tested in financial areas. Perhaps this is a test of our depth of faith. We as Christians often say we will give our all for the Lord. Would we truly or would we close our hearts and eyes to the commands of the Lord when we feel the commands are too costly and justify our disobedience?"

"Babe, I am not about to disobey God. I am trying to rationalize and face facts. We had a swimming pool put in a couple of months ago. We cannot return it and get our money back. Our savings is presently nothing to speak of. If we adopt the boys, we will not receive assistance in supporting them. I alone must cover their expenses. We are talking five children to financially support. I would like to have my own child. There is no way if we would adopt the boys we could afford the medical of the birth of our child. All through the Bible, God promotes husband and wife to produce children. I have only requested for one child, our child, yet I am not granted only one biological child." Kelley replied clearly expressing his frustration. Darla gently took her husband's hand into hers.

"Sweetheart, I know you want your own child. I know in my heart that God will grant you your heart's desire as He did for Karry and Katie. As He did for me when you took me as your wife and adopted Heaven. I do not know why the delays in my conceiving your child, but I will not question the Lord in His timing. I do not need to, for I know the Lord will grant you the desire of your heart. You are a good and faithful servant. You are deserving of this desire. God fulfills all His promises, not some of His promises, just as He will always supply our needs regardless the size of our need. Perhaps the Lord is simply testing your faith." Darla suggested compassionately, brining comfort to her husband.

"Perhaps." Kelley agreed, relaxing somewhat.

"If we would adopt the boys, I would have to work five days weekly for your dad instead of three, in addition to my one evening weekly tutoring and my position in the church. This would put more work on you. This concerns me, Darla. You have so much to do now and I often worry about your health."

"I have not become exhausted in five years. Michael and Carlos will be returning to their mother within two months. The three boys, Heaven and Karry are in school all day now. I will have the weekdays of solitude pampering myself and preparing my sewing room as a mini nursery for your son that I know the Lord will grant us soon." Darla encouraged with a tender smile, as she got up from the desk to sit on her husband's lap.

"I needed to hear you say this. I cannot explain why I feel it a must to have our own child. It is very important to me though, Babe. At times I feel almost obsessed by this want."

"I know and I do understand." Darla assured with a comforting smile, gently kissing her husband's lips.

"Do you recall when my mother and I were conversing in the kitchen in our home in Tucson the day we celebrated Heaven's fifth birthday?"

"I remember, you politely ordered me out of the kitchen." Kelley answered with a smile bringing a soft laugh from his wife.

"Mother informed me I handled my husband quite well." Darla shared, bringing a chuckle from Kelley.

"Mother was teaching me my duties as a wife. I was annoyed because I felt the subject was not debatable in regards to my conceiving. I did not feel comfortable discussing my relationship with my husband to anyone. In my eyes, this was a closed book. Mother, in her insisting 'hear me out' way, explained the importance and the beauty of a child being conceived to the husband as well as the wife. She said the child silently represents the beauty of the love between husband and wife, showing the entire world their love toward one another. Therefore, Sweetheart, I do understand your desire, for no husband loves his wife more than you love yours." Darla shared, looking into her husband's eyes with a tender smile. Kelley tightened his arms around his wife, drawing her closer to him, his face now most tender as her words warmed his heart.

"You always know how and when to make me feel okay and

special all in one." Kelley shared with both pride and tenderness on his face and in his voice.

"Good. I must be fulfilling my duty as a wife."

"Most definitely." Kelley assured, pleased.

The young couple remained up until Katie had returned home safely and then called an end to their late Friday night, in the comfort of one another's arms.

Up early enjoying her quiet time as her family continued sleeping, Darla went to her husband's desk. Sitting down in his chair, she searched his desktop. Opening the long center drawer, she found what she wanted. Removing papers from an envelope, she carefully read over the papers that were necessary to fill out in order to begin adoption proceedings on the three brothers. On each blank, requiring her signature, she signed her name in ink. The blanks requiring income status she lightly wrote in pencil, the Lord will supply our needs. She carefully folded the papers, returning them inside the envelope, placing the envelope in the drawer where she had found it. She unlocked the bottom drawer. Removing their savings book and checkbook, she laid them on the desktop. With her eyes closed in reverence, she prayed over their finances and then returned the booklets to the proper place.

Spending the day in San Diego with Katie enjoying their special time together, Darla's heart was overjoyed, for she knew without a doubt the Lord would work everything out. She and her husband would be confronted with in all areas of their life, in their present and their future. She served a God who owned the heavens and the earth. She served a loving and a just God, a God who made promises to His faithful servants, fulfilling His promises. Her God would never forsake nor leave His children and she knew that without any doubt she was a child of the King.

Katie's shopping completed, Darla drove to the beach just as the sunset.

"How about a hotdog and a stroll on the beach?" Darla asked as she parked her car.

"I would love to." Katie answered excitedly.

Removing their shoes, leaving them in the car, they went to the snack bar. With a hotdog and coke in hand, they slowly walked in the wet sand, allowing the water to hit their feet and legs as the waves came in.

"Are you ready to share my secret?" Darla questioned with a tender smile.

"Yes. I thought you had forgotten to tell me." Katie answered curiosity clearly on her face.

"I think I am pregnant." Darla informed as she looked into Katie's eyes for her response.

"Really?" Katie asked, thrilled.

"Yes, really." Darla answered with a happy smile, as Katie hugged her excitedly.

"Is Dad happy?"

"I said I have a secret. You are the only one I have told. You are not to tell anyone. I want to be positive before telling Dad. He has wanted this for so long and I do not want him disappointed if I am wrong."

"This is cool." Kate replied overjoyed.

"Do you want to have a son or a daughter?"

"Dad says he must have a son. I hear this is every man's dream. It would be nice to fulfill dad's dream. He works so hard at fulfilling our dreams."

"Dad is a special person." Katie agreed with a pleased smile.

Darla put her arm around Katie's waist as they both silently held Katie's comment close to their hearts, admiring the beautiful sunset. This was a special time for Katie, having her mother sharing her special secret with her first as though she was recognizing Katie not only as her daughter, but also as an adult.

"We had better leave, Sweetheart. If we are too late, Dad will worry."

Katie returning to college for another term left a void in her family's hearts. Though she was faithful to call home every weekend, her absence was dearly missed.

"Daddy." Six-year-old Heaven called, entering her parents' room as they prepared for Sunday evening service.

"What Princess?" Kelley questioned as he tied his tie.

"May I sit on your lap at church tonight? Carlos always gets to sit on your lap." She complained.

"Are you feeling left out?"

"Yes." Heaven answered barely above a whisper.

"Sometimes I get tired of sharing you and Mommy with all these kids."

"I am sure you do, Babe." Kelley replied, understanding.

"Do you know it takes a special person to share their home and their family with others?"

"It does?" Heaven asked, looking into her daddy's eyes.

"Sure, especially to share your parents and there are not many kids that would share as you do. This is most pleasing to God, Mommy and me."

"Do you think God is upset with me because I want to sit on your lap?"

"No, Sweetheart." Kelley answered with a tender smile.

"God wants you to have your parents as you need them. He wants you and me to have a special date, so your 'left out' feelings will go away. I am sure Mom will be glad to hold Carlos so we may have our date. Do we have a date?"

"Yes, Daddy." Heaven answered with a big smile.

Heaven had her date with her daddy. Her special time as requested and as needed. Her lonesome feeling was quickly replaced with reassurance and love.

The children each tucked in bed for the night, Darla and Kelley slipped under their covers. Snuggling up to her husband, Darla rested her head on his chest as Kelley put his arm around her shoulders.

"Tom said he wants to be a preacher when he grows up." Kelley shared with pride in his voice.

"It appears you have a fan." Darla approved pleased.

"Perhaps. I filled out the adoption papers on the boys. I thought

I would turn them in tomorrow. My conclusion is to leave the final decision in the Lord's hands. I cannot possibly know what our future holds."

"The Bible does say the future is not to be a concern of ours." Darla replied, approvingly.

"As the word says the Lord will supply our needs. I erased this notation of yours a few times from the forms. You are one of a kind, Babe."

CHAPTER SIX

Darla and Kelley kept busy with their five foster children, Heaven, Karry and Kelley working five days weekly for his father-in-law instead of three. The young couple found great joy in working with the children. Their lives always filled with surprises from them, never leaving a day of boredom.

Standing at the back door, Darla and Carlos waved goodbye to Kelley and the kids. Like every weekday morning, Kelley would drive the kids to school on his way to work. Carlos now tagged along behind Darla as she smoothed wrinkles out of the younger children's bedspreads from the children's attempts at making their own beds. Becoming faint, Darla put her hand on the wall to steady herself. The faintness leaving, feeling sick to her stomach, she hurried to the bathroom, vomiting until her stomach ached terribly.

"Darwa, Darwa." Carlos said standing outside the bathroom door. His face filled with freight as Darla flushed the toilet.

"Darla is okay, Sweetheart." Darla replied with a comforting smile, as she washed her face.

"Get your puzzles out, please. I will be with you in a minute."

"Okay." Carlos agreed, running off toward the den.

Her stomach settling, yet feeling slightly faint, Darla joined Carlos in the den, lying down on the sofa.

"Baby Jesus." Carlos informed, as he proudly displayed his completed puzzle.

"Yes." Darla agreed with a happy smile. She briefly closed her eyes as Carlos picked out another puzzle.

"Oh, Kelley, you have been granted your heart's desire. You will have your child you have so desperately wanted." She thought thrilled.

"Thank you Lord, he is so deserving of this wish. Thank you for this wonderful, precious miracle."

Feeling better, Darla now sat up on the sofa, making over Carlos' puzzle completions.

"Darwa, may I answer the telephone?" Three and a half-year-old Carlos questioned excitedly, as the telephone rang.

"Yes, you may." She answered kindly, going to her husband's desk where the telephone sat.

"Hello."

Darla patiently sat down at Kelley's desk.

"Yes, Ma'am." Carlos spoke in his grown-up tone.

"A lady wants you, Darwa."

"Thank you." Darla replied, smiling at his manner as she took the telephone.

"Good morning."

"Is this Mrs. Kelley Peterson?"

"Yes."

"I am Sally a charge nurse in emergency at Memorial Hospital." She informed.

"Yes?" Darla questioned, her face turning white and her heart beating faster.

"Your husband has been in an auto accident. Is it possible for you to come to the hospital?"

"Of course." Darla answered quickly.

"Will he be okay?"

"The doctor is presently with him. I do not have all his medical facts."

"I will be there shortly, thank you." Darla replied hurriedly.

With watery eyes, fearing the unknown of her husband's condition, she dialed her sister-in-law's telephone number.

"Roberts." Paula answered.

"Good morning, this is Darla."

"Good morning, Darla. How are you?"

"I am not sure at the present moment." She answered nervously. "I need to go to the hospital. Kelley has been in an accident. I just received the call."

"What may I do to assist you, Darla?" Paula questioned quickly.

"I need someone to watch Carlos for me. In addition, Michael will need picked up from kindergarten at noon, should I be detained at the hospital."

"The hospital is halfway between our homes. I will meet you there and care for Carlos. I will pick Michael up also." Paula informed.

"Thank you, Paula. I will see you shortly."

Blinking hard to keep her tears back, with trembling hands, she quickly dialed her parents' number. After several rings with no response, Darla put the telephone down. Hurrying from the den, she entered her bedroom, snatching her purse and car keys from her dresser.

Praying silently nonstop, she drove as quickly as the speed limit would allow her. Entering the hospital parking lot, Darla parked next to her sister-in-law's car.

"Hi." Darla greeted with a nervous smile as both women vacated their cars.

"Hi." Paula greeted with a sympathetic smile.

"Do you know anything of Kelley's condition?" Paula inquired as she opened Darla's car door for Carlos to vacate his foster mother's car.

"No." Darla answered nervously.

"I tried to call Mother, but there was no answer. Judging by the hour, I am sure Dad is wondering why Kelley is not at work."

"I will stop by your Father's work and inform him of Kelley." Paula offered.

"Thank you. I truly appreciate your help." Darla assured, giving Paula a quick hug.

"Bye, kiddo, be good for Aunt Paula." She instructed, giving Carlos a quick kiss and then hurried toward the hospital entrance.

Hurriedly entering through the emergency room doors, Darla's heart pounded faster and faster.

"Excuse me, Ma'am." Darla spoke nervously as she reached the desk.

"I am Kelley Peterson's wife."

"I have been waiting for you. I am Sally." The nurse greeted with a pleasant smile.

"Come with me, please." She instructed as she left the desk area to another nurse.

"The doctor has moved your husband to the intensive care unit." She informed as the women started down a long hall.

"Intensive care?" Darla questioned with tears quickly beginning down her thin cheeks.

"Yes, apparently a semi-truck ran a stop sign, hitting your husband's car."

"Oh." Darla sighed, her tears coming more quickly, her face drawn, drained and pale as they approached the intensive care unit.

"Dr. Porter." Sally spoke, as she and Darla approached the doctor, who was studying a medical chart.

"This is Mrs. Kelley Peterson."

"Hello, Mrs. Peterson." Dr. Porter greeted, extending his hand kindly to Darla.

"Hello, Sir." Darla replied, quickly wiping her tears away.

"How is my husband?"

"Very fortunate. Quite honestly, I do not know how he survived the accident.

"The Lord knows how much he is needed." Darla said, forcing a weak smile.

"Perhaps." Dr. Porter replied with a kind smile.

Darla listened attentively as the doctor explained her husband's condition. Although Darla had been forewarned of Kelley's condition, she turned white as a sheet as she approached Kelley's side with the doctor.

"Oh, Kelley." She spoke barely above a whisper, taking his motionless hand in hers.

"With the amount of blood loss alone, is a miracle. He apparently is a fighter." Dr. Porter remarked.

"Yes, Sir." Darla agreed with a pleased weary smile as her tears streamed down her cheeks at the sight of his injuries.

"He will pull through just fine." She added confidently.

"I agree, Mrs. Peterson. We are seeing a miracle before us simply with him surviving the accident. I do not mean to discourage you nor will I promote false hope. Until your husband regains consciousness, we will not know the extent of his head injuries."

"He will be fine, Doctor. The Lord will see to it. He is busy healing his body at this very moment." Darla replied, determined.

"I hope you are right, Ma'am."

Darla stayed at Kelley's side for some time. With his hand held securely in hers, she silently prayed for a quick and complete recovery.

Leaving the intensive care unit, Darla entered the waiting room.

"Darla." Spoke her father, entering the waiting room behind her.

"Oh, Daddy." Darla said as she released her tears once again.

"How is Kelley, Babe?" Dad Roberts questioned, putting his arms around his daughter, comforting her.

"Considering, quite well. I know he will be okay, Dad, but he does not look like Kelley at the present." She answered, gaining control of herself.

"I need to call Kelley's mother. If you would like, we may go see Kelley together."

"I would like this."

"I would like for you to pray for Kelley, Daddy, when you see him."

"Sweetheart, I have been praying for Kelley since I saw his car."

"The car looks bad?" Darla questioned, as they approached the telephone booth.

"Very bad. It is at the junk yard. I am surprised Kelley is still with us."

"This is what Dr. Porter has said. Kelley will be upset about the car. We just paid the car loan off."

"Honey, the driver's company will have to replace your car. The guy ran a stop sign." Her father explained.

"This is one consolation." Darla replied, removing a dime from her wallet.

"I dislike calling Kelley's mother. She will be heart broken when she sees Kelley." She informed, as she dialed the telephone, glancing at her father's strong compassionate face.

"Mom Peterson." Darla greeted slowly.

"I dislike being the bearer of bad news, but Kelley was in an auto accident. Yes, Ma'am, he will be okay with time. Yes, I am at Memorial hospital. No, he will not be leaving the hospital for a while. Yes, Ma'am. I will be waiting in the waiting room on the second floor. Bye." Darla hung the telephone up, letting out a long sigh.

"How is Kelley?" Bill inquired as he now joined his sister and father.

"He is going to be okay, Bill." Darla answered, forcing herself to be strong and believe in the healing power of her Jesus.

"We may visit him now."

Arriving at Kelley's side, Darla's father and brother looked at one another at the sight of him. Both of Kelley's legs were in casts. His left arm also had a cast on it. His head was shaved of his hair and his head had several stitched areas, as did his chest. His ribs were broken. His eyes, nose, cheeks and lips were swollen. There were tubes and machines connected to his body and he appeared lifeless.

"Babe, what did the doctor say in regards to Kelley's condition?"

"He said it is a miracle that Kelley is alive. Will you pray for him now, Daddy? I am believing for no brain damage." She explained as her tears slid down her cheeks.

"Sure, Babe." Her father agreed without hesitation.

The three adults bowed their heads in reverence as Dad Roberts prayed aloud for complete healing in Kelley's body. When opening their eyes at the completion of his prayer, Mom Robert's silently stood near her daughter, with her arm around her shoulders offering her comfort. Her face bore the concerns of her heart, shocked at her son-in-law's condition.

"He will be okay, Mother." Darla assured, looking into her mother's saddened eyes.

"I know he will be, dear. We serve a loving God." Mom Roberts said with a comforting smile, as she quickly brushed her tears away to be strong for her daughter.

"I must return to the waiting room. Kelley's mother will be here soon." Darla informed, gently placing Kelley's hand back on the bed.

Looking at her husband's face for a few moments in silence, she silently said another pray. Leaning close to his ear she whispered, "I love you, Kelley. We need you honey." She gently kissed his lips and then left his side with her family silently at her side.

"I trust Kelley's dad is with Sister Peterson." Darla said as they entered the waiting room.

"I think this would be wise, also." Mom Roberts agreed.

Darla went to the window looking outside watching for her in-law's car to pull into the parking lot as her family sat down. Darla thought about the tiny child within her that Kelley had so longed for. She had hoped to share her news with him that evening.

"Babe, come sit down. You look drained." Dad Roberts encouraged. Darla silently did as her father requested to ease his concerns.

"Dad says our station wagon is totaled." Darla informed, breaking their silence.

"I am trying to picture squeezing seven children into Kelley's tiny Vega." She shared with a weak smile, attempting to lift her family's spirits.

"I will loan you my pickup truck." Dad Roberts offered with a chuckle, bringing smiles to his family's faces and a soft laugh from Darla.

"Kelley has wanted to get rid of the Vega and get a truck." Darla shared. Her head seemed to fill with only Kelley's wishes, thoughts and ideas. She took her eyes from her family now. She silently sat looking at her wedding rings on her finger, thinking of all the love she and Kelley held for one another.

"Sis, Paula and I will be glad to help you with the kids until Kelley is well." Bill offered.

"I am sure I will need some assistance. Kelley has a unique way of keeping the boys corralled. There is no way I could begin to fill his shoes." She confessed, her tears quickly coming again.

Mom Roberts quickly went to her daughter's side, putting her arm around her and hugging her.

"Sweetheart, it is okay for you to cry. Both you and Kelley's family will see you and Kelley through this. Neither one of you will be alone." Mom Roberts assured as Darla broke down, sobbing in her mother's arms.

Kelley's parents arrived in the waiting room with frightened expressions as they silently witnessed their heartbroken daughter-in-law. Dad Roberts quietly got up from his chair stepping out into the hallway with them.

"Pastor, how is our boy?" Dad Peterson questioned as though fearing his answer.

"Darla has offered very little information. From what I saw and according to Darla, he survived the accident by the grace of God. Come, see him." Dad Roberts answered, putting his hand on Dad Peterson's back to comfort him.

Kelley's mother began to cry as she looked at her son lying motionless, with tubes and machines connected to him.

"It is okay, Mama. God is taking care of our boy. He is resting and getting his strength back. He is a strapping lad. He will be fine." Dad Peterson comforted.

With her composure regained, Darla joined her in-laws at Kelley's side.

"Mom Peterson, it is okay to touch Kelley. I find comfort in holding his hand." Darla suggested, gently lifting Kelley's glass scratched hand toward her. Mom Peterson gently took her son's hand into hers.

"Kelley will heal. The only question the doctor has is whether Kelley will have brain damage. I personally do not believe God spared Kelley's life to allow him to be left with any handicaps. I simply refuse to accept this. I know the Lord is giving us each one our Kelley back, either as he was or better, if better is possible." Dad Peterson put his arm around his wife's shoulders as she held her son's hand, her tears streaming.

"Miss Darla is right, Honey. We must believe in the healing powers of our Jesus' stripes He bore and claim our son's healing." Dad Peterson comforted.

"I will believe this, I must." Mom Peterson replied, wiping her tears away.

Darla stood near the head of Kelley's bed with her eyes upon his face, silently praying and silently loving him.

"Kelley we are each here for you, Honey." Darla spoke; leaning near his face as she gently touched his face.

"Even when you do not hear our voices, we are with you in spirit. Fight to get well, Sweetheart. We are each counting on you. We need you and we love you."

"Mrs. Peterson, I do not believe the doctor would approve of more than two visitors at a time." A nurse informed.

"Why not, we are Kelley's family." Darla spoke looking at the nurse.

"It is policy two visitors at a time, Ma'am."

"I presently do not care about your policy. I only care about my husband's needs being administered to. I do not mean this with disrespect." Darla replied in her gentle yet determined tone.

"I assure you, we will give your husband the best care possible."

"I believe medically you have done a superb job and will continue to do so. Is your staff able to pray for my husband twenty-four hours a day?"

"Why no, but…"

"If your staff is not large enough to have at least two people sitting at my husband's side twenty-four hours a day to pray for him and talk to him until he regains consciousness, then I will be in charge of his mental and spiritual well-being." Darla informed.

"If you will give us just a few more minutes, with the understanding of my obligations, we will limit to two visitors, please."

"I am sorry, Mrs. Peterson, but I will have to speak with Dr. Porter about your request for two people in here twenty-four hours." The nurse informed.

"Five more minutes and then two visitors until I have a reply from Dr. Porter." She added.

"Thank you." Darla replied politely.

"Honey, you are not able to stay here twenty-four hours a day." Mom Roberts said, putting her arm around her daughter's shoulders.

"I know I am not able alone, Mother, but the Bible says if two or more agree on anyone thing, asking in Jesus' name, it shall be done." She explained looking into her mother's eyes as though she was desperate.

"I know what the Bible says. I believe prayers are just as effective whether at one's side or miles away."

"I suppose you are right. I do not want Kelley left alone though. He needs to know he is not alone."

"I agree Honey and we will fight for this." Sister Peterson said, determined.

"Babe, let us give the Petersons some time with their son." Dad Roberts suggested, putting his hand on his daughter's back as though prepared to guide her from the room.

Darla gave her husband a light kiss and then silently left her husband's side as her father had suggested, as did her parents and brother.

"Sis, maybe you should go home and rest." Bill suggested, putting his arm around her shoulder.

"Kelley's parents, I am sure would welcome this time with their son."

"I want to be with Kelley also, Bill." Darla informed, looking at her brother as though surprised with his suggestion.

"Kelley does not know you are here, Dar. You are drained and you will need your strength to be strong for Kelley when he regains consciousness." He advised.

Dr. Porter entered the waiting room before Darla could respond. "Mrs. Peterson."

"Yes, Sir?" Darla questioned, hoping for a change in her husband's condition.

"I am assuming this is your family."

"Yes, my parents and brother."

"I have informed the nursing staff to grant you your request on your husband's behalf. I am familiar with your husband's faith in God. We met a few years ago when he would come here to pray for the sick or injured. I know he would expect of you what you have requested. You are also right in assuming your husband is able to hear you. It is most likely that he hears. If you are able to arrange someone at his side talking with him, this may bring him out of unconsciousness sooner. I have explained this to your in-laws already. It is a pleasure to meet Preacher Kel's wife." Dr. Porter extended his hand to Darla with a reassuring smile.

"I sincerely appreciate your understanding." Darla replied, feeling great relief as she shook the doctor's hand.

"So much for brotherly advice." Bill remarked as the doctor departed.

"I appreciate your concern dearest brother." Darla assured, giving Bill a kiss on his cheek.

Darla sat at her husband's side each day while her children were in school. Mom Peterson would relieve Darla, staying with her son into the late night. Friends and family members filled in the hours as needed so Kelley was never alone. Bill, Paula, Cindy, Dan, and Mom and Dad Roberts saw that Darla had help with her family and many duties both inside and outside of the home.

Calling the children to dinner, they each quietly took their places at the dinner table. The children had been overly quiet and helpful after Kelley's accident. Dan and Cindy, along with Darla, also sat down at the table.

"When are you going to bring Kelley home, Darla?" Five-year-old Michael questioned as they ate their dinner.

"I do not know, Sweetheart." Darla answered.

"You are a nurse and we would help you take care of Kelley." Tom encouraged.

"It isn't this simple boys. Kelley has machines to help him get better. We do not have these machines here." She explained compassionately.

"Mommy, is Daddy going to die?" Heaven questioned with watery eyes.

"No, Honey, this much I promise you."

"Your dad will not die, Heaven. He is too important to God. Kelley says Christians are God's helpers. Kelley is the best Christian God has. He cannot die." Tom said confident of his advice.

"Amen." Dan agreed.

Darla and Cindy smiled at Tom's positive attitude and support for Heaven. He was trying hard to be a daddy to all the kids since Kelley's accident. His attitude was a big help to Darla.

"Excuse me." Darla said, getting up from the table, she going to the ringing telephone.

"Hello."

"Honey, this is Mom Peterson. I have someone who would like to speak to you."

"Okay." Darla agreed slowly, assuming her mother-in-law was still at the hospital.

"Hi, Sweetheart." A low shaky voice greeted.

"Kelley?" Darla questioned quickly, her eyes filling with happy tears.

"No, this is your other boyfriend." He answered, bringing a tickled laugh from his wife.

"It is so good to hear your voice, Honey." She replied smiling through her tears.

"Is Daddy okay?" Heaven questioned excitedly.

"Daddy is okay, Sweetheart." Darla answered happily, looking at her family's happy faces.

"Are the kids okay?" Kelley inquired.

"They are fine."

"How about my wife? I hear I have been occupying this hospital bed much too long."

"Your wife is fine. Yes, you have been away too long."

"This bossy nurse says I must get off the telephone." Kelley informed, his voice sounding weaker.

"Mom says you will be up to visit in the morning. I will be looking forward to your visit."

"Me too, Honey, I love you. We each miss you. Bye."

"How did Kelley sound, Dar?" Cindy questioned excited.

"Like Kelley." Darla answered happily.

"He sounded weak, but I detected no changes otherwise. Our prayers have been answered." She added with tears streaming down her cheeks.

"Mommy, do not cry. You said Daddy is okay." Karry said compassionately.

"These are happy tears, Sweetheart." Darla assured quickly wiping her tears away with her napkin.

"Darla, go see Kelley. Dan and I are quite able to handle these guys." Cindy suggested, smiling at the seven children.

"Oh, I would love to. Tomorrow seems so far off." She confessed.

"You are a mind reader." Darla said, giving her cousin a tight hug.

"Dar, you do not have to hurry home." Dan informed.

"Thank you." Darla replied, with a kind smile.

"Give Daddy kisses for us, Mommy." Heaven reminded.

"I will. Each of you be good, do your chores and your homework." Darla instructed.

Darla released her tears as she left her home. It had been a long rough couple of weeks waiting for Kelley to regain consciousness. She thanked the Lord repeatedly for answering her prayer that Kelley would not have brain damage.

Parking her car in the hospital parking lot, she almost ran to the hospital entrance. Her heart pounded faster and faster with excitement. Arriving at Kelley's room, her heart leaped with joy. The head of Kelley's bed was raised for the first time. He had his head turned toward his mother with his eyes open.

"Hi." Darla greeted with a radiant smile, as she approached her husband's bed.

"There is my Baby doll." Kelley said his voice shaky and his smile weak, his choice of words causing her to blush in her mother-in-law's presence. Darla gently gave him a kiss.

"He looks great." Darla commented with a soft laugh, giving her mother-in-law a tight hug excitedly.

"I look real good. I would like to get my hands on the person who cut my hair." Kelley said, bringing laughter from the women.

"Your hair will grow back. You will be as handsome as ever." Darla assured with a loving smile.

"You did have a few stitches in your head, Deary."

"This is what I hear. I have been told I am extremely fortunate to be here." Kelley replied, his face growing serious as he looked into his wife's eyes, knowing how frightened she must have been.

Darla's eyes quickly filled with tears, she silently knowing he was concerned for her days of heartache.

"We just could not let you leave us yet, Sweetheart." Darla said with a tender smile, as her tears escaped.

"Come here, Babe." Kelley instructed with tenderness on his face.

Darla neared her husband. Kelley slowly lifted his weakened arm. He gently put his hand on his wife's face, brushing her tears away

"I love you, Babe."

"I love you." Darla said with a tender smile.

"You will not be alone much longer. I will be home soon." He assured, returning his hand to his side as it tired quickly. Darla took his hand in hers.

"I have always known this." Darla assured.

"Good. Give me a kiss." Darla did as requested.

"Go home and get some rest. I will be waiting for your visit in the morning. Make Mom go home. I will be okay now."

"You are the boss, Honey." Darla replied with a tender smile.

"I love you. Goodnight." She added.

"I love you, Babe." Darla kissed her husband once more and then left his side.

"Mom, I will be waiting in the hall."

"Okay, Honey." Mom Peterson agreed.

Darla left her husband's room. She felt complete now. Kelley would be okay. With time, he would be home, busy in his many activities.

Each morning Darla visited Kelley. When his pain from his broken bones became intense and the pain he endured showed on his face, Kelley would insist she leave. He in his protective manner would not have his wife burdened more by seeing how intense his pain could become. Though Darla disapproved, she kept her comments to herself. She had learned over her married years, Kelley's need to protect her in every way he could was necessary for him to fulfill his husbandly duties.

"Good morning." Darla greeted pleasantly as she entered her husband's room.

"Hi, Babe." Kelley greeted, his face drawn and tense as a nurse handed him some pills and a glass of water.

"Nurse, is there a problem?" Darla questioned with concern in her eyes.

"No problems, I just exercised your husband's legs. I wore him out." She answered with a kind smile.

"His leg casts are off?" Darla asked, hopeful.

"Yes."

"Great. When will you begin walking him?" Darla questioned excited.

"Within a couple of days."

"How is his shoulder and arm?"

"Healing nicely. We get him walking and he may go home."

"Oh, this day I am looking forward to." Darla said happily.

Darla gave her husband's lips a kiss as the nurse left them alone.

"You had a rough workout?" Darla asked sympathy on her face.

"Yes, Ma'am." Kelley answered, forcing a weak smile, attempting to conceal his pain as he took his wife's hand into his.

"Are your ribs still causing you discomfort?"

"Some. How about you take your husband out of here. I am homesick."

"I would love to more than anything, Honey." Darla assured, her heart going out to her husband. She gently put her hand on his face and then gave him another kiss.

"Surely I will not be here much longer." He remarked, shaking his down mood.

"Surely not." Darla agreed pleasantly.

"Perhaps if I would exercise your legs again we could get you home sooner." Darla teased to cheer her husband.

"Wife, do not touch my legs." Kelley ordered with a grin, bringing a laugh from her.

"How are the kids?"

"Missing their daddy terribly." Darla answered with a pleased smile.

"I am to deliver seven kisses to you. One from each child."

"Even Tom?" Kelley questioned, surprised.

"This was Tom's idea."

"I am ready for the kisses, Babe." Kelley informed with a boyish grin as he put his arm around his wife, pulling her closer to his bedside.

"There is nothing wrong with my lips."

"Mine either." Darla assured, kissing her husband.

"Would you like all seven kisses now?" She asked playfully, looking into her husband's eyes.

"Of course, quickly before my roommate returns and you chicken out."

"I was not aware you have a roommate." Darla replied quickly glancing toward the doorway.

"As of last night I do. He will not be back for another fifteen minutes."

"In that case, I best hurry." Darla said with a smile and then gave her husband another long gentle kiss.

Now looking into her husband's eyes, she gently ran her fingers through her husband's hair.

"Your hair has grown back nicely. You look as handsome as ever."

Taking Darla's hand into his, he raised her hand to his lips, kissing it.

"Thank you, Babe. Sit down by me." He suggested.

Darla carefully sat down on the side of his bed as not to wiggle the bed, adding to his painful discomfort.

"The morning of my accident, I had turned in the paperwork in regards to the three boy's adoption. Had I known I would be spending weeks in a hospital, I would not have been so hasty turning the papers in. I guess you not becoming pregnant yet is a blessing. I am not able to support my family while I am lying here. I would like you to impose on your brother for me. He deals with insurance policies and claims. Ask him to visit me to talk business. We are not able to survive without my working."

"Honey, surely this can all wait until you come home and you feel better. This is not the time for you to be concerned about financial matters."

"Sweetheart, I have been here over six weeks. Too much time has already lapsed. I should have dealt with such matters weeks ago. Please give Bill my message."

"I will give him your message." Darla agreed releasing a sigh.

"I am assuming by your sigh, I am becoming as stubborn as my wife when wanting my wishes granted." Kelley said with a relaxed smile, bringing a smile to his wife's young tender face.

"This is necessary to deal with now." He assured, touching her long hair, soothing her from her concerns.

"I do not believe you, Peterson." A thin, frail young man spoke, pushing himself into the hospital room in his wheelchair.

"You are not able to get out of bed, yet you have a girlfriend ready to wait on you hand and foot."

"Some of us have it and some of us don't." Kelley remarked kindly.

"Honey meet Frank Silvers, my roommate. We attended junior high school together. Frank my beautiful wife Darla."

"Pleased to meet you, Darla." Frank greeted politely, shaking her hand.

"I am sure the pleasure is likewise."

"How did you get a wife this pretty?"

"Our marriage was in God's plan." Kelley answered.

Kelley's reply immediately brought a serious expression to Frank's face.

"Sure buddy." Frank replied now pushing himself in his wheelchair to his side of his room.

"Sweetheart, I want you to go home now, so you are able to rest before the kids return from school. I realize how much you have to do without my help."

"Kelley, I have not been here long. Besides, our families are constantly assisting me."

"You look tired and your face is flushed. I thought with Carlos and Michael reunited with their mother a few days ago, your color would look better by now. Give me a kiss please and then go home."

"I wish you would not do this." She complained lightly barely above a whisper, although she got up from his bed. Leaning close to Kelley's face, she looked into his eyes.

"You really are in no condition to be giving me orders." She reminded with a gentle smile, bringing a weak laugh from her husband.

"You will humor me though, right?" He questioned, his face beginning to grow tense again as his pain medicine began to wear off.

"Only until you are fully recuperated." Darla answered honestly with a soft laugh.

"Then I intend to have my way." She added.

"I am sure you do." Kelley replied with a weak smile.

"Give me a kiss, please."

Darla gave her husband a kiss and then reluctantly left his side. Stopping at the payphone, she called her brother's office informing Bill of Kelley's wishes along with a brief update in Kelley's condition. She left the hospital, heading for her home.

Entering her large country home, she slowly walked through each room. With Carlos and Michael's absence, she felt a void. She missed Carlos' tiny arms around her neck, giving her hugs and kisses during the school hours while the older children were away. She now stood in front of the full-length mirror in the hallway observing her tiny firm stomach. No one had yet noticed her small, slightly swollen stomach from the baby growing inside her. Her arms longed to hold a baby, her and Kelley's baby.

"Oh, Kelley, God has truly granted you the desire of your heart and you are concerned with finances. Why must you be so conservative? When will you learn the Lord will truly supply our needs without you working day and night?"

Changing her dress slacks for a pair of jeans and a loose comfortable sweatshirt, she left her bedroom. Passing the closed door that led to the tiny room that had served as her sewing room, she opened the door.

"Kelley will be so surprised." She thought as she smiled, pleased with the tiny room she had repainted and decorated as a nursery during Kelley's stay in the hospital.

Reclosing the door that hid her secret away, she entered the kitchen. With a sandwich and a glass of milk, she sat down at the breakfast table having her lunch with her thoughts quickly going to Kelley lying in the hospital. Hearing a car in the drive, she left the table to look through the window. Pleased with the arrival of company, she eagerly opened the back door.

"Hi." She greeted happily, as her brother approached.

"Hi, Sis." Bill greeted, giving his sister a kiss.

"May I interest you in a sandwich?"

"Sure, thank you." Bill answered politely, as he removed his suit coat.

"I just left your husband. I told the nurses to quit being stingy with the pain medication. I do not understand how he keeps his cool."

"I have not been permitted to witness the extent of his pain. Kelley always sends me home when the pain medicine begins to wear off."

"Trust me; he is in a lot of pain."

"I assumed as much." Darla shared, releasing a worried sigh.

"He is being thick headed also." Bill remarked.

"He reminds me of my sister."

"Alright, you leave me out of your and Kelley's disagreements. What is the problem?" Darla asked, as she placed her brother's lunch before him and then returned to her lunch.

"Kelley has a legitimate lawsuit against the trucking company, but he refuses to sue."

"Bill, Kelley will not sue. He would not sue anyone for any reason. He believes this is wrong to do."

"I understand Kelley's reasoning. Sis, he says he will not even accept severance pay. He said if the company pays his medical expenses and replaces his car, this is all that is due him."

"You are kidding." Darla said surprised also with her husband's wishes.

"I am dead serious. He is due his loss in wages until he is able to return to work. He said if he is not on the job, he should not receive a paycheck."

"He will receive his pay if I have to declare him temporarily insane and sign the necessary paperwork myself." Darla replied in her stern tone.

"Convince your husband of this. The trucking company is more than willing to do right by Kelley. They do not want a lawsuit."

"Are you willing to deal with the trucking company in Kelley's behalf?" Darla asked.

"I will be glad to."

"You work out the arrangements with the trucking company and leave Kelley out of the picture. When you have completed this, go over the arrangements with me and I will deal with Kelley and his stubbornness." Darla instructed.

"Darla, Kelley will not approve of this." Bill warned, hesitant.

"He will get over it. He is not the only person in this family capable of making decisions. You know as well as I do, his thinking is ridiculous in this matter. I will deal with Kelley." Darla insisted with firmness.

"I will do as you have requested." Bill agreed.

"I honestly do not believe Kelley realizes he is going to be off work for some time yet. I am right in assuming at least another four to six weeks?" He questioned, looking at his sister.

"At least. They just removed his leg casts this morning. He has not walked in six weeks. His ribs are not yet healed or is his shoulder completely healed. He is still considerably weak. I know he is concerned with our finances. Maybe he will be able to face his limitations if we are able to get his salary for him. I would like to relieve him of this worry as soon as possible, Bill. He does not need to be focusing on finances. He needs to focus on fully recuperating."

"I agree with you, Sis."

Within a couple of weeks of therapy, Kelley was once again walking. His pace was slow and painful with the aid of a crutch.

Darla waved goodbye to the children as the school bus arrived like every weekday morning. Closing the back door, she went to the laundry room. With a load of clothes washing, she entered the children's bedrooms re-tidying their rooms. Returning to the kitchen, she began washing breakfast dishes. Her mind quickly drifted to Kelley. She missed him most when the children were away and the house was quiet. It had been so many weeks since the accident. She missed him terribly. Drying her hands, she answered the ringing telephone.

"Good morning, Peterson's."

"Good morning, Baby doll." Kelley greeted, his voice quickly bringing a happy glow to Darla's face.

"Baby doll? What kind of pain medicine do they have you on?" She questioned with a soft laugh.

"Apparently the right kind. What were you doing when I called?"

"Washing dishes. Why not come home and keep me company?"

"Come get me, the doctor has released me to your care." Kelley informed anxious.

"Should I leave this very minute or may I tarry?" Darla asked teasing, bringing a laugh from her husband.

"You have thirty minutes or I will be calling a cab. Come get me, Babe. I want to come home, I miss you."

"I miss you too, Sweetheart. I am on my way. Love you."

"Love you, Babe."

Hurrying to her room, Darla removed her purse and car keys from the dresser. Driving into town, she felt almost as excited as she did on her wedding day. It had been way too many weeks of Kelley's absence from the family.

Entering Kelley's hospital room, Kelley sat ready and waiting in a wheelchair at his roommate's bedside.

"Good morning." Darla greeted pleasantly, as she neared her husband's side.

"Hi, Babe." Kelley greeted, giving her a kiss.

"Good morning, Darla." Frank greeted.

"Preacher, I guess it is goodbye for now."

"You take care, Frank. You have my telephone number, so call anytime. Read your Bible and you will be in my prayers." Kelley assured.

"Thank you." Frank replied, his face pale, as he appeared weak.

"It has been a pleasure knowing you Darla."

"Thank you, Frank. I assure you, the feeling is mutual."

Sitting in a wheelchair, a nurse pushed Kelley through the hall. Darla hurried ahead to move her car near the hospital entrance.

"I did not think about the difficulty you will have getting in this compact car." Darla said concern on her face as Kelley slowly and carefully stood up.

"You should not have wrecked the station wagon." He teased forcing a weak smile, as he slowly neared the car.

"I should have borrowed Mother's car." Darla replied, going to her husband's side to assist him.

"I am okay, Babe. I can manage." He insisted in his independent manner.

Darla glanced at the nurse as they both doubted Kelley would manage alone. His face was flushed and tense from the pain as he finally seated his tall frame inside the car. The nurse looked at Darla, shaking her head with disapproval.

"You have your work cut out for you." The nurse whispered, sympathetic.

"I see this." Darla replied with concern on her face.

Kelley silently sat in the car with his eyes closed as though fearing if he moved another muscle, he would not be able to endure the added pain.

"Kelley." Darla spoke as she closed the passenger door for him.

"Let us go home, Babe." He said, barely above a whisper, with his eyes still closed.

Darla silently went to the driver's side. Kelley remained silent for several blocks. Opening his eyes, Kelley glanced at his wife as she drove, he seeing her concerns for him.

"May I hold your hand, Miss Darla?" He asked forcing a weak smile in hopes to ease her concerns.

"Yes, you may." Darla answered, she also forcing a smile as she attempted to conceal her concerns.

"Frank accepted the Lord last night."

"Great, some good came out of you being in the hospital."

"Yes, it did. Frank is not expected to live much longer. Thank God he will be going to heaven when his time does come." Kelley now stared out the window as Darla turned onto the country road that would take them home. With each bump the small car hit, pain seemed to shoot through Kelley's body. Darla drove slow and careful, yet her attempts did not seem to ease his pain.

"Kelley, I am sorry this ride is so rough for you." Darla apologized, feeling terrible for not thinking to borrow a more suitable car.

"It cannot be helped, we are almost home."

Parking her car, Darla sat a second looking at her aching husband.

"Take a few minutes to catch your breath, Honey." Darla suggested, gently wiping the perspiration from Kelley's forehead.

"Perhaps we should trade your mother cars, should we attempt a ride in the near future. I am baffled how such a normal doing still seems to zap me of my strength."

"Honey, your body has been through a great trauma. It will take time for you to feel as you should. As you know, it is a miracle you are even here. Please be patient with yourself. You are making excellent progress." Darla encouraged, wiping his forehead once again.

Getting out of the car, Darla unlocked the back door propping it open. Returning to the car, she opened Kelley's door, placing a kitchen chair on the ground next to the car seat.

"Kel, it will be more difficult getting out on your ribs then getting in the car. Slide unto the chair when you are ready and then take your legs out of the car." She instructed.

Kelley carefully did as instructed. He sat on the chair for some time, remaining silent.

"Use the car door to pull yourself up and I will help."

"I will manage." Kelley assured.

Darla's face flushed with Kelley refusing her assistance. Now standing, Kelley took his crutch from his wife. He stood looking at the distance between himself and the back door. His expression clearly showed he questioned if he could make the walk.

"I will be right behind you with the chair. If you need to rest, you rest."

"I will try to make it." Kelley insisted as he slowly began to walk.

"I never realized how uneven this ground is before."

Almost to the door, Kelley looked at his wife, his color turning white.

"Sit down, Kelley." She ordered, quickly assisting him onto the chair.

"I am sorry, Babe." Kelley said, closing his eyes.

Darla went inside the house, quickly soaking a hand towel in cold water. Returning to her husband, she placed it around his neck. His face had broken out with perspiration.

"Kelley, I do not expect, nor do I wish to hear you apologize anymore. The facts are you are not well and you will accept my help. I am giving the orders. If you are not able to put aside your pride so we may get you well together, then I will take you back to the hospital where you will be forced to accept help from others. You might as well decide now before we go any further." Darla insisted.

"Dar, I want to be home with you and the kids."

"Then you will accept my help?" Darla questioned, looking into her husband's eyes.

"You are leaving me with no choice."

"No, you have the choice. Which way will you decide?"

"I said I want to be home. It isn't easy for me to burden you." He answered as though embarrassed.

"Neither is it easy for me when you treat me as if I am a child and reject my assistance. I am a big girl and I will not break, Honey." Darla assured, looking into Kelley's eyes with tenderness and understanding.

"You are the boss, Babe." Kelley agreed with watery eyes.

Darla's heart was deeply moved. She knew this was one of the most difficult tests he had been put through. He, like his father, felt it a terrible weakness to lean on their wives. Wives in his eyes were to be pampered, protected, and unburdened by their husbands. Darla kissed her husband's lips.

"I am so glad you are home, Kelley." She informed with a comforting smile.

"Let us get you inside."

Resting again halfway between the back door and bedroom, Darla quickly prepared the bed for her husband. After rearranging pillows several times, Kelley was able to rest.

The first few days of Kelley's convalescing at home were difficult on everyone. It was difficult for Kelley giving in, allowing his wife to care for him. Visitors were in and out of their home daily to visit Kelley. Their visits often disrupting Darla's work schedule, mealtime and family time. The children disliked having their time with Kelley limited, which often caused hurt feelings within them, making Darla's parenting role more hectic. Due to her pregnancy, she was becoming irritable easily. She was gaining weight much sooner than she had when she was pregnant with Heaven. This was irritating to her. She was finding it difficult to fit into her clothes.

With the children in school, no visitors for Kelley yet, Darla entered the den. Turning the stereo on, Darla relaxed on the sofa enjoying the gospel music and time of brief resting. Kelley was busy in the bedroom doing his exercise to lengthen his legs and arms.

"Are you okay, Darla?" Kelley questioned, as he arrived at her side.

"Yes, I am catching a break before your many visitors arrive." She shared with a tender smile.

"It should not be much longer, Babe, and I will be fully recuperated. Then I will give you a vacation. I thought I would send you to Chicago to visit Sonja after I return to work and get our finances straightened out."

"Sweetheart, I do not need a vacation. I have only one request, for you to get well so we are able to be a complete family again. I do appreciate your thoughts though." Darla replied, now sitting up on the sofa.

"I could use some of your special attention. Come, sit down."

Kelley sat down next to his wife, taking her hand in his. Darla rested her head on her husband's shoulder, allowing him to sooth her hair, pampering her.

"Babe, it is not necessary for you to continue sleeping on the rollaway bed. Other than my ribs, my pain is gone."

"I will not take the chance of me bumping you during the night causing you added pain. When you have absolutely no pain, I will gladly give up the rollaway bed." Darla replied, looking into her husband's gentle eyes.

"Gladly." She repeated with a gentle smile.

Kelley kissed his wife several times until interrupted by the ringing of the telephone.

"I will answer the telephone, you relax." Kelley offered.

Going to his desk, Kelley answered the telephone. With only a few comments made on Kelley's part, Darla knew the caller was from the insurance company.

Getting up from the sofa, she went to her husband's side, leaning against his desk. Kelley looked into his wife's eyes with disapproval clearly on his face. Darla patiently held his stare calmly, yet silently expressing she was prepared to stand her ground.

"As you say, my wife has been overseer of my affairs. I will converse with her and get back with you. Thank you, Sir. Goodbye." Kelley spoke.

Putting the telephone down, Kelley looked at his wife.

"May I please see the papers the insurance company has given you?"

"Of course."

Unlocking the bottom drawer to Kelley's desk, Darla removed the papers along with their checking and savings books. She quietly waited Kelley's response.

"Why did you go behind my back agreeing to this? This is not what I told Bill to do." Kelley said, fully irritated.

"I did not go behind your back; I simply took charge where you failed to do so."

Kelley's face flushed with his wife's response, only bringing more irritability to him by her accusation.

"I agreed to what was right by you, in regards to your wage loss and what was right by your family. Your pride does not pay the bills, Honey."

"So I am prideful? I appreciate the compliment." Kelley snapped, leaning back in his chair, picking the papers up again, re-reading them, and silently trying to calm himself. Darla remained silent, not wanting to add fuel to the fire. Kelley now picked up the checkbook. Opening it, he discovered a check made out to him from the insurance company.

"What is this for?" He questioned, as though in shock.

"To purchase another car. You will have to take care of the picking and choosing to replace our car. That check is only made out to you."

"I am surprised you did not find a way to take care of this without my knowledge." Kelley said as he looked over their checkbook.

"Honestly, Kelley." Darla scolded sternly, attracting Kelley's full attention by her tone.

"I did what was necessary and right. If you have a problem seeing that the Lord has supplied our needs regardless of your misfortune, then it is your problem alone to deal with. I will not allow you to make me feel guilty. I will not apologize for looking out for this family's best interest. The Lord has even presented you with the opportunity to be eligible to adopt the boys and have our own child. Surely you have not forgotten we requested this financial need to be met."

Kelley rubbed his head wearily, yet remained silent. Darla now was silently awaiting a response. With none offered, she released a sigh and quietly left the room.

Darla changed her slacks for a pair of jeans. Leaving her home, she saddled her horse. She rode for some time, calming herself, re-evaluating her doings and Kelley's ways. She knew Kelley was at home doing the same, searching his heart for what was right regardless of self's ideas. After an hour and a half of slowly allowing her horse to walk at a slow pace, Kelley approached in his car.

"Hello, beautiful." Kelley greeted pleasantly as he remained in his car.

"Hi." Darla greeted with a smile.

"I normally have lunch with my wife at this hour. I promise to control my tongue if you will join me."

"I will consider your invitation after I ask you one question."

"Ask your question." Kelley encouraged in his calm manner.

"Why are you driving when you know you are not supposed to yet?"

"I missed my wife and her nagging, scolding ways." Kelley answered, bringing a laugh from her.

"I will meet you at home, please park the car."

"Yes, Ma'am."

Kelley was standing near the corral leaning against the fence when Darla arrived on Princess. As she neared the corral, he opened the gate for her to enter.

"Thank you."

"You are welcome."

"What would you like for lunch?" Darla inquired as she dismounted.

"A couple of tacos if you do not mind driving into town for lunch."

"I do not mind." Darla agreed, removing the saddle from her horse.

Leaving the corral, Kelley put his arms around his wife.

"I apologize for being short with you and for being prideful." Kelley said sincerely.

"Your apology is accepted."

"Thank you. May I treat you to lunch now?" Kelley asked, now taking her hand into his.

"You may, as soon as I change and freshen up. I will not be long."

Darla drove her and her husband to their favorite Mexican restaurant.

"It feels good to be out around people." Kelley said as they briefly conversed with acquaintances as they entered the restaurant.

"I am sure it does, you have been isolated for so long. Do you still intend to try and sit through church this evening?"

"Yes, Ma'am. If I feel up to it, Pastor Finks wants me to preach Sunday night."

"Do not push yourself before you are ready, Kelley." Darla advised concern on her young face.

"I am going stir crazy, Babe."

"I am aware of this, I live with you." Darla reminded, bringing a smile to her husband's face.

"I have tried to conceal my restlessness. You seem to catch me every time I try to fulfill it." He confessed with a grin.

"Tom tried to warn me that you hear and see all." He added with a laugh, his face turning red. Darla smiled at her husband's confession.

"You see the doctor Friday. Hopefully he will have good news for us." Darla encouraged in her gentle way.

"Hi." Candy greeted, Darla's high school girlfriend.

"Hi, Candy." Darla greeted pleasantly.

"How are you, Miss Candy?" Kelley questioned as Candy placed glasses of water before the couple.

"I cannot complain. Tom tells me you are doing much better. He says you are able to play catch with him now." Darla looked at her husband as though in shock. Kelley's face turned its reddest.

"I take it Kelley is not supposed to be playing catch?" Candy questioned blushing with innocently letting the cat out of the bag.

"He most certainly is not." Darla answered, surprised at her husband's doings.

"Sorry, Kelly, I have my girlfriend's best interest at heart." Candy said.

"Your apology is not accepted." Kelley replied with a chuckle, bringing a laugh from Candy.

"As Darla says, 'be sure your sins will find you out.'" Candy teased.

"Would you take our orders please? You have caused me enough trouble." Kelley suggested with an embarrassed laugh, knowing his wife was upset with him again.

"This definitely is not my day." He added with a grin, looking at his wife as though to say, 'I am guilty as charged, please spare me the lecture.' With their lunch orders given, Candy left their table.

"Kelley Peterson!"

"Honey please, I am still feeling guilty from my actions this morning. Let us have a nice lunch."

Darla looked into her husband's eyes. Though her expression clearly showed her concerns in regards to his ribs mending, she remained silent.

"I thought we might look at station wagons after lunch." He informed.

"We really do need to do this, so we can give Mother's car back." Darla replied.

Though Darla conversed with her husband, she remained preoccupied. She so desperately wanted Kelley to obey every rule, so the doctor would release him. She disliked not being able to share her news with him of their baby.

Darla was overly quiet as she and Kelley looked at automobiles to replace their station wagon that had been wrecked. Driving toward home, Kelley was also quiet. He respected his wife's right to her silence. He knew she was concerned with his health. Darla remained quiet through the remainder of the day. Her face looked drained as she allowed her concerns to consume her.

Arriving at church for the Wednesday night service, Kelley was surrounded by many welcoming his return. Darla pleasantly greeted several and then made her way to the pew where her daughters were already sitting. Tom, Pete and Bobbie sat on the pew in front of her with two of Tom's friends. Kelley joined Darla's side as the service time neared.

"Kelley." Spoke Pastor Finks.

"Do you feel up to leading testimonies?"

Kelley glanced at his wife with eagerness on his face. Darla looked away from her husband.

"I best wait and see if I am able to sit through a service first." Kelley answered, though hesitant in his decision.

Kelley managed to stand as long as the congregation did. He appeared to do fine sitting until the sermon began. Darla secretly noted his face growing tense from the position he was forced to sit in. Heaven got up from the end of her parents' pew, as did Karry. Karry sat down next to Darla, leaning her head against Darla, as she grew tired. Heaven started to pass her mother.

"Where are you going, dear?" Darla asked in a whisper.

"I want to ask Daddy something."

Darla kindly moved her legs so Heaven could get past her to Kelley.

"Daddy, may I sit on your lap?" Heaven asked, whispering in her father's ear.

"Sure, Princess." Kelley put his hands around Heaven's waist intending to lift his six and a half-year-old daughter.

Darla quickly put her hand on Kelley's wrist, bringing both his and Heaven's eyes on her as though surprised at her.

"Kelley, do not lift her." Darla scolded.

Silently, with flushed cheeks, Kelley removed his hands from Heaven's waist not wanting to upset his wife further.

"Heaven, sit here by Daddy." Darla suggested moving down, allowing her room to sit between her parents.

"Daddy lets me sit on his lap." Heaven complained, still standing.

"Sit down now." Darla ordered sternly. Heaven did as ordered.

Darla felt drained as she now stared at her open Bible. She felt she was fighting a losing battle in assisting her husband to a complete recovery. It was as though her every effort was in vain. Her own children were working against her efforts and Kelley allowed them. Finally calming herself, she returned her eyes toward the pastor. As Heaven grew sleepy, she leaned against her daddy's side, causing him to flinch as her weight pressed against the side of his ribs. Darla and Kelley exchanged glances.

"I will have her move, Dar." Kelley assured quickly, understanding his wife's concerns.

"Princess, put your head on my lap." Kelley instructed.

By Friday, Darla felt she was a bundle of nerves. She often felt like crying or snapping at Kelley or the children. She was finding it difficult to remain patient and understanding with the tiniest unimportant happening.

Patiently waiting in the waiting room of Kelley's doctor's office, Darla desperately tried to calm her feeling of irritability. She was sure Kelley would not be released from the doctor's care with this visit, yet she wanted to believe he would be released. Kelley returned walking even slower than he was walking when arriving at the doctor's office.

"Two more weeks, Mrs. Peterson providing Kelley does not lift a finger. See to it he obeys doctor's orders this time." The nurse advised.

"Okay." Darla replied, appearing as though she was already defeated.

"I am sorry, Babe." Kelley started as they left the doctor's office.

"Kelley, I warned you. Why is it you pay no attention to my opinions?" Darla asked, her eyes filling with tears as she got inside their car.

"Darla, I know you warned me and your opinions are important to me. I have been foolish. I am not able to erase what is done. I will back off from doing things I should not have done yet with the kids. It is difficult to tell them no when they have asked so little from me. I will do as both you and the doctor say. I honestly want these injuries healed as much as you do." Kelley assured, rubbing his wife's shoulder to comfort her as she drove.

"I do understand why you have done things you should not have done with the kids, Honey. It has been nearly three months since your accident. I need you to be well." Darla said wiping her tears away as she glanced at her husband with tenderness on her face.

"I am becoming unbearable."

"A bit short at times, but not unbearable, Babe. I have

unintentionally caused most of your upsets. I will correct my mistakes. I assure you this."

Beginning dinner preparations early for their coming guests, Darla again became abnormally nervous for no apparent reason. She hoped the children and Kelley stayed out of her way. She did not want to be rude, snapping at them and hurting their feelings.

"Hi, Deary." Mom Roberts greeted, as she entered the kitchen through the back door.

"Hi, Mother." Darla greeted pleasantly. Did Dad have a safe trip to Los Angeles?"

"Yes, he called me before I left the office. Dinner smells good."

"Thank you. It will be ready shortly."

"Hello, Mom Roberts." Kelley greeted slowly entering the kitchen.

"Hi, Kelley. You are walking slower?" She questioned concerned.

"The doctor tightened the wrap around my ribs. I should be better in a couple more weeks."

"Dar, would you like the girls to help you? You look tired."

"No, thank you. My patience is wearing thin. It will be best if I avoid everyone as much as possible." She answered honestly.

"I appreciate the warning." Kelley replied, bringing a smile to his wife's face.

"I am in the doghouse with my wife. I best exit while I am still able." He added with a grin, causing Darla to blush.

"Your face does look flushed. Are you coming down with something?" Mom Robert's inquired, as Kelley left the kitchen.

"No, Mother, I am pregnant." Darla whispered with a pleased smile.

"Kelley does not know?" Mom Roberts questioned, surprised with her daughter's secret.

"No, I want to tell him more than anything. Yet if I do before he is completely well, he will try to do everything he can to help me. This would delay his healing even longer. I am so nervous over the tiniest thing. I was not like this when I was pregnant with Heaven.

I am gaining weight much sooner too. I will not be able to fit into my clothing much longer."

"Darla, tell Kelley. It is not wise to be easily upset and your husband not understand why. You did not have five children and an injured husband when you were carrying Heaven. You only had yourself to look after."

"I almost told him today. I became terribly upset when the doctor did not release him. I literally wanted to have a tantrum and this just isn't me, Mother."

"How long have you known about your pregnancy?"

"Since Kelley's accident. I was going to tell him when he returned from work that evening." Darla answered with watery eyes.

"Kelley and I had been trying to have a child for the longest time. The very day I learn I can tell him, making him the happiest man in the world, he nearly dies." She shared, as her tears were released.

"Sweetheart, you truly are a strong woman." Mom Roberts said, putting her arms around her daughter and hugging her.

"Get your cry out, Deary, you are long overdue."

"Mommy..." Karry started, stopping quickly in her tracks.

"Mommy needs Daddy, Karry. Will you get him please?" Grandma Roberts asked.

"Yes, Ma'am." Karry answered, running from the kitchen.

Kelley arrived alone with concern on his face.

"Your wife needs you." Mom Roberts informed, removing her arms from around her sobbing daughter.

Kelley put his arms around his wife, yet looked at his mother-in-law questioning.

"Darla is four months pregnant. She learned this the day of your accident. That was to be the day of you hearing this."

"Darla." Kelley said, laying his head on hers as he held her.

"I wish I had known, Sweetheart."

"Have you known this?" Kelley asked, looking at his mother-in-law.

"No, I just learned this myself." Mom Roberts answered, wiping her tears away.

"This is why she is extra nervous."

"I am sorry, Babe. You have been through four months of a second pregnancy alone. We were supposed to share this together from day one, Sweetheart." Kelley said soothing her until calming her sobbing.

"I have five more months for you to endure my moodiness with me." Darla said with a soft laugh, as she looked into Kelley's eyes with sparkles in her eyes though her tears continued.

"We are having a child." Kelley said pleased.

"Yes, maybe even a son." Darla answered with a radiant smile.

"Are you happy?"

"I'm more than happy. This is a dream come true. This is fantastic. I cannot wait to tell the world." Kelley answered with an excited laugh, bringing laughter from both his wife and mother-in-law.

"Now I know why you have picked up weight."

"You noticed." Darla said, surprised.

"I do notice you, wife." Kelley informed, bringing a tickled laugh from Darla, she blushing in her mother's presence.

"Six years of marriage and you still blush?"

"You have said more than enough, husband." Darla warned, with a nervous laugh, not trusting him to quiet his line of talk as she removed his handkerchief from his back pocket.

"I only carry handkerchiefs for Darla." Kelley informed, smiling at his mother-in-law.

"Kelley, are you telling me you make my daughter cry often?" Mom Roberts questioned, putting her arm around Darla's waist.

"No, Ma'am. You will never hear me say this." Kelley answered quickly, bringing smiles to the women's faces.

It was a joyous evening in the Peterson home. Immediately following dinner, Kelley called each of their relatives sharing their exciting news. He was as an excited boy at Christmas time. Darla felt a tremendous burden lift from her shoulders now that she had shared her secret with her husband. She proudly displayed the tiny nursery she had decorated also in secret with her mother and husband.

"Good morning, sleepyhead." Kelley greeted, placing a breakfast tray next to his wife's roll-a-way bed.

"Kelley..." Darla started with a sigh and then grew quiet.

"Darla, I did not make breakfast." Kelley informed, sitting down on the bed and then giving her a kiss.

"Mom and Dad came early to have breakfast with us. Mom insisted you be pampered this morning. I have no problem with this. My wish is to pamper you every day of your life." Kelley shared, quickly relieving her concern.

"I do not intend to upset you again by breaking rules. I am anxious to return to work to support my son you are carrying. I do not wish my wife anymore upset. I have caused you enough to last a lifetime." He assured with tenderness in his voice and sincerity on his face.

Darla put her arms around her husband's waist. She looked into his eyes with sparkles in her eyes, with a radiant smile.

"As you said, everything will be back to normal in our home soon. It seems Satan will stop at nothing in his attempts to destroy Christians. What a fool he is. He cannot withstand our Master. When you were in the hospital, I realized most thought I was overreacting, perhaps too emotional. There was a spiritual warfare going on for your life, Kelley. I had to obey the scriptures. I had to send up the prayers and I had to believe God's word in healing you. God truly honors obedience. We, you and I, will continue our fight as a team. We are on the winning team." Darla shared in all sincerity.

"You bet we are. Are you sure you have not missed your calling to be a minister?"

"I am a minister. I minister to my husband and children daily. Have you not noticed my nagging?" Darla asked with a soft laugh, bringing a grin to her husband's face.

"I have noticed you promoting obedience, Babe." He answered, setting her breakfast before her, removing his cup of coffee from her tray.

"Thank you for always making my ways sound special; I love it when you pamper me. This is just one of the many benefits I have with being your wife. I wish every wife was as fortunate as me."

Their Saturday was a refreshing day. Mom, Dad Peterson, and fifteen-year-old Matt spent, the day with their son and his family. Aaron arrived near noon, he also sharing in the joyous event of Darla being with child. Darla was ordered to take the day off. She was loved and pampered by each one present. Kelley had Aaron and Matt remove Heaven's baby furniture from the attic, arranging the furniture in the nursery under Darla's supervision. Kelley even insisted the boxes with Heaven's baby clothes be brought down from the attic. Mom Peterson and Darla excitedly went through the clothes, separating what could pass as boys clothing from the frilly girl outfits.

"Make sure you only leave out clothing that is appropriate for a boy." Kelley said, as he and the guys now joined the women and girls in the front room.

"We are having a son, wife."

"Kelley, if Darla has a baby girl, will you give the baby away like Karry's mother did her?" Seven and a half-year-old Bobbie questioned.

"That is a dumb question, Bobbie." Pete remarked, shaking his head at his brother.

"It is not." Bobbie defended, aggravated at his brother.

"Alright guys, calm down." Kelley instructed.

"Pete, Bobbie was speaking to me."

"Sorry." Pete apologized.

"Bobbie, if Darla has a girl, I will gladly accept her." Kelley answered, quickly relieving his foster son's concerns.

"Our dad wants to give us away." Bobbie informed, his knowledge surprising all present.

"Who told you this?" Kelley asked, his heart going out to the three brothers.

"Tom did. Our dad wrote him a letter and said he doesn't want us."

"Then you, Pete and Tom will have to live with us. We did not want you to leave anyway." Darla said with a tender smile.

"Really?" Bobbie questioned with an excited grin.

"Kelley." Darla said.

"Yes, really." Kelley agreed, tousling Bobbie's hair as he sat on the carpet near his foster dad's feet.

"I told you Kelley would never make us leave." Pete said, letting out a sigh, once again shaking his head at his brother.

"Daddy, are you going to make the boys Petersons like you did me?" Seven-year-old Karry questioned.

The three brothers looked at Kelley in silence. Their young faces expressed their eagerness and yearning to be permanent family members.

"Perhaps the boys and I will discuss their wishes in private sometime soon." Kelley answered winking at the boys, bringing hopeful smiles to their faces.

"How many kids do you intend to have?" Aaron asked, surprised at his brother's suggestion.

"However many the Lord requires of us to train in His ways."

"When do you intend to settle down, Aaron?" Darla asked.

"You have been out of college for some time." She added.

"I enjoy my bachelorhood. I like being foot loose and fancy free." He answered in his happy go lucky manner.

"He also likes living off his father and building a bank account." Dad Peterson informed, bringing laughter from the adults.

"Dad, you taught me the importance of saving." Aaron reminded, bringing a chuckle from his Irish father.

"Now I understand where Kelley gets his conservativeness." Darla sided, smiling at her father-in-law.

"Uncle Aaron would you play Darla's guitar for us?" Tom asked.

Aaron gladly entertained his family with his superb musical talent. He seemed to make the guitar strings dance. Tom was soon playing his guitar with his Uncle and Pete with his drums. Karry, Heaven and Bobbie clapped their hands in time with the music.

Darla welcomed the busy activity Sunday mornings brought in her home, as her family dressed in their best to attend the Lord's house.

"Babe, we are going to be late." Kelley informed as he entered their bedroom.

"I am hurrying. I have tried four dresses on and they are each too tight." Darla explained.

"Apparently your son is going to be a big boy."

"As Dad would say, 'a strapping lad.'" Kelley replied with a pleased grin, as he politely zipped the zipper on his wife's dress for her.

Kelley managed to sit through Sunday school class with little discomfort. Attending the morning worship service directly following Sunday school, Darla noted midway through the service Kelley's face growing tense from his prolonged sitting. This was his first attempt attending Sunday services since his accident.

"Will you be able to endure the entire service?" Darla questioned in a whisper, concern on her young face.

"I will make it, I have endured worse." Kelley answered, putting his arm around his wife's shoulders to comfort her from her concerns.

Returning home from church, Kelley rested while Darla prepared their Sunday dinner. Kelley appeared to feel better when joining his family at the dinner table. After dinner, he spent some time at his desk with his Bible open before him. When growing weary of his sitting position, he stood with his Bible in his hand, engrossed in his reading.

"You look like a preacher." Darla said with a gentle smile, as she entered the den.

"Are you speaking this evening?"

"I thought I would give it a try." Kelley answered, briefly taking his eyes from his reading as his wife leaned against his desk.

"You will remember our agreement, right?" Darla questioned

in her slow, gentle manner, putting her arm around her husband's waist.

"Yes, Ma'am."

"Will your parents be visiting the service to hear their son?"

"Probably."

"I believe I will make a dessert in case your parents visit after the service." Darla informed.

"This is not necessary, Babe. The remainder of the cake we had earlier for dessert will be fine." Kelley assured.

"I would rather you rest."

"Your boys and Tom's friend Roger with the bottomless pit for a stomach just finished off the cake." Darla informed with a tender smile.

"I will make my dessert and allow you to return to your studies." Darla gave her husband a quick, light kiss and then left his side.

Darla had a sense of excitement within her as she arrived for Sunday evening services with Kelley and her children. Other than Kelley's slow walk to remind her he was not entirely recuperated, she knew Kelley would soon be in full charge. Kelley greeted several in the congregation, as did Darla before the service began. It pleased her to see her in-laws sitting with her parents. Not only would Kelley receive his parents' support, but they also were enjoying spending a service with their dear friends of many years. Bill, Paula, Dan and Cindy sat together in the pew behind Darla. She felt privileged to have her family both near and supportive through everything. She and Kelley were blessed with loving and devoted families.

Kelley reverently joined Pastor Finks on the platform. Darla silently sat on her pew now with Karry and Heaven at her side. The boys silently sat on the pew in front of Darla. Each had their eyes on Pastor Finks as he neared the pulpit to begin the service. Kelley silently sat through the song service. Darla assumed Kelley was saving his strength for his message he would bring forth shortly by not singing.

As the song service ended, the song leader left the pulpit. Pastor

Finks once again went to the pulpit. Instructing the congregation to stand, Pastor Finks lead them in prayer.

"You may be seated." He instructed.

"How many have missed Brother Kelley?"

Several raised their hands and others answered 'Amen'.

"Amen." The pastor agreed.

"Kelley, come minister unto us."

Kelley walked slowly to the pulpit. Laying his Bible on the pulpit, he stood tall and straight, as he looked out over the congregation.

"Thank you. It feels great to be able to be in the house of the Lord."

"Amen, Amen."

"I want to thank each of you for your weeks of prayers and visiting me in both the hospital and in my home. I am incapable of thanking you enough."

"I assured my wife I would speak only this evening, not preach. Since I intended to speak on obedience, I best hasten to her advice." Kelley informed with a grin.

"Sweetheart, come join me briefly."

Darla looked at her husband as though puzzled, yet did as he requested.

"While my wife is coming, I would like to say Mom and Dad, it is good to have you in the service this evening."

"Amen." Pastor Finks said.

As Darla joined Kelley, she whispered and then silently stood. Kelley grinned at his wife and then looked at the congregation, as he put his arm around her waist.

"Darla has just informed me I best not embarrass her." Kelley shared bringing flushed cheeks and a tickled laugh to Darla, as the congregation laughed with Kelley's teasing.

"The Lord continuously blesses Darla and me." Kelley said his face growing serious now.

"Yes." Darla agreed.

"Darla and I have always had our needs supplied. We have had the desires of our hearts granted."

"Sometime before my accident, my wife and I decided to have a child. We are pleased to share that Darla is four months with child. Come May, I shall be granted the desire of my heart." Kelley shared, pleased.

The congregation was extremely happy for the young couple.

"Thank you, Babe."

Darla left the platform, returning to her pew, sitting next to her daughters.

"When my brother visited my family and me yesterday, he inquired as to how many children my wife and I intend to parent. My response was, 'however many the Lord chooses.'"

"Yes, Amen." Pastor Finks said as well as several in the congregation.

"I do not choose my occupation, my Heavenly Father does. I choose whether I will be obedient or disobedient in obeying our Father's orders. As Christians, we are commanded to be obedient."

"Amen, Amen."

"The older I become, the more I appreciate both my parents and my in-laws for enforcing obedience from my wife and myself during our youth. Being raised to have an obedient nature makes one's walk with the Lord easier."

"A few weeks before my accident, my wife and I were faced with a decision that would affect our future. In my inner search questioning, the Lord for His perfect will, I in my conservative nature, questioned what I was sure was the Lord's will. I questioned due to our financial funds not being what I felt was adequate before making my decision. When discussing this matter with my wife, she suggested perhaps the Lord was testing our faith, our obedience without hesitation. Several days passed and I felt assured the Lord's wishes in this decision. I removed the necessary forms from my desk to find my wife had already signed her signature. In the blanks requiring income information, my wife had lightly written for my benefit, 'the Lord will supply our needs.'"

"Amen, Amen."

"We are to be obedient to God's holy word in its entirety. Not just a small portion of the word and not just when we feel one-hundred percent comfortable. Our daily Christian walk is by faith. When I left for work four months ago, my family nor I had the slightest idea I would be involved in an auto accident. I believe my wife being obedient to the Lord according to the scriptures, the Lord spared my life."

"Amen." Pastor Finks said.

Kelley slowly leaned against the pulpit as he began to tire and then looked out over the congregation.

"My wife is not a large person or a boisterous person. She does know her Bible and she is obedient unto the Lord. The scriptures she recites as needed are more powerful than if a giant were speaking, these scriptures, the word of Almighty God." Kelley said with power in his voice.

"Amen, Amen!"

"I lie for several days not responding to my wife or my mother or whoever was at my side. I recall most of the talk around me. I recall hearing my petite wife demand that she was in charge of my spiritual and mental well-being. Darla knew prayer, faith, and obedience in the word was all she had to pull her husband back. Faith in Christ Jesus' stripes He bore that we might be healed. She had to believe the scripture. The doctor stood by my bed and told my wife, 'I will not give you false hope. I do not know whether your husband will have brain damage or not.' My wife said, 'He will be okay.' Her faith and her obedience unto the Lord daily, allowed her to collect on the Lord's promises."

"Yes, Amen." Pastor Finks agreed.

"We must instill obedience in our children. We must be self-disciplined as adults, lest our flesh sidetrack us from the leading of the Holy Spirit. We must be as children unto their biological parents. We, children of our Heavenly Father, must be obedient."

"Preach it brother."

Kelley looked at his notes as he removed his handkerchief from his pocket, wiping the perspiration from his face, as he silently calmed the excitement within him, controlling the urge to preach hard instead of speaking.

"During the past several months, I have been greatly ministered unto. I have been granted the opportunity to stand still, listen, observe, learn and apply to Kelley's character. My wife's brother and I have an understanding about Darla." Kelley started, his face flushed as he released a chuckle.

"She has a special talent with words. In a few brief words, she is capable of telling you how wonderful you are or how foolish you are."

The congregation laughed. Darla's face turned its reddest. She held her hand at the side of her face as not to allow anyone to see her embarrassment, as she shook her head at her husband, clearly expressing her disapproval.

"Amen, preacher." Bill agreed, causing the congregation to laugh once again.

Darla felt each of her children's eyes on her with their daddy and uncle's teasing. She silently stared at her open Bible on her lap, avoiding all eye contact.

"Bill." Paula scolded in a whisper from the pew behind Darla.

"Bill, I am the bearer of bad news. Again, this unique way Darla has with words is scriptural. Let your talk be yea or nay. Amen?" Kelley questioned, his face quickly growing serious again.

"Amen! Amen, brother!"

"In my days of convalescence being still and learning, my helpmate automatically took charge in areas I normally would have dealt with. In doing so, Darla was forced to make a few decisions in my behalf. My wife, being stubbornly obedient unto the Lord, made a couple of choices in decisions, knowing I would disagree. As I began to recuperate and discovered these decisions had been made, I expressed my disapproval to her. She patiently, in her gentle way, attempted to explain her reasoning. I was not hearing her. I disagreed merely because her choice was not my choice. I am the head of the house. My choice had to be right. Are you hearing me out there?" Kelley questioned, looking into the faces of the congregation.

"My choice was wrong. My choice was made while thinking in the flesh. My wife's choices however, were made due to being obedient unto the Lord. Regardless our position, perhaps you have many years of wisdom. If we fail to be one-hundred percent in tune with the Lord through prayer and if we fail to read God's holy word, lacking the knowledge, we will each at some point in time be disobedient."

"Amen."

"You see folks, being obedient to God overrules all rules."

"Amen!"

"As I prepare to close, my advice to each of us is this." Kelley started; pausing as he once again wiped the perspiration from his face with his handkerchief.

Returning his handkerchief to his suit coat pocket, he once again leaned against the pulpit, supporting his tiring body.

"Let us search our hearts. Have we allowed self-pride to blur our vision of the Lord's rules for our daily walk with Him? Have we allowed our position within our individual homes, on the job, in society, within the church, to take preference over obedience in our lives? Perhaps some have forgotten, regardless if your position entitles you to leadership, whom the 'boss' and the 'leader' are. Have you become as though 'the blind leading the blind', simply because your pride wishes to be in charge? Your pride wishes to make each decision? Disobedience? It is extremely dangerous folks. We must continually examine ourselves. Being obedient allows our Master to increase and self to decrease. Seek only the ways of our Lord." Kelley encouraged sincerity on his young, strong face.

"Praise God." Kelley said, as he slowly left the pulpit, going to Pastor Fink's side on the platform whispering to him.

Kelley remained near the chairs where Pastor Finks had sat with his eyes closed in prayer. Pastor Finks went to the pulpit. With the close of Pastor Fink's prayer, Kelley slowly sat down closing his eyes in prayer. Pastor Finks quietly walked to those whom knelt in prayer. He encouraged the older Christians to go to the alters and pray with others. Darla, as did Sister Finks, prayed with the women at the altar that seemed overly burdened.

CHAPTER SEVEN

Springtime had arrived. Flowers were blooming; the grass was once again a pretty green. A time of new birth. The Peterson children witnessed the beautiful miracle of the birth of baby chicks as they were hatched. They witnessed the wonderfulness of the birth of the four tiny kittens Katie's cat had. A beautiful experience of new birth and new beginnings.

Dressed for a busy Friday morning in dress slacks, a delicate maternity blouse and dress shoes, Darla stood in front of her full-length mirror.

"You look beautiful." Kelley complimented as he completed dressing, putting his arms around his wife lovingly.

"Thank you." Darla replied turning around to face her husband.

Slipping her arms around his waist, she looked up into her husband's eyes with sparkles in her eyes.

"You look most handsome. I am hoping our son looks like his daddy." She happily shared, bringing a pleased expression to her husband's face. Kelley put his hand on his wife's stomach.

"How do you feel this morning, Babe?"

"Slightly overweight." She answered with a soft laugh.

"Only four more weeks and you will be slim and trim again. I for one am finding it difficult to contain the excitement of wanting to see and hold our child."

"Me too." Darla agreed her face radiant with happiness.

With the five children ready for school, Kelley prayed for protection and guidance for his family during their day. Kisses exchanged, Kelley watched as the children went to the bus stop and boarded the bus, while Darla went to her room for her purse. Returning to the kitchen, Darla turned the light out and locked the back door.

"Mom, the kids are waving goodbye." Kelley informed as the bus slowly pulled away. Darla quickly waved goodbye before the bus disappeared. Now going to the family car, Kelley politely opened the car door for his wife.

"It will be nice having Katie home for spring break." Darla said as Kelley backed their car out of the drive.

"A few more weeks and Katie will be graduating from college. She will be home for good, Babe."

"I have been looking forward to this for a long time."

"I will be glad to have a telephone bill without long distance calls on it. I have been looking forward to this day for a few years." Kelley shared with a chuckle as he drove toward the big city of San Diego, bringing an understanding smile from his wife.

"Please do not share this with our Katie. She will feel forever indebted to us if you do. Although, we have been her parents for nearly seven years, she still finds it difficult to burden us."

"I assure you Dar; my comment will remain between you and me."

Vacating the parking garage, Darla excitedly put her arm around Kelley's arm as he escorted her to the airport terminal their foster daughter would be arriving at shortly.

"Oh, Kelley, our Katie is all grown-up." Darla voiced barely above a whisper, as Katie entered the airport from her flight.

"Yes, she is." Kelley agreed, pride in his eyes as well as his wife's.

"I am surprised she doesn't have a boyfriend."

Kelley now escorted his wife toward the approaching passengers.

Holding his hand up to attract Katie's attention as she neared the crowd of awaiting friends and family members. Katie's face expressed her happiness with spotting her father. In her patient, lady-like manner, she slowly made her way through the crowd to her God-given parents.

"Welcome home, Sweetheart." Darla greeted excitedly as she hugged her eldest daughter.

"Thank you." Katie replied happily, as she remained in Darla's embrace hugging her tightly in return.

"Katie, do I get a hug?"

"Of course." She answered with an excited laugh, quickly pulling away from her mother, giving her father a hug.

"You have been dearly missed, Babe." Kelley assured.

"Thank you." Katie replied with happy, moist eyes.

"I have missed you and Mom terribly." She shared blushing as though sharing a forbidden secret.

"You will be a graduate soon and home for good." Kelley comforted with pride in his eyes as he kindly relieved Katie of her tote bag.

"You are a beautiful young woman." Darla complimented in a whisper as they began their walk to leave the terminal. She lovingly put her arm around Katie's waist. Katie silently smiled at her mother. Her compliment warming her heart. This seemed to be her God-given parents' specialty; making others feels special.

With Katie's luggage loaded in the car, Kelley opened first the back door for Katie, politely closing the door behind her. Opening the front door for his wife, he secondly assisted her inside the car.

"Mom, are you sure you have four more weeks until the baby arrives?" Katie questioned as Kelley walked around the car to the driver's side.

"According to my doctor. It would not offend me in the least if he were wrong. I would not mind delivering early. I have been overweight long enough, not to mention a bit short with my family once or twice."

"Honey, once or twice?" Kelley questioned with a grin, though his expression was as he was scolding his wife for telling an untruth.

Darla laughed, her face turning its reddest. Katie smiled at her parents' well-mannered and loving, honest ways. They had an air about them that made one feel pure and innocent of all sin when sharing their company.

"I have been difficult, Katie. Bear with me, Sweetheart, if you witness my patience wearing thin during your vacation. Had Dad known I would have spells of no patience, he probably would have decided against he and I having this child." Darla said, giving Katie a tender smile.

"Honey, you know better." Kelley scolded, glancing at his wife as he briefly took his eyes from his driving.

"I have waited three years for this child. Do not imply I may have regrets."

"I take it back. Katie, scratch my remark." Darla said with a soft laugh, blushing with her husband's scolding.

"Perhaps I should be still, dear." Darla said looking at Katie.

"I am getting deeper and deeper in trouble with Dad."

"Perhaps this is wise." Kelley agreed with disapproval in his voice, bringing tickled laughter from both women.

Darla kindly put her hand on her husband's shoulder, as to call a truce. Nearing the outskirts of San Diego, the three adults were silent shortly, observing the beautiful mountain scenery.

"Mom in your last letter you said you intend to be at my graduation. I will not be offended if you do not make the trip. I know Dad is concerned with you traveling near your due date."

"Whom may I ask informed you of Dad's concerns?"

"Aunt Cindy."

"Aunt Cindy had no right to burden you with this. Besides, if the doctor is right, the baby will be 2-4 weeks of age by your graduation date. Dad and I had thoroughly discussed my attending your graduation before I sent you the letter. Your family will be there for you." Darla informed.

"Right, Dad?" Darla questioned, looking at her husband for support.

"Right." Kelley assured.

"Aunt Cindy has been known to speak when she should be silent."

"Uncle Dan used to say this also." Katie replied, with an understanding smile.

"I am afraid Uncle Dan is still saying this, Babe." Kelley said with a chuckle, bringing smiles to the women's faces.

Arriving in their hometown of Ragweed, Kelley pulled into the parking lot of Katie's favorite restaurant as the lunch hour was upon them.

Kelley sat across from his wife and daughter as they waited for a server to approach their table.

"I have been granted a job in Japan for a year upon graduation." Katie informed.

"Japan?" Darla asked, her face clearly expressing her concerns.

"Yes. I will be teaching at a mission orphanage. The pay is nothing to speak of. I believe the work will be both challenging and rewarding. It will also be a terrific history lesson." Katie shared, pleased.

"We thought you would come home. Your dream has been to work here with the street people. Why the change of heart?" Darla asked.

"I have always enjoyed seeing and learning first hand of other places. This is a fantastic opportunity. I will still be involved in a work for the Lord. I and one other person were chosen from the Bible College. I accepted the offer for a year of duty."

"Oh, Katie." Darla said, releasing a long sigh. I wish you would have discussed this with Dad and me."

"I honestly thought you would be pleased, Mom." Katie shared, searching her mother's eyes with hers, her face now flushed with knowing she disapproved.

"I believe Mom is confused, Babe. Frankly, I am confused."

Kelley informed, his expression also bearing his concerns, though his voice was calm and gentle.

"You have shared openly for the past several years the Lord has called you to work in the park ministry. Are you saying the lord has changed His mind?"

"No, I do intend to return to the park ministry. I do still believe this is the Lord's chosen work for me. Surely, one year in Japan, in a Christian work is acceptable though. It is an opportunity of a lifetime for me."

"Mom, Dad, I will not be going alone. The Lord will be with me." She assured, bringing relaxed expressions to her parents faces.

"I do not go anywhere that the Lord is not with me."

"This gives me great comfort." Kelley replied with a pleased smile.

"I guess I am forced to wait another year before I can be selfish with you." Darla said with a weak smile. Though she worried with her daughter's news, she also understood her adventurous nature. She too wanted Katie to feel she had her support. Katie excitedly explained her adventurous missionary plans with her parents as they now listened attentively.

Darla enjoyed having Katie home for spring break. She was both a joy and a help, quite often insisting on relieving Darla of her duties so she could rest. Katie enjoyed pampering her mother.

Darla seemed to work in slow motion as she and the girls did dinner dishes. She seemed to tire quickly as she approached her baby's due date.

"Mommy, when are we getting our baby?" Heaven asked excitedly as she and Karry dried the dishes.

"It could be any day now, Deary. The sooner the better." Darla answered with a tender smile.

"May we hold the baby?" Karry questioned just as excited as her sister.

"Of course you may."

"Daddy said he intends to be stingy with the baby." Karry informed.

"Daddy was teasing, Sweetheart." Darla assured.

"Bobbie says Daddy will not have much time for us after the baby comes." Heaven informed, looking up into her mother's eyes awaiting her opinion.

"Bobbie is wrong. Daddy will have the same amount of time for each of you as he has now."

"I think Bobbie thinks Daddy will like the baby better then him." Karry shared, feeling sorry for her foster brother.

"I think Bobbie feels left out sometimes because he is a foster son and not a Peterson."

"Have you girls shared your thoughts with Dad?" Darla asked as she removed the stopper from the sink.

"We are not tattletales." Karry answered.

Darla removed a paper towel from the roll. Dampening it with cold water, she put it across the back of her neck. Her cheeks flushed, she slowly went to the kitchen table, sitting down.

"Are you okay Mommy?" Heaven questioned quickly.

"I am okay, Deary." Darla answered, forcing a weak smile.

"I will inform Daddy of Bobbie's concerns. Karry, if someone is hurting it is okay to repeat what another says. You should tell either Dad or me in private as not to embarrass the person that is hurting. If no one knows another is hurting, then no one will know to make the person feel better, right?"

"Right, Mommy."

"Why not offer to help Bobbie with his chores? I am sure your kindness will make him feel better."

With the girls outside to offer their assistance to their brother, Darla slowly got up from the table. She felt tremendous pressure in her lower stomach as she slowly left the kitchen for the den. Entering the den, Darla sat down at her husband's desk. Picking up the telephone, she dialed her chosen number.

"Hello." Dad Roberts answered in his husky, cheery way, bringing a smile to Darla's face with his manner.

"Hi, Daddy." Darla greeted.

"You sound happy." She added.

"Why, of course. We Christian folk are never supposed to have a bad, or should I say a sad, moment. Am I right?"

"I will say you understand people very well." Darla answered with a pleasant smile.

"How are you, Babe?"

"Miserably overweight. I feel like my stomach is about to explode." She answered with a soft laugh.

"You have five more days until your due date. Do you think you will deliver early?"

"Yes, actually I have thought all day I would begin labor, but I have not as yet; perhaps another day or two."

"You sound tired. Would you like Mom to come give you a hand?"

"No, thank you. Kelley and the children are tending to the chores as we speak. I had this sudden loneliness to call my parents and hear their voices."

"Sweetheart, you know you may return home whenever you would like. In doing so, leave your army of children with your husband. Mom and I are getting too old for the parenting role of young children." Dad Roberts replied with a chuckle, bringing a soft laugh from his daughter, quickly fading her lonely feeling.

"You always know how to uplift my spirits. Have I told you lately I love and appreciate you?" Darla asked with a weary smile, yet tenderness in her voice, as she leaned back against her husband's chair.

Kelley entered the den as Darla's father answered her question. He patiently stood near his wife with concern on his face. Darla now bore an expression of concern, her relaxed smile no longer present as she wondered what was troubling her husband. She looked into his eyes, searching his eyes with hers.

"Daddy, Kelley has come in. May I call you later?" She inquired politely.

"Sure, Babe. You call regardless of the hour when you have your first labor pain."

"I promise, I will." Darla agreed, pleased with her father's orders.

Putting the telephone down, Darla returned her eyes to her husband's troubled face.

"The girls said you are not feeling well." Kelley informed.

"I am tired, but I am okay, Honey. I did not tell the girls I feel ill." Darla assured, gently taking her husband's hand into hers to calm him of his concerns.

"Dar, your face is flushed."

"I know. I should have left the dishes for you to do. I am tiring so quickly. Surely our baby is soon in arriving." Darla shared with a weary smile, her explanation relaxing her husband's face. With his hand remaining in his wife's, Kelley sat on the edge of his desk.

"You have not had any labor pains then?"

"No, although, I keep praying for them to begin." She answered with a soft laugh.

"My arms long to hold our child." She added.

Darla's words touched Kelley's heart. His face now expressed the pride he felt with being both husband and father.

"Perhaps my overprotective husband will tend to the milk and eggs as the boys bring them in?"

"I will be glad to. I will also make your prayer my prayer. I too am longing to see our baby." Kelley said with sparkles in his eyes as he spoke of the special moment he held dear to his heart.

"Do request from our Lord the labor pains not be too painful. Since we are asking, why not ask big?"

"I know of no reason not to." Kelley answered, tightening his hand on his wife's as to comfort her.

The girls and Bobbie entered the den. Turning on the television, the children sat down on the floor to watch their half-hour program.

"Did the girls tell you of their concerns for Bobbie?"

"Yes. I will talk with him before bedtime. Karry seems to think if we adopt Bobbie, changing his last name to Peterson as ours, all Bobbie's worries will vanish." Kelley shared with a gentle smile.

"I do believe your Irish father has sprinkled magic dust on Karry. She believes in the Peterson name wholeheartedly as he does."

"Perhaps." Kelley replied with a tickled laugh with his wife's suggestion.

The three youngest children momentarily turned their eyes from the television program, glancing at Kelley with his laughter. They silently smiled at one another, turning back to their program.

"If you will excuse me wife, I will tend to the milk and eggs." Kelley gave his wife a quick kiss and then left the room.

Darla started to pick the telephone up when Pete entered the room, approaching her.

"Hi, kiddo." Darla greeted with a pleasant smile, returning the telephone back to its cradle.

"Hi." Pete replied hesitant, his face flushed as he put his hands in his front pockets of his jeans.

Darla was silent for a few moments, awaiting her foster son to share with her his apparent burden.

"Peter, what is troubling you, Deary?" Darla inquired in her gentle, patient way.

Pete's expression quickly changed from burden to shock. His mouth flew open and his eyes grew moist.

"Honey, what is wrong?" His foster mother questioned, quickly putting her arm around his shoulders, drawing him closer to her.

"You have never called me Peter before." The bewildered child said, looking into his foster mother's eyes.

Darla patiently searched Pete's eyes with hers, as she waited for him to explain, as she knew he would.

"My mom would call me Peter when she knew something was bothering me or if I was in trouble." He added with a half-grin, his face flushed.

Pete remained with his hands in his pockets as Darla remained with her arm lovingly around his shoulders. He continued to look in her eyes as though he had seen a ghost from the past.

"If you would rather I not call you Peter again, I will not. I never want you to feel as though I am trying to take your mother's place."

"I do not care if you call me Peter. Besides, Mom is in heaven.

I kinda need a mom now, one that I am able to see and touch. I get kinda lonesome sometimes since Mom went to heaven.

"I am sure you do." Darla said, her eyes filling with tears as her heart was touched by the young boy's sorrow.

"Darla, do you think Tom, Bob and I are okay kids? I mean, we are not horrible, are we?" Pete asked nervously.

"Yes, I know you are okay kids. No, you by no means are horrible. You are very good boys. I know your mother must be very proud of each of you." Darla answered with a tender smile, as she quickly caught her tears, wiping them away before they could escape.

"Why are you asking this? I and Kel thought you understood that we are proud of you and your brothers."

"Bobbie and I heard Grandma Roberts say you and Kel have too many kids." Pete answered slowly, not wanting to tattle or share he had heard a conversation that was not meant for he or his brother to hear.

"Oh..." Darla released a sigh. Her face now looked sad and drained, as she now understood the fear the two brothers secretly harbored. They had fear of non-acceptance because they were not a blood relative and the fear of a permanent home and permanent family because they were foster children. Little, young Karry understood these fears.

"How wise you are, Karry." Darla thought as her tears came more quickly, soon managing to escape, making their way down Darla's cheeks.

"Honey, I assure you, Grandma did not intend for you boys to hear this. She loves you each very much. Surely you know she loves you, right?"

"Yes." Pete answered his face flushed again for doubting his foster grandmother's love. Pete lowered his head, no longer looking at his foster mother.

"Did you hear any other comments by accident?" Darla asked, pulling Pete even closer to her side as she silently comforted him by her gesture.

"No, Ma'am."

"You know, Kelley is forever teasing me for worrying when you boys play football. He says I worry most of the time before there is a need or a reason to worry. My worrying never seems to stop you or your brothers or Kelley. You rough guys ignore my wishes and do as you please because this is what you enjoy. Am I right?"

"Yes." Pete answered, raising his head up, looking into his foster mother's eyes.

"Sometimes, I really become aggravated because Kelley deliberately ignores my wishes. You know this, but this disagreeing does not change the love between any of us. Grandma worries I will become ill. She feels I have too many children, too large of a home to care for, too many activities I am involved in. Grandma and Grandpa worried before I even became a mother or Kelley and I married. They worried when I was your age, as I worry over each of you now. Though Grandma worries, she still loves each of you very much. She does not wish any of you to leave this family. In fact, I know she would take you each home with her before she would allow any of you to not have a home."

"Even if all us kids drive Grandma crazy?" Pete asked with a big grin, as though surprised.

"Yes." Darla answered with a soft laugh.

"Although I am sure Uncle Bill and Grandpa Peterson would feel left out if Grandma Roberts had you children all to herself." Pete grinned his biggest grin. His self-confidence in his place with his foster family had been restored.

"Foster moms need hugs as much as foster sons. Are you game?" Darla asked with a tender smile.

Pete hugged Darla's neck tight, as she hugged him in return.

"Kel and I love you, Sweetheart, with all our hearts. Do not ever question this." Darla whispered in Pete's ear as she hugged him for a very long time, allowing him to freely take her love for him, to replace the empty spot within, from his biological mother's absence. As Darla and Pete removed their arms from one another's embrace, Darla noted Kelley quietly standing in the doorway, observing each member of his family.

"I will tell Bobbie you are not sending us away." Pete informed excited.

"You may do this after you do your homework. In addition, here on out, I demand at least one hug from my children each day. This helps me get through my rough moments also. Do we have a deal?"

"Yes." Pete answered with a pleased grin.

"My Mom would tell us this."

Darla smiled at Pete, knowing her ways that were as his mother's, meant the world to him. She lovingly patted him on his back.

"You had best get to your homework. I believe Kel is checking up on each of us." Darla whispered.

"I am out of here." Pete replied in his humorous manner, bringing a laugh from Darla.

"Excuse me, Kelley. I have homework to do." Pete informed politely, as he reached the doorway where Kelley silently stood.

Pete glanced over his shoulder at his foster mother as Kelley stepped aside, allowing him to exit. Darla smiled at Pete as he in his cleverness handled his foster dad.

"Kids, turn the television off." Darla instructed as she got up from her husband's desk, starting for the sofa.

"Mommy, we want to watch this program." Heaven informed and then quickly turned her eyes back on the television set.

Darla sat down on the sofa, untying her tennis shoes.

"Kids..."

"Please, Darla?" Bobbie questioned, interrupting Darla.

"Perhaps the three of you would like to express your wishes to Dad." Darla suggested her voice stern now.

The three children quickly turned around noticing Kelley's presence for the first time. Karry quickly got up from the floor to begin her piano practice. Heaven lingered, keeping her eyes on the television set, wanting to catch every second possible of the program. Bobbie turned the set off and then started for his room to do his homework. Heaven departed behind Bobbie to take her bath.

Darla lay down on the sofa, resting her weary body from her

busy day. Kelley silently went to his desk. It was not long before she was sleeping soundly.

"Darla." Kelley spoke as he gently soothed her hair, awaking her.

"The kids are ready for bed." He informed, as Darla sleepily looked at her husband.

"What time is it?" Darla questioned, holding her hand out toward her husband for him to assist her up.

"Nine, I prepared your bath water."

"Thank you." Darla replied slipping her arm around her husband's waist as the young couple vacated the den.

Entering the girl's room, Kelley and Darla prayed with the girls and then tucked them in their beds for the night.

Entering the boy's room, the couple repeated their nightly ritual as with the girls. With each of the children securely tucked in their separate beds for the night, Darla took a leisurely bath.

Leaving the shower room across the hall from the bathroom, Kelley knocked on the bathroom door.

"Are you okay, Sweetheart?" He inquired.

"Yes, thank you." Darla answered, removing the stopper from the tub.

Dressed for bed and the bathroom tidy, Darla left the bathroom. Entering her bedroom, she removed her robe, slipping under the covers.

Kelley politely put the book aside he was reading while lying in bed. Darla snuggled close to her husband, laying her head on his chest.

"Still no sign of labor pains?" Kelley inquired, putting his arm around her shoulders lovingly.

"No, you must pray harder, dear." Darla answered pleasantly.

"Yes, Ma'am, I will."

Another day had come and gone with still no sign of labor beginning. It was a beautiful Thursday morning in early May. Awaking early before the alarm rang, Darla turned off the alarm, quietly vacating her bedroom. She felt extra excitement within. She quietly walked through her home while her family was fast asleep. She checked each room, mentally making notes of her day of house cleaning. Entering the laundry room, she checked the hamper, sorted the clothes and then started the washing machine. Returning to the kitchen, the percolator finished producing coffee; she poured herself a cup of coffee, and then left the kitchen. Going to the corral with her cup of coffee in hand, she silently admired the beauty of the sun rising. The family horse and pony soon made their way toward her wanting to be petted and noticed. She gently and lovingly petted first the pony and then the horse.

"Good morning." Bill greeted as he approached, riding a bicycle.

"Good morning. I was not aware your exercising began this early."

"I am much like my sister. I adore seeing the sunrise along with the early hour only hearing the sounds of nature."

"You and I are blessed, dearest brother." Darla said in her slow, gentle manner, slipping her arm through her brother's arm as he stood near her.

"Do you recall Mother teaching us the beauty in the sun rising and setting?" She asked, looking up into her brother's eyes with sparkles in hers and a happy, radiant glow about her face.

"I remember. Mom seemed to see the beauty of God in every act of creation." Bill answered with a pleased smile as he recalled their childhood days.

"Mother taught us so much. She could make the impossible sound simple and possible."

"I recall, 'there is no such word as can't.'" Bill said with a chuckle.

"I confess I doubted Mom's advice as a teenager."

"Mother taught us strength to endure all and the beauty in everything. Dad, by simply being his child, made one feel safe, secure and loved. I do not recall ever questioning our parents' love for us. Did you ever question?"

"No." Bill answered, looking down at his sister.

"Why are you dealing with our parents' ways this morning? Is there a problem I have not been made aware of?"

"No, I am simply counting my blessings by appreciating having loving Christian parents. Karry's past, Katie's and the boy's past, as well as their present, often remind me how blessed you and I have been from our birth. You do realize we are blessed, right?" Darla inquired, her face growing serious as she quickly looked up into her brother's eyes.

"Yes, preacher, I realize." Bill answered bringing a tickled laugh from his sister.

"You do keep in mind the early hour. Conversing and sharing I am able to deal with. Do not deliver me a sermon of any kind at this hour. If you attempt in doing so, being a bit older than you, I will pull rank on you without hesitation."

"I promise, besides my husband is the preacher." Darla reminded with a smile.

"Sis, you have been preaching since you began talking." Bill informed, bringing laughter from his sister again, his remark causing her to blush.

"Good morning." Kelley greeted, approaching with two cups of coffee.

"Good morning." Bill greeted cheerfully as Kelley joined he and his wife, handing his brother-in-law a cup of coffee.

"Good morning, Honey." Darla greeted with a happy smile and then greeted her husband with a kiss.

"Did you sleep well?"

"Yes, thank you. Did you?"

"Yes, I would sleep much better if junior were here with us. He must weigh ten pounds." Darla answered with a soft laugh. Kelley put his arm around his wife's waist.

"I think you are just as beautiful now, Babe, as before you gained weight due to junior." Kelley said with genuine pride in his eyes.

"In fact, I think you are more beautiful now."

"Why is it Kel, our wives do not seem to see the beauty in being with child?"

"Wife, you are giving your brother a false impression of how you truly feel. Perhaps you should clarify his question." Kelley suggested.

"Truly Bill, I do see, understand and feel the specialness and beauty of conceiving my husband's child." Darla shared.

Putting her arm around Kelley's waist, she looked up into his eyes with sparkles in her eyes.

"This child represents the endless and abundance of love Kelley and I have toward one another. The stretch marks I will be left with after the birth of this child, I will never forgive you for, Kelley." She added with a tickled laugh, bringing laughter from both men, as she surprised them with her added comment.

With Bill on his way, the Peterson couple returned inside their home. Kelley woke the children while Darla began breakfast preparations. Kelley assisted the children with their outdoor chores as most weekday mornings. Chores completed and the children dressed for school, the family met at the breakfast table for breakfast.

"Honey, I would appreciate your assistance this morning after the children leave for school." Darla informed, pushing her saucer of uneaten toast aside.

"You want the kids to ride the bus this morning?" Kelley questioned, secretly concealing his suspicions of his wife beginning labor in front of the children.

"Yes, please." She answered as she slowly leaned back against her chair, concealing her reasoning.

"Go brush your teeth, kids." Kelley instructed, anxious to have a moment alone with his wife.

Kelley began the dishwater as each child took their dishes to the sink, before leaving the kitchen. As the last child left the kitchen, Kelley looked at his wife with eagerness on his face.

"I have had two labor pains." Darla shared in a whisper.

"I do not know how long before the pains are close enough to leave for the hospital. Perhaps soon, or perhaps not for several hours. I would like for you to stay with me."

"I want to be with you, Babe." Kelley agreed, quickly going to her side, taking her hand in his.

"I love you, Dar." He said as he already began showing his nervousness.

"I love you, Honey. I am fine, remain calm and do not worry."

"I will try to do as you wish."

"We may call our parents after the children leave for school if you would like." Darla suggested with a gentle smile to ease her husband's nervousness.

"I will be thrilled to call them." Kelley assured with excitement in his voice, bringing a pleased smile to his wife's face.

Hugs and kisses given to the five children, Darla and Kelley watched at the back door until the last child had boarded the bus for school.

"How do you feel now, Babe?" Kelley questioned with the departure of the school bus.

"Like I will be giving birth to our child sometime today." She answered with a child-like excited laugh as she put her arms around her husband's waist, giving him a tight hug.

Kelley hugged his wife in return until she loosened her arms around his waist. Now looking up into her husband's gentle, protecting face, Darla stood on her tiptoes giving him a kiss.

"You are the best father and husband in the world. I will always cherish this special time."

"So will I, Sweetheart. You are a beautiful lady." Kelley said with a look of one romantically in love, as he kissed his wife long and gently.

Removing his lips from his wife's, Kelley looked into her eyes.

"May I please call our parents before our dads leave for their jobs?"

"Yes, you may."

Darla began washing a skillet breakfast, as Kelley dialed the telephone.

"Dar, do not do the clean-up. Please sit down." Kelley instructed as he held the telephone to his ear.

"I am fine, Honey. I will do what I am able to do. The time will pass more quickly." She replied as she continued the task before her.

With Kelley on the telephone, Darla leaned against the sink as another pain came. As the pain left, she took a deep breath and then let out a sigh. This pain was definitely harder. She glanced at the clock on the kitchen wall to time her pains, as she now hurried to complete washing the stove top.

"Darla, your mother says for you to either sit or lie with your feet propped up." Kelley informed as he held the telephone to his ear.

"I am a nurse, Kelley, I know how I feel." Darla replied in a low voice so her mother would not overhear her, as she completed her task.

Putting the telephone down, Kelley went to his wife's side as she now began to dry the pans.

"Honey, humor me please." Kelley said, taking the dishtowel from his wife's hand.

"No more working, come sit down on the sofa. Our parents will be here soon. If I am not pampering you when our parents arrive, I will be in serious trouble by each parent. I want this special time to be pleasant for myself as well as our families."

"Yes, dear." Darla agreed with an understanding smile, bringing some relief to Kelley's face.

He escorted her to the sofa in the front room. Sitting down on the sofa, Kelley politely brought the ottoman close. Darla obediently propped her feet up as her mother had instructed.

"Come sit with me, Kelley while we have this time alone."

Kelley politely sat down by his wife, putting his arm around her shoulders.

"Gladly." He agreed with a boyish grin and then kissed his wife causing her to blush with his play.

"Oh, oh." Darla said barely above a whisper as a labor pain came.

"Dar." Kelley said, his face turning white, he not knowing what to do.

Darla closed her eyes tightly and squeezed Kelley's hand until the pain passed.

"I forgot how painful child bearing is." She said with flushed cheeks.

"I am sorry you must endure pain, Princess." Kelley said gently soothing his wife.

"When we get to heaven, be sure and give Eve a piece of your mind for me." Darla replied with a soft laugh, hoping to ease her husband's concern for her.

"This I will do, Angel." He agreed kissing the top of her head.

"Anyone home?" Dad Roberts questioned from the kitchen.

"We are here." Kelley answered. Darla's parents entered the front room.

"Are you ready to go to the hospital, Babe?" Dad Roberts questioned.

"Not yet, have a seat Daddy."

"How close are your pains, dear?" Mom Roberts inquired, sitting next to her daughter patting her on her leg.

"Twenty minutes apart. I will leave for the hospital when the pains are five minutes apart."

"Do you have a name picked out for my granddaughter, Kelley?" Dad Roberts questioned with a grin, teasing his son-in-law.

"No, I assure you, you will be granted a grandson not a granddaughter." Kelley answered politely.

"You are hoping, anyway." Dad Roberts replied with a chuckle, bringing smiles to each one's face.

"Do you have your suitcase ready for the hospital, dear?"

"Yes, Mother. It has been ready for two weeks." She confessed with a weary smile as a labor pain began again.

Slowly resting her head on Kelley's shoulder, she once again closed her eyes, squeezing her husband's hand until the pain had left. Opening her eyes, her parents' and husband's eyes were on her.

"Darla, why not lie down, dear?" Mom Roberts questioned, getting up from the sofa to make more room for her daughter.

"Mother, please come sit down. I am fine as I am. I would like you to be near. This is our special time as well as Kelley's and mine." Mom Roberts silently returned to her daughter's side.

Darla lovingly held her mother's hand with her free hand, giving her a tender smile.

"I cheated you and Dad out of being part of Heaven's birth and I will never forgive myself for that. Stay near my side even if I become unbearable."

"I will, Sweetheart." Mom Roberts agreed with watery eyes as her daughter touched her heart.

"I was expecting to see my grandson when my wife and I arrived." Dad Peterson informed as he and Kelley's mother entered the front room with expressions of pride on their faces.

"Dar's Dad seems to think you will gain another granddaughter, Dad." Kelley informed, surprising Dad Peterson with this knowledge.

"Do not dare sic your father onto me." Dad Roberts scolded, as though threatening Kelley, bringing laughter from each.

"Miss Darla, how are you doing, Honey?" Dad Peterson questioned in his protecting way, his strong face expressing tenderness and his voice gentleness.

"Anxious to have this child, Sir." Darla answered with a pleasant smile.

"Yes, of course, Missy." He replied, understanding.

"Excuse me, please." Darla said, getting up from the sofa quickly, hurrying from the room.

"Honey?" Kelley questioned springing to his feet.

"I will go with her, Kelley." Mom Roberts offered, hurrying after her daughter.

Entering the bathroom behind her daughter, Darla stood bent over the toilet stool vomiting.

"Mom Roberts?" Kelley questioned, his face clearly expressing his worries.

"I am sure Darla will be okay, dear. I would put her suitcase in the car. When she has freshened up, I suggest you not allow her to delay going to the hospital any longer."

"Yes, Ma'am." Kelley agreed.

Kelley immediately left the bathroom door for his wife's suitcase.

"Mother." Darla started as she washed her face.

"Did you or Kelley call Bill and Cindy?"

"Dad did this for Kelley. I thought they both would be here by now."

With her face washed and teeth brushed, Darla slowly sat down on the toilet stool.

"I suddenly do not feel so well, Mother. I did not become ill with Heaven." Darla informed, looking into her mother's eyes, her voice sounding troubled.

"It is very seldom a mother has two births alike. Am I right? You are the nurse."

"Yes." Darla answered with a weary smile.

"Perhaps Kelley should take me to the hospital now."

"I will help you to your feet."

"I will assist her, Mom." Kelley offered politely as he returned to the bathroom. Darla bit her tongue, concealing the pain, as her labor pains were extremely hard now and much closer together.

"Kelley, not so fast, please." Darla said with watery eyes, as they neared the kitchen.

"I am sorry." He apologized, his face flushed by his wife's scolding as he slowed his pace.

"Ignore my sarcasm, you are the greatest. I am simply a grouch at present." Darla replied, glancing up, looking into her husband's frightened face. Her heart now went out to him, seeing his fear.

"I will be okay, Sweetheart. A bit of discomfort and then we will have our beautiful child."

"Our son." Kelley corrected with a comforting smile as they neared their car. Though tears were now streaming down Darla's face from the intense pain, she laughed at her husband's correction.

"I do not care if we have four sons, I just want this over." Darla said with a soft laugh, as Kelley assisted her inside the car.

"Yes, Ma'am, we are off to the hospital."

"Kel, where is Mother?" Darla questioned before he could close her car door.

"In her car with your dad."

"Do you mind if she rides with us? It would mean the world to her."

"I do not mind, Babe. I will get her."

Kelley returned to the car with his mother-in-law. Darla moved to the middle of the front seat, making room for her mother.

"I am counting on you to keep me in line, Mother. I have already snapped at my husband, hurting his feelings." Darla shared with a weak smile, taking her mother's hand into hers.

"I know you best not snap at me." Mom Roberts warned with a soft laugh, bringing smiles from both her daughter and son-in-law, as Kelley backed their car out of their drive.

"Kel, remember when we get to the hospital not to allow the doctor or nurses to give me anything for pain."

"Why not?" Mom Roberts questioned, clearly disapproving.

"I want to have natural childbirth as I did with Heaven. I do not want any drugs. Oh, oh…" Darla said as the pain struck.

"I am hurrying, Dar." Kelley said nervously.

"Kelley, you stay within the speed limit and concentrate on your driving, Darla is fine." Mom Roberts advised.

Putting her arm around her daughter's shoulders, she kindly wiped the perspiration from her face.

"Your face is terribly warm, dear."

"It is warm today." Darla replied, leaning her head on her mother's shoulder, closing her eyes with another labor pain.

Kelley glanced at his mother-in-law, as she did him. She knew Kelley was silently questioning his wife's comment on the temperature. It was a beautiful spring day. It was nice, not warm at all. It was a perfect, cool day.

"Who took you to the hospital when Heaven was born? Surely you did not drive yourself?" Mom Roberts questioned, attempting to distract her daughter's thoughts from her pain.

"No, I arrived at the hospital in a taxi, although I could have driven. I was not in this amount of pain during my ride to the hospital with Heaven. Perhaps this baby is different because we are having a boy, Kel." Darla spoke, forcing a smile.

"I have never doubted this, Angel." Kelley agreed as he turned into the hospital entrance.

Kelley parked near the hospital doors.

"I will get a wheelchair, Babe." Kelley quickly vacated the car.

"Darla, I believe you have a temperature." Mom Roberts informed as she once again blotted the perspiration from her daughter's face.

"I know. I feel ill, Mother. Something seems wrong. Do not tell Kelley, he is already frightened. We will tell the doctor."

Kelley returned with a wheelchair. Darla felt light headed as she vacated the car. Sitting down in the wheelchair, she closed her eyes as Kelley quickly wheeled her inside the hospital. Kelley checked his wife in at the desk, as his parents and father-in-law arrived. Darla glanced at her mother. Her face, as Kelley's now bore her concerns as she harbored her daughter's secret. Darla silently reached out toward her mother, taking her hand in hers.

"Perhaps Dad could pray a quick prayer?" She asked, seeking comfort for her loved ones.

"I know Dad would feel honored." Mom Roberts answered.

"Let us get you upstairs, Mrs. Peterson." A nurse informed, as she swiftly approached Darla.

"One minute please, my dad wishes to pray first. Daddy." Darla instructed, holding her hand out to her father. Dad Roberts obediently took his daughter's hand in hers. Reverently each family member bowed his or her heads. At the close of his prayer, Dad Roberts gave his daughter a kiss on her forehead.

"Thank you, Daddy."

The ride in the wheelchair seemed rough as the nurse quickly pushed Darla toward the elevator. Darla was finding it difficult to silence the moans and groans that wanted to escape her, as her pains seemed unbearable. Her eyes were watery. Blinking hard, she desperately managed to prevent her tears from escaping. Kelley put his hand on his wife's shoulder as the elevator took them higher to the OB ward, desperately wanting to comfort her.

The hours in labor, as Darla lay in the labor room, seemed to last forever. Although Darla managed to control her tears and not snap at anyone, the pain was so intense she felt she was near losing control of her emotions. She did not want to lose control, bringing added worries to her family and husband.

"Princess, I will return. The women would like to come in." Kelley informed as he tightly held her hand in his.

"Okay. Kelley, please do not go far, I find comfort in your presence."

"Your husband will be right outside this door, Missy. I will make sure he will not be far." Dad Peterson assured, putting his arm across his eldest son's shoulders.

"He will do right by his bride."

"I know, Dad. Kelley has always done right by me." Darla replied giving her husband's hand an extra tight squeeze as she looked into his gentle, frightened face, knowing her words gave his heart the comfort and reassurance he needed to aid him through his helpless feeling.

"I love you, Princess." Kelley said, wiping the perspiration from his wife's face with a Kleenex, followed by a kiss.

Both Darla's father and father-in-law also gave her a kiss before departing. Mom Roberts, Mom Peterson and Cindy entered the labor room.

"Darla." Mom Roberts began, taking her daughter's hand into hers.

"Do take something for the pain. Why must you always feel the need to be unnecessarily brave?"

Darla did not answer her mother's question. She closed her eyes tight, flinching. She silently gripped her sheet as hard as she could. She briefly opened her eyes as she turned her head from her family's eyes, catching sight of Bill and Paula entering her room.

"Honey, do as your mother asks. You look terribly weak." Her mother-in-law encouraged.

"Surely it will not be much longer. It seems I have been here forever." Darla replied, becoming terribly restless from the pain.

"Mother, did you tell the doctor I believe there is a problem?"

She asked, as she now continuously moved first her head from side to side and then her legs, as though her restlessness was consuming her.

"Yes, I did. He said everything appeared normal except your temperature being slightly elevated."

Darla let out an irritated sigh as she rubbed her head wearily.

"Do you want me to get your doctor, dear?"

"No, perhaps I am getting too soft and old for this ordeal." She answered, releasing another sigh.

"Sis, do not speak in this manner in front of Paula or I will never have a child. You are younger than she is."

Darla momentarily glanced at her brother, he bringing a laugh from her.

"I am sorry. I feel like being spiteful. I could almost slap Kelley at this moment for wanting a child." Darla shared, with a nervous laugh, bringing both laughter and shocked expressions with Darla's liberal confession.

"If either of you repeat what I say in my time of weakness, I will deny it."

"Bill, do take Paula out of here. I do not trust your sister's further comments at this point." Mom Roberts suggested.

"Oh, oh, oh, the baby is coming." Darla said in a weakened tone, as she became extremely restless. Mom Peterson quickly went for her son.

"Kelley." She called barely above a whisper as tears began down her cheek with the added pain of the contractions.

"I am right here, Sweetheart." Kelley said, taking his wife's hand into his.

"Mother?"

"Yes, dear."

"Something is wrong, Mother. Please tell the doctor." Darla said mumbling, as she felt herself drifting into sleep.

"Darla." The doctor spoke in a demanding tone, as he shook her, noting her weakness as he arrived.

"Yes?" She questioned, fighting to open her eyes.

"You have a baby wanting to be born. Come on, hang in there, I need your help. You may sleep later."

"Keep her talking." He instructed.

Darla felt herself being pushed in her bed into another room. She heard both her mother's voice and Kelley's continuously speaking to her. It seemed several people were busily moving around the room in white coats. She barely felt a needle going into her arm. She was not sure what was happening around her, yet she felt safe. She heard her mother's voice, her husband's voice and she felt big strong arms around her. She knew the arms belonged to Jesus. She felt a peace and she knew everything would be okay now, for her Jesus was in control of her well-being.

"Push Darla." The doctor ordered as though he was angry to get her attention as she fought sleep.

"Push, Princess, our baby is almost here." Kelley encouraged as he held his wife's hand and gently soothed her hair.

"Once more, Sweetheart and you may rest." Mom Roberts encouraged.

Darla did as her mother instructed. She faintly heard a baby cry.

"A handsome baby boy." The doctor reported. Darla felt happiness flood her heart.

"Sleep now, Princess." Kelley said and then gave his wife a kiss on her forehead.

"Baby, healthy?" Darla questioned mumbling.

"Yes, our son is a strapping lad." Kelley answered with pride.

Several hours after giving birth to her child, Darla slowly opened her eyes. Feeling extremely weak, she glanced around her room.

"Hi, Princess." Kelley greeted, tightening his hand on his wife's hand.

"Congratulations, Daddy." Darla replied, barely above a whisper in her weakened state, yet with a peaceful smile on her face.

"Thank you. Thank you for the most beautiful baby in the nursery."

"You are welcome." Darla said with a weak, excited laugh, her eyes dancing with sparkles.

"Have you held our son?"

"Yes, Ma'am, and he is precious, Dar." Kelley answered with pride on his face as he lovingly soothed his wife's hair, pampering her.

"Did you doubt how precious our child would be?"

"No, I am overwhelmed by all that is involved to receive a child. I had no real understanding prior to witnessing our son's birth. This was a breath-taking experience."

"The most marvelous experience a couple is granted to share." Darla replied slowly, lifting her weakened hand once again. She gently touched Kelley's lips with her fingers.

"I for the life of me do not understand why we waited seven years to experience this wonderfulness."

"I agree this was not one of our wisest moves." Kelley said, gently kissing his wife's lips.

"Honey, what happened in the delivery room? I am disappointed I was not in charge of my faculties. I too, am aware of my terribly weakened state."

Kelley's face grew serious as his hidden pain clearly showed on his face for his precious wife's health.

"You began hemorrhaging." Kelley started, his eyes growing watery.

"You were given a blood transfusion. You were also right in your thinking you were ill. The doctor discovered a serious infection. This was why you felt warm and why your temperature was elevated. I did a lot of fast praying."

"My loving husband had to witness all of this." Darla said once again slowly lifting her weakened hand as she touched Kelley's face, her face bearing her great compassion for him.

"I vowed to be at your side in sickness as well as health, Princess." Tears came to Darla's eyes with his reply.

"Come closer so I may properly thank you."

Kelley bent over his wife as she lay in her hospital bed. Darla gently kissed his lips and then looked into his eyes, her eyes sparkling with happiness.

"Thank you for being mine."

"Sweetheart, the pleasure is most definitely mine."

"Mm, perhaps I will grant my husband a second child in a few years." Darla replied with a weakened child-like laugh, her talk bringing a smile to Kelley's face.

"Kiss me please." Kelley kissed his wife's lips gently and passionately.

"You two best not be thinking about having another child." Cindy advised as she stood just inside Darla's room. Her appearance made both Darla and Kelley blush. Their talk was private, not intended for another to hear.

"I guess I should have closed and locked the door." Kelley said, looking into his wife's eyes, she knowing how he detested others butting in. Darla's face flushed even more with Kelley's remark.

"Cindy, I say this out of love, not to be rude..." Darla started slowly.

"How many children I choose to bear is between Kelley and I, okay? This is a special time for Kel and I. We intend to enjoy each moment to its fullest as the Lord permits." Cindy's face now flushed.

"I apologize. I had no right to voice such an opinion. You gave us each a scare, Dar. We never want to lose you." Cindy explained with tear-filled eyes.

The young couple's hearts were quickly touched by hearing Cindy's pain.

"I could use a hug from my favorite cousin. I did not intend to take away from your joy."

Kelley politely let go of his wife's hand, leaving her side and making room for Cindy.

"You know me, I will accept all the hugs I am offered." Darla replied with a gentle smile.

Cindy went to her cousin's side, the two women exchanging hugs.

"I was fine, Cindy, even when my condition looked bad to each of you. Jesus had His arms around me the entire day and even presently as I speak. Actually, I was at peace in His arms, well protected and loved. Share this with my and Kelley's families. Do also tell our families not to express their concerns of my being with child in the future with Kelley. This is a special time for him and me. He is worried enough. He does not need any negative lectures or advice. Would you tell them now, please?"

"Yes." Cindy answered with an understanding smile, as she quickly wiped her tears away.

"Kelley?" Cindy questioned, looking into his face.

"Why not." Kelley answered and then gave Cindy a hug.

"If Dan has not been able to quiet you by now, no one can." He added with a grin, bringing a laugh from Cindy.

"Darla is right, Kel, you are tops. Congratulations."

"Thank you." Kelley replied, his face now serious, yet tender.

Cindy was still wiping tears from her face as she left her cousin's room.

"Honey, I want to see our son. Please see if they will bring him for a few minutes." Darla suggested with excitement in her voice.

"You look terribly weak and tired, Baby." Kelley replied concern on his face as he held his wife's hand once again.

"I just want to touch him and give him a kiss. I then will be able to sleep like a baby." She shared with a weak smile.

As Kelley left his wife's room wanting to fulfil her every wish, Darla's parents, in-laws and Cindy entered her room. When Kelley returned with a bundle in his arms followed by a nurse, everyone's face seemed to light up. The nurse slowly raised the head of Darla's bed.

"Look who I have, Mom." Kelley said his face radiant with happiness.

"Oh, Kelley, he is beautiful."

"Hi, Sweetheart, Mommy loves you." Darla said, holding her son's tiny hand as Kelley held him close to her.

"We want to take our baby and go home now." Darla informed

with a child-like laugh, as she glanced at the nurse, her honesty bringing understanding smiles to everyone.

"When you regain your strength, Ma'am. He is a beautiful baby and he is the picture of health." The nurse noted.

"Thank you, he takes after his daddy." Darla said, smiling at her husband, her words bringing a pleased smile to his face.

"I will be in the hall. Five more minutes please and then you must rest, Mrs. Peterson." The nurse instructed.

"We will leave now, Son. This is your time and Miss Darla's time." Dad Peterson informed.

With his statement, each relative gave hugs and kisses and then left the young couple alone with their baby.

"Are you a proud Daddy?" Darla asked happily, slipping her fingers through her husband's hair.

"The proudest ever." Kelley answered with a boyish grin as he looked into his infant son's face.

"Who is tending to the needs of our other five children?" Darla asked as she gently rubbed her son's tiny hand.

"Your brother and his wife. I have called home and each of the kids is equally excited as you and I."

"May I give our son a kiss before he is taken away from me?"

"Sure." Kelley held Curt close to his mother. Darla gently kissed baby Curt's tiny cheek. He soon wrinkled his nose and began to fuss.

"Oh, Sweetheart." Darla said sympathetic.

"Perhaps he is hungry, Kel. It has been hours since his birth."

"A nurse fed him earlier. You will not be able to nurse until your physical condition has improved." Kelley informed, reading his wife's thoughts.

The nurse now entered Darla's room.

"One more kiss Mom?" Kelley asked.

"Yes." Darla answered, pleased and then kissed her precious son.

Kelley stayed at his wife's side until she was sleeping soundly. Quietly leaving her room, he stopped at the nursery looking through the large window at his tiny son, also fast asleep. No longer needed at the hospital, he left for his children waiting his return home.

Within a couple of days, Darla was strong enough to hold baby Curt during feeding time. With her medication changed and on her way to a quick recovery, she was also now permitted to nurse her baby, as was her desire.

At the end of a ten-day hospital stay, she was more than thrilled to be going home to her family she so dearly missed. Sitting in the front seat of the station wagon, with Curt sleeping on his mother's lap, Kelley put his arm around his wife's shoulders.

"I broke a rule this morning. I best confess before we arrive at home."

"My husband does not break rules, he is obedient." Darla replied with a smile, bringing a chuckle from Kelley.

"What terrible act of sin have you committed behind my back? You left dirty dishes in the sink, or perhaps you left your shoes in the den?"

"I allowed the kids to stay home from school today."

"Honey, they should be in school if they are not ill." Darla scolded lightly.

"One day will not hurt. This is a special day, Baby doll. They have missed Mom terribly, not to mention they are quite eager to meet their brother." Kelley reminded, gently rubbing his wife's shoulder as he drove.

"When I was attending school, Bill and I had to be near death before we could miss."

"Sweetheart, you did not have me for a dad. I am a nice, compassionate and understanding guy." Kelley replied with an excited, boyish laugh.

"You are a softy. The kids know how to work you. If the truth was known, their skipping school was probably your idea." Darla accused, looking at her husband, searching his eyes for her answer.

"Does it matter whose idea it was?" Kelley asked with flushed cheeks and a tickled laugh.

"No, the issue is you confessed to rule breaking." Darla answered with an understanding smile.

"I suppose you have also approved a day of party?"

"The party is the kid's idea. They have prepared you a special lunch."

"Aye, no more hospital food." Darla said with a pleased smile.

Excitement arose in Darla as they neared their home. The children eagerly waited outside for sight of their daddy bringing their mommy and brother home.

"We each truly missed you, Mom." Kelley assured, bringing a soft excited laugh from his wife, as he turned into their drive. The kids hurried toward the car.

"I believe you." She agreed with another happy laugh as the kids now eagerly opened her car door for her.

"Mommy!" Heaven and Karry greeted excitedly giving their mommy kisses. The three foster brothers stood close behind the girls quietly, though they each had expressions of excitement also.

"May I give the boys a kiss also, girls?" Darla asked happily.

The girls quickly moved aside, allowing the boys to near Darla as she still sat in the car. Darla excitedly gave each boy a quick hug and kiss as she had her daughters. Kelley now neared his wife, carefully taking baby Curt from her.

"May we see our baby brother, Daddy?" Heaven asked excitedly.

"A quick look until we get Mom and Curt inside."

The children were fascinated with the arrival of the newest member to their family.

"Dad, would you like for me to carry Curt while you help Mom?" Eleven-year-old Tom asked. Kelley looked at his wife and then Tom.

"What do you think, Mom?" Kelley questioned hesitant with turning his ten-day-old son over to an eleven-year-old.

"I am sure Tom is quite capable of carrying Curt. They each have been practicing with dolls." Darla answered, pleased with Tom's offer.

Darla silently questioned Tom's sudden change in addressing her as Mom and Kelley as Dad, as Kelley escorted her inside their home. Sitting down in the front room, Darla happily observed as Kelley carefully allowed each child a turn holding baby Curt.

"Dad says Tom's the only kid big enough to pick Curt up all by himself." Bobbie informed as he looked at Darla carefully and proudly sitting on the sofa, taking his turn holding the baby.

"I agree with Dad." Darla said pleasantly, she now keeping her eyes on her youngest foster son, noting him also referring to her husband as Dad.

"Oh." Darla said with an excited laugh, surprising her family with her tickled laughter.

"Kelley, why are the boys calling you Dad?" She asked, putting her hand over her mouth to conceal her excitement.

"They became Peterson's a few days ago. The boys and I thought Mom and Dad sounded more appropriate. Do you have any objections?" Kelley asked, winking at the boys as he teased his wife.

"No, I have absolutely no objections." Darla answered, releasing her laughter freely now.

"This is fantastic!" She exclaimed, her eyes quickly filling with tears.

"I knew it." Bobbie said, shaking his head no, letting out a big sigh.

"What do you know?" Kelley questioned as he carefully took Curt from him.

"I knew Mom would cry. We are supposed to make her happy."

"Mommy is happy, Bobbie, those are happy tears." Karry explained, going to her mother and giving her a hug.

"Mommy always cries over us kids, even Katie and she is all grown-up. You will get used to it." Heaven shared as she now held her baby brother. Heaven's comment brought another laugh from her mother as her happy tears continued.

"Here you go, Mom." Pete offered, handing Darla some Kleenex.

"Thank you, dear." Darla accepted, blowing her nose and wiping her eyes.

"I knew Daddy would make the boys Petersons like he did me,

Mommy." Karry informed as she sat on the edge of her mother's chair as Darla held her hand.

"How did you know this? Did you pray and ask Jesus to make this happen?" Darla asked as she looked into her seven-year-old's big brown eyes and soothed her long blonde curls.

"Yes, Heaven and I prayed one of our secret prayers." She answered proudly.

"Uh, Karry!" Heaven scolded, to hush her sister.

Karry quietly put her hand over her mouth saying no more, blushing over accidentally betraying her sister by sharing their secret.

"I will tell you later in private, Mommy." Karry whispered.

"Okay." Darla agreed, whispering also, bringing a smile to Karry's face, and quickly setting her at ease.

"Dad, I thought it is rude to tell secrets in others company." Tom reminded, teasing.

"It is for us guys, but girls do it all the time. Especially your sisters and Mom." Kelley sided.

"Only in private, Daddy, Mommy said this is okay." Heaven assured as her daddy cautiously stayed at her side while she held Curt.

"I am teasing, Princess. Moms and daughters should share secrets, as should dads and sons."

"Dad, why is a guy a sissy if he chooses to tell his mom a secret instead of his dad?" Nine-year-old Pete questioned in his most serious manner.

"I have never heard this said before. Apparently you have been told this?" Kelley asked, all teasing aside, noting the heavy burden on his young son.

"Yes, Sir, by our other dad. I would not talk much to our real mom if my dad was home. He said Tom was a sissy too when he fell on his bike and Mom helped Tom." Pete answered.

"May I answer our son's question, Dad?" Darla asked her voice gentle and her face expressing her tender heart.

"Please do." Kelley answered, politely giving his bride the floor.

"Peter." Darla spoke in her slow, sensitive way, secretly touching her adopted son's heart by calling him Peter, making him feel as special as Darla truly felt he was.

"God intended for children to have a mother and a father. God gives us a mother to go to with any problem at any time, regardless whether you are a son or a daughter. God gives us a father to also go to whenever needed, whether son or daughter. Dad and I are peculiar parents, right?" Darla asked with a gentle smile.

"Yes, you are Christians." Pete agreed.

"Dad and I believe sons and daughters should always follow their heart in knowing which parent to go to. It is impossible for one to be a sissy if a son needs his mother, if God says children need a mother and a father. I would not want to argue with one as great and mighty as God myself."

"Me either." Pete agreed, in his serious manner.

"When I was very young, I was my daddy's little girl. I felt I could tell him all my secrets. As I got in junior high school, I began to share more with my mother and less with my father. Sometimes, I wanted both my parents at the same time. Each of you boys, allow your heart to be your guide. Dad and I will never call you a sissy. You have been given two parents. You choose which one of us you need and when you need us. We will be sensitive to your feelings and needs. You are our sons and we love you deeply."

"Mom, Dad says baby Curt, Tom, Pete and I are quadruplets because you got us all at the same time." Bobbie shared with a pleased grin.

"Quadruplets." Darla repeated, her eyes dancing with sparkles, as she released a soft laugh.

"I agree with Dad."

"You had best agree with me." Kelley advised with a smile, his comment bringing laughter from his family.

Shortly leaving Heaven's side, Kelley went to his wife's side.

"Welcome home, Mom. We guys have missed you and need you as much as your daughters need you." He assured, giving her a tight hug followed by a kiss.

His loving gesture brought tender smiles to his children's faces. Kelley clearly expressed by his actions as well as by his words, a mother is a unique family member. A mother is one to be honored, cherished, and pampered, and to receive comfort and love from.

With Curt safely put to bed in the basinet in his parents' room, his family went to the table for their special lunch, enjoying one another's company.

"Mom, would you like to ask the blessing?" Kelley inquired as each one took hold of their neighbor's hand.

"Yes, thank you." Each family member reverently bowed his or her head.

"Our Heavenly Father, we come before you overflowing with blessings, joy unspeakable and full of glory. We appreciate Your love and we thank You. I ask You bless this meal to the nourishment of our bodies. I thank You for allowing me these beautiful, special children to mother that have prepared this feast before us. I thank you for a healthy baby, a God-loving husband for myself and father for our children. We are incapable of loving and thanking You enough. In the name of our precious Jesus, I pray, Amen."

"Amen." Kelley said in agreement.

"Yum, our children are excellent cooks, Dad."

"Daddy helped us." Heaven informed.

"I thank you each, including Daddy for a special morning, a special lunch and a special family."

"You are welcome, Babe." Kelley replied.

"You certainly are deserving of the best, right kids?"

"Yes!" The kids exclaimed all at once, bringing a soft laugh from Darla as her eyes seemed to dance with happiness.

"Daddy, are we going to stop adding to our family now?" Karry questioned as though hopeful.

"I do not see any reason to limit our family's size." Kelley answered, winking at the kids and then glancing at his wife with a boyish grin.

"Kelley..." Darla warned with a gentle smile.

"We presently have four sons and three daughters. Most of our friends have one to three children at the most. Surely you do not want to drive your wife insane."

"Sweetheart, have you already forgotten your comment you made at the hospital when Cindy rudely interrupted us? Need I remind you?"

"No." Darla answered with a soft laugh, blushing.

"Karry, if Daddy brings anymore children home, they along with he will sleep in the barn." Darla informed as though her solution was a promise, bringing laughter from her children.

The children tucked in bed for the night, Darla went to her baby's aid. His diaper changed, she picked up her tiny son from his basinet. Sitting down in the wooden rocker Kelley had also placed at her bedside, she softly sang to her son as he nursed. Her actions, her touch, and her tone were already teaching her son a mother's love. The special children chorus she sang during nursing hour held special words of Jesus' love and Bible characters. Again, beginning immediately to teach her child to know and love Jesus."

Entering his bedroom and closing the door behind him, Kelley quietly dressed for bed as his wife continued softly singing to their son. Nearing his wife's side, shortly observing his son nursing, Darla looked in her husband's gentle face.

"I do not believe I have ever known you to be this happy and excited." Darla said in her soft, gentle way.

"I have never experienced a more beautiful and satisfying feeling as I have experienced with the birth of our son. You have fulfilled my last dream, Dar by giving me a child. You, my lovely wife, are responsible for making me happy and fulfilled." Kelley shared as he looked upon her beautiful face.

"You have just described, my love, the way I feel about you. God has truly blessed you, me and our family."

"Yes, He has." Kelley agreed in all sincerity.

Kelley gently gave his infant son a kiss on his cheek. Gently lifting his wife's chin, he looked into her eyes and then lightly kissed her lips.

"I love you, Princess."

"I love you, Sweetheart." Darla replied with a tender smile.

CHAPTER EIGHT

Awakened early by baby Curt's crying, Darla sleepily got out of bed.

"Shhh, Shhh, Mommy is here, Curt." Darla whispered, hoping to quiet her newborn before he woke his daddy also.

Quickly changing his diaper, speaking in her soft, gentle tone did not seem to comfort the infant. He cried his hardest.

"Shhh, Shhh, Sweetheart, you will wake Daddy." Darla whispered, as she picked up her infant son, holding him close to her as she sat down in the rocking chair, preparing to nurse him.

"Daddy is awake." Kelley informed, rubbing his head wearily as he released a sigh.

"I am sorry, Honey. I tried to hush him quickly." Darla apologized, Curt now quieted, finding contentment as his mother allowed him to nurse.

"You owe no apology, Babe." Kelley assured, as he sat up on the bed, picking up the alarm clock and checking the time.

Without further conversing, he left their bed and then their bedroom. Darla softly sang to her baby as she heard her husband turn the shower on. She sleepily looked at his tiny face as he nursed, now fully content. She happily smiled at her precious baby and then gently kissed his tiny head.

Returning from his shower, Kelley dressed in his work clothes for his day away as a carpenter. Dressed for the new day, Kelley sat down on the edge of the bed near his wife and son, his face clearly expressing his pride with the presence of his tiny son.

"How long before Curt will sleep later than five o'clock?" Kelley asked as he gently touched his son's tiny hand.

"Considering he is only thirteen days old, perhaps a month or two."

"Is this normal the way Curt had you in and out of bed all night?" Kelley questioned, looking into his wife's gentle, yet very tired eyes.

"Perhaps normal for a baby whom has had his sleep interrupted due to visitors since he and I have returned from the hospital. I trust, as the uninterrupted visits cease, I will be able to establish a normal schedule for Curt. I realize the excitement a new baby brings to others. Curt and I have entertained for two days. It is time for him and me both to have a break and then I will be able to establish somewhat of a schedule."

"Are you suggesting we tell our visitors not to visit?"

"I am not quite sure how to deal with this. I am working on a solution." Darla answered pleasantly, as she leaned her head back against the rocker.

"Babe, we must develop a solution without further delay. You are not yet recuperated from giving birth, yet you are up and down like a yo-yo. You appear terribly tired this morning, as you did all day yesterday."

"With today being Monday, most of our friends and family members will be busy with their jobs. I thought I would see how today goes, before smoothing out the edges of my solution and sharing it with you. I realize you are concerned in regards to my health. I am quite tired and still considerably weak. If you will grant me one more day before appearing rude and sending our visitors away, I will present you with my solution this evening."

"I will be silent until this evening, but no longer than this. We all three could use a quieter sleeping time. I am surprised such a tiny child is able to cry so loud."

"He is more demanding than Heaven was. He appears terribly impatient." Darla sided with a beautiful smile.

"Whom did he acquire these traits from? Neither you nor I are spoiled or impatient."

"My dad's temper and your brother's impatience." Kelley answered with a grin

"Poor Curt, with the combination, he will have the sorest sitting-down area of all the children." He added with a chuckle.

"My son will be an angel." Darla replied happily, laying her baby against her chest to burp him.

"Sure he will be. Curt will be the perfect son, just as I was as a child." Kelley said with a boyish grin.

"But Deary, your father and your brother Aaron are often telling me stories of your youth. They have clearly expressed you were not the perfect child as I was led to believe you were upon marrying you. In fact, I was given the impression your sitting down area was sore more often than not." Darla's added comment brought a tickled laugh from her husband as his face flushed.

"I was simply all boy, Babe, which I am sure our son will be also. As Tom says, at least boys do not act prissy, bossy and cry over everything." Kelley shared with a smile, he now bringing a tickled laugh from his wife.

"I believe I will take a half-hour nap. Would you like to put our perfect son to bed, Daddy?"

"Dad would consider this an honor. I surely am the first father with a perfect son. I am not able to contain this knowledge for long. The congregation at church will finally witness their heart's desire." Kelley said beginning to laugh as he put his son to bed and his wife slipped back under her covers.

"Which is?" Darla questioned smiling at her husband, enjoying his sense of humor.

"Wife, I have produced the first perfect preacher's kid. A miracle has been performed. If any dispute my word, I will tell them to take this matter up with my wife."

"Kelley, you best not repeat your word of knowledge to the congregation. I do not want to hear them prove this knowledge wrong to me. If you do this, you will find your sleeping arrangements have been moved to the den."

"As Tom says…" Kelley started, bringing a tickled laugh from his wife as he sat down on the edge of the bed, pulling the covers up over her shoulders, looking into her eyes.

"Girls are prissy, bossy and they cry over everything." Kelley now kissed his wife's lips.

"Mm, stay home with me and keep me company." Darla suggested with a tender smile.

"Shame on you, you are the wife of a preacher, yet you are forever tempting me."

"Only because my love for you is so great, Sweetheart. I do not apologize for being madly in love with you. I intend to always enjoy you and your abundance of love."

"You are precious to me, Babe." Kelley said, kissing his wife once more long and gentle.

"Rest now, I will wake you before the kids leave for school."

It did not take but a few moments of silence for Darla to drift into sleep.

"We love you baby Curt." Heaven said as she, Karry and Bobbie stood next to the basinet, gently patting their brother.

Slowly opening her eyes to the faint sounds of voices, Darla's eyes fell upon the children.

"Good morning." She greeted in a soft whisper.

"Good morning." The children greeted in their normal tone.

"Shhh, Shhh, you must whisper. Your baby brother had a restless night. He needs his sleep."

"You guys are in trouble." Pete whispered as he entered his parents' bedroom.

"Dad wants you in the kitchen for breakfast."

The three children silently left their mother's room to join their daddy. Pete lingered a few seconds, admiring his baby brother as he slept. Pete's young face bore love and tenderness.

"Peter, is Dad waiting breakfast for you also?" Darla inquired with an understanding smile.

"Probably." Pete answered with a grin, his face flushed.

Pete quietly left his parents' room. Slowly getting out of bed, Darla slipped into her robe. Freshening up, she joined her family in the kitchen having their breakfast.

"Good morning." She greeted.

"Good morning." Her family greeted.

Going to the counter, Darla poured herself a cup of coffee. With her coffee cup in her hand, she took her seat at the breakfast table.

"We are sorry we disturbed you, Mommy." Karry apologized with watery eyes.

"Me too." Bobbie said, his fact its reddest.

"I am sorry too, Mommy." Heaven said, looking at her mother as though she was about to cry.

"Your apologies are accepted." Darla replied with tenderness in her voice, her heart going out to her saddened children.

She glanced at her husband as she sipped her coffee. His expression of disapproval informed her, he had scolded their children. She knew the children understood they were not to enter their parents' room without permission, although, her heart still silently ached with her children's sadness.

Kelley left the table to prepare his wife's breakfast.

"It looks like a pretty day out." Darla said pleasantly, attempting to cheer her family.

"It is a beautiful day." Kelley agreed in his calm manner.

"Dad said we get to fill the pool in a couple of weeks." Tom informed excitement on his face.

"Perhaps it will be warm enough to have a swimming party for your birthday." Darla suggested.

"Maybe." Tom replied, pleased with his adoptive mother's suggestion, as well as her remembering his birthdate was nearing. Kelley silently placed his wife's breakfast before her.

"Thank you."

"You are welcome, Babe." Kelley placed his breakfast dishes in the sink and then refilled his coffee cup.

"Good morning." Mom Roberts greeted as she let herself inside her daughter's home through the back door.

"Good morning." The Peterson family greeted.

"Have a seat, Mom." Kelley offered, setting a cup of coffee on the table for her at his place.

"Thank you, Kelley."

"Eat up, kids." Kelley encouraged as he glanced at the clock.

"You girls are in for a treat. Mommy will brush your hair for you this morning. I have resigned." Kelley said, winking at the girls, bringing smiles to their once saddened faces.

"Perhaps Mom will fix your hair-do for you also, Bobbie." He teased, bringing a grin to the eight-year-old's face.

Darla's heart was now uplifted as her husband released their children of their sadness.

Mom Roberts visited with her daughter and son-in-law as the children left the table to brush their teeth. The girls soon returned with their hairbrush, requesting their mother's assistance.

"Mommy, if you need Heaven and me to stay home from school to help you care for baby Curt, we want too." Karry offered sincerely.

"I appreciate your offer." Darla assured, as she brushed both her daughter's hair.

"I want you both to learn all you are able to. Grandma will help me until you girls return from school. When you return, I will gladly accept your help." Darla's response brought smiles to the girl's faces as they were made to feel needed.

With kisses given to her children and husband, Darla waved goodbye from the back door. Closing the door, she went to her mother's side as she began washing breakfast dishes, putting her arm around her mother's waist.

"Thank you for your assistance. I have truly been blessed with a terrific mother." Darla said kindly, followed by a hug and a kiss.

"Thank you for the compliment, dear. I am equally appreciative of my daughter."

Darla enjoyed having her mother's company. Mom Roberts enjoyed pampering her daughter, assisting with her grandson as well as taking charge of her daughter's home.

Returning from the shower, Darla discovered her mother changing Curt's diaper. She talked to her grandson in her most gentle voice. Darla smiled at the proud look on her mother's face. Silently, Darla went to the rocking chair patiently awaiting her mother to finish with Curt.

"Curt definitely has strong lungs." Mom Roberts voiced with a soft laugh as she presented her grandson to his mother.

"Kelley made this comment also at five o'clock this morning." Darla informed with a smile as she fed her baby, quickly quieting his crying.

"He seems impatient, this reminds me of Bill."

"Me also." Mom Roberts agreed with a pleased laugh.

"Although your brother has learned much patience since his marriage to Paula."

"In what manner are you referring to?" Darla questioned, detecting concern in her mother's voice.

"The most pressing issue is your brother's desire to become a father. He and Paula have been married nearly nine years. According to your brother, Paula refuses to have a child."

"Why? Bill adores children. He would make a wonderful father."

"I have not been told the why not's dear. I do know your brother is extremely upset. He has wanted a child since he and Paula accepted the Lord as their Savior. Six years is a long time to try one's patience.

"My children adore Paula. Kelley said she and Bill both did a superb job with the kids while he was with me at the hospital. I do not understand why Paula would not want a child. She and Bill even have everything materially to offer a child."

"Paula is pleasant to Dad and me, dear, but she has yet to confide in me with anything of importance. Besides seeing her briefly at church and reading about her activities in the society section of the newspaper, I hear very little of her doings or wishes. She seems to place distance between herself and our family at least."

Awaking from a nap, Darla's thoughts immediately went to Paula and Bill. Peeking in the basinet, Darla found it empty of her son. Leaving her bedroom, entering the hall, Darla heard voices coming from the front room. Reaching the entrance to the front room, her heat seemed to swell with love. Leaning against the wall, she silently observed her mother and mother-in-law enjoying their grandson with pride clearly on their faces. Their eyes seemed to sparkle and their voices held laughter.

"Allow me to burp Curt, Mary." Darla's mother-in-law requested, as Darla's mother completed giving the baby his bottle.

Quietly returning to the hallway allowing their special time alone with their grandson, Darla freshened up, slipping into a comfortable, floor length housedress. Sitting down at her husband's desk, she dialed the telephone.

"May I speak with Bill please? This is his sister." Darla spoke into the telephone.

"Hello, Sis." Bill greeted cheerfully.

"Hello. I am concerned about you, big brother."

"Why is this? I am a born again Christian." Bill reminded with a chuckle bringing a smile to his sister's face.

"I am not concerned about your relationship with the Lord. However, I am concerned about your relationship with my sister-in-law."

"Did my wife speak with you today?" Bill questioned, his tone growing serious.

"No, I have not heard from Paula since you and she visited yesterday afternoon."

"I thought she might visit you today. She mentioned last night calling you to see if she could assist you."

"It is possible she has tried to contact me today. I have been a lady of leisure. Mother has been in charge of both visitors and telephone calls." Darla explained slowly leaning back against the chair.

"Why the royal treatment? You have only presented Mom with a handsome grandson."

"This is true, I have." Darla agreed with a soft laugh, bragging.

"Does your preacher-husband realize your prideful nature?"

"I doubt he is able to see past his own pride to notice mine." Darla answered bringing a laugh from her brother.

"Mother says you wish to become a daddy."

"I believe I would find great pleasure in being a father. Unfortunately, Paula does not share my opinion. In fact, we had words with one another this morning. I was everything but patient and understanding. I have wanted a child for some time. Paula says she is not ready to have a child, yet she will not explain why. This is irritating to say the least."

"Would I offend Paula if I approach her on this subject? I would like to assist you both, but I certainly do not want to but in."

"Sis, I honestly do not know what my wife would prefer. I have been married for nine years. As shameful as it is, I still do not know my wife completely."

"Paula does not confide in you?" Darla questioned, her heart bearing her brother's burden, also saddening her.

"Not really."

"Perhaps she confides in her mother." Darla suggested, hopeful.

"Sis, Paula does not share anything with her parents. They barely speak to her since she accepted the Lord."

"Then she must feel she is all alone. I suppose she feels as irritated and frustrated as you do, perhaps more so than you. You do have a loving, understanding family to turn to whenever you feel the need."

"I certainly slammed the door in her face this morning, had she chosen to confide in me. She left our home this morning in tears. I have tried all morning to locate her."

"Oh, Bill, if she confides in no one, then she has no one to run to with her pain." Darla said, releasing a sigh, her face expressing her concerns for her aching sister-in-law.

"I am well aware of this, and yes, I am most concerned of her whereabouts as well as realizing how foolish I was earlier. I almost called the lounge at the country club to see if Paula was there."

"Bill, she has been a Christian for six years." Darla scolded.

"I know this. Satan enjoys toying with one's head. I did rebuke him. The Lord took over the fight for me. Darla, Paula honestly means the world to me." Bill shared though his voice was strong; he still expressed his heartache over his lack of understanding his wife's needs.

"I know you sincerely love your wife. I will be in prayer. If I should hear from Paula I will call you."

"Thanks, Sis. I would appreciate this."

Returning the telephone to its cradle, Darla bowed her head and closed her eyes as she prayed. She began to weep, interceding in prayer for both her brother and his wife. She prayed for understanding between one another, creating a bond as never before.

"Darla." Paula spoke, hesitant with entering the den, concerned she was intruding with her sister-in-law's state.

"Hi, Paula, come in." Darla welcomed with a gentle smile as she reached for a Kleenex.

"If I have come at a bad time, there is always tomorrow." Paula replied compassionately as she stood by Kelley's desk.

"No, tomorrow is too far off. I could use your company this very minute."

"What is troubling you?"

"I have been praying for my favorite, dearest brother and sister-in-law." Darla answered, looking into Paula's eyes with gentleness on her face

"Oh, Bill has spoken with you about our argument." Paula said, now blushing.

"Bill gave me little information in regards to your misunderstanding. He is kicking himself for upsetting you. He said he has called everywhere looking for you. You know me, I am not capable of withstanding a family member enduring pain. I immediately take the burden to the Lord. He is the healer of all pain." Darla shared compassionately, searching her sister-in-law's eyes with her eyes seeing her heartache.

"May I use your telephone please?"

"You most certainly may. Please, sit down." Darla suggested, getting up from the desk chair.

"Thank you."

"Paula, I love you." Darla informed, giving her a quick hug.

Darla's gesture brought tears to Paula's eyes and tenderness to her saddened face. She silently sat down at the desk picking up the telephone. Darla went to the sofa, silently searching and praying the Holy Spirit would use her to be Paula's guide through the wilderness and the valley until obtaining the victory over her sorrow.

"Hello, this is Paula; please inform my husband I wish to speak with him."

Paula was on the telephone with Bill for several minutes. Darla patiently waited for her sister-in-law to join her on the sofa as she continued in silent prayer. Paula remained at the desk briefly with the close of her conversing with her husband. Wiping her eyes with a Kleenex and blowing her nose, she had regained her composure.

"Your brother has a way of bringing tears to my eyes often, lately." Paula shared as she sat down on the sofa near Darla, once again blotting her eyes with a Kleenex.

"If Bill is bringing tears to your eyes from granting you happiness, I approve one-hundred percent. On the other hand, if he is upsetting you, I will gladly slap him for you. I owe him a hard slap from my youth anyway." Darla replied with sincerity on her face.

Paula smiled at Darla. She leaned back against the sofa.

"I need a real friend, Darla. I did not realize until Bill and I began to spat a few days ago that I have not one close friend, yet I have many friends. I would like you to help me if you are able to and keep our conversing in confidence. May I impose?"

"A family member needs being met, never fall under the category of imposing. In our family, we each have a silent understanding of this. As we have needs, we freely take. As another member has needs, we freely give. The Roberts' love, as well as the Peterson's love, is free without conditions. I want to be your best friend throughout our lives if this is your wish. If not, regardless, I am your sister. Sisters are allowed to share secrets. My daughters do this often." Darla assured with a gentle smile, patting Paula on her hand.

"I have wanted this type of relationship with you for several years. At least since, I accepted the Lord into my life. I am not one to reach out to others as your family seems to do on a daily basis."

"I am truly sorry for not realizing your wishes, Paula." Darla said her young face expressing her heartbreak toward her sister-in-law. She took Paula's hand into hers, holding it and hoping to begin a bond and bring comfort.

"This is my doing by not expressing my needs or wishes. This, I did not realize until today. Bill has said practically from the start of our marriage he is not a mind reader. I am guilty of not expressing myself even to him. This is terribly annoying to Bill. I feel foolish; perhaps childish is more correct that I do not know how to share my feelings. I was not raised as your family. In many ways I was probably raised more like your children before you and Kelley adopted them." Paula explained, her eyes filling with tears.

"I am so sorry, Paula. I honestly had no idea you have been hurting all these years that I have known you. You must feel terribly lonely."

"Yes, I do." Paula confessed, beginning to sob now, as though she were a broken woman.

Darla put her arm around Paula, hugging and soothing her, allowing her to release and undo the years of bondage that entrapped her of having complete victory of her past sorrows. Paula cried for the longest time allowing Darla to soothe and comfort her.

"Darla." Mom Roberts spoke barely above a whisper.

"I am sorry to disturb you, dear. The children are tended to as well as dinner awaiting Kelley's return from work. Curt will want his feeding shortly. You only prepared me one bottle."

"I will nurse Curt if you will inform me when he wakes, please."

"Okay, dear. May I be of assistance to my daughters?"

"If you would call my husband to come get me, I would be appreciative." Paula answered, removing her head from Darla's shoulder.

"Here, Paula." Darla offered, placing the box of Kleenex near her.

"Bill is here, dear." Mom Roberts informed, putting her arm around her daughter-in-law, giving her a tight hug.

"We love you, Paula."

"Thank you." Paula replied with a weak smile, her tears quickly coming again.

"I will get Bill, dear." Mom Roberts offered.

"Will you come spend tomorrow with me?" Darla asked with a kind smile, as she once again took her hand into hers.

"I would welcome this. Perhaps I will have my cry out by tomorrow."

"If you do, fine, but if not, this will be fine also." Darla assured and then gave Paula a tight hug.

"We are conquerors through Christ Jesus. We will not be defeated. Right?"

"Right." Paula answered as she now looked up into her husband's face as he patiently stood at her side.

Paula held her hand out for her husband to assist her from the sofa. Bill silently did as requested. Standing next to her husband with the elegant look of a wealthy model, Paula looked into his eyes. Her eyes saddened, filled with tears.

"Please hold me, Bill." She requested, as she began to sob again. Bill quickly put his arms around his wife.

"I will hold you for as long as you wish, Babe." Bill replied.

Darla quietly slipped out of the den, closing the door behind her.

Darla nursed Curt in the privacy of her bedroom. She sang to him, gently talked to him, hugged and kissed him.

"You are so fortunate, Sweetheart. You will never be neglected your rights to be loved, guided and protected." She whispered, as her eyes grew moist with thinking of all the hurting, lonely children in the world that were less fortunate.

"There is my wife." Kelley said as he entered their bedroom from work.

"Hi, Sweetheart." Darla greeted with a gentle smile.

"How was your day?"

"Tiring as most, your father is a slave driver." Kelley answered with a chuckle, bringing a smile to his wife's face as he removed clean clothes from the closet for his shower and then went to his wife's side.

"How was your day?"

"I had a restful day. We will talk later. Mother has dinner ready. You best take your shower after you give our son and me a kiss." Darla spoke, looking up into her husband's eyes.

"Do not limit me to one kiss. This is only your third day home from the hospital. I have been away from you all day. I want many kisses, wife." Kelley informed with a grin, bringing a tickled laugh from his wife.

"It is nice to know you have missed me." Darla said happily, as Kelley took her hand into his and leaned down to kiss her and then his son.

"Your absence definitely makes my heart grow fonder." Kelley replied and then kissed his wife again before leaving for his shower.

Gently laying her sleeping infant in his bed, Darla vacated her bedroom. Entering the kitchen, Darla smiled as her children assisted their grandma with dessert dishes to be placed in the refrigerator.

"Mother, may we talk you into moving in with us?"

"And Grandpa too." Bobbie offered hopefully, his wishes bringing a soft laugh from Grandma Roberts.

"Speaking of grandpa, I best get home to him. Darla, your messages are on the counter. I will see you in the morning."

"Okay, thank you, Mother."

"Kids, I will see you also in the morning. Help your mother."

Grandma Roberts instructed and then gave each child a kiss goodbye.

Darla quickly glanced at the list of messages. With Kelley entering the dining room from his shower, his family took their seats at the table. With the children and Darla seated, Kelley then sat down. Darla seemed to notice every minor detail of her family members as they enjoyed dinner together. She did not have a perfect husband, perfect children, nor was she the perfect wife and mother. What she and her husband did have was genuine love toward one another and each of their children. Their love alone united them, creating a family. What a strong bond love formed.

"Mom, will you feel well enough to come to open house Friday night?" Bobbie asked.

"Most certainly, I never miss special events."

"Dad, in case Mom is not well enough to go to open house will you go anyway?" Tom asked.

"Of course."

"Thanks." Tom replied, letting out a sigh.

"Our other dad never went to see us kids if our mom was not able to attend." Pete explained, allowing his adoptive dad to understand his brother's question.

"Daddy and Mommy go to everything." Heaven assured pleased.

"Uh huh." Karry agreed.

"They are never ashamed of their kids either." The girl's opinions brought pleased smiles to their three brothers' faces as well as their parents.

"Girls, will you help me bring dessert in, please?" Darla asked as she pushed her chair out away from the table.

"Mom, stay put." Kelley ordered, he quickly getting up from the table, picking up his dinner plate.

"Kids, bring your dishes to the kitchen." Kelley instructed, picking up his wife's dinner plate for her."

Darla remained seated as her husband and children cleared their dinner plates. Returning to the table with their desserts, Kelley set his wife's dessert before her.

"Thank you, Honey."

"You are welcome, Babe."

Kelley gave Darla a kiss on the top of her head and then returned to the head of the table. Kelley no sooner sat down when the doorbell rang. Wiping his mouth with his napkin, he went to the front door.

"Good evening, ladies." Kelley greeted.

"Come in, please. Heave a seat while I get my wife."

Kelley returned to the dining room. Darla looked at her husband, silently questioning who had ringed the doorbell.

"Gail and a couple of ladies from the church are here to visit you. Gail said they came by earlier, but you were napping."

"Not again." Bobbie voiced, leaning his head on his hand. Heaven folded her arms as though aggravated, leaning back against her chair. Karry now looked at her mother with sad eyes. Kelley and Darla glanced at their children's sudden mood change and then looked at one another.

"Am I not allowed to have company?" Darla asked, looking at the three children as though disappointed in their actions.

Heaven unfolded her arms. Bobbie quickly removed his elbow from the table, sitting up straight. Karry no longer looked at her mother, as though pouting. The children did not answer.

"Excuse me." Darla said after several moments of silence.

Darla visited with her visitors for an hour while her family were busy with their after dinner chores.

"Curt had so many visitors during the weekend interrupting his sleep. He had a very restless night. If Kelley does not receive proper rest tonight, I am in serious trouble." Darla shared in her pleasant manner.

"It will not disturb Curt if I take you to quietly peek at him if you would like."

The women were more than pleased with Darla's solution to end her infant's disrupted schedule. With the conclusion of her visit, Darla politely excused herself from visiting, walking her visitors to the door. Again, the women were understanding with

Darla just returning from the hospital and having a large family to contend with.

Entering the den, Karry, Bobbie and Heaven were watching their half-hour evening television program. Darla quietly sat down with the children. The girls quickly sat down on each side of their mother. Bobbie left the beanbag chair, leaning against the sofa, near his mother's legs. As the program ended, Bobbie turned off the set.

"You each know what you are to do now. When you are finished, how would you like to help feed Curt his bottle?"

"Yes." The children agreed excitedly.

"Good, we have a date then. Perhaps tomorrow evening Pete and Tom would like to feed Curt." Darla suggested.

While the girls took turns practicing their piano lessons and their baths, Darla entered the kitchen. Pete, Tom and Kelley tended to the milk and eggs, preparing them for the icebox.

"Who washed the dinner dishes?" Darla asked as she stood between the boys, putting her arms loosely around their waist as they washed the eggs.

"Dad and the girls." Tom Answered.

"Pete and I covered Dad's outside chores for him."

"With all the rules and chores, are you boys sure you will remain happy being Peterson's?"

"Yes, Ma'am." Tom answered quickly.

"Without a shadow of a doubt." Pete answered with his biggest grin.

"Good because you are stuck with Dad and me for life." Darla informed with a loving smile as she gave each son a hug and a kiss.

"How about you, Dad?" Darla questioned in her slow, passive manner as she now put her arm around his waist.

"Are you willing to hang in with each of us moody dependents even if you are overworked and underpaid?"

"Overworked and underpaid, this is true, Lassy. Aye, the fringe benefits I delight in." Kelley answered speaking as his Irish father would, his play bringing laughter from his sons and wife.

The Peterson couple had a more restful night. Curt awoke only at his feeding times during the night. Awakened by Curt for his five o'clock feeding, Darla quickly hushed him as not to awaken her husband. Slipping out of her bedroom with her infant in her arms, she went to the rocking chair in the front room. With the drapes opened, she adored the view of the sun rising as she softly sang to her baby as he nursed. How beautiful the outdoors looked. How beautiful the indoors felt.

"Thank you Heavenly Father for being granted not only the privileges of seeing your beauty all around me, but also the beauty of feeling your presence of love around me as well as within me." This brief, special prayer put a smile on Darla's face as well as a song in her heart.

With the completion of Curt's feeding, she returned to her bedroom. Turning off her husband's alarm before it could ring, she sat down on the edge of her bed near her sleeping husband.

"Good morning, Daddy." Darla spoke happily, as she woke Kelley.

"We love you." She added as she carefully laid baby Curt next to his daddy, he opening his eyes.

Slowly turning on his side, putting his head close to his son, his face quickly expressing fatherly pride, he gently kissed his son on his tiny head.

"Good morning, Mom." Kelley spoke putting his arm around his wife.

"Your face is radiant with happiness. What pills are you taking?"

"Honey, it is the best medicine known to man. It is called the love of Jesus." She answered, bringing a pleased smile to her husband's face.

"It seems I have drunk so much of this marvelous medicine, that I am full and overflowing with this special love."

"You are not only a pleasure to fall asleep with, Sweetheart, you are also a joy to wake up to." Kelley said, gently pulling her close to his face, so he could kiss her lips.

Darla picked Curt up from the bed. Standing up with the baby in her arms, as she allowed her husband room to get out of bed, she placed Curt in his basinet and then left the room. With the percolator plugged in, she set the breakfast table.

"Is Curt joining us for breakfast?" Darla asked as Kelley entered the kitchen with the basinet.

"In a way." Kelley answered as Darla poured their cups of coffee.

"With Curt's arrival into our family being this new, the excitement within the kids to see their baby brother must be overwhelming. This solution is solved. They may wake up to their brother's presence."

"My children have a clever father." Darla said approvingly, sitting down at the table with her coffee.

Each child eagerly, yet gently went to the basinet as they entered the kitchen. They gently patted their baby brother, touched his tiny hand, or kissed him. Their individual visit with Curt was brief with having their morning chores to tend to. Though their visits were brief, each child appeared to be satisfied with simply being allowed to see their brother.

Feeling stronger, yet still moving a bit slower than her normal pace, Darla made breakfast with Kelley assisting her.

"Petersons." Kelley answered into the telephone.

"Dar, it's Cindy, she says it is urgent."

"Hello, Cindy." Darla greeted with concern on her face.

Kelley kindly removed the cooking utensil from his wife's hand, taking over breakfast preparations.

"Hi, Darla." Cindy greeted, her voice sounding shaky and distance.

"Cindy, are you crying?" Darla questioned compassionately.

"Yes."

"Why?"

"Because Dan is a jerk." Cindy answered as she began to sob.

"What? I do not believe what I heard you say. What could Dan possibly do to have you speak this way?" Darla questioned her expression as though she was in shock causing Kelley to glance at his wife with concern on his face.

"He does not want me to become pregnant."

"Why?" Darla questioned surprised.

"Because our savings is not as large as he feels it should be. He said if I should allow myself to become pregnant at this time, I would have to continue working after the arrival of our baby for two years, taking the baby to a sitter all day." Cindy answered, she now crying harder.

"I am sorry Cindy. I do not understand Dan's attitude in the least."

Letting out a deep sigh, Darla glanced at her family now arriving at the breakfast table. Putting her hand over the receiver, she looked at her husband.

"Kel?" she questioned, seeking his approval.

"We will start breakfast without you." He answered giving his approval.

Darla stepped just outside of the kitchen into the dining room, as she politely listened to each of Cindy's upsets with her husband's opinions.

"I believe I am already pregnant." Cindy informed, crying her hardest.

"Oh, Cindy." Darla said barely above a whisper as her own eyes filled with tears.

Darla smiled a weak smile at her mother as she entered the kitchen, planning to spend another day assisting her daughter.

"I bet Mommy will be too busy to fix our hair this morning Karry." Heaven complained, looking at her sister.

"I bet she has Daddy fix our hair." Karry agreed also complaining, the girls blunt talk surprising each present.

With the telephone still to her ear, her hand once again on the receiver, Darla stepped back into the kitchen. She tapped both her daughter's on their head, getting their attention. Heaven and Karry looked up seeing the stern look their mother now had on her face.

"I will deal with both of you for being selfish, as soon as I am able." Darla assured in her stern tone and then slipped back into the dining room to concentrate on her cousin's grief.

"I tried to warn you girls and you Bob, Mom was going to get tired of you being babies." Tom said shaking his head at his sisters as he removed his dishes from the table.

"Oh, well, Tom it is their sitting down area that will be sore, not ours." Pete sided, as he also removed his dishes from the table.

"I did not say anything." Bobbie reminded, glancing at his brothers and then his dad nervously.

"Not this time. Mom should bust you too." Tom scolded, as the three brothers left the kitchen to wash their faces and brush their teeth.

Kelley smiled at his mother-in-law as she quickly put her hand over her mouth as not to allow the laughter to escape her with the boys talk. With flushed cheeks, the girls silently removed their breakfast dishes from the table, leaving the kitchen also.

"You may laugh now, Grandma." Kelley said with a grin, as he politely refilled his mother-in-law's coffee cup.

"Cindy, please stop crying." Darla pleaded, she now sounding desperate.

Both Kelley and his mother-in-law grew silent as they quickly looked toward Darla.

"I would like to give Dan a piece of my mind, but..." Darla started and then grew silent.

Heaven and Karry returned with their hairbrush. They walked past their mother, starting for their daddy. Darla snapped her fingers at the girls. Gaining their attention, she motioned for the girls to go to her. Growing tired from standing, Darla sat down on the stool near the kitchen counter.

"I will be praying, Cindy. We love you, bye."

Heaven and Karry looked into their mother's face as she combed their hair. They noticed her moist eyes and saddened tone as though extremely concerned for their Aunt Cindy.

"I am sorry, Mommy for being selfish with you." Heaven said with flushed cheeks.

"I am sorry too." Karry sided, she also with flushed cheeks.

"Sometimes I feel like being stingy with you." She confessed.

"We missed you when you were in the hospital. Tom says we are babies. We still miss you, Mommy, even though you are home. This does not mean we are babies."

"Daddy missed you and he is a grown-up." Karry explained putting her tiny hand on her mommy's shoulder as her mother combed Heaven's hair, as though she needed to touch her even at that very moment.

"Ten days is a long time to children when they miss their mother's love and presence." Grandma Roberts sided in her gentle way, as she ceased washing breakfast dishes.

"In fact, I recall my daughter at the age of twelve going away to church camp for two weeks. At the end of the first five days, she called her daddy pleading for him to bring her home."

"What did your daughter's dad say?" Bobbie questioned in his serious tone as he, his brothers and dad waited for their sisters, so they could leave for school.

"He said he could not bear her missing her family. He drove several hours to the camp to bring his daughter home."

Darla's face was tender now as her mother's example explained the deep lonely feeling even a properly loved and well-adjusted child at times experienced.

"I will be sensitive to your feelings." Darla said looking into her daughters' eyes, giving them each a tight hug.

"You must also be sensitive to Mommy's feelings and speak respectfully. Am I right?"

"Yes, Mommy." The girls answered.

"Bob, come here please."

Bobbie silently went to his mother's side looking into her gentle eyes. Darla put her arm around her eight-year-old son's waist, giving him a tight hug.

"Do you and I have the same understanding as your sisters and I?"

"Yes." Bobbie answered with a happy grin.

"Mom, it is getting late." Kelley reminded.

"Kids, give Mom and Grandma a kiss goodbye."

With kisses exchanged, her five school age children each held hands as Kelley prayed a prayer over his family.

"We love you, Mom." Kelley said, followed by a goodbye kiss.

"We will discuss a solution to Cindy's upset this evening if you would like." He added in a whisper.

"Please, have a good day."

Getting up from the stool, Darla went to the back door, watching as her family left for their busy day. Leaving from the back door, she began drying dishes.

"You look stronger and more rested this morning."

"Curt slept better last night, which enabled me to receive more sleep. As far as my strength, I do feel stronger this morning."

"We must be taking good care of you." Mom Roberts said with a gentle smile.

"Yes, Ma'am. I receive the best of care. I thank you Mother for another day, being blessed with your assistance."

"You are welcome, dear. I am concerned about my niece. Are you sworn to secrecy?"

"I do not believe Cindy would object to my sharing her upset with our family. She and Dan are also spatting as Bill and Paula in regards to having a child."

"I do not believe this." Mom Roberts said as though heartbroken.

"Apparently, Dan feels they need a specific amount of money in their savings before having a child. Cindy protested this, making her wishes known, her wants to be a mother. Dan informed Cindy if she would become pregnant at this time, she would have to continue working regardless for two years. This would mean childcare for their baby. Cindy is one-hundred percent against mothers leaving their babies all day with sitters."

"I often question whether Christians today even bother reading the Bible to know the ways of the Lord. Dan and Cindy, Bill and Paula, each Christians, yet their actions are far from acts of love. What more does Dan feel he must acquire materially?"

"I honestly do not know, Mother. They appear to have more

than enough to provide nicely for a child. The worst part is Cindy believes she is presently pregnant."

"Is Dan aware of Cindy's suspicions?"

"I do not think so. Cindy was crying terribly hard. I barely understood her. I am like you, Mother. I do not understand. Are children becoming an inconvenience to even Christian couples?" Darla questioned as though bewildered with the thought, as she searched her mother's eyes with hers, seeking her years of wisdom.

"I pray this is not fact, Sweetheart. It does appear this generation is determined to destroy the family. These selfish actions within my family truly break my heart." Mom Roberts answered her face weary and drawn.

"We will intercede in prayer for Cindy and Bill, Mother. We will not allow Satan to continue to cause strife within our families. We will witness both Cindy and Bill's stand for the family is to their advantage. For this is right in the eyes of the Lord." Darla said with a sudden boldness.

"Yes, dear, we will intercede in prayer. We each are overcomers through Christ Jesus." Mom Roberts agreed, she also gaining boldness, eliminating negative concerns.

"We best begin praying for the Holy Spirit to lead me. Paula is visiting this morning to discuss her and Bill's conflicts." Darla shared as she put the last of the dishes away.

"My prayers have already begun, dear. Praying without ceasing has always been my way."

Curt began to fuss as his eight o'clock feeding arrived.

"Oh, Sweetie, you will be just fine." Darla said as she carefully picked up her fourteen-day-old son.

"Mother, how could one look at this precious baby and not want to shower him with love?" Darla asked with an excited laugh, as she held Curt in her arms, blushing with her bragging.

"If any would dare not agree with you, dear, I order they be declared insane." Mom Roberts answered with a smile as she looked at her fussing grandson with admiration on her face.

Leaving the kitchen, Darla carried her infant to her bedroom.

She gently bathed him, speaking to him and loving him with her gentle tone and kind words.

"Sweetheart, you are living proof of a couples love as God intended." She said with sparkles in her eyes and a radiant smile on her face.

Her baby bathed and dressed, Darla went to the rocking chair near her bed. Preparing herself and positioning her son, she allowed him to nurse. She smiled as baby Curt's facial expression changed from eagerness to nurse to contentment with feeding.

"Darla." Her mother spoke as she lightly tapped on the bedroom door.

"Yes, come in."

"Paula is here, dear. She says she is not able to stay long."

"She is welcome to come in here." Darla suggested.

Picking up the lightweight baby blanket next to her, Darla gently draped the blanket over her shoulder giving she and her nursing infant their necessary privacy.

"Good morning, Paula." Darla greeted with a happy smile.

"Good morning. I apologize for interrupting. Your mother said you were feeding Curt. I did not understand you nurse Curt."

"I am quite aware that my old-fashioned ways often surprise others due to my young age." Darla replied with an understanding smile to Paula's surprised expression.

"You may bring the chair near from my vanity or you are welcome to sit on the bed."

"The edge of your bed is perfectly acceptable." Paula assured as she sat down near Darla.

"Kelley does not mind you nursing?"

"I trust he is not offended by my doing the most natural act between a mother and infant. He has never voiced an opinion." Darla answered, surprised with her sister-in-law's question.

"What are you to do when you are away from home?"

"Oh." Darla said, followed by a soft laugh, her face flushed with realizing Paula's thoughts.

"I use bottles. Curt would rather I not, he is not fond of the rubber nipples. If I know a head of time I will have company visiting where I am granted ample time to prepare, I will usually bottle feed at home also."

"I did not realize anyone breast fed in this day and age." Paula confessed.

"Not many do, most mothers are too busy with a career or activities to have enough time to donate to breast feeding their child. My roommate at the hospital was under the impression it was morally wrong. She was barely twenty. No one had implied this opinion to her. She simply assumed this with never knowing personally anyone whom breast fed."

"I suppose most are guilty of going along with the crowd without thinking."

"I know I have often been guilty of this." Darla agreed.

"It would be a wise move for ones investing to invest in a company that makes baby formula. With the percentage of mothers nursing being so low, one should make a fortune." She added with a gentle smile.

"Then you feel it is wrong to bottle feed?" Paula inquired as though taking notes.

"No. In fact, in some cases a mother has no choice. Perhaps the mother's milk is not healthy for her child, or perhaps a single mother, who is forced to work being away from her child for many hours. I was not able to nurse Heaven. I wanted to, but my circumstances of being a college student and working when she was a baby did not allow me to do so. In many ways, Curt has brought me the opportunity to experience ways I was not blessed with experiencing with Heaven. The most beautiful feeling of all is to look at this tiny child and know he represents the love Kelley and I have toward one another."

"You make giving birth sound beautiful." Paula voiced with a pleased smile.

"The most beautiful experience shared between husband and wife."

"Darla, I have a luncheon date." Paula voiced, glancing at her watch.

"You look as though you could use a nap. May I return later? I really need to talk."

"Of course you may. Our door is always open, Paula. Do truly know this."

"I believe you and I thank you. I will see you in three hours, perhaps?"

"I will be awake from my nap by then." Darla agreed as she placed Curt against her, patting him to burp him.

"May I give my nephew a kiss?" Paula asked, her face lightening up with the appearance of Curt.

"You may, he appreciates kisses." Darla's answer brought an even bigger smile to Paula's face.

"He is so precious." Paula said, gently rubbing his tinny head.

"I best go before I am late." She said, yet hesitating, giving Curt another kiss.

Darla napped until Paula returned. Mom Roberts kindly tended to Curt and household duties. Paula shared her heats secrets with Darla behind closed doors in the family den. Shortly before the arrival of the children from school, Paula vacated her sister-in-law's home.

With Curt tucked in his basinet, Darla joined her mother in the kitchen to assist in dinner preparations. Upon the arrival of the school bus, Darla watched through the kitchen window as each child vacated the school bus.

"Did you count five heads?" Mom Roberts asked with a gentle smile, bringing a soft laugh from her daughter.

"Yes." Darla confessed.

"They each appear happy and content." She added.

"Dear, I do believe you feel it an honor to mother an army of children." Mom Roberts said, sharing her daughter's excitement to greet her approaching children.

"I truly do, Mother. You and Dad taught me to share and I recall being told often 'it is better to give than to receive.'"

"You were a good student. Do take a break when the children arrive. You need one another as much as you should sit down and rest. You being in the hospital nearly two weeks, surely felt like eternity to you and the children by being separated."

"Thank you, Mother. You are the greatest." Darla replied happily, giving her mother a tight hug and kiss.

"Mm, thank you."

Darla visited with her children in the front room as they each excitedly shared their day with her.

"Darla, I will go home now dear. Kelley's mother will come help you tomorrow. Kids, help your mother. Do not allow her to overdo it."

"Okay, Grandma." The children agreed sincerely.

"Bye, Mother, thank you for everything." Darla said.

One by one, the boys requested to be excused. Tom wished to ride his mother's horse, while Pete and Bobbie wished to ride their bikes. The girls soon grew restless. Soon they had their dolls in the front room floor, playing near their mother. With five o'clock nearing, Darla went to her newborn. Changing his diaper, he awoke. Taking her son into her arms, she returned to the front room. The girls quickly left their dolls to see their brother. They continuously touched his tiny hand, patted his leg or gently rubbed his tiny head while Darla nursed him behind the draped baby blanket.

"Mom, Aunt Cindy is here." Pete informed, his face flushed as though he was troubled.

"Will you invite her in? I am feeding your brother."

"Yes, Ma'am." Pete answered slowly.

"Peter, what is troubling you?"

"Aunt Cindy is crying and she has a suitcase with her."

"Come here, Deary. Aunt Cindy has been terribly upset. We will be kind, loving and understanding toward her. We will not question her. Do show Aunt Cindy in. Perhaps you would offer to carry her suitcase for her if her desire is to bring it inside."

"Yes, Ma'am."

"Pete, explain to your brothers, especially Bobbie to be extra polite to Aunt Cindy. Thank you, and do not worry. Jesus has our Aunt Cindy in the palm of His hand this very minute. We will pray she will be happy again. The Lord will honor our prayer because we serve the Lord, right?" She inquired with a gentle smile, giving Pete a tight hug.

"Right." Pete answered with a smile.

"I will be a cheerful gentleman." He added

"Thank you. I thought you would." His mother replied, pleased. "Go get Aunt Cindy."

"Karry and Heaven, you heard Pete and my talk. With knowing Aunt Cindy has an upset, will you be offended by me for speaking with Aunt Cindy in private?"

"No, Mommy. Aunt Cindy needs a friend if she is crying." Karry answered sincerely.

"Jesus would not be happy with Karry and me if we were selfish with you when we should share." Heaven answered thoughtfully.

"I believe my daughters have become more grown-up since this morning." Karry and Heaven smiled at their mother.

"Perhaps you will play with your dolls elsewhere?"

"Yes, Mommy." Karry and Heaven answered as they quickly picked up their dolls from the carpet.

"Hi, Aunt Cindy." The girls greeted politely, as their aunt entered the front room.

"Hi." Cindy greeted forcing a smile.

The girls left the room. Pete politely set his aunt's suitcase on the floor and then silently returned to his play outside.

"Have a seat next to me please. Tell me why you have been crying." Darla instructed compassionately.

Cindy sat down on the sofa next to her cousin whom was as a sister to her.

"I went to the doctor and I am pregnant." Cindy informed, her eyes quickly filling with tears.

"Congratulations!" Darla exclaimed happily putting her arm around her cousin, giving her a hug.

"Which do you prefer, a beautiful sweet daughter or a handsome strong son?"

"I have no preference. I just want Dan to want our baby and love our baby." Cindy answered, her tears quickly streaming down her cheeks.

"Have you told Dan of your news?"

"No, nor do I intend to. He does not want this child for at least two years. I am pregnant now."

"Cindy, what is your plan to keep Dan from knowing of his child?" Darla questioned slowly, her face bearing her heartache for her cousin's happiness.

"Hello, ladies." Kelley greeted concern apparent on his face as he returned from work.

"Hi, Kelley." Darla greeted her face troubled, as she looked up into her husband's eyes. Cindy did not greet Kelley. She kept her head lowered as her tears streamed.

"Good evening, Cindy." Kelley greeted.

"Hi. Excuse me, Kelley, I have had an upsetting day." Cindy replied, briefly glancing at her cousin, with reddened cheeks, yet not looking toward Kelley as her tears continued.

"This is what I hear. What is the problem between you and Dan where you feel you must leave him?" Kelley questioned, sitting down on a chair.

"Cindy." Darla scolded, her scolding making Cindy's cheeks redden more.

"I do not believe you intend to throw ten years of marriage away over this misunderstanding."

"I should not have come here." Cindy said closing her eyes as she desperately tried to stop her tears.

"Yes, you should be here. In fact, I am glad you are here. Dan will do right by you, if I must go to him and tell him myself. I have never heard of such nonsense from an unsaved husband, yet Dan is a Christian and even ministering. Surely, there is a huge communication gap between you and him. I simply find this devastating." Darla voiced as she secretly buttoned her blouse under the baby blanket.

Removing the blanket, she picked Curt up; laying him against her shoulder to burp him.

"Honey, what is the problem?" Kelley asked for the second time.

"Dan does not want a child for at least two more years. He does not feel their savings is presently large enough. If Cindy would be pregnant before this time, she would have to continue working, leaving her baby with a sitter everyday regardless of Cindy's wishes for at least these two years."

"Cindy, Dan said this?" Kelley questioned, stunned. Cindy shook her head yes, though she kept her head lowered.

"Is there anything else?"

"I learned this afternoon that I am pregnant." Cindy answered as she began to sob.

Holding Curt to her shoulder with one arm, Darla put her other arm around Cindy to comfort her.

"Dan did not have a change of heart when you told him you are pregnant this afternoon?" Kelley questioned, getting up from his chair, carefully taking baby Curt from his wife.

"She did not tell me she is pregnant." Dan informed, standing in the doorway, he also appearing deeply hurt.

"There was no reason to tell you." Cindy mumbled between sobs.

"You do not want our baby."

"Cindy, please." Darla calmed, hugging and soothing her.

Darla and Kelley both looked at Dan with disbelief on their faces. His face turned its reddest, as he looked at first Kelley and then Darla.

"Surely Cindy is misunderstanding you." Kelley voiced, looking at Dan, awaiting an explanation.

"I did not know Cindy is pregnant, otherwise I would have been more careful with my expressing." Dan answered, feeling badly for upsetting his wife so deeply.

Darla released a long sigh as she now took her eyes from Dan.

She glanced at her husband, knowing he was baffled and stunned with Dan's actions. Looking at her weeping cousin, Darla silently prayed.

What do you say you and I go for a walk?" Kelley asked, looking at Dan.

"I want my wife to come home. She and I are capable of working out our differences alone." Dan answered too embarrassed to share, discuss or admit any wrong on his part.

"My home and my baby's home are in Los Angeles." Cindy informed, lifting her head from her cousin's shoulder, wiping her tears with her hands. Kelley quickly handed Cindy some Kleenex.

"You do not mean this, Cindy." Darla said quickly, searching her cousin's eyes with hers.

"I mean this. If my child is not wanted by his own father, I will not be a part of him either."

"Cindy..." Dan started.

"You call yourself a Christian? God is love, Dan, not money and not selfishness."

Dan appeared as though he had been slapped in his face several times with Cindy's comments. Dan started to leave the front room. Kelley quickly took hold of his arm.

"Hey guy, come on. You cannot walk out on her. You have been married ten years and you have a baby on the way. Where is your fight, Dan?" Kelley questioned desperately wanting the couple to make amends.

"It is gone, everything is gone." Dan replied, he appearing as a broken man now.

"What is gone?"

"My job for one. I am going to lose our home and everything. Cindy might as well go home to her parents. My own wife will tell you my relationship with the Lord is no longer genuine."

Darla and Cindy looked at Dan with compassion as he shared his burdens with disbelief on their faces.

"I do not buy it. I know your love and dedication to the Lord is genuine. Get ahold of yourself Dan and your family. Take a stand against Satan. He is your enemy, not your wife." Kelley took hold of Cindy's hand as she sat near Darla on the sofa.

"Come here." Kelley instructed.

As Cindy stood, Kelley placed her hand in Dan's hand.

"Are you willing to allow Satan to rob your child of a father and yourself of your husband? He is your enemy, not Dan. Stand together, steadfast in the ways of the Lord. We are in the Lord's army. We are overcomers. We shall not faint from being weary."

Cindy looked into her husband's eyes as he looked into hers.

"Talk to one another. Level with your wife in regards to your finances, Dan. Work this out. Reach out by faith and believe your every need will be met. I promise you both, all your needs will be met. God will bless you for being obedient through these rough times. When the Lord sends His blessings, He seems to shower us with them." Kelley assured.

Darla got up from the sofa, nearing the three adults. She took both Dan's and Cindy's free hand. Placing Cindy's hand into Dan's hand as her husband had done with their other hand; she put her arm around her husband's waist.

"Cindy, look into Dan's eyes and see his pain. Perhaps you will see some fear with him losing his job. How is he to take care of a family without work?"

"Dan, look into your wife's eyes and see her pain. She is carrying your child. This should be the happiest moment for the two of you. This is a priceless gift. We wives feel that we are truly blessed when we learn we will present our husband's with their baby."

"Dan, Cindy, after you see one another's pain, also see the love your partner truly has for you and you have for your partner. Call a truce, please. Join Darla and our family for dinner. After dinner, we will bind together in prayer and work out a solution in regards to your finances. I feel assured the Lord is already working your future out." Kelley instructed.

"Dar, I will call the children in if you will tend to Curt please." Kelley instructed, handing his sleeping infant to his wife.

Dan put his arms around Cindy, hugging her as Darla and Kelley left the young couple to privacy.

"Pray without ceasing, Sweetheart." Kelley whispered to his wife.

"I intend to. In fact, Mother and I began doing so this morning. I too feel an answer is within their reach, as you do."

"Good, you and I must be in one accord." Kelley replied, bringing a smile to his wife's face.

"Put our son to bed, wife. I am starved." He added and then gave her a light kiss on her lips.

Cindy and Dan were quiet as they had dinner with the Petersons. Their faces appeared as though they were both drained and weary from their upsets. They appeared to have calm within them now; their previous strife among them appeared to be silenced.

The children busy about their evening chores, Kelley instructed the four adults to hold hands. He prayed a powerful prayer in Dan and Cindy's behalf. It felt as though the room was filled with the spirit of the Lord. There was a peace of reassurance within each that the promises the Bible contained for believers would once again be fulfilled.

Kelley began to council the couple. He reminded Dan of his obligations to his wife, stressing how strong his love is to be toward his wife according to the word of God. He reminded Cindy of her duties, elaborating on reverencing her husband and being submissive unto him as the head of her family. He shared his own shortcomings in fulfilling his duties and being obedient unto the word made all the difference.

"Excuse me, Dad." Tom spoke, standing barely inside the den as not to invade the adult's privacy.

Kelley silenced his talk with looking toward his eldest son.

"Curt will not quit crying."

"Excuse me." Darla spoke and then left the den, closing the door behind her.

"I tried to rock Curt, but he continued to cry." Tom informed.

"He is a bit stubborn when he is hungry." Darla replied.

"I had not realized the time." She added.

"Curt sure can cry loud."

Darla smiled at Tom's remark, as they entered the nursery. Darla talked to calm her crying infant, as she changed his diaper. Tom stood near his mother in silence, observing his baby brother's actions.

"Bobbie said you will allow Pete and me a turn to feed Curt tonight. May we feed him now?"

"Yes, you may."

Tom excitedly left his mother's side to find Pete.

Darla silently admired both Tom and Pete's gentleness as they gave Curt his bottle. Their activity soon brought Karry, Heaven and Bobbie, observing their tiny brother.

Within the next couple of weeks, Cindy visited Darla often, sharing her concerns and progress made between her and Dan that created their horrible upset. Dan too, often visited Kelley. The two men would spend time alone in private. As Dan, like most men, was a private person in regards to important matters. Paula often visited Darla as Bill confidently called in regards to their upsets.

Darla placed the last dish on the table for her luncheon date as her guests arrived. With greetings of hugs exchanged with Paula, Cindy and Candy, the women took their places at the table. Requesting they hold one another's hands, Darla asked the blessing over their meal and requested the Lord protect their separate homes and families.

"Candy, how have you been, and the twins?" Cindy inquired politely.

"How much should I share, Darla?" Candy questioned jokingly, though her cheeks flushed.

"Whatever you wish, as much or as little, you are among friends. What is said will remain between us." Darla answered in all sincerity.

"I have my good days and my bad days like everyone, I guess. With the twins being seven, near eight-years of age, they are a handful. They both definitely are all boy. It is difficult raising them without a father. They feel cheated also. On my waitress earnings, I am not able to afford to have our own home. I do not feel I have become successful with my life. Compared to each of you, I know I'm not successful." Candy shared with a weak smile.

"If you are unable to afford a home, where do you and your sons live?" Paula questioned, her face expressing her concerns.

"With my mother and her newest husband." Candy answered, glancing at Darla.

"If I speak out of turn, Candy, pinch me." Darla advised with a gentle smile.

"Candy and her sons live in a beautiful home. They each have their own room. Candy must take a back seat to mothering her sons in order to supply them with a nice home, plenty of food and plenty of clothing. Her mother rules Candy and her sons. If Candy disagrees with these arrangements, she must go elsewhere to live and her mother will fight for custody of her sons."

"This is cruel." Cindy voiced disbelief on her face.

"Candy, your mother sounds like my parents. They will do anything for me, providing I allow them to rule my husband and me. By this not being allowed, they rarely even speak to me. Trust me when I say I sympathize with you. Hear me when I advise you to get out from under your mother's control. Your sons belong to you. Do not allow her to deprive you of a normal mother-son relationship. If you do, your sons will not have the one on one relationship between their mother as God intended. You see the boys lack without having their father. They will be lacking even more if their mother is as a sister instead of a mother." Paula suggested.

"I have tried, Paula. I am not able to afford rent on my wages. I realize none of you has been forced to survive on my wages, therefore, you do not understand my situation completely. I only have one alternative at present, move my sons into a housing project. I would give my sons to my mother before I would raise them in the highest crime area in town and cry nightly over their future." Candy explained.

"There simply must be a solution." Paula insisted, as though in deep thought.

"You sound like Darla." Candy said with a smile.

"She says if I would become a Christian, God would solve my problem."

"Yes, of course, the Lord will solve all your problems." Paula assured in all sincerity

"It is up to each of us quite often how soon our problems are solved. One must learn obedience unto the Lord by reading, understanding, and putting the Bible scriptures into action by living the word daily. Being patient and waiting upon the Lord to supply our needs and believing that He will, is difficult for some of us at times. I have never experienced money problems, this is true. But Candy, I never knew the meaning of love until Darla led me to the Lord. I was simply a piece of property or possession my parents had acquired. I would have rather lived in a shack and been permitted parents whom put their arms around me and told me they loved me. All the insecurities that I have had to deal with after years of being a Christian still at times haunt me."

"You appear overly confident." Candy replied, surprised with Paula's confession. Candy's reply brought a smile from Paula.

"Darla has been my counselor in the flesh, the Holy Spirit my guide and comforter, while I slowly learn what I should have learned as a child. I have been well trained to be confident, strong-willed and in control. Darla is younger than I am. Due to her loving home life as a child, she is much wiser than I in most every area of my life. My husband would like to have a child. He says if he could just have one child, he would be grateful. I am afraid I will not be a good enough mother. I did not grow up with a mother figure. I could not hurt my child by being insensitive to his or her needs out of ignorance. I have not yet conquered this fear nor have I learned all that is necessary yet to be a parent. Yet, I will win this battle. I will be a mother someday. The Lord uses his word to instruct me and others to assist me. All I had to do was admit my fear and then get busy overcoming it. Trust me Candy when I say this is only one of several areas the Lord has reconstructed within me. He is able to solve your every problem."

"I was blessed with wonderful parents, Candy. Until a few weeks ago, I did not understand financial crisis in other's lives. My parents gave me most everything during my youth. Dan had a good job and then he lost his job. We both felt our world had crumbled. I learned I was pregnant the same day I learned Dan no longer had an income. We fussed a bit with one another and we both said some cruel things during our moments of weakness, due to fear in regards to our future. Yet, our Jesus put his arms around us, gave us both a good shaking, getting our attention. Jesus says, He will never leave us or forsake us. It was so silly and childish of both Dan and I when we both know the Lord has and always will supply our every need." Cindy shared.

"I am sorry, Cindy. I had no idea." Candy sympathized with flushed cheeks.

"What will you do? You have a big beautiful home, surely it is costly."

"Dan did begin a new job this week. The salary is half his previous salary, so we put our home up for sale. There are good neighborhoods without being extravagant. I had not realized, Candy, how foolish I was with Dan's money until we experienced this crisis. Dan was often lecturing me in this area. I did not listen to his warning. Believe me; Dan has my full attention now." Cindy answered with an embarrassed laugh.

"Dan and I both have learned a lot through this. The most important lesson was not to take man's capabilities in success or providing for granted. Always know we must lean on the Lord to supply, not man. Man's best is not good enough to endure all obstacles Satan puts in one's path in a lifetime. Our home was my pride and joy. As Paula said, I would rather have a shack and have my husband and our child I am carrying, than our beautiful home that is pending sale. Salvation, love, and family, money does not purchase these ingredients to happiness and security."

"You know, Candy, whether a Christian or not, we each have

our share of trials. We each are sinners. Some of us are sinners saved by the grace of Jesus because we have chosen to be His servants. Jesus makes the unbearable bearable, and the impossible possible. He is so loving and forgiving even through our whining and complaining spells." Darla said in her compassionate way.

"Darla, you and Candy were friends in high school?" Paula questioned.

"Yes, we attended one year together." Darla answered.

"I am surprised, Candy. You have known Darla much longer than I, yet her Christian ways have not rubbed off on you." Paula voiced.

"Yes, Candy, what must I do for you to get smart and receive Jesus into your heart?" Darla inquired, with a soft laugh as Candy blushed at the women's questioning.

"Is this what some refer to as club preaching?" Candy questioned, bringing laughter from the women.

"I thought each of you understood, 'No man cometh to the Father, less the Holy Spirit draws him.'" She added, surprising Paula and Cindy with her knowledge of scriptures.

"You see, Paula, I have attempted to lead Candy to the Lord for many years. She has learned many scriptures to prove this." Darla shared giving Candy a warm smile, not wanting her to feel as an outsider.

"In these many years, you have never felt the Holy Spirit tug at your heart to accept salvation?" Cindy questioned, doubting her question was fact.

"Darla, your cousin must want me to pinch her." Candy said with an embarrassed laugh. Her reaction clearly expressing the Holy Spirit had most certainly dealt with her a time or two.

"We each had our time of being stubborn, not obeying, yielding to the Holy Spirit." Cindy assured.

"In fact, had I owned a set of ear plugs when I first moved into Darla's home as a teenager, I would have used them. It was very difficult ignoring the Holy Spirit tugging at my heart when living in a minister's home, although I held out for a few months."

She confessed her cheeks now flushed from sharing her past stubbornness.

"We have each been there. Salvation is not inherited; it is a personal repentance of one's sins unto God the Father through Jesus Christ His son. Had Salvation been inherited, Bill and I would have been near perfect, as my children would be. I confess my children are near perfect." Darla spoke, her face quickly blushing as she laughed at her bragging. She seldom bragged because this was prideful. Her joking sharing her true inward feelings of pride toward her children brought pleasant understanding smiles to her guests' faces.

"Having a family truly is a beautiful gift."

"I agree." Paula informed with a radiant smile.

"I feel blessed Bill is my husband, even though he is not near perfect, Darla."

The women tried to plan a luncheon once a week. It was their time to share, uplift, encourage, learn and grow in many areas. They let down their guards, as they were free to laugh or cry as they were united in one accord.

CHAPTER NINE

Summer had brought several changes in the young Peterson couple's lives. Their children had matured considerably. Tom, Pete and Bobbie appeared to have adjusted to their adoptive parents' ways. They seemed to be secure in their new home and at ease within the family. A stranger would not know one of the Peterson's children was adopted. When the Lord is the head of a family, He tends to choose family members perfectly.

Dressed in jeans, boots and a lightweight sweater for the cool fall morning, Darla quietly slipped out the back door of her home. Entering the corral, she mounted her horse bareback as she often did just as the sun began to rise. She enjoyed being silent, observing the wonders of the creator. Riding to the far field, she dismounted her horse. Walking slowly, leading her horse, she stopped near a canal. Picking up some rocks one by one, she tossed them into the water.

"Howdy, neighbor." Aaron greeted, as he drove along the ditch bank in his father's truck.

"Good morning." Darla greeted pleasantly.

"What on earth are you doing out at this early hour?"

"Admiring my property." He answered, pointing to the land on the opposite side of the canal.

"May I ask what you intend to do with your land, dearest brother-in-law?" Darla questioned, as she leaned against her father-in-law's pickup truck.

"I intend to use the land to fulfill a secret dream I have." He answered with a mysterious grin, knowing quite well he had aroused his sister-in-law's curiosity even more.

"Tell me dear, Aaron, will you ever outgrow your teasing stage?"

"I doubt it, I enjoy having fun. My older brother is the serious one of us Peterson brothers."

"Are you implying my husband lacks the ability to have fun?" Darla asked with a smile, though clearly expressing he best not badmouth her husband.

"No, Ma'am." Aaron answered quickly, in his serious manner, bringing a laugh from Darla.

"You appeared to be in deep thought when I arrived. Is my brother doing right by you?"

"Yes, of course. I am fortunate to have a husband like Kelley. I am often reminded how fortunate I am when women confide in me with their marital upsets."

"Good, I was about to suggest telling Dad if Kelley is not staying in line. I owe my brother a few heartaches. He caused me my share during our youth." Aaron shared with a grin, as though he would have enjoyed telling on Kelley.

"This knowledge is strange. Kelley says the same about you. As I recall, Kelley says had it not been for you snitching on him, he rarely would have gotten caught at doing his wrong acts."

"Perhaps." Aaron replied with a chuckle.

Aaron got out of the truck, standing near Darla.

"How does Kay like Japan?"

"She says Japan is an interesting country. Her letters are so far in between. She only gets mail once a month. She has not expressed this in her letters, but I detect she is homesick."

"Have you or Kelley suggested she come home?"

"No, whether my suspicions are correct or incorrect, Katie would not leave. She agreed to one-year missionary duties there. She would not go back on her word, regardless of her own needs or wishes."

"Personally, I was shocked to learn of Kay's missionary plans. She has expressed for years her desire to minister to the homeless, unfortunate street people."

"Kelley and I were shocked also, yet Katie does have an adventurous nature. She would be the first in line to go to any country, state or town if for no other reason than to explore the unseen in Katie's world. Until she became our daughter, Katie had not been out of this town. When we pastored the church in Arizona, on Katie's visits home she visited most of the state to learn and see all she could. In some ways, she is still as a child, searching, eager to learn and see all she feels she has missed out on with her neglectful childhood."

"For this reason, I am glad for Kay, she has the opportunity to visit Japan. Perhaps this adventure will calm her restless nature down, if this is possible." Aaron voiced, looking doubtful, with a boyish grin.

"Katie is independent, strong-willed and occasionally unpredictable." Darla confessed with a gentle smile.

"You may say that again." Aaron agreed, rubbing his cheek as though he had been slapped, bringing a tickled laugh from Darla, her face turning red.

"Aaron, I do apologize for Katie slapping you when she was fifteen. I had not been her mother long enough at that time to teach her proper manners as a young lady."

"Dar, Kay did not slap me, she punched me with her fist." Aaron informed.

Darla's mouth quickly flew open as though she was in shock. Her response brought a chuckle from Aaron.

"Kel tells me Kay is presently taking lessons in martial arts for self-defense. When our dear Kay does return home, I for one intend to keep my distance." Aaron's remark brought laughter from both adults.

With goodbye's said, Darla felt a deeper longing to see Katie, with she and Aaron talking of her.

Returning inside her home, Darla slipped her boots off at the back door. She washed her hands and then prepared the percolator with coffee. Her family still sleeping, she entered the den. Going to the huge bookshelf behind her husband's desk that served as the family's mini library, she stepped up on the stepladder. Removing Katie's eight-by-ten portrait of her in her college graduation cap and gown, Darla's eyes grew moist as she looked at the picture of her eldest child.

"Darla?" Kelley questioned, his face troubled as he noted his wife's sadness.

"Good morning." Darla greeted politely, forcing a weak smile. "You have caught me at an awkward moment."

Now standing at his wife's side, Kelley briefly looked at the framed picture his wife held with great care in her hands. He put his arm around her waist, pulling her close to his side and then kissed the top of her head.

"She is a beautiful and special young lady. I miss Katie also, Babe." Kelley spoke, comforting his wife.

"I realize Katie is a young adult. I am aware she is capable of surviving on her own. In some ways honey, you know as well as I, Katie is lacking in maturity due to her neglect as a child."

"I know this, Babe." Kelley agreed, looking down into his wife's tear-filled eyes.

"If only we had Katie much earlier than the age of fifteen. She has overcome a great deal, but she has not conquered all of her insecurities."

"Not yet, but I have faith she will. She is both a fighter and a go-getter. When she returns home in seven months, you will be granted the time needed to mother Katie, assisting her to eliminate the last hauntings of her youth. I truly believe this. She is fine, Sweetheart. She is safe in the hands of our Lord." Kelley reminded.

Looking up into her husband's eyes, Darla smiled as his words comforted her heart.

"Would you like to have a cup of coffee with your wife before your younger children awake, taking our time away from one another?" Darla asked, as she placed Katie's picture on the desk and then put her arms around Kelley.

"I would appreciate this."

"I would appreciate a good morning kiss if you are able to spare me one." Darla informed with a tender smile, looking into Kelley's gentle eyes.

"Your wish is my command."

Darla silenced her concerns for Katie. She came to peace within herself in regards to Katie's well-being. She felt restlessness within herself, as she had often noticed in Katie when she was bored with her activities. It appeared Kelley was too showing symptoms of restlessness. Much time was spent in silent prayer, questioning this. Darla seemed to arise early more frequent, going off riding alone. She felt closer to the Lord out among nature in the early quiet of the morning. She searched her heart for her answers, yet felt frustrated with finding no answers, no apparent reasoning for the restless feeling that continued to remain within her.

With Curt tucked in bed for the night, the older children busy with their studies under Kelley's supervision, Darla left her home. Pulling her lightweight jacket tight around her, folding her arms across her chest, shielding herself from the chilly desert night air, she slowly walked through her yard.

"Lord, what is my problem? Why do I feel emptiness when you have blessed me so? Am I too, becoming spoiled, unappreciative as many in my generation seem to be?" If I am, I beg of you to forgive me. I truly must appear ungrateful to you, Lord, after all you have done for me and continue to do for me. I will work harder at ridding myself of this empty, restless feeling."

Darla kept busy while the kids were away at school and Kelley was away at work. Though she physically was busy, within her large home and with Curt, the silence often gave way to she dwelling upon the emptiness that refused to leave regardless how busy she planned her weekdays.

Dressed in warm clothing for the chilly fall morning, Darla entered her mother's office with Curt in her arms.

"This is a nice surprise." Mom Roberts said happily.

"Hi, Mother." Darla greeted pleasantly, giving her mother a kiss. "Curt and I were bored and lonesome."

"Deary, how is it possible for you to ever become bored or feel lonely with parenting six children?" Mom Roberts questioned, surprised with her daughter's remark.

"I have been asking myself this question for weeks. I need something more, Mother, something for Darla. I trust I do not sound selfish."

"I know you dear and you are not a selfish person. Do you know what would feel this void?"

"Yes, I believe so." Darla answered slowly, looking into her mother's eyes.

"I want to become involved in nursing."

"Oh, Darla, just when I thought everything would be peaceful in our family. Dad will be upset; Kelley's dad will most likely voice his disapproval with Curt still a baby."

"I know this, Mother. I have not spoken with Kelley yet. He will most likely disapprove also. I know a full-time position would be too much at this time. I would be thrilled if I only worked one day a week. You understand my need to feel complete, right, Mother?" Darla questioned as though desiring to hear someone understood her need.

"I understand, but will Kelley understand?"

"He will learn to understand." Darla answered with a soft laugh, her face flushed.

"You have already decided to do this with or without Kelley's approval?"

"Yes."

"Let me know when you intend to tell Kelley, so I may take a vacation. I do not care to hear any opinions from the male folk in our family. They at times, are a bit narrow-minded when it comes to our capabilities as women." Mom Roberts suggested, with a weary smile.

"Perhaps you will speak with Kelley for me of my need before you leave on your vacation?"

"No, thank you, dear. I have Dad to deal with. You are on your own with Kelley." Mom Roberts answered, bringing a laugh from both women.

With conversing with her mother, Darla felt good for the first time since becoming restless. Her mother did not see her desire to return to nursing as a selfish desire.

"May I interrupt you ladies?" Russell, Mom Roberts' cousin and employer questioned as he entered the office in a hurried manner.

"Of course you may." Mom Roberts answered pleasantly.

Darla quietly went to the office window, allowing five-month-old Curt to see the wonders outside. The huge semi-trucks slowly entered and left the warehouse across from the office building, as her mother and her mother's employer discussed business.

"You might see if Darla would be interested in filling our well needed typing position." Russell suggested. With his goodbyes said to Darla, he left the office.

"What are the details in regards to the typing need in this office building that employees four typist?" Darla inquired, walking away from the window, nearing her mother's desk.

"The business is growing. We do need a part-time typist, but then you are a nurse."

"True, although my nursing skills are probably as rusty as my typing. It has been so long since I have been involved with either." Darla confessed with a smile.

"Where are you and my handsome grandson off to from here?"

"By Cindy's work to meet her for lunch. The way I have planned my day, Curt and I should return home in time for me to prepare dinner." Darla answered as she put Curt's coat on him.

"You truly are bored, avoiding your home." Her mother voiced, allowing her wishes for her daughter's contentment to show.

"Maybe dear, you could contain your boredom for a couple more months? It would be nice to enjoy the holidays without strife within our family."

"Mother, surely my working one or two days a week will not be that upsetting." Darla replied, as though surprised at her mother's suggestion.

"Dear, have you forgotten the disapproval both your father and Kelley's father expressed when Heaven was a baby?"

"Perhaps I had forgotten the depth of their disapproval." Darla answered, her face flushed as she released a sigh.

"I have been merely dwelling on Kelley's reaction. His dad gave him a hard time for agreeing to me working when Heaven was a baby. I best pray about this desire a bit longer before confronting Kelley. He clearly expressed when I became ill when we were newlyweds; my nursing desire is a want not a necessity. I suddenly recall this also." Darla answered with a disappointed smile.

"I do not have a strong enough case at present to win." She confessed with a soft laugh.

Darla enjoyed her luncheon date with Cindy. She attentively listened while Cindy shared the magnificent way the Lord was answering each of her and Dan's financial needs.

"Do you recall me expressing my opinion of Dan's decision to go into the ministry shortly after you and Kelley married?" Cindy asked with excitement in her voice.

"No, I am afraid that period of my life is vague. Mother refreshed my memory of that particular time in my life also today. Refresh my memory."

"I complained saying we or I would become a spectator for all to observe and judge."

"Yes, I recall you making that statement." Darla replied with a soft laugh.

"Seven years later, I will learn firsthand if my sarcastic comment will become a fact. Pastor Finks called Dan last night. He has asked Dan if he would fill the youth pastor position that will be available next month and Dan accepted."

"This is fantastic! I am thrilled for Dan. He has both studied and prayed for all these years." Darla voiced.

"Dan said had he still been working for his previous employer, he would not have been able to accept the youth pastor position, due to the often long hours and out of town trips. We never thought we would see any good from him losing his previous job five months ago. We were both so wrong. It is true, Dan and I have been faced to lean on the Lord as never before. This has been a time of deep soul searching. I for one have learned to be more humble unto the Lord, more attentive to my husband's wishes and opinions and less self-centered."

"I have noticed a major change in you. You have grown spiritually in many areas. It seems, at times, the Lord allows a drastic event to get our full attention." Darla complimented.

"Dar, do you and Kelley at times feel as though you are unable to be involved enough for the Lord?" Cindy questioned excitedly.

"Yes." Darla answered with a pleased smile.

"More often than not, one will feel this way if one is a yielded vessel. Welcome to the Lord's ministry of long hours, yet the most fulfilling occupation. The harvest is plentiful, yet the labors are few. Trust me, the Lord never runs out of tasks for us, providing we are obedient unto His leading."

Darla felt revived with Cindy sharing the many ways the Lord was working within her and Dan's life. The modest home the couple was able to purchase from the sale of their extravagant home left them with minimum financial obligations. Though Dan's income was less, he was able to accept a position in the ministry. This had been a desire of his heart for so long. Dan's number one goal was to please his Heavenly Father above others and himself.

"I believe I am as excited over Dan accepting the youth pastor position as he is. Dan's involvement with the park ministry to the street people is a ministry he and I are not involved in together. We have been praying for a ministry we could work together in. I have been terribly bored with having no activity I enjoy. I will be able to fill this void with assisting Dan with the youth."

"I am happy for you. You relate very well with teens."

"I do not easily admit to shortcomings." Cindy stated with a weak smile, her face flushed.

"Other than Dan needing a different job to allow him the proper time to be available for the Lord's leading, Dan did not deserve these past five months of financial battles. I am the one whom the Lord needed to shake to get my complete attention. When I realized this, I must have cried for hours, especially for thinking Dan did not want our baby. I harbored several mean thoughts at that time. I do not believe I have ever been as embarrassed or humiliated as I was then. When one feels they have hit bottom, one tends to let down all one's guard, taking a good look in the mirror. Dan has always been one-hundred percent sold out to the Lord. I learned I was seventy-five percent." She shared, her face now turning its reddest with her confession.

"Most of us are guilty of becoming somewhat or temporarily sidetracked." Darla defended sympathetically, taking Cindy's hand into her hand and giving it a tight squeeze.

"I have never questioned your walk with the Lord." Cindy smiled at her gentle, loving cousin.

"You always have a kind word." Cindy said, squeezing her cousin's hand in return.

"I was too self-centered and too materialistic and definitely not humble enough to be a minister's wife. This crisis has truly been a valuable lesson for me. I am sorry Dan has been forced to endure for my being a slow learner. Dan has always said, as I have often heard Kelley say, he is 'a pleaser of God, not man.' Dan and I have been married for ten years. This piece of scripture has just recently been whole-heartedly applied to my life. I did not intend, or realize this flaw in my Christian walk with the Lord. I truly want to be a 'pleaser of God and not man.'"

"I have always known this, Cindy. You are being too hard on yourself. We each learn at different stages. Kelley, Dan, and I were each raised in Christian homes. We have been reared to understand the Bible and a Christian's duty. You were not taught this until you came to live with my family when you were nearly out of high school. The issue is you have never turned your back on the Lord since you accepted salvation. You have continued to learn and grow closer and closer to the Lord. We each are still learning and still growing. I believe it takes many years to acquire wisdom through trial and error. Mother often says, 'one never reaches the age of not learning.'" Darla comforted.

Getting up from her side of the table, Darla sat down next to her cousin, giving her a tight hug.

"I am so happy for you and Dan." She added.

"Thank you." Cindy replied happily, hugging her cousin in return, her eyes growing moist.

"In four months you will be a mother. You have a comfortable home you are able to afford and you and Dan will be working for the Lord as a team shortly. Is there anything I have left out?" Darla questioned, with a gentle smile, as she looked into her cousin's eyes.

"Yes." Cindy answered excitedly.

"The youth pastor position even has a small salary attached. This is more than Dan and I requested."

"God is good."

"He is the best!" Cindy replied with an excited laugh, her eyes sparkling and her face aglow.

"Mama, Mama." Curt said loudly, as he completed his soda cracker.

"Shhh…" Darla replied, quickly wiping her son's face and hands with a napkin.

"He is demanding." Cindy voiced, smiling at five-month-old Curt.

"Very demanding." Kelley and I have decided Curt has Bill's characteristics.

"Impatient, most definitely." Cindy agreed admiring her nephew as his mother lovingly removed him from the highchair.

"His appearance is definitely Kel all over again."

"I agree he is quite handsome." Darla said as she looked into Curt's eyes and then gave him a tight hug.

"I will be so glad when my child is born. It will be the greatest feeling when I hold and hug our baby." Cindy shared excitedly.

"Most definitely. You and I will have the first perfect preacher's kids ever." Darla replied with a soft laugh, bringing a laugh from Cindy as Darla slipped Curt's coat on him.

Darla was relieved Cindy and Dan were steadfast in their walk with the Lord. Their obedience during their trials had been very profitable for them in every area of their life. Cindy was still Cindy, with her spunky side, yet she had become humble. She seemed to be completely at peace within. She and Dan appeared to have grown much closer together through enduring their tests and trials together. They experienced firsthand the accomplishment of being overcomers and of being dedicated soldiers in the Lord's army. They had gained the victory through their faith and obedience unto the Father, their Savior, and their Master.

Putting the last of dinner dishes in the dishwasher, Darla leaned against the counter. Silently, she stared through the window above the kitchen sink, as though her thoughts were millions of miles away from her present environment.

"Mommy." Seven-year-old Karry spoke, standing near her mother.

"Yes, Ma'am?" Darla questioned as she turned away from the window.

"Uncle Bill is on the telephone."

"Thank you."

Going to the end of the counter, Darla picked up the telephone as Karry and Heaven left the kitchen for outside.

"Mama, Mama." Curt said, coming toward his mother in his walker, with his arms raised.

"Hello." Darla greeted pleasantly, as she removed Curt from his walker.

"Hi, Sis, are you sitting down?"

"No, should I be?"

"With the news I am about to deliver to you, this might be best." Bill answered with a chuckle.

Darla sat down on the stepstool near the counter with Curt on her lap.

"I am sitting."

"Paula is pregnant." Bill informed, followed by laughter.

"Congratulations! I am so happy for you, Bill." Darla replied, her face radiant with happiness.

"How is Paula? Is she as thrilled as you are?"

"I am on the extension, Darla. Yes, I am thrilled, although your brother is already giving me a hard time in regards to the baby that has not yet arrived. He wants a son to go fishing with him. His plans sound selfish to me." She shared.

"I on the other hand, would like to have a daughter."

"To go shopping with..." Bill explained.

Bill's comment sent Paula into excited laughter. Darla smiled as her brother and sister-in-law's happiness touched her heart. This was a major turning point in the couple's lives. Paula was ready to be a mother. She had worked hard to overcome her fears of being a failure as a parent. Now, her heart was assured of her wants and capabilities. She not only felt happy and fulfilled with her accomplishments, her husband reaped the joys with her.

"Dada..." Curt said, holding his arms up, reaching toward his father as Kelley entered through the back door, carrying a bucket of milk for Tom.

"Bill, Kelley has just come in. Would you like to share your news with him or shall I?"

"I would appreciate this honor." Bill answered proudly, bringing a tickled laugh from Darla.

"Honey." Darla instructed, holding the telephone out toward her husband as Curt continued to chatter wanting his daddy.

Taking the telephone, holding it to his ear with his shoulder, Kelley quickly washed his hands at the sink.

"Hello." Kelley greeted, now taking Curt from his mother's arms into his, consoling his son.

"Congratulations. I am happy for you." Kelley said followed by a chuckle.

Darla tended to the milk their cow had generously produced for her family. One by one, the children began entering the kitchen from outside. Bobbie placed the basket of eggs he had collected on the counter near his father. Bobbie started to hurry from the counter when his father quickly prevented him by taking hold of his son's arm. Kelley's action startled both Darla and Bobbie, they both silently looking into Kelley face, questioning his action. Letting go of Bobbie's arm, Kelley turned his son's head toward his wife.

"Oh, Bobbie..." Darla said barely above a whisper, seeing the red swollen bump on his cheek.

"What happened to you?" Her heart going out to her eight-year-old.

Bobbie looked at his father with flushed cheeks, as though fearing he would be punished.

"Bobbie?" Darla questioned again, not understanding his silence.

Suddenly Bobbie pulled away from his mother. He wrapped his arms around his father's waist, burying his face against him. Darla was silent. Kelley handed Curt to his wife and then put his hand on Bobbie's back, patting him until his telephone conversation was completed.

"Who punched you, Bob?" Kelley questioned, as he hung the telephone up.

Bobbie remained silent with his face buried.

"Call the kids in, Babe." Kelley instructed, looking at his wife with concern on his face.

Kelley silently continued to pat Bobbie on his back while Darla sought their other four children.

"Karry is not talking either." Darla informed, holding her unhappy daughter's hand in her hand, as she showed Kelley a red mark on Karry's arm.

"Who is doing the hitting?" Kelley questioned, now fully irritated.

"Pete?" Kelley questioned in his stern tone.

"I did not touch anyone, Dad, honest." Pete answered quickly.

"Heaven?"

"I did not hit anyone either." Heaven answered nervously looking at Tom.

"Tom?"

"I did not hit Karry, Dad. I would never hit a girl."

"Yet, you punched your brother, am I correct?"

"Yes, Sir." Tom answered with flushed cheeks, now staring at the floor.

Kelley removed Bobbie's arms from around his waist.

"Look at me, Bob." Kelley ordered.

Bobbie slowly raised his head looking into his father's eyes.

"Are you going to whip me?" Bobbie questioned with watery eyes.

"For what reason, do you ask?"

"I slapped Karry." Bobbie answered slowly.

"She would not quit bossing me."

"You slapped Karry, so Tom punched you because you slapped your sister."

"Yes, Sir." Bobbie answered.

"I suppose I should punch Tom now for him striking you." Kelley voiced.

The children each looked at their father and then Tom.

"Would this make you feel better?"

Bobbie shook his head no.

"Sometimes girls are bossy, Bob. I do not understand why they feel this need, but nonetheless, we guys must learn to either grin and bear this or quietly walk away until they calm their bossy ways. You best learn this. If you dare to hit again, I will paddle you. There will be no slapping or punching from girls or boys. You dare to lay a hand on your brother again, Tom, you will not be able to sit down for a while." Kelley assured in his sternest tone, noting the bump on Bobbie's face was now blue, not only red.

"Yes, Sir." Tom replied with flushed cheeks.

"I am sorry, Bob."

"You said you would stop punching on me." Bobbie glared, as tears came to his eyes, his anger flaring, surprising his family by his outburst.

"Tom, you have punched on your brother in the past?" Kelley questioned.

Tom now stared at the floor with flushed cheeks. Slowly putting his hands in his front pockets of his jeans, he remained silent.

"Tom, answer me." Kelley ordered his tone more stern.

"A couple of times." Tom answered slowly, though he continued to stare at the floor.

"Someday when I get big, I will bust you a good one like our other dad did to you for punching on me." Bobbie threatened.

Eleven-year-old Tom quickly looked at Bobbie, his eyes filling with tears.

"Be quiet, Bobbie." Nine-year-old Pete scolded his face now as flushed as Tom's face. Pete stepped in front of Tom as though prepared to protect his older brother.

"Girls, you may be excused." Kelley informed, as Heaven and Karry quietly left the kitchen.

"I am having a problem understanding you boys. You each must help me out." Kelley informed, patiently leaning against the kitchen counter.

The three biological brothers looked at their adoptive father as though stunned by his calm nature.

"Bob, are you implying your previous father hit Tom with his fist?"

"Yes, for punching on me." Bobbie answered quickly, as though this form of punishment was acceptable.

Kelley looked at his wife shaking his head in disbelief.

"Were we not told the boys had a good home life?" Kelley questioned.

"We were told this." Darla answered with watery eyes, secretly questioning their adoptive sons' past upbringing.

"Peter, please move from in front of Tom. Dad is not going to strike your brother." Darla instructed with compassion on her face, as she sat Curt in his walker and then silently and wearily sat down at the table, looking at her husband.

Pete slowly moved from standing in front of Tom. The three brothers looked at one another again, as though shocked with their parents' calm ways.

"What now, Kel?" Darla questioned, releasing a sigh.

"I will be good Darla, I promise." Tom assured quickly, as though devastated by her question.

"Me too, Karry may boss me all she wants." Bobbie sided as though frightened.

Pete silently backed up, as though he had seen a ghost as tears streamed down his cheeks.

"Honestly, Kelley." Darla said, as tears quickly began down her cheeks, by the boy's scared reactions.

Kelley seemed to be frozen from shock as the boys reacted, expressing a side he did not know existed among the brothers.

"Kelley." Darla said as though pleading for him to snap into action.

Kelley got ahold of himself.

"Tom." Kelley spoke compassionately.

"Please do not call your mother Darla."

"Yes, Sir." Tom replied nervously wiping his tears away, hoping his adoptive father was about to forgive him.

"I am sorry, Dad." Tom said, as his tears continued, even though he tried hard to make them stop.

"I know you are, Son, just as I know how sorry Bobbie is for upsetting Karry. Come here guys."

The three brothers slowly went to Kelley. He silently put his arms around the boys. The boys eagerly hugged Kelley in return. They seemed to hug Kelley forever. With tears still streaming, Darla silently observed the boys. Her heart felt as though it was broken with her new knowledge the three brothers harbored scars of some neglect and perhaps some abuse from their biological father. Nonetheless, they certainly were not without insecurities, even though they bore the last name of Peterson for the past five months.

One by one, the boys removed their arms from around Kelley, each wiping their eyes with their hands.

"Boys, there is Kleenex on the counter." Kelley instructed as he removed his neatly folded handkerchief from his back pocket.

"Mom has dibs on my handkerchief." He informed with a gentle smile.

The boys each smiled as did Darla with Kelley's spoken words and his gesture, handing his wife his handkerchief.

"What will you use for your tears, Dad?" Darla asked, looking up into her husband's gentle, compassionate face, his eyes moist.

"Mom, everyone knows men do not cry." Kelley answered, winking at the boys, bringing another smile to the brothers' faces as they threw their Kleenex away.

"Besides, I used my shirt." He added with a grin, bringing big grins to his sons' faces, as he lightly teased his wife.

Darla released a sigh as she shook her head at Kelley, as though giving up on him using manners. Kelley looked at his sons rolling his eyes up at his wife's ways. The three boys laughed at their father's play.

"I saw you mocking me. You are being a terrible example." Darla said, though she also laughed with her husband's often-humorous ways.

"Do not ever attempt doing as I did to Mom, boys. I doubt she will notice the humor behind your actions." Kelley explained, pulling out a chair from the kitchen table to sit on.

"Come sit down, guys." He instructed, his face growing serious.

With the three brothers silently seated at the table, Kelley asked many questions digging deep inside the boys' minds and past. He would work for hours on end if necessary, to fully understand one harboring pain or insecurities to assist one in feeling complete and without bondage.

Removing her weary five-month-old from his walker, taking Curt into her arms, Darla quietly left the kitchen. Entering the front room where Karry sat before the piano practicing her nightly lesson.

"Karry." Darla spoke and then waited for her daughter to remove her hands from the piano.

"I will be in the nursery preparing Curt for bed. When you are finished practicing, I would like you and I to talk."

"Okay, Mommy." Seven-year-old Karry agreed.

With a gentle smile and a light kiss on the top of her daughter's head, Darla left Karry's side. Entering her daughter's room, Darla found Heaven removing her nightclothes from her drawer.

"Are you okay, Sweetheart?" Darla asked, noting the worried look on her daughter's face.

"I am okay, but everyone else is upset." Heaven answered, releasing a long sigh as her mother often did when baffled or feeling defeat.

"I told the boys and Karry that Daddy will never send them away because they are all Petersons. They do not believe me. I have been the Peterson the longest, but they never listen to me."

"I am sure they each listen to you, Deary." Darla comforted, with a tender smile, patting Heaven on her back.

"Perhaps they want to believe you more than anything, but they are afraid to. Daddy and I thought the boys and Karry knew we would never send them away with them being adopted. We did not know until tonight they questioned this. You have always had Daddy and me. Dad and I have always had our parents. Perhaps we never being without parents do not understand how scared Karry and the boys must feel at times when they recall their past when not having parents. We will work harder at convincing them they will always be your brothers and sister, even when they have a tough day being good." Darla said, with her arm around Heaven's shoulder.

"You and Curt are so fortunate, Sweetheart. You do not have these fears within you. I wish not one child in all the world was without loving parents."

"Me too, Mommy. Bad parents must make Jesus cry a lot. Jesus loves children and Daddy says Jesus even loves children when they do bad things. I hope I never make Jesus cry or you or Daddy." Seven-year-old Heaven shared looking up into her mother's gentle eyes.

"I appreciate your kind thoughts. I know both Daddy and Jesus would also appreciate this. You always do your best to please Jesus no matter what and you will help keep His tears from shedding. This I assure will also keep you happy." Darla replied as Curt began to fuss, becoming impatient from his long, tiring evening.

"Take your bath, dear, while I get your sleepy brother to bed."

Curt dressed for bed, Darla sat down in the rocker near his crib. She softly sang, 'Jesus loves you,' as he nursed and she rocked him.

Gently and lovingly, Darla looked at her baby. He was safe, loved and content. She and Kelley held his future in their hands whether their baby of only a few months would continue to grow in a loving, safe environment or not.

"How could any parent hurt their child for any reason, purposely?" She silently questioned as she gently rubbed her baby's head, he beginning to fall asleep without a worry or a care.

Karry arrived outside the nursery door.

"Mommy." She spoke, barely above a whisper through the slight opening of the door.

"Come in, dear." Darla instructed, putting a lightweight baby blanket over her and Curt, as he continued to nurse.

"May I see your arm?"

Karry obediently showed her mother the light red mark on her arm.

"It does not hurt anymore."

"I am glad for this. I am afraid Bobbie will be in a bit of pain at least throughout the night. His cheek is swollen and bruised." Darla said.

Karry looked at her mother with saddened eyes.

"Is Daddy real angry at me for being bossy?" Karry questioned slowly, starting to bite her nails, expressing her nervousness.

Darla quickly removed her daughter's hand from her mouth, holding her hand in hers.

"No nail biting allowed. I keep telling you a princess must have nice nails. You do still intend to be Daddy's princess, right?" Darla asked lovingly giving her tiny hand an extra tight squeeze.

"If Daddy wants me to be." Karry answered slowly.

"Do you question Daddy's wants?"

Karry shrugged her shoulders and then looked down at her baby brother, no longer looking at her mother.

"Daddy not only wants this, he will expect this. You, Heaven and I will always be princesses in Dad's eyes, even when we have our bossy or grouchy spells. Dad may tell you to quit being bossy, lest you receive a punishment. But, Sweetheart, if you were the most terrible daughter in the world, you would still be a princess in Dad's eyes."

"Just because I am Daddy's daughter?" Karry asked, now looking into her mother's eyes once again.

"This is why." Darla answered with an understanding smile.

"I thought Daddy might send the boys away for hitting. Then I thought if I had not bossed Bobbie, he would not have hit me. I know Daddy likes having sons to do boy things with." Karry said with watery eyes.

"Karry, you have been a Peterson the second longest of all you children. You thought Dad would blame you for Bob's and Tom's actions sending you away also?"

Karry slowly nodded her head yes. Darla put her arm around Karry's waist pulling her close to her.

"You are not going to any other home ever, or your brothers. You each are a member of this family. As upset as Dad or I may become at times with your behavior, your brothers' behavior, Heaven's behavior, or baby Curt's behavior, we will not quit being your parents. You are each stuck with Dad and me forever." Darla clarified sincerely, looking into Karry's brown eyes.

"Please believe me, Karry. You have been my daughter for a year. I believe it is time you learn to stop questioning our love for you as well as you need to stop thinking Dad and I would ever send you away."

Karry gently touched her mother's long hair as she looked into her mother's eyes that seemed to be pleading with her to be happy.

Pulling her daughter even closer to the rocker she occupied, Darla gave her a kiss.

"Daddy and I love you, Sweetheart."

"I love you and Daddy, Mommy, more than anyone." Karry replied and then suddenly hugged her mother's neck tightly. Karry deeply touched her mother's heart.

"Karry, come sit on my lap, I feel the need to hold you." Darla instructed, moving Curt to make room for Karry also.

Karry, sitting on her mother's lap with Darla's arm around her, she leaned her head back against her mother's chest, feeling safe, secure and loved.

As the hour grew late, Darla tucked her daughter's in bed for the night without the aid of her husband. Dressed for bed, Kelley and the three brothers still conversing in the kitchen, Darla slipped under her covers with a book. Her pillows arranged she sat up in bed, leaning against her pillows as she read her choice book. Her reading appeared to be in vain. Her mind continued to wander to her family's upsets.

"Mom." Tom spoke, as he and Pete arrived in the open doorway.

"Yes?" Darla questioned, laying her book down.

The boys now approached, stopping near her bedside.

"Pete and I wanted to tell you goodnight."

"I appreciate your thoughtfulness." Darla replied with a kind smile.

"Where is Bobbie?"

"He fell asleep, so Dad carried him to bed. Mom, I got Bob some ice for his cheek before he went to sleep." Tom informed, his cheeks quickly turning red.

"Sit down, boys." Darla instructed, patting the empty bed space next to her. Both boys obediently sat down.

"I am pleased you prepared an ice pack for your brother. Did

Dad tell you to do this, or did you do this because you knew this was right?"

"Dad did not tell me, I wanted to make Bob feel better." Tom answered in all his sincerity.

"Good. This, your compassion, I am sure made Bobbie feel better. Do you boys feel okay inside now?"

"Yes, Ma'am." Tom answered, his face flushing again.

Tom looked at Kelley as he entered the bedroom. Keeping his eyes on his adoptive father, Tom slowly stood up. Darla silently looked at Tom and then her husband, puzzled once again by Tom's actions.

"Sit down, Son, until Mom has excused you, please." Kelley instructed his face sensitive to his son's silent uncertainties.

Tom's face was once again relaxed, as he silently sat back down next to his brother.

"Perhaps I should allow you boys to call it a night. It is terribly late and you must be exhausted." Darla said as she took the boys' hands into hers.

With a kiss and a hug given to both sons, Darla said her goodnights. Kelley walked the boys to bed. Nearly an hour passed before he left his sons' room, returning to his wife.

Laying her book on her nightstand, Darla turned her lamp off.

"I was about to give up on you." Darla informed, as Kelley prepared for bed.

"Are the boys truly okay, Honey?"

"They will be with time. Pete and Bob mainly feared you and I would feel their behavior was unacceptable, therefore, we would send them to another home to live. Apparently, Karry has shared her past foster homes with the boys. They thought if they pushed you or me too far, we would no longer want them."

"Have you convinced them this is not true?"

"I believe so." Kelley answered as he got into bed.

"Tom will take some time to put his dad's ways aside. Apparently, Tom was allowed to corral Pete and Bob when their dad was away. He assisted his mother in most matters. When the boys' dad was home, he expected Tom to take a back seat. Tom put the hammer on Bob a couple of times when his dad was home. According to Pete, the boys' dad worked Tom over good."

"Explain worked over."

"He blackened Tom's eye and bloodied his nose. Tom was also either punished or put down if he appeared to need or want his mother for any reason. This was why Tom was uncomfortable talking with you when I entered our room earlier."

"Yet, Bobbie and Pete were allowed to have a normal relationship with both parents?" Darla questioned, looking into her husband's eyes.

"From what I understand, yes. With the boys' dad away from home most of the time, these upsets were few and far between, nonetheless, the upsets left a lasting impression. Pete says they each were very close to their mother. He said, 'our mom was a fair lady and she did not pick favorites like our dad did.'"

"We thought the boys had adjusted so well and quickly. I am beside myself with seeing how frightened the boys were, especially Pete standing in front of Tom as though you were going to punch an eleven-year-old." Darla said, resting her head on her husband's shoulder.

"I was rather shocked myself to learn of each of their hidden fears."

"Brace yourself for the latest update on Karry." Darla advised.

"Karry asked me if you were sending her away for creating these upsets by bossing."

"This is unbelievable. What am I, a villain? Karry has been with us over a year and the boys a year. You would think by now they would each feel secure."

"Maybe the children will truly find their place now. Maybe this upset was needed for the children to have their proof how deep our love is for them." Darla suggested.

"Perhaps."

Kelley and Darla were overly attentive to their adoptive children's moods in the weeks to come. Kelley spent extra time alone with the boys, often inventing errands to run involving the boys with him. When home, uninvolved with the boys, Kelley gave of himself to the girls, reassuring Karry of her specialness in their family as well as Heaven's. He often encouraged Tom to assist his Mother, teaching his son it was both natural as well as acceptable by Kelley for him to be involved with his mother.

The alarm awoke Darla early. Reaching for the alarm to turn it off, she noted her bed was empty of her husband. Dressed for the day, Darla entered the kitchen.

"Good morning." She greeted pleasantly.

"Good morning, Babe." Kelley greeted, briefly taking his eyes from the notepad in front of him.

"Were you not able to sleep? You are up earlier than usual." Darla inquired as she poured herself a cup of coffee.

"I slept well, I awoke early is all." Kelley answered, though keeping his eyes on his notepad in deep concentration.

Darla went to her husband's side.

"May I ask what you are doing?"

"Seeing where we might cut corners next month. It costs a fortune raising six kids." Kelley rubbed his head wearily.

"Things are tight." Darla agreed after carefully checking over her husband's figures.

"Too tight for me."

"What do you suggest we do to loosen the rope we have placed around our necks?" Darla questioned, bringing a smile to her husband's face by her choice of words.

"I do not know, Babe." Kelley answered, laying his pencil down and giving his wife his full attention.

"You could call the dentist today, asking if he would give us a refund on the braces we allowed him to put on Tom's teeth last month."

"I am sure this would please Tom to be relieved of the metal in his mouth." Darla replied with a smile.

"You know, Honey, you are blessed in many ways. Have you

forgotten you are married to a nurse?" Darla questioned, looking into her husband's eyes.

"What are you driving at, Babe?" Kelley asked his voice gentle, yet his face now serious.

"I would like to return to nursing. I had intended to discuss this with you several weeks ago before we began working overtime with the boys and Karry."

"No, Darla." Kelley replied without batting an eye.

"You have enough to do as it is."

"Kel..." Darla tried again.

"I am surprised at you, Darla." Kelley informed, scolding.

"The Lord has given you ministry after ministry for Him. He is forever filling your time with work. Years ago, you chose between your nursing career and a ministry for the Lord. Your present ministry is meeting the needs of six children." He reminded, as though put out with his wife's suggestion.

With flushed cheeks from her husband's scolding, Darla sipped her coffee saying no more.

"Dar..." Kelley spoke, taking his wife's hand into his, his voice gentle once again.

"I will always find a way to provide for our family. This I assure you."

"Honey, I have never doubted your capabilities to provide for your family in the past nor will I in the future." Darla replied supportively, concealing her disappointment with Kelley not realizing her desire to return to a work she found fascinating.

"Mom, I do not feel well." Tom informed, his face flushed as he slowly entered the kitchen in his pajamas.

Quickly vacating her chair, Darla went to her eldest son's aid. She put her hand on his forehead.

"You feel as though you have a fever, sit down, dear." She instructed.

Going to a cabinet, Darla removed a thermometer. Tom had laid his head down on his crossed arms on the table.

"Where do you hurt, Son?" Kelley questioned.

"All over, but my head hurts most." Tom answered with his eyes closed.

"Here, kiddo." Darla said.

Tom opened his mouth allowing his mother to insert the thermometer, though he did not raise his head from the table.

"I had hoped you would bypass the flu this winter, dear." She gently rubbed her son's back to sooth him, as she stood at his side waiting to read the thermometer.

"I spoke with Vera at the youth detention center yesterday. She says the majority of the kids presently have the flu." Kelley shared.

Darla removed the thermometer from her son's mouth.

"Four kids were absent from my class yesterday with the flu." Tom informed.

"You make number five." Darla informed.

Cleaning the thermometer and then returning it to its proper place, Darla dealt with Tom. Returned to his bed, Darla gave him a kiss on his forehead.

"Thanks, Mom." Tom said, holding his aching head.

"You are welcome, Sweetheart. I will be in later to check on you."

Returning to the kitchen, Darla began breakfast preparations. Kelley approached his wife from behind. Slipping his arms around her waist, he kissed the top of her head.

"You are a wonderful nurse, Miss Darla. We truly need your services here. Will you please grant us our request? We are in need of a nurse on call, twenty-four hours daily, and seven days weekly. The pay is not worth mentioning. The fringe benefits are endless." Kelley said, bringing a laugh from his wife.

"You and your crew of children have yourselves a nurse." Darla answered with a smile.

"I thank you; our children thank you, as well as we each appreciate you, Baby doll." Kelley said with another kiss.

"I will wake the children."

Darla nursed and pampered Tom through his illness, as well as Heaven and Pete. She felt badly for the children being ill. Her nursing abilities being needed was a good feeling. Nursing the children, and waiting on them seemed to eliminate her desire to work away from home.

"Darla." Paula called.

"Hi." Darla greeted pleasantly, entering the kitchen with a tray of dishes.

"How are you?"

"Happy and excited." Paula answered her face radiant with happiness.

"I have something to show you." She informed, setting her purse and shopping bag on the table.

Paula eagerly removed the clothing items from the bag.

"Maternity outfits. I thought you had a difficult time seeing the beauty in being with child." Darla teased.

"You are as skinny as a rail, yet you are wishing to physically fill these outfits someday?" She inquired with a happy smile.

"Yes." Paula answered without hesitation.

"I want the entire world to know Bill and I will be granted a child." She shared with a child-like laugh.

Darla gave her sister-in-law a hug.

"I am so happy that you and Bill are happy."

"I believe you are. Bill and I are the happiest we have ever been." Paula replied, removing a glass from her sister-in-law's cabinet.

"When my children are through passing the flu to one another, Kelley and I must have a party in your and Bill's and Cindy's and Dan's honor. You each have been through some difficult struggles. We should celebrate while everyone is on the mountain top at the same time." Darla suggested kindly filling Paula's glass with iced tea.

"I for one would enjoy a party with the family. It seems more often than not, we each are too busy for quality time together unless there is a crisis."

"We are guilty as charged." Darla agreed.

"You and I must put an end to this. How does a once a month get together for our family with no family member allowed to be absent sound?"

"Yes, this would be great. I want my child to be close to each of her relatives. This is very important to me for this is important for the child." Paula answered, thrilled with Darla's idea.

"My child will have a close family, like her daddy grew up with."

"We each will love her or him, endlessly." Darla assured with a pleased smile.

"This I know without any doubt. Your family does not lack in the area of love by any means. I still at times feel overwhelmed by the depth of love your parents have for you and Bill. I find this even more overwhelming to see this love expressed between you and Bill." Paula replied with a look of pride, as the women sat down at the table with their drinks.

"Mom." Pete spoke entering the kitchen in his pajamas.

"Yes?" Darla questioned, putting her hand on his face and forehead, finding his flushed face still terribly warm.

"May Heaven and I watch television if we lie down?"

"No, you are ill; therefore you will stay in bed. Besides, since when do you watch television in the middle of the day?"

"My other mom let me watch television whenever I wanted."

"Oh, Peter, you have such a tough life." Darla said, putting her arm around his waist, pulling him to her and giving him a hug.

"You know what times you may watch television. Do not give me a hard time."

"Pete occasionally has a difficult time dealing with the endless rules we Peterson's have, Aunt Paula." Darla said, smiling at her sister-in-law.

To Darla's surprise, Pete did not find humor in his mother's comment, which was unusual for his humorous nature.

"I do not feel well." Pete said, looking into Darla's eyes as though pleading to feel better.

"I know you feel miserable, Sweetheart. Sit with us for a bit until you feel sleepy."

Pete sat on his mother's lap. With her arm around him, he laid his head on her shoulder, closing his aching eyes.

"With the boys living with you and Kelley, at least a year, you are still compared to their biological mother?" Paula asked with disbelief on her face.

"Peter only compares aloud when he misses her most.'

Pete slowly opened his eyes. Looking up into his adoptive mother's eyes, she looked down at him, giving him an understanding smile. With a kiss to Pete's forehead, he slowly reclosed his eyes, putting his arm around his mother's neck. The women smiled at one another with Pete's gesture.

"Kelley tells me Bill will be our new Sunday school teacher for the young adult class."

"Yes, Bill seemed eager to accept the position. Now that he has accepted, he has complained to me about having to stand in front of people." Paula shared with confusion on her face.

"This is our often complaining, Bill. Bill does not like being in front of people, so this comment is a legitimate complaint, yet he is quite capable of teaching. He does well with small groups. He was a fine youth leader during his teen years."

"I did not know Bill was involved in the leadership of anything in his past."

"You must be kidding?" Darla questioned looking at her sister-in-law as though in shock.

"Visit my parents and have Mother give you Bill's high school and college yearbooks. You will probably learn more your neglectful husband has not shared with you. Have you any further questions in regards to Bill's past before you and he met? I will gladly answer all I know." Darla assured with a soft laugh.

Pete slowly opened his eyes. He lightly put his fingers to his mother's lips, gaining the women's attention.

"Uncle Bill says you tell all his secrets." Pete informed, bringing laughter from both women.

"Trust me, Sweetheart; I owe it to your Uncle Bill to tell his secrets." Darla replied with a soft laugh, blushing.

Pete smiled a weak smile at his mother, approving of her spunky response and then slowly closed his heavy eyes again.

The children eventually ceased spreading the flu to family

members. With each child well and returned to school, Darla felt a lonely tugging at her again to return to her nursing desire. Waving goodbye to her husband and five school age children, she lingered at the back door until the family car was out of sight.

"Mama." Curt said, holding his arms toward his mother.

"I am coming, dear."

Preparing a washcloth, she approached Curt in his highchair. Though Darla gently spoke to Curt as she washed his face and hands, she continued with a preoccupied expression. Setting Curt on the floor, she quickly closed the wooden folding gate, blocking the doorway so Curt was unable to leave the kitchen. Silently, she filled the dishwasher with breakfast dishes.

"Good morning, dear." Mom Roberts greeted, entering through the back door.

"Hi, Mother."

"I have been concerned about your silence."

"My silence?" Darla questioned puzzled, as she started the dishwasher, looking into her mother's gentle eyes, seeing her concerns.

"Yes, your silence. Please sit down and give me a few minutes of your time."

Darla politely sat down at the table.

"You have openly and kindly assisted Cindy with her upsets. You did a superb job counseling with Paula, assisting her through her insecurities. Dad tells me Kelley is involving himself with the street ministry again to fill his void. You have spent long hours to relieve your adoptive children of each of their insecurities, but what about Darla? I have yet to hear any word in regards to Darla's void being filled."

"I have no answer, Mother. When I feel as though I have my answers, I quickly am faced with cancelling them."

"You are a mother. You know as a mother if one of your children is restless, you are concerned for that child until you have a solution. We must find your solution, so you and I will feel better."

"Perhaps I am becoming spoiled, Mother. Perhaps I want my cake and eat it too." Darla replied with a weak smile.

"This is a cop out on your part. You are definitely showered with love. You are not acting in a spoiled manner whatsoever." Have you discussed your desire to be involved in nursing with Kelley?"

"Not entirely, I chickened out. Kelley was going over our finances early one morning and he expressed his concerns with our lack of finances. I reminded Kelley he was blessed with a wife that is a nurse. He did not see this as a blessing. He gave me a speech saying I chose years ago between my nursing career and a ministry for the Lord. He says the children are my ministry and I have enough to deal with."

"You must be softening, dear. I have not known you to give in so easily if you whole-heartedly believed in something."

"This is my true problem. I am not clear on what is actually right. It is a fact that I long to be involved in nursing. I miss it terribly, Mother. It is also a fact that Kelley's salaries from being associate pastor and his carpentry salary is barely keeping us going with six children to provide for. In my eyes, one to two days nursing would solve both these needs. Kelley assures me he will provide for us alone without my assisting. He also worries I will become overworked and become ill. If one of the children should be ill from school on a day I had to work, I would feel terribly guilty not being with them. Karry and the boys have been through so much. I do not want to spoil their accomplishments by not being available for them as they have need of me."

"Therefore, everyone's needs are considered and met except my daughter's needs." Mom Roberts replied, releasing a weary sigh.

"You and Dad did teach Bill and me to put others first, Mother." Darla reminded with a tender smile, bringing a smile to her mother's face.

"You were also taught each individual is responsible for his or her degrees of happiness, accomplishments, and fulfillment. You are lacking in being fulfilled. I promise you, if I notice the often restless faraway look in your eyes, your husband will also notice."

"You are right, Mother. I best quit ignoring my need and find a solution. Perhaps you came equipped with a solution?"

"Now that you are ready to stand up for your needs, I will offer you the perfect suggestion for your solution. You will still have your husband to deal with on your own." Mom Roberts answered with a smile.

"We both know I am capable of handling my husband." Darla confessed, bringing a laugh from her mother.

Darla listened attentively to her mother's suggestion. Her heart longed to fulfill the restlessness within her. With Mom Robert's visit completed, Darla felt she truly had a lasting answer, a solution even Kelley could not find fault in or her own guilt tug at her, preventing her of fulfilling her desires. She once again had a song in her heart. Busily preparing dinner for her soon arriving children and husband, Darla's eyes seemed to sparkle. She would inform her husband of her plans with the completion of dinner.

"Hi, Mommy." Heaven and Karry greeted, entering their home.

"Hi, Sweethearts." Darla greeted happily, giving and receiving hugs from her daughters.

"Where are your brothers?"

"Daddy picked them up from school." Karry answered.

"Again..." Heaven added with a sigh.

"Daddy said to give you this note, so you will know the boys are really okay."

"Are you upset because Daddy did not take you and Karry with him also?" Darla questioned, noting her daughter's unhappy expression.

"Yes." Heaven answered slowly, picking up her baby brother from the kitchen floor, avoiding eye contact with her mother.

"Whom did Daddy take out for ice cream cones Sunday afternoon?" Darla questioned, looking at Heaven with disapproval on her face.

Heaven's face flushed with her mother's question, as Heaven now looked into her mother's patient face.

"Karry and I. I forgot, Mommy." Heaven answered, now wishing she could withdraw her complaint.

"Do try harder to remember your Daddy is fair to each of you."

"Yes, Ma'am."

Heaven set her baby brother back on the floor near his toys. Curt quickly crawled behind his sister, chattering. Going to the fruit bowl, Heaven removed an apple from the bowl and then sat down at the breakfast table. Karry sat at the table drinking a glass of lemonade she had gotten herself.

"Daddy said he is bringing a guest for dinner." Karry informed, she now picking Curt up, returning to her chair with her brother on her lap.

"Does Dad's guest have a name?"

Karry shrugged her shoulders to answer, 'I do not know.'

"He works with Daddy and he has a ponytail." Karry answered.

"He has sad eyes."

"We will be extra pleasant and happy at dinnertime, in hopes Dad's guest will replace his sadness with happiness." Darla suggested.

Darla waited dinner for her husband, sons and the unknown dinner guest. She patiently sat at the table while her daughters excitedly chattered away, filling her in on their school day.

"Hi, Mom." Tom, Pete and Bobbie greeted.

"Hello to each of you. What has Dad had you boys doing?" She inquired, noting the sawdust on her younger son's clothing.

"Whoops." Pete said, looking down at his dusty clothes.

"We forgot to brush our clothes off, Bob." The two brothers quickly returned outside.

"We were helping Dad and Grandpa." Tom informed, pouring himself a glass of water.

"Hi, Babe." Kelley greeted pleasantly, giving his wife a kiss.

"Hi, welcome home." Darla greeted, glancing at her watch, reminding her husband of his late arrival.

"Your Dad would not allow us to leave. He is to blame for our late arrival." Kelley explained, reopening the back door for Pete, Bob and his dinner guest.

"Mike?" Darla questioned, as though seeing a ghost as her eyes and Kelley's' friend's eyes met.

"Darla?" The young man questioned, he expressing his surprise with seeing her as well.

"Mike, my wife Darla. Dar, my new coworker, Mike." Kelley introduced, teasing, they depriving him of a proper introduction and his comment bringing smiles to each adults face.

"Pleased to see you again, Darla." Mike assured, politely.

"My ex-wife and your wife were good friends in high school." He informed, looking at Kelley.

"Kelley, Mike is Candy's ex-husband."

"Kelley, if you would rather I not stay for dinner, I will understand. I assume Candy and Darla are friends to date." Mike offered, he now expressing his awkward position.

"Mike, we would like to share our dinner with you regardless of your relationship with Candy. Neither my wife nor I sit in judgment of others."

"Darla?" Mike questioned politely.

"My husband speaks for both of us. We would enjoy keeping your company." She answered kindly, her heart going out to her husband's guest.

"Kel, if you and Mike would wash, we may have dinner before it is ruined."

Mike's company was very much enjoyed. He had returned to town to work and live near his children. After eight long years of parties and different women, he found he was still empty inside.

"I have cheated my sons long enough. They should be granted their father." Mike had said at the dinner table when briefly conversing in regards to Candy, his ex-wife and his twin sons.

The Petersons' long busy evening ending, Darla lightly knocked on the shower door.

"Kelley..." She called.

"I will be outside on the swing. Come join me when you have finished."

"I will join you shortly."

Slowly swinging the glider swing Darla enjoyed the chilly winter desert air. Pulling her legs up unto the glider, she wrapped her coat tighter around her chilled body. Looking up toward the Heavens, she smiled as she silently thanked her Heavenly Father for the many blessings He showered her and her family with. Kelley soon vacated their country home through the back door, carrying a blanket in his arms as he approached his wife.

"It is winter time, wife." He reminded, tucking the blanket around both of their shoulders. Darla snuggled close to her husband.

"I would ask you to build a fire if the hour was not so late." Darla informed with a happy look of romance, looking up into her husband's face.

"Baby doll, my fire for you has never gone out." Kelley informed, bringing a laugh from her.

"It would be nice if you and I could go off together for a few days, preferably our honeymoon cabin in the mountains."

"This would be refreshing. I recall a couple of months ago when our wedding anniversary date arrived, suggesting this. You did not want to leave the children. At present, we are not in a position to afford such luxury."

"Sweetheart, where is your imagination? Look at the beauty around us we have been blessed with. We will pretend we are in the mountains. This glider is the rowboat in the beautiful lake. The air is chilly due to the breeze blowing across the water. The children are each sleeping; therefore, we will pretend they are presently spending this night with relatives. You do not even have to carry firewood for our cabin fireplace. You are my fireplace and I feel very warm and comfortable next to you." Darla happily brought a pleased smile to her husband's face. Kelley tightened his arms around his wife.

"It is nice to see your sparkles have returned to your eyes. You must have had a good day."

"Your youngest son and I had a most rewarding day. Mother visited, which was nice. Curt and I ran some errands. Being out, mingling with others was refreshing. To learn Candy will finally have the long overdue assistance, she and her sons are entitled to from Mike, is breathtaking. Paula, Cindy and I have been praying for a solution for Candy's situation. I wanted to tell Mike it is about time he grew up."

"I am glad you refrained from fulfilling your want." Kelley said.

"I had no idea Mike was Candy's ex-husband. Your Dad hired him Monday. All I knew was his skills came highly recommended. He said he has lived in Texas for the past five years. I hope he is sincere about doing right by Candy and the twins. She has not had an easy life and those boys could definitely use a father. They rule their mother. I dread to see their behavior as teenagers if some drastic changes are not made soon."

"Candy feels defeated. When she disciplines the boys, her mother defends them. As long as she is living in her mother's home, she is fighting a losing battle." Darla explained.

"We will pray Mike makes a major change for Candy and the boys. It would be marvelous to see the entire family reunited. Candy is much too young to be single." Kelley voiced.

"This would be marvelous. I do not believe Candy has ever gotten over caring for Mike. I know she has dated, but she has never become serious about anyone."

"What errands did you and my son fulfill?"

"I found a solution to our present financial squeeze. Yours truly will be typing in the comfort of our home, earning a weekly paycheck."

"Typing for whom?" Kelley questioned, surprised with his wife's news.

"For Russell, Mother's cousin and employer. I begin next week. I would be at home, Honey. Are you pleased?"

"Impressed would describe more how I feel. I did speak with your Dad about my hours. He has agreed to grant me overtime for the next couple of months. Therefore, Babe, I will be able to loosen the rope around our neck without you assisting. I told you I would work this out."

"Are you implying you would rather I not type for Russell?" Darla questioned, her face growing serious as she looked into her husband's eyes.

"No, Babe. I know you well enough to know you need your empty hours filled during the school year with the older kids away from home all day. I am simply reassuring you, I will always provide for my family's needs." Kelley answered in his protective manner, gently kissing the top of his wife's head.

"Then you will understand my need to give three hours each Tuesday morning as a volunteer nurse at Memorial Hospital?"

Kelley looked into his wife's eyes, remaining silent for some time. Darla silently in return, held her husband's stare awaiting his response.

"Kelley, I would be doing this for me. Please understand I find nursing fascinating and rewarding. I truly want your understanding and support. Moms and wives are also individual people, Honey."

"I know this." Kelley agreed, releasing a sigh, rubbing his head as though defeated.

"I am sure you have a suitable sitter in mind for Curt."

"Paula volunteered. She says watching Curt would be good practice for her while she awaits the arrival of her baby." Darla shared with a smile, as she lovingly ran her fingers through her husband's hair, hoping to calm him of his uncertainties.

"We do not have to allow your father to know of my three-hour nursing need." She added pleasantly.

Kelley laughed with his wife's remark, as he recalled their early months of marriage with his father protesting Darla working away from her home and family.

"I am perfectly capable of handling my father as well as his opinions in regards to what works best for my family."

"I told Mother this morning this in regards to my dealings with you." Darla confessed with a tickled laugh, knowing she surprised her husband with her confession.

"You speak the truth. You are most capable in handling me." Kelley agreed with a pleased smile.

"I will be the first to admit I have enjoyed spoiling you, Mrs. Peterson. I intend to continue spoiling you. I will do right by my wife, as the Lord commands of me. I am a pleaser of God, not of man."

OTHER BOOKS BY SHERRY DEE

Trials Of A Christian Teenager